Rotten to the Core

ALSO BY T E KINSEY

Lady Hardcastle Mysteries:

A Quiet Life in the Country

In the Market for Murder

Death Around the Bend

Christmas at The Grange

A Picture of Murder

The Burning Issue of the Day

Death Beside the Seaside

The Fatal Flying Affair

Dizzy Heights Mysteries:

The Deadly Mystery of the Missing Diamonds

The Baffling Murder at the Midsummer Ball

Rotten to the Core

A Lady Hardcastle Mystery

T E KINSEY

THOMAS & MERCER

This is a work of fiction. Names, characters, organizations, places, events, and incidents are either products of the author's imagination or are used fictitiously. Any resemblance to actual persons, living or dead, or actual events is purely coincidental.

Published by Thomas & Mercer, Seattle

www.apub.com

ISBN-13: 9781542031462
ISBN-10: 154203146X

Cover design by Tom Sanderson

Cover illustration by Jelly London

Printed in the United States of America

Rotten to the Core

Chapter One

The hedgerow along the lane was alive with birds of every shape and hue as we walked into the village in the Monday afternoon sunshine. All of them were contemptuously ignoring the tabby cat stalking hopefully along the road in front of us. She flicked her tail as the smaller birds flitted above her, and once dropped into a low prowl as a blackbird landed nonchalantly on the road to peck at the base of the hedge.

The cat wound up to pounce and I would have sworn the blackbird rolled his eyes as he lazily flapped away. I fancied it was the same one that had visited us in the garden a short while before. He knew us, and was sure that we would share his low opinion of this inept predator. The cat, meanwhile, had resumed her tail-flicking walk as though she had never been interested in catching birds anyway.

'Is that the doctor's cat?' asked Lady Hardcastle as we watched her hop through a gap in the hedgerow. She cast us a disapproving look as she disappeared, as if she considered us responsible for her failed hunt.

'It looks like it,' I said. 'She has a butterfly pattern across her shoulders.'

'I've always thought of it as an infinity symbol.'

'Have you? Have you indeed? Well, I always think of it as a butterfly.'

'Ever the poet.'

'It's the Welsh in me. Did you know that butterfly in Welsh is *glöyn byw*? It literally means "living ember". How could I not be poetic with ancestors who thought like that?'

We reached the end of the lane and crossed the road to the village green. A couple of young men, watched by a gaggle of gawping children, were busy dismantling the stage that had been hurriedly built beside the cricket pavilion for the village show the day before.

Even though lunchtime was well and truly over, the tables outside the Dog and Duck were still busy with farmhands, taking their ease in the last few days before the harvest got properly underway and their free time disappeared.

Our route took us past the tables, and my friend Daisy, the pub's indefatigable barmaid, gave us a cheery wave.

'Afternoon, Flo. Afternoon, Lady H. I can't stop – it's bedlam out here. Will you be in this evenin'?'

'Possibly,' I said. 'I think we're having a quiet supper at home but we might be persuaded to come out.'

'I might see you later, then. Ta-ta for now.'

She hurried back to the bar with her tray of empties.

We carried on to the little parade of shops and in through the open door of the grocer's, where Mrs Pantry, the shop's owner, sat on a stool behind the counter, sipping a cup of tea. She looked up as she heard our footsteps on the wooden floorboards. Despite the stifling heat, she was draped as always with her heavy woollen shawl, her hair wrapped tightly in a thick cotton scarf.

'Good afternoon, Mrs Pantry,' said Lady Hardcastle, breezily. 'And how are you this fine day?'

''Ot,' said the grocer.

'It is a trifle warm, isn't it? Does it affect your stock at all?'

Mrs Pantry was a curmudgeonly woman whose low opinion of the upper classes always clashed with her desire to make a profit from anyone who came into her shop. On the few occasions when Lady Hardcastle had accompanied me there, I had never been entirely certain whether she was intent on trying to win the grumpy shopkeeper over or just enjoyed teasing her.

Hilda Pantry was impervious to teasing, if teasing it was, and answered honestly.

'The butter's on the turn and them chocolate bars won't last another day,' she said, sourly, indicating the wooden box behind her containing bars of Fry's Chocolate Cream. 'I can let you have two for a penny.'

I never bought chocolate, but I'd have been surprised if the bars were more than a ha'penny each even when they weren't melting into their wrappings.

'Not today, thank you,' said Lady Hardcastle. 'I was wondering if you have my chemicals.'

With a sigh, Mrs Pantry heaved herself up from her stool and stooped to rummage under the counter. She re-emerged a few moments later and plonked a pint bottle and a phial on the countertop. They were of blue glass, and the larger bottle bore a maker's name below the neck.

'Absolutely splendid,' said Lady Hardcastle. 'Thank you very much indeed.'

Mrs Pantry held on to the bottles.

'What do you want 'em for?' she asked.

'Smoke effects for a moving-picture project.'

'I can't be held responsible for you settin' fire to your house. You takes these at your own risk.'

'There shall be no fire, Mrs Pantry, have no fear.'

'How you goin' to make smoke, then?'

Lady Hardcastle smiled and said, 'Chemistry.'

Mrs Pantry let out a 'Pfft', but wrapped the bottles in brown paper before taking the money and locking it in her till.

Back out on the pavement in the sunshine I said, 'How *are* you going to make smoke?'

'Some potassium permanganate,' said Lady Hardcastle, 'and some hydrogen peroxide. Mix them together and Bob's your uncle. It's a bit messy, but it won't burn the house down. The "smoke" is very impressive, though.'

'I see. Wear your overalls, won't you.'

'I shall look like a railway engineer, tiny servant, worry not.'

'See that you do. I can't even begin to guess what "a bit messy" might look like, but I'm willing to bet it'll be a devil to wash out of a summer dress.'

Her no doubt devastatingly witty rejoinder died on her lips as we were accosted by a young woman walking along the pavement towards us.

'Do you live around here?' said the young woman, with an intensity that might easily be mistaken for aggression.

'We do, dear, yes,' said Lady Hardcastle. 'How can we help you?'

The woman was strikingly beautiful. Auburn curls framed a delicately featured face set with green eyes. She had a small port-wine stain on her left temple which she had attempted to conceal with the brim of her hat. She was almost as tall as Lady Hardcastle, and I judged her to be about five and twenty years old. Her clothes were clean and well cared for, but a few years behind the fashion. She was clutching a threadbare carpet bag as though she feared we might steal it from her.

'Does the pub still have rooms?' she asked with no further preamble.

'The Dog and Duck? Yes, Joe keeps a couple of guest rooms. The food is . . . well, it's filling at least. If you—'

'Thank you,' said the young woman. She turned on her heel and walked off towards the pub.

'What did you make of that?' asked Lady Hardcastle once the woman was out of earshot.

'Brusque and businesslike,' I said.

'She was certainly that. I wonder who she is. Or where she's from. Or what she's doing in dear old Littleton Cotterell.'

'To judge from her accent,' I said, 'she's not from round here, though I'd say she's from the West Country somewhere. She's not well off, but she's proud – her clothes aren't new but they're well cared for and she's obviously concerned about how she appears to others. I can't decide whether her direct manner is the result of ignorance and rudeness or whether it's a way to overcome some level of innate shyness. But we'll have all the answers we need by tomorrow lunchtime.'

'What makes you think that?'

'She's going to the Dog and Duck. Daisy will find out everything about her before she sends her up to her room with her evening cocoa.'

Lady Hardcastle laughed.

'I rather think she will at that,' she said.

We dined early that evening. After the disruption of the investigation at the aeroplane factory over the previous few weeks and the excitement of the village show on Sunday, Lady Hardcastle had decided that a little peace and quiet was in order.

We were in the garden, sitting on the new furniture under the apple tree, enjoying the unusually warm weather. Lady Hardcastle sighed contentedly.

'This is the life, eh, Flo?' she said as she tucked into her mackerel. 'Dining in an English country garden in the last rays of the summer sun. I don't think there's anything to beat it.'

'The south of France has its charms,' I said. 'Bengal, too. I loved the sounds as the wildlife changed shifts and the night-time creatures came on duty.'

'True, true. But I do love being at home in the peace and quiet. We should potter a while. I enjoy a bit of excitement as much as the next girl, but it's all the more exciting if it's set in contrast to periods of the humdrum and the mundane, wouldn't you agree?'

'I would,' I said. 'I'm all in favour of a few days of humdrum. A few weeks if it's on offer.'

'Splendid. What shall you do?'

'Well, there's always mending to be done – if I live to be a million years old I'll never work out how an intelligent, capable woman like you manages to cause so much damage to her clothes. Miss Jones wants to give the kitchen a proper scrub-down so I might give her a hand with that. I need to sort out the kitchen accounts, too – she tries her best but her arithmetic skills sometimes let her down. And then—'

'No, dear, that will never do. I'm suggesting we need a few weeks off and you're trying to find ways to fill the time with drudgery.'

'A lady's maid's work is never done,' I said.

'Well, I declare it done for now. Or at least in abeyance.'

'But—'

'Hang the mending,' she said, waving her fork at me. 'If my dresses are unwearable I shall buy new ones. Edna can help Miss Jones with the deep cleaning of the kitchen. And unless and until we are issued a summons to appear before the debtor's court for non-payment of household bills, Miss Jones's poor arithmetic will have to suffice. So what, Miss Florence Armstrong, shall you do with this unexpected period of leisure?'

I smiled and shook my head.

'I have no idea,' I said. 'I have my exercises and my reading—'

'But you do those all the time. Something new. Something exciting.'

I thought for a few moments.

'I have been wondering if I might try my hand at writing,' I said. 'You've tried to teach me to paint, and to play the piano – both with a dismaying lack of success – so I thought I might attempt some other creative pursuit.'

'Splendid. I look forward to reading it.'

'Oh, I don't think there's any chance of that. I shall write for my own amusement.'

'Then I look forward to your being amused. What shall we do this evening, though?'

'A trip to the pub while the weather's still nice? I did suggest to Daisy that we might.'

'A stroll in the dusk and a drink on the green with our friends in the village. An excellent plan. I shall find my hat.'

'I'll tidy the dinner things and we can get going as soon as you like.'

With the evenings still so warm, even after the sun had gone down, we were expecting the new tables outside the Dog and Duck to be busy but we weren't at all prepared for the sight that greeted us as we crossed the green. The tables were heaving and a good many drinkers were standing. Some were leaning against the tables where their companions sat, and one was propped up by his bicycle.

'So much for our plans of sitting outside,' said Lady Hardcastle.

'We could stand,' I said. 'Perhaps one or two of those fine young men would be gracious enough to offer us their seats if they saw two ladies having to stand with their drinks.'

'Perhaps they would at that,' she said. 'I like to imagine that the young men of the village are gracious and charming. Let's go inside and get some drinks so we can put it to the test. Perhaps Daisy might be able to tell us why things are so busy.'

I had expected to find the public bar almost as busy as the benches outside, but it was nearly deserted. For some reason, the dozen men gathered around the tables at the far end by the skittle alley had the place to themselves.

'This is most peculiar,' said Lady Hardcastle.

'You'd certainly have thought that one or two of the standees outside might have come in for a bit of a sit-down,' I agreed. 'It's lovely out, but a comfy chair indoors beats leaning on a bicycle any day.'

Daisy was behind the bar.

'They's all afraid of that lot down there,' she said, tilting her head to indicate the twelve men at the other end of the room.

Lady Hardcastle cocked an eyebrow. 'Afraid?'

'Well, perhaps that's the wrong word. "Wary", p'raps. People tends to mind their Ps and Qs when that lot's in here. And they don't like havin' no one about when they has their meetin's.'

'Then why have their meetings in the pub?' asked Lady Hardcastle. 'If it's all so private, why not meet in someone's kitchen under cover of darkness, wearing cloaks and using secret passwords?'

'It's tradition, i'n't it?' said Daisy with a shrug. 'They's always held their meetin's in the pub and no one round here wants to tell 'em to do anythin' different.'

'Who are they?' I asked.

'They's the Weryers of the Pomary,' said Daisy, solemnly.

Lady Hardcastle snorted. 'The what of the where?' she said, trying not to laugh.

Daisy looked over at the group of men to check that they hadn't heard.

'The Weryers of the Pomary,' she repeated in a stage whisper. 'It's old-fashioned talk for the Guardians of the Orchard.'

'They're the ones who do all the charity fundraising,' I said. 'They're quite well known. Sir Hector has mentioned them. Inspector Sunderland, too. They usually go by the Cider Wardens – I believe they think it's a bit more friendly.'

'Oh, that's them?' said Lady Hardcastle. 'Why didn't I know they were called the Worriers of the Pomeranian?'

'Probably because you expended so much mental effort trying to come up with "amusing" variations on the name that you forgot what they were really called.'

'That definitely sounds like me,' she said with a grin. 'But leaving aside for the moment the obvious question of why the orchard might need guardians, one still wonders about the fanciful name. You can't blame me for being amused.'

'All I knows, m'lady,' said Daisy, 'is they's just always been called that. It goes back hundreds of years, they say.'

'And when they're not doing good deeds, what do they do, these . . . "Weryers"?'

'It's all to do with the cider. They oversees the apple harvest and the cider makin'. They done it for generations. It's a great honour to serve as a Weryer and they takes it all very serious. And so does everyone in the village.'

'Then I apologize for laughing. I love these village traditions. Perhaps we should have two ciders if we're to fit in.'

'Comin' up,' said Daisy, taking two glasses from the shelf above the bar.

'And one for yourself, dear.'

'That's most kind. I'll have the same.'

Daisy filled three glasses with the local cider and set them on the bar. A farmhand came in and looked nervously over at the assembled Weryers before quietly ordering eight more glasses of the local brew for himself and his pals. Lady Hardcastle, meanwhile, eyed the door to the snug.

'If the public bar is out of bounds for the evening,' she said when the young man had gone, 'and the tables outside are all full, I suppose it's too much to hope that there's room for a couple of weary old ladies in the snug?'

'You speak for yourself,' I said. 'I'm in the prime of life, me.'

'Very well. Is there room in there for one weary middle-aged lady and one tiny lass bursting with youthful vigour?'

'That's more like it.'

Daisy laughed.

'Not tonight, I'm afraid – Joe's had a delivery. He couldn't put it in the public 'cos of the meetin' so he had it all stacked up in the snug. I'n't no room in there for ladies young or old.'

'A delivery of what?' asked Lady Hardcastle.

'All will be revealed in the fullness,' said Daisy with a wink. 'I reckons you'll enjoy it, though.'

'You're a dreadful tease, Daisy dear. But sufficient unto the day, and all that. I'm a patient woman.'

I snorted.

During this brief exchange I'd been taking a look at the twelve men at the other end of the bar. I recognized a few of them. Old Joe Arnold, the pub landlord, was sitting next to Septimus Holman, the baker. There were a couple of men with their backs to us who could have been Bob Slocomb, the local dairyman, and Lawrence Weakley, the village greengrocer, but I couldn't be certain. Most of the others looked vaguely familiar, as though I'd seen them about the place over the years, but I couldn't put names to them.

They had been ignoring us at first, but from the increased frequency of the inhospitable glances coming our way it was becoming clear that our time at the bar was up.

'I think we ought to take our drinks outside,' I said. 'I don't think we're welcome here.'

'Oh, pish and fiddlesticks. They can put up with us for a few minutes,' said Lady Hardcastle.

'You were the one who expressed her love for the village traditions. And one of them is that the—'

'Whisperers of the Pomegranate,' she interrupted.

'Don't start,' I said with a sigh. 'You've heard Daisy say "Weryers" twice. You said it once yourself. And don't even try to pretend that you can't remember "Pomary" now you've been told it means orchard.'

Lady Hardcastle grinned.

'One of the village traditions,' I continued, 'is that the Weryers of the Pomary have the public bar to themselves when they meet.'

She had opened her mouth to reply when a man of middle years stomped noisily through the door and slammed his empty glass on the bar.

'Another pint in there, if you will, Daisy, my love,' he said. 'That is if the Weryers will allow it,' he added loudly. One or two of them looked up. He grinned and tipped his cap towards Lady Hardcastle and me. 'Evenin', ladies. Sorry for interruptin' but I gots a thirst on.'

We both smiled and inclined our heads in synchronized acknowledgement.

'Comin' right up, Mr Swanton,' said Daisy as she took his glass. 'How you gettin' on?'

'Can't complain,' he said.

'I'd not pay you no mind if you did. How's your Mercy?'

'She's not so bad. Her hips are still playin' her up, but it don't stop her.'

'I'm pleased to hear it.'

Daisy took his money, and with a final ironic salute to the assembled Weryers, he stomped back out.

'Am I to take it that Mr Swanton has no fondness for our friends the Cider Wardens?' said Lady Hardcastle.

'Mr Swanton?' said Daisy. 'No, he don't like 'em one bit.'

'Why's that?' I asked. 'I've always found him to be quite an equable chap.'

'I have, too,' said Lady Hardcastle. 'He serves on one of Gertie's village committees, though I can't for the life of me remember which.'

'He's a decent fella,' agreed Daisy, 'but the Weryers turned him down and he bears them a grudge.'

'Turned him down?'

'A few years ago when old Billy Baker passed on – you remember Billy Baker?'

'Before our time, I think,' I said.

'Well, when he passed, a space opened up on the Weryers and Pat Swanton thought it was his. He'd been anglin' for it for years.'

'And they said no,' said Lady Hardcastle.

'They did. Never gave him a reason, neither. It only takes three members to object and once they's said no, that's it. He's held a grudge against 'em ever since.'

'How do you know so much about them?' I asked.

'That'll be 'cos of me,' said a voice from behind us.

We turned to see Cissy Slocomb standing there with an endearingly cheeky grin on her face.

Cissy was the dairyman's daughter and very much looked the part. In times gone by she would have been described as a 'buxom wench' and she had the cheery disposition and filthy sense of humour to go with it. I'd always got on famously with Cissy. I knew her reasonably well and had spent many a raucous evening in the pub with her, Daisy, Lady Hardcastle's cook Blodwen Jones, and the rest of their disreputable gang.

'Hello, Ciss,' I said. 'And how do you know, then?'

'Our dad's one of 'em, look.'

With none of the Weryers looking our way I was able to cast a proper eye over the group. Sure enough, the man I thought might have been Bob Slocomb turned slightly to address his neighbour and I could see at last that it really was the dairyman.

'So he is. But still . . . it's all meant to be secret, isn't it?'

'Meant to be,' she said. 'But you knows our dad – he couldn't keep a secret if his life depended on it.'

'I thought milkmen were supposed to be discreet,' said Lady Hardcastle. 'They see all the comings and goings first thing in the morning.'

'Well, if our dad sees any comin's and goin's first thing, half the village'll know about 'em by lunchtime.'

We laughed.

Lady Hardcastle sipped her drink and regarded the earnest men.

'What on earth do they find to talk about all evening, I wonder?' she said.

'Weryer business,' said Cissy, sagely.

'The charity work?' I asked.

'Nowadays, yes. Our dad says there used to be . . . what did he call 'em . . . "Mystic Rites", that's it. In the olden days they used to do ceremonies and that, to "ensure a bountiful apple harvest", but now, like you says, they mostly raises money for charity. And gets drunk, o' course. They mostly gets drunk. Oh, and come Christmas time, they does a bit o' wassailing. They loves to wassail.'

It was my turn to chuckle.

'Who doesn't?' I said.

'I love to wassail, certainly,' said Lady Hardcastle. 'Or I'm sure I would if I were fully au fait with the details. Hold on, though, ladies, best behaviour. Here comes one now.'

A handsome man with greying hair and smiling eyes had left the Weryers' table and was approaching the bar.

'Might we trouble you for another round, please, Daisy?' he said with a cheerful smile.

'Certainly, Mr Cridland,' said Daisy. 'You just sit yourself back down and I'll bring them over.'

'At least let me help,' he said, still smiling. 'You'll be trudging back and forth all evening.'

'Don't you worry about that, Mr C – I's paid to trudge.'

'You're a credit to your parents. How are they, by the way? I've not seen either of them for a while.'

'Can't complain,' said Daisy. 'Well, they can, and they do, but they's no need to.'

Mr Cridland laughed, then seemed to notice the rest of us for the first time.

'I'm sorry, ladies,' he said. 'Look at me being so rude. Cissy I know. And Lady Hardcastle, isn't it? We've not met, but I know you by reputation, of course. Claud Cridland. I run a farm over on the way to Woodworthy. Some arable land and an orchard. Nothing grand.'

'How do you do?' said Lady Hardcastle. 'And if you've heard of me, you'll no doubt have heard of Miss Florence Armstrong, too.'

'I have indeed. Saviour of the Littleton Cotterell village show. We all had a wonderful time yesterday. Thank you.'

'Entirely my pleasure,' I said.

'Well, I ought to be getting back to the meeting, I suppose. Lovely to have met you all.'

He returned to the table on the other side of the room.

'He seemed nice,' I said.

'Lovely fella,' agreed Cissy. 'Though he's not much of a judge of character if he thinks Daisy's a credit to anyone.'

''Ere,' said Daisy. 'Less of that. I'm a paragon, I am.'

'You are, dear,' said Lady Hardcastle. 'And don't let anyone tell you different.'

Cissy rolled her eyes.

'I know what I wanted to ask,' I said. 'Do you have a new boarder?'

'We has, as a matter of fact,' said Daisy. 'How'd you know about that?'

'We met her outside this afternoon. She asked if we knew of anywhere that did rooms and we sent her here.'

'Well, thank you very much. Old Joe can always do with a few extra bob. We don't get many people stayin' here.'

'What did you learn about her?' asked Lady Hardcastle.

'Not a lot. I tried – you know me. But she i'n't very forthcomin'. I got her name from the visitors' book – Miss Grace Chamberlain – but other than establishin' that she don't care for black puddin' on her breakfast, I couldn't get a word out of her.'

'Is she about? Perhaps we should introduce ourselves.'

'I a'n't seen her since I took her some pie an hour ago. She'll be in her room, I reckon.'

'That's a shame,' said Lady Hardcastle. 'I was hoping she might be out on the green – it would be more than a little intrusive to knock on her door and demand her life story. Some other time.'

'If I finds out anythin', I'll let you know,' said Daisy.

'You're a poppet.'

During this exchange, I had been keeping a weather eye on the Weryers and noticed that we'd been getting increasingly obvious looks of disapproval. I was about to point it out to Lady Hardcastle, but I was pre-empted. With a placatory wave of his hands to his companions, Mr Cridland rose from the table and approached us once more.

He looked slightly troubled, but nevertheless resolute. 'My apologies for interrupting again, ladies,' he began, 'but . . . you see . . . the thing is, my fellow Weryers and I would be grateful if you would let us have the bar to ourselves. I'm sorry to have to do it,' he added apologetically, 'but . . . well . . . you know . . .'

'Of course, Mr Cridland,' said Lady Hardcastle, amiably. 'Give us a few moments to say our goodbyes and we'll get out of your hair.'

'Thank you, my lady. Please don't take too long.'

She frowned at him but said nothing further. He turned on his heel and left.

'Marching orders have been given, ladies,' she said. 'We'd best be off. If there are no seats outside, Flo, what say we return home for a game of cards?'

We said our goodbyes and checked the tables outside. They were still full to overflowing, so we went home.

As usual, I was up early the next morning, and was pottering in the kitchen when Edna and Miss Jones arrived together. They were uncommonly animated.

'Have you 'eard the news?' said Edna.

'Terrible news,' said Miss Jones.

'I'm afraid I've only been up an hour,' I said. 'You two are the first bearers of news I've met since last night. What's happened?'

'There's been a murder,' said Miss Jones.

'A stabbin',' added Edna.

'Good heavens,' I said. 'Who? Where?'

'Claud Cridland,' said Miss Jones. 'Constable Hancock said someone found his body in the cider orchard first thing this morning. Stabbed, he was.'

'With an apple in 'is mouth,' said Edna with indelicate glee.

My own mouth fell open and I swore quietly in Welsh. Edna looked at me in confusion but she could see from my face that whatever it was I'd said had been an expression of shock.

'That's horrible,' I said. 'We met him for the first time last night. Did you know him?'

''E ran the apple orchard what supplied the cider mill. Lovely man, 'e was. Never 'ad a bad word for no one. Generous, too – 'e does a lot of work for local charities.'

'But he didn't live in the village, did he?'

'No, the orchard's the other side of the village. He didn't never come over this way much. Didn't 'ave no cause to.'

''Cept for Weryers' meetin's,' said Miss Jones. 'He would have been over here last night at the Dog and Duck.'

'Yes,' I said, 'the Weryers of the Pomary – that's where we met him. They'd taken over the public bar so the tables on the green were packed and we ended up not staying. Cridland seemed like a very pleasant chap. Handsome, too.'

'Oh, 'e was,' agreed Edna. 'Broke a few girls' hearts in his day, I can tell you.'

'The poor man. Does anyone know what he might have done to get himself stabbed?'

'Constable Hancock didn't have no more to say,' said Miss Jones. 'He was in a hurry to get back to the police station and I didn't care to linger.'

'Back from where?'

'You know what Constable 'Ancock's like,' said Edna. 'I'n't no way 'e was goin' to 'ang on to a bit of gossip like that without tellin' everyone in the village. Like an old woman 'e is, sometimes. 'E'd been over the greengrocer's to tell Weakley. 'E's another one of the Weryers, Larry Weakley.'

'Yes,' I said. 'We saw him at the meeting, too. Well, I'm sure we'll learn more in the fullness of time. I've no doubt Lady Hardcastle will try to find out all she can.'

There was a yawn from the kitchen doorway and we turned to see Lady Hardcastle standing there in her nightgown.

'What will I try to find out about?' she asked, croakily.

'One of the Weryers was stabbed to death in the cider orchard last night,' I said. 'Someone found him and reported it to Constable Hancock this morning.'

'Good heavens. How awful. Which one?'

'Claud Cridland.'

'Oh,' she said. 'I rather liked him.'

'He told us to sling our hooks.'

'But he felt guilty about it. It was rather charming. But you're right – I'll certainly try to find out as much as I can. I can't abide an unsolved mystery, especially not the death of a good man.'

'Ooh,' said Edna, keenly. 'Will you be investigatin'?'

Lady Hardcastle smiled. 'I think we ought to keep out of the way. The police aren't nearly so keen on amateur interference as the detective stories would have you believe.'

'They'd be lost without you, m'lady. You've solved umpteen murders since you moved here.'

'I suppose we have at that. Still, I think we ought to keep our noses out unless someone actually asks for our help – I promised Armstrong a period of indolence, after all.'

'A few weeks of humdrum,' I said.

'Precisely so. We shall sit tight unless and until we are called upon. Is there any coffee?'

'I've just put the kettle on,' I said. 'Make yourself comfy in the morning room and I'll bring it through in a few minutes.'

At that moment, though, the doorbell rang.

'Actually, can you see to the coffee, please, Miss Jones – I'd better answer that.'

I opened the front door and was greeted by the sight of Sergeant Dobson, his face flushed and his tunic slightly askew as though he'd been in something of a hurry to get to us.

'Mornin', Miss Armstrong,' he said, tapping the brim of his policeman's helmet with a finger in casual salute. 'Is your mistress at home?'

'She is indeed, Sergeant. Won't you come in?'

'Thank you, miss.'

I led him through to the morning room, where Lady Hardcastle was sitting at the table with the newspaper open in front of her. She looked up as we entered.

'Good morning, Sergeant,' she said, closing the paper. She smiled as she noticed his embarrassment. 'You'll have to excuse my nightgown – I'm afraid I haven't the energy to run upstairs to change, and I judge from your own appearance that you're almost certainly in too much of a hurry to want to wait for my vanity anyway. What can we do for you?'

'I don't like to impose, m'lady,' he began, still not entirely certain where to look, 'but I was wonderin'—'

'If we'd come and poke our noses into the murder of Mr Cridland?'

He nodded, gratefully.

'To be honest, Sergeant, I thought you'd never ask,' she said with a smile. 'Do please make yourself comfortable while I get dressed. There's coffee on the way, apparently, but I'm sure we could run to a pot of tea if you prefer.'

She bustled out of the morning room and galumphed upstairs before Sergeant Dobson could respond. With a shrug to the bemused policeman, I followed her.

Chapter Two

The cider orchard was about a mile and a half away from the house, on the opposite side of the village, and Sergeant Dobson had arrived on his police-issue bicycle. This, I belatedly realized, accounted for his slightly dishevelled appearance, but it also meant that we would be unable to give him a lift in the Rolls. I found it hard to imagine him being happy perched on the luggage rack of the two-seater, though, even without his bicycle, so it was probably for the best.

'We'll meet you there, Sergeant,' said Lady Hardcastle as she eased the motor car out into the lane.

I looked over my shoulder as we sped off, and the weary old sergeant had only just begun to tie a length of string around the bottom of his uniform trousers to prevent the material becoming entangled in the chain. He still hadn't mounted his trusty bicycle by the time we rounded a bend and he was lost from view.

The village was already abustle – they're early risers in the countryside – and I returned the cheery waves of our neighbours as we sped by. Lady Hardcastle was very much of the opinion that if a motor car was capable of driving quickly, it should always be driven as quickly as possible. More than that, she believed it should *only* be driven quickly, and in less than five minutes we had covered the mile and a half and had parked at the end of the footpath leading to the orchard. A sign pointed the way and we disembarked to continue our journey on foot.

The footpath led through a dense wood and I began to wonder if we might somehow have taken the wrong route.

'I'm no dendrologist,' I said, 'but even I can tell that these aren't apple trees.'

'Indeed no, dear. They're mostly elm and alder, with at least one hornbeam thrown in. Isn't she a beauty? Like a craggy-faced old lady. I wager she has tales to tell, and wisdom to impart.'

'But no apples,' I persisted.

'No, just little clusters of seeds in the autumn. Samaras. They fly like sycamore seeds, you know.'

'No good for making cider, though. Are we on the right path?'

'Of course we are.'

'How can you be so certain?'

'Well, my first clue was the signpost pointing along this path that said "Orchard", but now there's . . . this.'

She gestured to indicate an expansive clearing in which grew row upon row of fruit-laden apple trees. Despite the grid-like formality of the planting, the orchard had an almost mystical feel to it. Hemmed in on all sides by woodland, it could easily have been an ancient sacred site. A temple to the goddess Idun, perhaps – the Norse guardian of the apples of immortality.

'This is beautiful,' I said.

'Utterly captivating,' she agreed. 'If a little inconvenient for commercial fruit cultivation. I mean, how do they get the apples to the cidery?'

'In handcarts to the road,' said a man's voice from behind us. 'And we loads the wagons there. The cidery's only a little way further along the road.'

We turned to see a middle-aged man dressed for manual work. His shirtsleeves were rolled up, revealing tanned, muscular forearms, and his cloth cap was set back on his head.

'Lady Hardcastle, isn't it?' he said. 'Sergeant Dobson said he'd be sending you up here. Though I'm afraid it's not a pleasant sight.'

'I am she,' she said. 'And this is Florence Armstrong. How do you do, Mr . . . ?'

'Mattick. Abel Mattick. Master Cider Maker.'

'How do you do, Mr Mattick? You work at the cidery?'

'How do you do? And yes. Claud ran his farm and tended the orchard; I run the cider mill.'

'You were friends? You must be devastated. I'm so sorry.'

'We were.' He paused for a moment, looking distractedly off into the distance. I thought I saw a look in his eyes that was more than grief – fear, perhaps? – but it was gone before I could be certain. He shook his head, as though suddenly remembering where he was. 'The sergeant said you'd want to see him. Claud, I mean. I confess I doubted him when he said it. I couldn't imagine two ladies wanting to . . . you know . . .'

'I'm afraid we would,' she said. 'We'd like to try to help find out who was responsible for your friend's murder, and it's a necessary first step.'

Mr Mattick pointed across the orchard.

'That way,' he said. 'Three rows over. I'll not join you if you don't mind.'

'I quite understand. Thank you.'

We set off in the indicated direction.

Three rows in, we came upon the body of Mr Cridland propped up against one of his apple trees, with a windfall stuck in his mouth. It was a grotesque sight, a deliberate humiliation. As if robbing the man of life with a stab to the heart wasn't enough, the killer had chosen to rob him of his dignity as well. I looked a little closer and saw bruising on Cridland's jaw where the killer had forced his mouth shut to bite into the apple.

Even in death he was still recognizable as the cheerful, handsome man we had spoken to the night before. He was no longer dressed in his smart tweed suit and instead wore a white shirt and dark cotton trousers. His shirt was open at the collar and blood had dried around a neat, circular hole in the shirt, exactly level with his heart.

Despite having left the house in something of a rush, Lady Hardcastle had still had the presence of mind to grab her sketchbook and pencils from her study on the way out. After minutely inspecting the area around the body, she took her drawing materials from her canvas satchel and began to sketch the scene. I knew she would be a while so I undertook a little exploration of my own.

The ground was baked hard by the summer sun so there was little chance of finding the traditional detective's clue: the incriminating footprint. There were scuff marks in the dirt, though, as if Mr Cridland's body had been dragged, and I followed the tracks as best I could, absently counting the trees as I went along the row.

Seven . . . eight . . . nine.

The tracks seemed to stop at the end of the row where the packed earth gave way to yellowing grass, and another quick search revealed that a patch of that grass might very well have been trampled in a scuffle. I knelt to examine it and found a few splatters of dried blood.

The grass was well tended and free of weeds or other encroachments, and ran the length of the orchard – probably about a hundred yards in all – to form a boundary between the untamed woodland and the regimented ranks of apple trees. There was little else to see, though, so I made my way slowly back towards my sketching employer.

I heard male voices coming from the other side of the orchard and had changed course to meet the owners of those voices when I saw that it was Inspector Sunderland and the police surgeon, Dr Gosling, standing, confused, in an almost-circular clearing in the centre of the neat rows of trees.

'Good morning, Miss Armstrong,' said Inspector Sunderland as he approached. 'We passed Dobson on the way and he said we'd find you here.'

'You didn't stop to offer him a lift, then?' I said.

'Nowhere to put the bike,' said Dr Gosling. 'The exercise will be of enormous benefit to him, I'm sure. Good morning, Miss Armstrong.'

'Good morning to you both,' I said. 'I confess to being a little surprised to see you – you're quite a long way off your beat. Oh, actually, do detective inspectors have a "beat"? But you're a long way from home, anyway.'

'I can never turn down a call for help from Littleton Cotterell. Constable Hancock telephoned the Bridewell first thing this morning on Sergeant Dobson's instructions. Apparently his mistrust of Gloucester CID continues unabated, and I seem to be his first call now whenever anything happens out this way.'

'Well, I'm delighted to see you. You too, Dr Gosling. How's Miss Caudle?'

'Dinah's fine, thank you. She sends her regards and wonders when we might see you again for dinner.'

Lady Hardcastle had known Dr Gosling since her university days, and she liked to claim responsibility for introducing him to his fiancée, the *Bristol News* journalist Dinah Caudle. We dined with them at Bristol as often as we were able.

'I shall have to ask Herself, I'm afraid – I'm not authorized to make dinner arrangements.'

'Ha! Jolly good. Where is "Herself"?'

'She and the body are this way,' I said. 'Follow me.'

'Jolly good,' said Dr Gosling. 'We've been wandering about the place for quite a while. Surprised to find that clearing.'

'It does seem an inefficient use of the space,' I said. 'Didn't Mr Mattick show you the way?'

'Mattick?' said the inspector.

'Medium height, white shirt, no collar, dark hair, runs the cider mill.'

'We've not seen a soul, old girl,' said Dr Gosling.

'How odd,' I said. 'Never mind, though – I've found you now.'

I led them between the trees to where Lady Hardcastle stood, still sketching the body and the area around it.

'Good morning, gentlemen,' she said, giving a little wave with one pencil while holding another in her mouth. 'Shan't keep you a moment. Just finishing off.'

'I keep meaning to put in a requisition for a camera,' said the inspector, 'but I'm sure I'd make a dog's dinner of it even if I remembered to bring it to the scene of a crime. My wife takes the most wonderful snaps but I waste a lot of film accidentally taking pictures of the sky, or cutting off people's heads in portraits. They'd be no use as evidence, but Lady Hardcastle's sketches have proven extremely useful.'

She nodded her acknowledgement, but carried on sketching without saying anything further.

Dr Gosling had been looking at the body from a distance.

'He's been stabbed,' he said, earnestly.

'You see, miss?' said the inspector as he took a notebook and pencil from his jacket pocket. 'This is why I need a trained medical man to accompany me on these trips.'

'He provides vital insights,' I said. 'Cridland wasn't attacked here, though.'

'No, I noticed the drag marks.'

I pointed towards the end of the row and the grass beyond.

'There was a scuffle down there between the woods and the orchard, about twenty yards to the right,' I said. 'There's a blood-stain on the grass so I'd say he put up a fight, took that blow to the chest, then the killer posed his body here.'

'With an apple in his mouth,' mused the inspector, making notes in his notebook. 'I wonder if that's significant or just a final humiliation.'

'Was he a pig, this fellow?' asked Dr Gosling as he bent to examine the body.

'We don't know much about him yet,' I said. 'We actually spoke to him briefly yesterday evening but we didn't learn anything other than that he was charming and friendly. He ran the nearby farm and managed the cider orchard. He was also a Weryer of the Pomary, but other than that and our housekeeper's high opinion of him we have no further information.'

'Worrier of the what?' said Dr Gosling.

'Local charity organization,' said the inspector. 'You probably know them as the Cider Wardens. He was well regarded, then?'

'Mattick seemed to like him.'

'Mattick – the man we didn't meet when we arrived.'

'Even he – the Master Cider Maker. He was definitely here when we arrived, though. I wonder where he went. He seemed quite distressed by his friend's murder – I hope he's all right.'

'I'm sure he is,' said Inspector Sunderland. 'It will have been a shock, that's all. I'd not be surprised to learn he'd gone home for a hot, sweet tea and a sit-down. We'll catch up with him later.'

'Well, he met us when we arrived and said that he and Cridland were friends. And Lady Hardcastle's housekeeper is definitely of the opinion that Cridland was a good egg.'

'I doubt your Edna Gibson used the phrase "good egg",' said the inspector with a smile.

'I may be paraphrasing, but it wasn't just not-speaking-ill-of-the-dead. She seemed genuinely fond of him.'

'Thank you. How did she come to be talking about him in the first place?'

'She was the one who brought us the news of the murder,' I said. 'She and Miss Jones had met Constable Hancock on their way to work and he couldn't resist telling them, apparently.'

'He's a promising young officer, that one, but he gossips like an old fishwife.'

'Edna said much the same.'

The inspector smiled.

'So, a good man is stabbed to death . . . in the early hours of the morning?' he said, looking to Dr Gosling for confirmation.

'I should say so, judging from his appearance and the state of the bloodstain. I might be able to get a better estimate once I've examined him properly,' said the doctor.

The inspector nodded.

'So, he's stabbed to death and posed in a humiliating way, beneath one of his own apple trees,' he said. 'It's not the sort of thing a robber would do. Nor a random attacker. There's meaning in this, I'm sure of it.'

Inspector Sunderland and I left the doctor to his examination of the body, and Lady Hardcastle to her sketches. I walked him along the avenue to show him the scene of the fight while we waited for the other two to finish their work. He agreed that it was the likeliest site of the murder and sucked pensively on his unlit briar pipe as he made more notes.

By the time we returned, Lady Hardcastle had finished and was packing her sketchbook and pencil in her satchel. Dr Gosling had finished his preliminary examination and made a few notes in his own notebook.

'I'll certify death,' he said. 'Obviously it appears to be as a result of the stab wound to the chest, but I'll only know what damage it did once I've got the poor fellow opened up. I'll check for evidence of the struggle on the body, too, but Flo's version makes a lot of sense.'

'What's your version, dear?' asked Lady Hardcastle.

I quickly recounted what I'd found at the other end of the avenue of trees.

'Any sign that he might have attempted to flee?' she said.

'Nothing obvious, but the ground's too hard to leave any detailed marks.'

'So he might have known his attacker,' she mused. 'He might have been engaged in a conversation before things turned ugly.'

'It's possible,' said Inspector Sunderland. 'But then again he was a big fellow. And I've not met many farmers who'd run from a fight, be they big or small. If he confronted someone he would have stood his ground.'

'Perhaps so,' she said. 'Odd that he should be in the orchard in the middle of the night, though.'

'Sunrise is at about five o'clock, don't forget,' I said. 'He might have been checking things before the heat of the day.'

'He might,' she agreed. 'Or he might have been summoned here. Or lured in some way.'

Before any of us could speculate further, we heard yet another voice, this one shouting our names.

'Over here, Sergeant,' called the inspector.

Moments later we were joined by Sergeant Dobson, even more red-faced than when we had seen him at the house.

'You found 'im all right, then?' he said, still puffing slightly.

'We did, thank you,' said Lady Hardcastle.

'When did Mattick find him?' asked the inspector.

'Accordin' to young Hancock's report, he called into the station about seven this mornin',' wheezed the sergeant.

'He telephoned?'

'That's right, sir. They gots a telephone at the cider mill. He called from there.'

'I see. And the cider mill is . . . ?'

'About ten minutes over that way on foot,' said the sergeant, pointing.

'So we'll give him a couple of minutes of shock and ten minutes to get to a telephone, which means he found the body no later than around a quarter to seven, probably a little earlier. It's a sizeable orchard so he might have been here some while before he stumbled upon Mr Cridland, which means he could have arrived as early as . . . shall we say six o'clock? That's rather odd, don't you think? What was a cider maker doing in the orchard at six in the morning, I wonder?'

'It's potentially suspicious,' agreed Lady Hardcastle. 'But it does leave more than an hour of daylight for Cridland to meet his killer, even if we assume it didn't happen in the middle of the night. And Mattick does have a vested interest in the state of the apples, so he does have business being here – his work depends upon them, after all. I shouldn't be at all surprised to learn that he visited the place often. I imagine there's a perfect time to harvest the fruit, just as with wine grapes. Do you remember that vineyard in the Loire, Flo? What was the winemaker's name?'

'Georges Rousseau,' I said.

'Ah, yes, dear Monsieur Rousseau. His winery produced one of the finest Pouilly-Fumés I've ever tasted, and he fussed around the vines as though they were his children. One imagines that someone worthy of the title "Master Cider Maker" would be equally fastidious.'

'You're probably right,' said the inspector. 'I'll speak to him in due course. Now then, Sergeant, have you made arrangements to have the unfortunate Mr Cridland's body moved?'

'I have indeed, sir,' said Sergeant Dobson, proudly. 'Young Hancock will be here presently with Dr Fitzsimmons's carriage. We'll get the body back to the surgery and you can have him picked up from there.'

'Good man. Well, I think that's all we can do for now. Dr Gosling and I will see you at the station later.'

'Would you care to come back to the house?' asked Lady Hardcastle. 'We dashed out before breakfast so I'm sure you did, too.'

'You read my mind, old girl,' said Dr Gosling. 'I've always imagined your cook makes a marvellous breakfast.'

'She does indeed. We'll see you there.'

Lady Hardcastle couldn't resist the temptation to race Inspector Sunderland back to the house. We all strolled companionably back towards the motor cars, but as soon as the gate came into view she increased her pace and I knew that it was only a last vestige of dignity and self-respect that prevented her from sprinting the last twenty yards.

Inspector Sunderland was as recklessly fast a driver as Lady Hardcastle, but we had the advantage of an electric starter motor courtesy of her friend Lord Riddlethorpe, as well as the superior power of the Rolls-Royce engine. As we sped off down the lane, the inspector was still cranking his engine to life.

We rounded a bend just outside the village at alarming speed, but I was distracted from my disapproving tutting by the sight of a tall young woman walking along the lane towards the village. It looked like Miss Chamberlain, the Dog and Duck's mysterious new lodger, but we passed her so swiftly that I couldn't be certain.

'Is that—' I began.

'Grace Chamberlain?' said Lady Hardcastle. 'It looks like it. I wonder where she's going.'

'She's going back to the village,' I said. 'I'm more interested to know where she's coming from.'

'Well, quite. Though that could be anywhere.'

We arrived at the house well ahead of the police vehicle, and the gleeful grin on Lady Hardcastle's face more than made up for the terror I had felt as we rounded the corner by the church almost on two wheels, and the embarrassment of frightening the milkman's horse as it waited outside the grocer's.

'Well done, me,' she said as she hopped out and straightened her dress. 'I knew we could beat them.'

'It was never in doubt,' I agreed. 'Shame about upsetting the milkman, though. Bob Slocomb's one of the Weryers and we're going to need to talk to all of them before we're done – we don't want them hostile to us before we've even begun.'

'Oh, don't be so wet. He'll not mind. He probably didn't even know it was us.'

'You.'

'Me, then. But there was no harm done.'

By the time Inspector Sunderland drew to a stop behind the Rolls, I'd already opened the gate and was on my way to the front door.

'Sorry we're late,' said the inspector. 'We had an altercation with the milkman. He said we were the second damn fool motor car to come haring past, frightening his horse.'

'The poor thing,' said Lady Hardcastle. 'Motor cars must be a terrifying addition to the life of the horse. Goodness knows they're fretful and skittish enough as it is.'

'He didn't see the first vehicle, but I assured him that we'd have words if we ever caught up with them.'

'As well you should. We can't have hooligans in motor cars careering about the countryside, frightening the horses.'

I led the party through to the morning room and went to ask Miss Jones if she wouldn't mind making breakfast for four.

I lent a hand with some of the preparation to help speed things along, and when I finally returned to the morning room they were setting up Lady Hardcastle's infamous 'crime board'. The school blackboard and easel she used to keep track of our investigations usually lived in the attic, and I was surprised to see it already standing by the window.

Lady Hardcastle caught my questioning glance.

'Simeon brought it down for me, dear,' she said. 'I thought we might make a start on the case.'

'Is that what we're doing? Isn't this your case, Inspector?'

'Officially, yes,' he said. 'But we all know there's no way I'd be able to stop you two interfering, so I thought we might as well acknowledge your involvement from the start.'

'You're a kind and patient man,' I said. 'What do we have so far?'

'The victim is Claud Cridland, a farmer who lived near Woodworthy,' said Lady Hardcastle, pinning one of her sketches to the board.

'I'll be visiting his home in due course to find out more,' said Inspector Sunderland.

'The body was found by Abel Mattick,' she continued, adding another, more hastily drawn, sketch. 'Master Cider Maker. Friend of the deceased. Both were Weryers of the Pomary. Both were at a meeting at the Dog and Duck the night before the murder, with ten other men.'

'We'll need to speak to all of them, too. They might know more about his enemies than his family. If there even is a family.'

'Do we know anything else about the Weryers?' I asked. 'Apart from the drinking and the charity work?'

'Not really,' said the inspector. 'I came across them a few years ago when they raised quite a bit of money to help some families in the city, after an accident at the docks left seven men dead and a dozen more unable to work. Clubs like theirs from the city, from Somerset, from Gloucestershire, all rallied round with offers of money, food, clothing, toys for the children – it was most touching. You'd think they were all parochial little cliques, but they came together when it mattered. I've a lot of time for the Weryers. Or the Cider Wardens, as they're known nowadays.'

'Is it just the local lot?' said Lady Hardcastle. 'Or are they a branch of a wider organization?'

'Just them as far as I'm aware. You know, I'd hate to think one of them was a suspect, but it's a sensible place to start.'

'I fear it is. Most people are killed by someone they know, after all. And they all knew Claud Cridland.'

'All true,' he agreed. 'But a tiny percentage are killed by complete strangers. Let's keep an open mind.'

Conversation was briefly halted by the arrival of Edna bearing a heaped tray of breakfast goodness.

'You knew Claud Cridland,' I said as she set it down on the table. 'Was he married?'

'Widowed,' she said. 'His wife died in childbirth about fifteen years ago. Lost the baby an' all. Poor fella. They'd only been married a couple of years. Married late, see? I don't think he ever got over it.'

'How old was he, then?'

'He had a big party for his fiftieth birthday last summer. His late wife – Annie, she was, lovely lady – she was a few years younger, but not much.'

'There's been no one else in his life since?' asked the inspector.

'Lady friends, you mean? Not so far as I know. He weren't never short of offers, mind.'

'Did he have any other family, do you know?' asked Lady Hardcastle.

'I doesn't 'ave no idea, I'm afraid, m'lady. I knew 'im to say hello to, like, but he wasn't one to stop and gossip.'

'Thank you, Edna, you've been a great help.'

'Yes,' said the inspector, 'you've saved me quite a bit of traipsing about.'

'My pleasure,' she said. 'Will there be anythin' else, m'lady?'

'No, this is splendid, thank you. And thank Miss Jones for us, too.'

Edna left us, and I passed the plates round. While everyone helped themselves to bacon, egg, sausage and fried bread, I examined the sparsely populated crime board.

'What are our next moves, then, Inspector?' I said at length.

'I think Gosling and I should return to the city.' He turned to the doctor. 'I'm sure you'd like to get on with the post-mortem, wouldn't you?'

'Live for them, old boy. It's been a quiet few weeks for murders.'

'Distressingly, it has,' agreed the inspector. 'In the meantime, I shall open a file and sort out the other necessary paperwork. You two ladies can . . . well, you can do whatever it is you do. I'm sure you have your own methods by now. You're well placed to delve into the minutiae of village life – by all means feel free to get delving. They trust you.'

'I'm a very trustworthy woman,' said Lady Hardcastle.

'She is,' I said. 'I can vouch for her.'

The inspector smiled.

'Then please find out as much as you can about the Weryers,' he said. 'I'm especially interested to find out what happened at that meeting.'

'Consider it done, dear,' said Lady Hardcastle. 'Can you do something for me, too, please?'

'If it's within my power, of course.'

'There's a stranger in the village who's going by the name of Grace Chamberlain.'

'"Going by the name of"? You think it might not be her real name?'

'Oh, I have no opinion on that one way or the other, but I've lost count of the false identities Flo and I have used over the years, so I never assume. Could you be an absolute poppet and make enquiries of your counterparts in . . . let's say Devon, Cornwall and Gloucestershire for now, and see if they've heard of her? She's around . . . what would you say, Flo, dear? Five and twenty?'

'I guessed exactly that,' I said.

'She's tall – about five foot seven – red hair, green eyes. She has a port-wine stain on her left temple. She's neatly turned out but not, I would say, well off. Her accent . . . I'm not familiar enough with the local nuances to be certain. I can usually tell precisely which district of London someone is from but the West Country voices elude me. She's definitely from somewhere between Cornwall and Gloucester.'

The inspector laughed.

'Well, that eliminates a fair swathe of the country, at least. Why the curiosity?'

'She's just a little . . . How would you describe it, Flo? Odd?'

'There's an oddness about her, certainly,' I agreed. 'She was abrupt and a little unfriendly, in a way that travellers usually aren't. Someone who troubles to visit a new place is more apt to be curious and friendly. She just asked about lodgings, then turned on her heel and walked off.'

'It was certainly unusual,' agreed Lady Hardcastle. 'The most puzzling thing about her, though, is that we can't for the life of us fathom why on earth she would come to Littleton Cotterell.'

'I have friends at Exeter and Truro, and there's a chap at Gloucester who owes me a favour,' said Inspector Sunderland with a smile. 'I'll make some discreet enquiries. But don't hold your breath – "not being as chatty as Lady Hardcastle would prefer" is hardly the sort of thing to bring her to the attention of the police. Pass the sausages, would you?'

Chapter Three

Inspector Sunderland returned to Bristol soon after breakfast, leaving Dr Gosling with us.

'If you could point me in the direction of Dr Fitzsimmons's house,' he said as we returned to the morning room for more coffee, 'I can get out of your hair. I'll wait there for the mortuary van and cadge a lift back into town with them. Unless you'd care to come over to see Fitzsimmons with me?'

'I always enjoy a chat with the doctor,' said Lady Hardcastle. 'I'm sure he won't mind.'

Half an hour later we strolled down the lane and across the green to the doctor's house. We were greeted at the door by his housekeeper.

'Good morning, Mrs Newton,' said Lady Hardcastle. 'You're looking well. Is Dr Fitzsimmons at home?'

'Is he expecting you?' said the black-clad housekeeper.

'He isn't, no. But he's performing a service for the police surgeon' – she indicated Dr Gosling – 'so I think he might be anxious to see us nonetheless.'

'So it was you as sent us a dead body first thing this mornin'? This is a doctor's surgery, you know, not a mortuary. You ought to—'

'Thank you, Mrs Newton,' said Dr Fitzsimmons from the hallway behind her. 'I'll take over from here.'

Mrs Newton returned grumpily to her work, muttering as she went.

'Don't have no respect, some people,' she grumbled. 'He's a doctor, not a mortician. Shouldn't be allowed . . .'

Dr Fitzsimmons smiled apologetically. 'Do come in.'

'We're not interrupting your work?'

'No, no, please don't worry about that. I've no patients to see until this afternoon. I'd be pleased to have some company, if I'm honest. Come in.'

We entered the hallway of the spacious Victorian house that Dr Fitzsimmons called home. It was darkly panelled, and hung with photographs and paintings.

'I don't believe you gentlemen have met, have you?' asked Lady Hardcastle.

'Oh, but yes. Yes, we have,' said Dr Fitzsimmons. 'During that business at Lady Farley-Stroud's moving-picture festival in '09.'

'We're old friends,' agreed Dr Gosling. 'We compared notes on that case quite a few times.'

Lady Hardcastle seemed mildly put out to be reminded, once more, that people continued to exist even when she wasn't there.

'Did you?' she said. 'Did you indeed? How splendid.'

'I've followed your career with great interest, dear boy,' said Dr Fitzsimmons. 'I often wondered if I might have enjoyed the life of a police surgeon.'

'It's not nearly so glamorous as you might suppose,' said Dr Gosling. 'For the most part it simply involves certifying death and agreeing with the attending constable's opinion that the unfortunate victim did, indeed, die from the adverse effects of being smacked on the head with a poker.'

'Ah, but sometimes one comes across something more interesting. I do hope you don't think me presumptuous, but I couldn't resist taking a look at the wound on Mr Cridland's chest. It's most unusual and I wonder if an expert might be able to satisfy an old man's curiosity and tell me what could have caused it.'

'I'd be happy to try,' said Dr Gosling. 'Would you care to show me?'

'I should like nothing more, dear boy. Nothing more. Would you like to see, my lady? And Miss Armstrong? I know you take a keen interest in these things, too.'

'I'm interested in anything that might help us find his killer,' said Lady Hardcastle. 'Lead on.'

We followed the doctor through a door at the far end of the comfortable consulting room, into a white-tiled surgery that had been built on to the back of the house.

'Well, I never expected this,' said Dr Gosling.

'Oh, I only carry out the most minor procedures,' said Dr Fitzsimmons. 'Ingrown toenails and the like, you know? But I confess to having a boyish enthusiasm for the latest medical technology.'

Mr Cridland had been laid carefully on the modern steel operating table. His shirt was open, revealing the small, neat puncture wound. No matter how many lives I had seen brought to a premature end, it still astonished and terrified me that life could be extinguished by such seemingly minor damage.

'You see here?' said Dr Fitzsimmons. 'The wound is perfectly circular with no sign of tearing. The weapon was very sharp, but with a round blade.'

'I've seen an ornamental Italian stiletto with a cylindrical blade,' I said. 'But the working versions tend to have a square or triangular cross section.'

My knowledge of edged weapons discomfited most people, and Dr Fitzsimmons, it seemed, was no exception.

'Ah . . . well . . . yes,' he said. 'But notice this small bruise here to one side of the wound.'

'That could just be the guard on the handle of the knife,' said Dr Gosling.

'But stilettos are famously symmetrical,' I said. 'The quillions – the arms of the guard – would leave bruises on both sides.'

'There, you see?' said Dr Fitzsimmons. 'Miss Armstrong has gone straight to the nub of it. One would imagine, too, that the cross-guards of a dagger – the . . . what did you call them?'

'Quillions.'

'The quillions, yes. One would imagine that they would leave their marks close to the entry wound. This bruise is small and offset by more than an inch.'

Dr Gosling looked more closely.

'I should love nothing more than to be able to dazzle you with my forensic knowledge, Dr Fitzsimmons,' he said. 'But I confess this one has me completely stumped.'

Further rumination was forestalled by the arrival at the surgery door of Mrs Newton.

'Two . . . "gentlemen" have arrived at the front door,' she began. 'The *front* door, if you please – claiming to be mortuary men from Bristol. I have sent them to the back.'

'Thank you, Mrs Newton,' said Dr Fitzsimmons.

The housekeeper left.

'Well, dear boy,' he said. 'He's all yours, now. I look forward to hearing the results of the post-mortem.'

Lady Hardcastle and I said our goodbyes and returned to the house.

◆ ◆ ◆

I had expected us to spend the afternoon tracking down Weryers and asking them probing questions about their relationships with the late Mr Cridland, but instead I was abandoned to amuse myself while Lady Hardcastle locked herself in her study.

She emerged shortly before two o'clock with a stack of envelopes ready for the post box.

'There,' she said, with a note of triumph. 'All done.'

'Aha,' I said. 'I wondered what you were up to.'

'If we're going to be up to our elegant knees in a murder investigation, I shan't have even a moment to myself. I can't leave my correspondents uncorresponded.'

'Goodness me, no,' I said. 'However would they cope without your wisdom to guide them?'

'Well, quite.'

'Of course, you've never had any trouble in the past.'

'With what?'

'With keeping up your correspondence while investigating murders.'

'Ah,' she said. 'I fear you might have found me out. The truth is, I have absolutely no idea where to begin with Mr Cridland's case. We know precious little about him, and only the tiniest amount about his associates. All we know is that they all met in the Dog and Duck and then he was stabbed with a pencil later that night.'

'A pencil?'

'Pointy, cylindrical . . . It could as easily be a pencil as anything else.'

'Perhaps Cridland was a vampire.'

'And the killer didn't have a stake to drive through his heart, so he pulled a pencil from his pocket—'

'Or from behind his ear – he might be a carpenter,' I said.

'I like the way you think, young Florence.'

'Thank you. There is a way we could find out more about the Weryers, though.'

'We could start talking to people? Yes, I know. But it's always daunting at the start, isn't it? A new job, a new project, a new case, a new . . . well, a new anything. Getting started is always the hardest part, wouldn't you agree?'

'I would. Would it help if I made the decision for you? Shall we go and speak to Mr Mattick?'

She thought for a moment.

'No,' she said at length. 'I think we should start with Miss Chamberlain.'

'Why? She's not a suspect, surely.'

'No, but we can treat it as a warm-up. I really can't bear not knowing more about her. We'll head to the Dog and Duck and see if we can catch her there.'

I laughed. 'That's the spirit. I knew if I tried to take charge you'd buck up and take over immediately. But what if she's still in her room?'

'She has to come out some time. We shall take the optimistic view and suppose that she'll be sitting in the snug with an improving book, enjoying the convivial atmosphere of an English village pub.'

'Pub, optimism, convivial atmosphere. Got it,' I said. 'Do those letters need posting?'

She held them out optimistically.

'Yes, they do,' she said.

'There's a post box on the village green outside the post office.'

I returned to my own work, leaving her chuckling to herself in the hall.

I heard the front door close a few minutes later as she left for the post box.

◆ ◆ ◆

We arrived at the pub to find the outdoor tables busy, but not jam-packed as they had been the previous evening. Inside, everything else was back to normal, with the sound of conversation and laughter in the public bar, and a game of skittles underway.

Daisy was flirting with a timid-looking young man who skittered away as we approached.

'You frightened him off,' she said, accusingly.

'He's too young for you anyway,' I said.

'I didn't want to keep him. I was going to play with him for a bit then throw him back. Now, his dad, mind you . . .'

I laughed. 'Oh? Who's his father?'

'Sid Palmer,' she said with a grin.

'Sidney Palmer of Palmer's Farming Equipment?' said Lady Hardcastle with a grin of her own. 'I can see how he might appeal. But he's happily married, dear.'

'I knows, but a cat may look at a king,' said Daisy. 'And he's gorgeous.'

'He does have a certain something about him, it's true. He's a charming chap, as well. I met him at one of Gertie's soirées. He has a delightful line in bawdy limericks.'

'See? We'd get on perfect.'

'I'm sure you would, dear, yes. But on to more mundane matters. Is your lodger at home?'

'She is, m'lady. She's in the snug.'

'It's back in business, then?'

''Tis. Joe moved his things out 'smornin'.'

'Is she alone?'

'She is now. Mrs Grove was in there with her pal, but they left half an hour since. Most of the other regulars don't like it in there.'

'Really? I think it's charming. But it's excellent news for us. Flo?'

'No time like the present,' I said. 'We'll have two ciders, please, Dais, and whatever you're having. We'll take them through and introduce ourselves to Miss—'

'Caldicott,' interrupted Lady Hardcastle.

'You're not funny, you know. We shall introduce ourselves to Miss—'

'Cummerbund.'

'To Miss *Chamberlain*, and see if we can find out a little more about her.'

Lady Hardcastle winked at Daisy. 'She used to be much more fun when she was young, you know,' she said.

I tutted and paid for the drinks.

Miss Chamberlain was, exactly as Daisy had said, alone in the snug. The small room could comfortably seat at least a dozen at its four tables, and it seemed oddly desolate with just one young woman huddled on the pew-like bench in the corner. The door was open to the evening air and we could hear the cheerful chatter of the drinkers on the green, but the young woman ignored them. There was a half-full glass on the table in front of her beside an open notebook with a pencil resting on top of it. She was reading a battered novel and didn't look up as we entered.

'Good evening,' said Lady Hardcastle brightly. 'Would you mind awfully if we joined you?'

The young woman finally glanced up from her book.

'There's plenty of room,' she said, indicating the empty seats with a slow wave of her hand. 'Help yourselves.'

Lady Hardcastle crossed the room and pulled out one of the two chairs opposite the young woman's bench and put her drink on the table. She indicated that I should do the same and we sat there, smiling across the table at the now-astonished woman.

'Good evening, my dear. I'm Emily, Lady Hardcastle, and this is Florence Armstrong. We met yesterday when you arrived in the village.'

The woman seemed somewhat taken aback by this brazen approach. There were three empty tables in the snug and she had clearly imagined that we might sit at one of those rather than at the one she was occupying. Despite being obviously a little irritated, politeness got the better of her.

'Grace Chamberlain,' she said.

'How do you do, dear? Have you come far to be with us at Littleton?'

'Quite a way, yes.'

'You must have important business to make such a journey.'

'Quite important, yes. To me, at least.'

'One assumes you must have come by train to Chipping Bevington?'

'I did.'

'I find travel so tiring. A long train journey wears me out, even though I'm sitting down the whole time.'

'It was only a couple of hours.'

'Chipping Bevington is a charming little town, though, isn't it?'

'I didn't see much of it. There was a man with a dog cart outside the station and he offered to bring me here for a reasonable price, so I didn't linger.'

'Ah, of course. We often pop over there for odds and ends. The village shops are marvellous, but there are some things one can't always get here. There's a lovely bookshop in Chipping, for instance.'

'I'm sure there is.'

'How did you come to hear about Littleton Cotterell? It's quite an out-of-the-way place.'

'My mother told me about it.'

'Was she from here?'

'Nearby.'

I admired Lady Hardcastle's tenacity, but this was like trying to get wool off a goat. I glanced down at the notebook. It was upside down but readable enough, and the open page bore a list in two columns. It was a list of initials, with a brief note beside each: *CS* – sol, Chip B; CC – orch; AM – cider; MP – coop, Glos Rd; GU – pub, WoodW; AR? – farm, PigH; LL – bank . . .*

I was startled by the sudden appearance in my field of view of Miss Chamberlain's hand as she removed the pencil and gently closed the notebook. I looked up but her attention was on Lady Hardcastle, who was still chattering amiably about the admirable qualities of the village and its surrounds.

'. . . and you really should make time to watch the local cricket team. They're rather good, aren't they, Armstrong?'

'Very talented,' I said.

Miss Chamberlain nodded.

'I'll bear it in mind,' she said, in a tone that suggested that even if Hell were one day to freeze over, watching the Littleton Cotterell cricket team in action would still be quite a way down her list of possible activities.

I decided to extricate us from the one-way conversation.

'Oh,' I said, as though suddenly remembering something. 'Didn't Daisy say she wanted to ask us about our plans for the Harvest Festival?'

Lady Hardcastle looked at me, briefly puzzled, but she, too, realized the folly of trying to get anything more from Miss Chamberlain.

'Yes, dear, she did,' she said after the briefest pause. 'It was lovely to make your acquaintance, Miss Chamberlain. I hope we meet again.' She reached into her bag and produced a calling card. 'We live up the lane. Do feel free to pay us a call if you feel the need for some company.'

Miss Chamberlain picked up the card.

'Thank you,' she said. 'Good evening.'

We returned to the public bar.

'Back so soon?' said Daisy.

'You weren't joking when you said she wasn't very forthcoming,' said Lady Hardcastle, 'but we might have learned a little more about where she's from.'

'Your prattle about the journey?' I said.

'Exactly so. We'll take a look at *Bradshaw's* when we get home – that might narrow it down a bit. If it comes to it, we can take a trip to Chipping and have a word with nice Mr . . . ?'

'Roberts,' I said. 'The station master is "Old Roberts" and the ticket office clerk is "Young Roberts".'

'What a memory you have. Yes, the Robertses. One of them will surely have noticed what train the attractive young lady with the faded carpet bag arrived on.'

'Bound to,' I said. 'Sadly, though, other than possibly being able to make a guess as to where she comes from, and Daisy's vital intelligence from yesterday about her abhorrence of black pudding—'

'Even that's supposition, mind,' said Daisy. 'I only knows she didn't want it for breakfast. She might love a bit o' black puddin' come supper time.'

'Perhaps you could offer her some to confirm,' I said.

'If you think it would help . . .'

I made a face.

'How would it help, Dozy?' I said. 'But apart from those two things, we know nothing new.'

'It's nice to have a bit of mystery,' said Daisy. 'We don't have nearly enough mystery in our lives.'

'Be careful what you wish for, dear,' said Lady Hardcastle. 'I fear Flo and I have altogether far too much mystery in ours.'

'Ah, but you thrives on it. I've seen the look Flo gets in her eyes when she's on a case.'

'I have a look?' I said.

'You do, dear,' said Lady Hardcastle. 'You have it now. What say we leave young Miss Spratt to her mighty labours and take your look back to the house where we can indulge in some wild speculation on the nature of Grace? Or her home town at least. And then cards.'

We said our goodbyes and returned to the house.

Back at the house, Lady Hardcastle bustled into the drawing room and lit the lamps before taking down our barely used copy of *Bradshaw's Guide* from the bookshelf and settling herself in an armchair. I briefly settled in the other and hurriedly made a note of what I had seen in Grace's notebook before she closed it. Notes made, I stood up again.

'Do you want a cup of tea while you do that?' I asked.

'Cocoa, please,' she said. 'With just the tiniest splash of brandy.'

When I returned a short while later, she was still flipping the pages of the railway guide while making notes in her pocket notebook. She murmured her thanks as I placed her cocoa on the side table, but she was still engrossed.

So as not to interrupt or distract her, I took a look at the bookshelves myself, where I lit upon a battered old dictionary. I took it to my armchair, opened it and began my own research.

'There's no entry for "weryer",' I said. 'It goes straight from "wert" to "weskit".'

'I did know thee well, sire,' said Lady Hardcastle without looking up. 'Thou wert ever a weskit-wearing weryer.'

'Did they make it up, then, I wonder?'

She set down her notebook and train timetables and put her reading glasses on top of her head.

'One presumes it's from the Old English *werian*,' she said. '*Siðþan he under segne sinc ealgode, wælreaf werede*. "Then under his banner he protected the treasure, defended the spoils of the slain." That's your actual *Beowulf*.'

'They're an old order, then, these Weryers of the Pomary.'

'Either that or they were founded a few years ago by someone with a fondness for Old English who knew a few obsolete words. We may never know.'

'That's another possibility, certainly. What have you found?'

'Well, now,' she said, reopening her notebook. 'We met Miss Chamberpot yesterday, not long after two in the afternoon. Working backwards, we allow her a few minutes to dismount the dog cart and stroll along the street; then, say, three-quarters of an hour to get here from Chipping. It takes another few minutes to disembark from a train and leave the station, so I'm working on the notion that she arrived at Chipping Bevington station about an hour before we met her. Some time, then, between one and half past. The only train to arrive at Chipping within our window was the 1.13 from Plymouth. She said she was on the train for "a couple of hours" which suggests she boarded somewhere around Exeter. Obviously she might have spent two hours on a trap getting to Exeter St David's, so we'll never glean her precise departure point, but I'd stake a considerable sum on our Miss Camembert setting off from somewhere in Devon.'

'And what does that tell us?'

'Not a thing, but I feel a cosy sense of achievement for having worked it out.'

'As you should.'

'Thank you. What did you see in the notebook before she spotted you and closed it?'

'It was a list of initials with notes beside them. Under any other circumstances it might have been notes about the book she was reading or even a cryptic shopping list, but one entry said "CC – orch" so I'm inclined to be suspicious.'

'Claud Cridland at the orchard, eh? What else?'

I briefly listed the other entries I'd been able to see, and she made notes on the crime board which I had hauled through from the morning room.

'AM would be Abel Mattick from the cidery, I presume,' she said, looking at the list. 'None of the others leap out at me, though I think the cooper on the Gloucester Road is called Peppard, so he could very easily be "MP – coop, Glos Rd", don't you think?'

'I do. He's called Moses.'

'Ah, yes, of course. I remember now. But why does she have a list with these men on it? And who are the others?'

'Now we're talking about him, I do wonder if I saw Peppard at the Weryers meeting. Could it be a list of Weryers?'

'It could. But we're still left wondering why.'

'It would help to know a little more about the Weryers,' I said.

'Indeed. I'll wager Hector knows all about them – I shall telephone him in the morning. But in the meantime, let's allow our minds to process things on their own while we turn our attention to other matters. Did you say something about playing cards?'

'No, that was you.'

'Ah, excellent – that makes me feel less guilty for declining the offer. I rather fancy a game of Go. Do you remember those old chaps in the park in Shanghai?'

'You tried to get them to teach you but they just laughed at you.'

'Quite right, too. I'm an absurd person at the best of times.'

'Very well, then, but you'll not win – you never do.'

'It's not about the winning, Miss Smug-Drawers. It's about the delicious feel of the stones and the pretty patterns on the board.'

'If you set it up, I'll get some fresh cocoa.'

I picked up the empty cups and set off towards the kitchen.

'With more brandy this time, dear,' she called. 'We're not on rations, you know.'

Chapter Four

Lady Hardcastle telephoned The Grange the next morning after breakfast, and we were warmly invited for elevenses. It left no time for me to start any of my own chores, so I helped Miss Jones in the kitchen for an hour.

She and Edna were both keen to hear about the events of the previous day, but I had little to tell them. Edna knew a little about the Weryers, but she did confirm that it was Lawrence Weakley that I'd seen with his back to us at their meeting in the pub. I made a mental note to tell Lady Hardcastle.

The lady herself appeared at the kitchen door just as I was putting away the last of the pans, and indicated that it was time for us to go.

'Gertie assures me that she will be exceedingly pleased to see us,' she said as we readied ourselves for the trip.

'She's always pleased to see us,' I said. 'We're delightful.'

'Granted. She has company, of course – Clarissa and Adam are still there with baby Louisa. But perhaps the joys of grandmotherhood are waning and she yearns once more for the company of adults who are not covered in sick.'

'Then we must do all we can to entertain and amuse her. Quizzing her on the local fundraisers might be the distraction she needs.'

'It might well,' said Lady Hardcastle. 'Have you seen my hat?'

'Yes, it's enchanting.'

'Most amusing. Where is it?'

'Your hat?'

'Yes.'

'The one you're wearing, or another one?'

She touched her head.

'Right you are. Well, I'm ready, then. How about you?'

'I'm always ready, my lady.'

We decided to drive the two miles to The Grange. It was yet another glorious day, but I argued – successfully for once – that we'd get more done in the afternoon if we drove. Not only would we save the half an hour it would take us to walk home, but we'd be less wearied. Walking any distance in the heat of the day would be sticky business.

The Grange never failed to impress and bemuse me with its mish-mash of architectural styles. The Palladian façade, the Tudor chimneys rising from the main hall, the Victorian wing with its neo-Gothic tower – all combined into a gloriously dotty home for a gloriously dotty couple.

The front door stood open as we approached, and we were greeted not by Jenkins the butler, but by 'the gels' – Sir Hector's three boisterous springer spaniels.

At the sound of our light summer shoes on the gravel, they bounded out to meet us.

'Good morning, ladies,' said Lady Hardcastle, delightedly. 'How lovely to see you all.'

She bent to ruffle the ears of two of them while I petted the other so she didn't feel left out.

'I've never been entirely certain which is which,' I said. 'I know they're Clotty, Lacky, and Troppo, but as to which moniker belongs to which dog, I've no clue.'

'Gertie told me once,' she said. 'Clotho is the one with the white patch on her back. Lachesis has the freckled legs. And Atropos is . . . well, she's the other one.'

As she named each of the Fates of Greek myth, she gave their canine namesake another scratch behind the ear. The wagging dogs pushed and barged at each other in their eagerness to be next in line for attention, but when we stood up to resume our walk to the front door, they quickly formed a guard of honour to lead the way, looking over their shoulders occasionally to make sure we were following.

They led us through the open front door, across the hall, down the passage to the ballroom, and out through the French windows on to the terrace. No humans needed to intervene, and Sir Hector and Lady Farley-Stroud seemed genuinely quite surprised to see us suddenly in their midst without an announcement from their butler.

'Oh,' said Lady Farley-Stroud. 'Hello, m'dears. Where on earth did you two come from?'

'The dogs let us in,' said Lady Hardcastle as we sat down. 'I hope you don't mind.'

'Hah!' said Sir Hector. 'Well, make yourselves comfortable, do. They've taken to doin' that lately, the gels. None of us can fathom why but it seems to make them happy, so I haven't the heart to try to stop 'em. Frightened the poor postman half to death, mind you, and I worry that poor Jenkins is going to feel a little put out.'

There was a polite cough from the French windows.

'Ah, there you are, Jenkins,' said Sir Hector. 'I was just sayin' the gels are doing you out of a job.'

'They do seem very keen, sir,' said Jenkins. 'My apologies for not greeting you properly, my lady, Miss Armstrong. Is there anything I can get you?'

'We're quite all right, Jenkins, thank you,' said Lady Hardcastle with a smile. 'I do hope Sir Hector isn't correct, though. I should hate to think our amusement at being shown in by the dogs was causing you distress.'

Jenkins laughed.

'Not at all, my lady,' he said. 'There's always plenty for me to do and I'm pleased to have their help.'

The three springer spaniels, meanwhile, had found a sunny spot on the flagstones and were taking their ease, their day's work done.

'If you could tell Mrs Brown that we're ready for elevenses now, please, Jenkins,' said Lady Farley-Stroud. 'Just the four of us, after all. Clarissa, Adam, and Louisa have gone into town for the day.'

'Very good, my lady,' said Jenkins. He disappeared back into the house.

'They've gone to the Zoological Gardens, you know,' said Lady Farley-Stroud.

'How lovely,' said Lady Hardcastle. 'We've still never visited, but Louisa will love it, I'm sure.'

'I'm sure she shall. We used to take Clarissa when she was young,' said Lady Farley-Stroud with a happy smile of reminiscence. 'But what an unexpected treat to see you both. I'd been hoping you'd drop by so I could thank you properly for being the saviours of our village show.'

'Just the one saviour, Gertie dear,' said Lady Hardcastle. 'I merely put on a spangly outfit and played the piano. Flo here did all the saviouring.'

I like to see my efforts appreciated as much as the next person, but I didn't want this adoration, well-meaning though it obviously was, to go on all morning. I decided to try to head her off.

'It's true,' I said. 'I'm an underappreciated marvel. I don't know what you'd all do without me.'

Sir Hector let out his familiar bark of laughter.

'That's the spirit, m'girl,' he said. 'You tell her.'

I gave him a smile.

'For all your self-effacing japery, young Florence,' said Lady Farley-Stroud, 'you really did save the day and we're all immeasurably grateful to you. Thank you.'

So much for heading her off, I thought. I smiled and said, 'Thank you. Though anyone would have done the same.'

'And made a complete pig's ear of it, m'dear. We need more people like you helping to keep our wonderful village moving.'

Lady Hardcastle laughed.

'No good deed, Flo,' she said. 'No good deed.'

'What?' said Lady Farley-Stroud. 'Can't quite hear you, m'dear.'

'Nothing, dear, just a private joke between Flo and me.'

Ever since we had got home on Sunday evening, Lady Hardcastle had been teasing me that I'd soon be drawn in to every village committee going. I was beginning to fear she might be a little too close to the truth.

'Right you are,' said Lady Farley-Stroud. 'As long as I'm not missing out. I find I miss a lot of things these days. But we do need people like you, Florence. Have you ever thought of serving on any of our many fine village committees?'

'I don't think I'm up to something so important,' I said. 'I'm more of a doer than an organizer. I haven't the first idea how committees work.'

'Nonsense. Why don't we break you in gently? The Harvest Festival Committee could do with your particular talents this year.

As well as the service at the church, we usually have separate events in the village hall, but thanks to the fire we can't use that this year. We need someone with your brand of unconventional thinking to think of ways the village can celebrate the harvest this year without it.'

'I'll see what I can come up with,' I said. 'Perhaps I could be some sort of non-voting adviser? That way no feathers would be ruffled and they could ignore me if they didn't like my ideas.'

Lady Farley-Stroud laughed. 'Not like you to shy away from a scrap.'

'I don't mind a scrap, but I'd hate to cause any lasting antagonism. I think I'm better placed as a consultant.'

'As you wish, m'dear. Don't want to force you. But I shall be pressing you for solutions to the Harvest Festival dilemma.'

'I thought Harvest Festival was in late September,' said Lady Hardcastle.

'It moves about,' said Lady Farley-Stroud. 'A little like Easter. Traditionally, Harvest Home is on the Sunday nearest the Harvest Moon.'

'And when's that, my little *chou-fleur*?' said Sir Hector with a cheeky grin, and a wink in my direction.

Lady Farley-Stroud seemed momentarily flustered – she clearly wasn't prepared for technical questions, and it was my guess that Sir Hector knew she didn't have the faintest idea when it was – so I stepped in to rescue her.

'It's the full moon nearest the autumnal equinox, isn't it?' I said. 'So it could fall anywhere between mid-September and mid-October.'

Lady Hardcastle had reached into her bag for her pocket almanac. I had no idea why she carried a pocket almanac, but she did, and this was one of the occasions when that little eccentricity came in handy.

'There are full moons on the eighth of September and the eighth of October,' she said. 'And the equinox is on the . . . twenty-fourth of September. Which means . . . Harvest Moon is in October, and Harvest Home is Sunday, the eighth of October.'

'So tradition would have it,' said Lady Farley-Stroud, getting back into her stride. 'But we celebrate the harvest when the harvest comes in. If the harvest is early, we celebrate early, and this hot summer means we'll be very early indeed. Several of our farmers are planning to start this week, and none will leave it beyond the end of next. We have, perhaps, a fortnight – three weeks at the most – to put our plans in place. The vicar will be announcing the date of the Harvest Thanksgiving service any day now.'

'What do you do in the village hall?' I asked, getting drawn in despite myself. 'Is it just the harvest supper?'

'Would that it were. We used to host that here, you know. It became too expensive for us, sadly – and it was always far too boisterous – so we turned it into a village affair and funded it through subscription and donations and held it in the village hall. Now I fear it's grown too large for us to host a return, even just for one year. Actually, that's not fair. We might manage at a pinch, but there are other things to consider. The village children need somewhere to make their corn dolls, and we need somewhere to store the decorations for the procession. You've seen the procession.'

'We never have,' I said. 'Somehow we always seem to be away.'

'Well, we store the banners and whatnot in the hall, and use it as a sort of marshalling point where people can change into their costumes, apply the finishing touches and what have you.'

'Could the children not make their corn dolls in the schoolrooms?' I suggested. 'And the cricket pavilion has space for storage. The season must be ending soon.'

'I believe they've played their last match, actually.'

'There you are, then. So all we need is to organize a harvest supper. Why not just an open-air gathering on the village green? Paper plates, picnic blankets. If this weather holds it would be wonderful.'

'How did we manage to miss the supper last year?' mused Lady Hardcastle. 'After missing it before, I remember we were especially keen to make an appearance.'

'You were certainly invited,' said Lady Farley-Stroud, 'but some important engagement kept you away again. You were in London, I believe.'

'Ah, yes. We were . . . Well, I shan't burden you with knowledge of what we were up to, but it was a good deal less charming than a harvest supper.'

Lady Farley-Stroud smiled. She had known us long enough to have an inkling of the sort of thing we might have been up to in London instead of attending the Littleton Cotterell harvest supper. She would never have guessed the details, mind you. It had involved the wife of a foreign diplomat, a West End actor, and a camera. Blackmail is an ugly business, but sometimes it's a splendid way of getting hold of secret embassy documents without the tiresome work of breaking in.

'Your suggestions are sound,' said Lady Farley-Stroud, 'and we've considered them already. My only concern is that supper on the green would descend into a wild bacchanalian carouse.'

'Sign me up for that,' said Sir Hector as he set down a tray of drinks on the table. 'I love a bacchanalian carouse. A genteel supper surrounded by corn dolls is all well and good, but it's not a proper celebration till they tap the cider casks.'

Lady Farley-Stroud tutted.

'You can see why we need a better idea,' she said as Jenkins and Dewi the footman arrived with the trays of elevenses.

◆ ◆ ◆

As we ate, Lady Hardcastle slowly but deftly manoeuvred the conversation round to our real reason for calling.

'Did you hear about Mr Cridland?' she said.

'Apple farmer from Woodworthy,' said Sir Hector. 'Terrible business. One of our tenants, y'know.'

'Was he really?' said Lady Hardcastle. 'I can never keep up with all your holdings.'

'Used to own the whole lot,' he said wistfully. 'Came with the house. Quite a few hundred acres, from the Severn up to Chipping Bevington. Had to sell most of it off over the years, though. Debts, expenses, duties and whatnot, d'you see? But we still have a parcel or two hither and yon, and the cider orchard and cider mill are both on Farley-Stroud land.'

'I had no idea you were a cider magnate.'

Sir Hector barked his familiar laugh and the dogs looked up in alarm.

'Hardly,' he said. 'We just collect the modest rent – all the fame and glory goes to Abel Mattick.'

'Is it big business, then, cider making?'

'It is in these parts. Most of the local farmers produce a few gallons of scrumpy in the autumn for themselves and their pals, so you'd think there was no money in it. More of a hobby, d'you see? But young Mattick sells to every inn and tavern for miles around. People seek his cider out.'

'If most farmers make their own cider, why does it take Mattick to make cider from Cridland's apples?' asked Lady Hardcastle. 'Why didn't Cridland just do it himself?'

'Scale, m'dear,' said Sir Hector. 'The farmers who make their own just press a barrel's worth and sup it at their leisure. Mattick makes hundreds of gallons of the stuff. Keeps him busy most of the year. Cridland's main line of work was his dairy farm.'

'Well, I never,' she said. 'I presume it's lucrative?'

'I'm told Mattick makes a tidy living.'

'I had no idea. So having control over the raw materials, as it were – the apples – would put a chap in a strong position? Cridland had quite a bit of power in their relationship.'

'I suppose he did, yes. It's like wine, d'you see? The cider depends on the apples the same way wine depends on the grapes. Different apples, different ciders. I'm sure Mattick could work his magic with any apples, but he built his reputation on the ones from Cridland's orchard. So you're right, m'dear – whoever controls the apples controls the cider.'

'Of course, you know, Hector dear, that this makes you a suspect.'

'How's that?'

'Well, if your tenant's dead, those apples are yours.'

Again the bark of a laugh. 'I suppose they are, ain't they?'

'He doesn't have what it takes to murder a man and steal his apples,' said Lady Farley-Stroud.

'And what does it take?' I asked.

'A good deal more than that old fool has, that's for certain.'

'My little *chou-fleur* has it right, as always,' he said. 'Complete duffer, me.'

'We shall eliminate you from our enquiries, then,' said Lady Hardcastle. She leaned menacingly towards Sir Hector. 'For now.'

Sir Hector chuckled.

I had more questions.

'Is it like wine in other ways?' I asked. 'Does it improve with age, for instance?'

'Not so much. It'll keep for six or seven months, but it doesn't age like a vintage wine.'

'You said the cidery keeps Mattick busy most of the year. So presumably they don't just make one batch, sell it, and then sit back and wait for the next harvest.'

'No, he's able to spread it out. The apples will keep for quite a while if they're stored correctly, d'you see? Mattick knows what he's about and he makes several batches a year. Different character depending on the age of the apples.'

Lady Hardcastle rummaged in her bag for her notebook and pencil.

'What do you know of the Weryers of the Pomary?' she asked.

Jenkins's arrival with fresh tea and coffee gave Sir Hector time to consider his reply. Once the pots had been refreshed and Jenkins had returned to his other duties, Sir Hector took a sip of his tea and answered.

'I was High Protector for a time at the turn of the century,' he said. 'I'm not at liberty to reveal all the secrets of the order – oaths were sworn and all that – but I can give you the gist. The High Protector is entrusted with the documents of the order, d'you see? So I know, for instance, that it was founded in its current form in 1721 in the reign of whatshisname . . . George the First. But it's much older than that. There are references in parish records as far back as Edward the First, when Chipping Bevington got its charter and became a town. But the rites . . . well, I'm not allowed to tell you about the rites, but they're ancient – back to the Anglo-Saxons. What I *can* tell you is that it's all about protecting the orchard and ensuring a bountiful harvest.'

'Getting drunk and singing songs, more like,' said Lady Farley-Stroud.

Sir Hector chuckled.

'There's a fair bit of that,' he said. 'Can't deny it. But since they became known as the Cider Wardens, they mostly dedicate themselves to good works.'

'There are rites?' I asked. 'Like pagan rituals?'

'I think that might be overstating it a bit but there are rituals, yes.'

'How fascinating,' said Lady Hardcastle. 'And you were High Protector? Is that the head of the order?'

'It is, yes. There are always twelve Weryers. The High Protector of the Pomary heads the order. Then there are four Custodians of the Arbour, and seven Stewards of the Orchard. Always twelve.'

'Why did you give up your office?'

Sir Hector looked uncharacteristically serious for a moment.

'Let's just say there were . . . there were certain things about the order I wasn't quite comfortable with. There's a . . . well, let's not beat about the bush – there's a darker side to the Weryers. They might have moved towards philanthropic works and called themselves the Cider Wardens to sound a touch more friendly, but at its heart, the ancient order of the Weryers of the Pomary is about power.'

'Power and . . . influence?' asked Lady Hardcastle.

'I knew you'd understand.'

'Corruption, too?' I said.

'And I knew you'd get to the nub of it,' he said with another chuckle. 'No beating about the bush for our Armstrong. Yes, indeed. Pressure is applied, or palms are greased, and Weryers get on much better in life than they otherwise might. Not at all my sort of thing, d'you see? Can't abide all that nonsense. A chap succeeds or fails by dint of his own efforts, not because his pals have made dark threats or offered bribes.'

A mouth fitted at birth with a silver spoon helps enormously, though, I didn't say. Instead, I said, 'So a Weryer is a very desirable thing to be?'

'Extremely. I might be overstatin' the unseemliness of it all, but it wasn't for me.'

'One would have thought they'd keep themselves a bit more hidden if that's the sort of thing they get up to,' said Lady Hardcastle.

'Time was when membership was a closely guarded secret – back when the order wielded real power – but they don't keep it hidden any more. Haven't done for years.'

'Do you happen to know who the current Weryers are?'

'Of course, m'dear. But why are you so interested? Are they involved with Cridland's death?'

'We've no idea at this stage,' she said. 'We're aware that he was a Weryer and it seemed as good a place to start as any.'

'Well . . . let me see . . . the present High Protector is a chap from Chipping called Cornelius Starks. He's a solicitor. Bit dull for my taste, but a steadfast fellow.'

'So he's the biggest of the wigs,' said Lady Hardcastle, writing the details in her notebook. 'Who else?'

For the next half an hour, while we sipped our coffee and ate Mrs Brown's delicious cakes, Sir Hector enumerated and evaluated the remaining eleven Weryers of the Pomary. We left The Grange shortly before lunch and made our way home.

As we rounded the village green we saw Cissy Slocomb coming in the other direction on her bicycle. She flagged us down.

'I'm glad I caught you,' she said. 'I been up to your house but Blodwen said you was out.'

'And so we were, dear,' said Lady Hardcastle as she shut off the engine. 'But here we are now. What can we do for you?'

'I was just goin' to ask about old Cridland.'

'Why ask us?' I said.

'Everyone knows you's doin' one o' your investigations.'

'They do?'

'Of course. I knows because Blodwen told me. And everyone else from here to Nempnett Thrubwell knows because Edna Gibson told . . . well, she told everyone she met, didn't she. You knows what she's like.'

'The whole district is always fully aware of what we're up to, dear, you know that,' said Lady Hardcastle with a smile.

'But we knows when we has to keep our mouths shut,' said Cissy, earnestly. 'Like when you was in London last year. No one said a word.'

'You see? We are among friends.'

'I never doubted it,' I said. 'So what do you know about Claud Cridland?'

'I don't know much more about him than you already do but' – she looked cautiously about and lowered her voice – 'I do know I saw Moses Peppard out on his bike just afore dawn on Tuesday mornin'.'

'One of the Weryers,' I said.

'The Master Cooper,' said Lady Hardcastle. 'And the number-one Custodian of the Whatsits.'

'Of the Arbour,' I said.

'That's him,' said Cissy. 'He come past the dairy while we was loadin' up our dad's wagon. Turned his face away, he did, like he didn't want to be recognized. But he's a burly fella so it weren't difficult to know who it was, even in the half-light with his face turned away.'

'Could you tell where he was going?' I asked.

'He was comin' down from the main road, that's all I can say for sure.'

'The coopery's on the main road,' said Lady Hardcastle.

'It is,' confirmed Cissy. 'He lives in a cottage next to his workshop.'

'And where does the road lead to? The one that passes the dairy, I mean.'

'Down to the orchard.'

'Oh, so it does. I remember where you are now. That's very suggestive, wouldn't you say, Flo? One of the Weryers heading towards the orchard on the morning of the murder.'

'It is,' I agreed. 'Though he might also have turned off and come to Littleton. Or gone up to Woodworthy.'

'Surely it would be easier to go up the Gloucester Road and through Chipping Bevington if he wanted to get to Woodworthy from the coopery,' said Lady Hardcastle.

'Well, no,' said Cissy, sounding slightly disappointed at pouring cold water on her own gossip. 'Not on a bicycle. There's a wicked hill up the main road. You goes round it if you goes down past the orchard.'

'Hmm,' said Lady Hardcastle. 'But he could still have ridden past the orchard at or about the time Cridland was murdered. At the very least he might be a witness. We should tell Inspector Sunderland.'

I nodded.

'What else do you know, dear?' she continued.

'About what?'

'About Mr Cridland. About the Weryers. Who among them, for instance, might have borne him a grudge?'

'I never come across no one who didn't like him. He was always kind and generous. Since his Annie died, he threw hisself into helpin' others. He was a good man.'

'No secret indiscretions? Hidden vices?'

'He was as honest as they come. You always knew where you stood with Claud, and he didn't put up with dishonesty from no one else, neither. He'll be missed.'

'He didn't put up with dishonesty?' I said. 'How do you know? Was there any friction over it?'

'Oh, there was never nothin' bad,' she said with a smile. 'Like, there was one time when he caught Noel Gregory cheatin' at dominoes. He just made a big joke of it and everyone was still best pals after, but he wouldn't let him get away with it.'

'Ah,' said Lady Hardcastle, 'but if one of them were up to something properly dodgy and he caught them at it, they'd know he wouldn't just keep it to himself. His honesty would become a liability to them, and a potential danger to him.'

'I knows what you means,' said Cissy, 'but aside from a little good-natured cheatin' at dominoes, they's all as honest as he was.'

'But still you're suspicious of Moses Peppard,' I said.

'Well . . .' she began, slowly. 'I mean, you gots to admit it was odd him cyclin' past the dairy at that time o' day. It's not like coopers keep the sort of odd hours we does. Or the farmers – they's up afore us some days.'

'We'll look into it, dear,' said Lady Hardcastle. 'Thank you. You've made our trip very worthwhile. And I'm sure Inspector Sunderland will be pleased with the information, too.'

'It's a pleasure, m'lady. But I'd better let you get on. See you later, Flo.'

And with that, she cycled off.

Chapter Five

Back at the house, Lady Hardcastle made straight for the drawing room and her trusty crime board. I fetched a jug of cordial and two glasses from the kitchen and made myself comfortable in an armchair while she went through her notes.

'So, we have the High Protector, Cornelius Starks,' she said, writing his name and rank on the board. 'I shall do sketches later once I've met all these people. He's a solicitor from Chipping, so he's definitely one of the ones on Miss Chamberlain's list.' She linked the new entry to the list she had copied on to the board the night before. She consulted her notes again. 'Then there's Moses Peppard.'

'The Master Cooper,' I said. 'And First Custodian of the Arbour. Also from Miss Chamberlain's list.'

'And who was seen on his way past the dairy before dawn on the day of the murder. Hector said he was a "bluff fellow", which I took to mean not entirely to Hector's taste. He prefers his fellows to be a little more easy-going and fun.'

'I didn't get the impression he was a wrong 'un, though.'

'Nor did I until we heard from Cissy. We shall put a question mark beside his name. Who's next? Ah, yes, Griffith Uzzle, Second Custodian.'

'And landlord of the Mock of Pommey at Woodworthy,' I said.

She linked him to GU on Miss Chamberlain's list.

'We never go to Woodworthy,' I said.

'We shall remedy that at our earliest opportunity. Especially if the local tavern is known as the Mock of Pommey.'

I stood and retrieved the dictionary.

'Mock . . .' I said. 'Mock . . . Oh, here we are. "Another term for a cider cheese." That's not marvellously helpful . . . One moment . . . Cheese . . . "Solid curds of milk" . . . No . . . "Fruit of the common mallow" . . . No idea what that might mean at all . . . Ah, this is it: "Parcels of apple pulp (pomace or sometimes pommey) built up into a stack for pressing in the cider-making process."'

'How very West Country. We're very much in the land of cider, aren't we?' she said. 'Who's next?' She consulted her notes. 'The Third Custodian is our Master Cider Maker, Abel Mattick – also on our list of initials. And the Fourth Custodian was the late Claud Cridland.'

'Dairy farmer and looker-afterer of huge apple orchards,' I said.

She examined the board and doodled a cowled man holding a staff.

'So those are the five leaders,' I said. 'Who would benefit from Cridland's death?'

'Well, Starks is a country solicitor so I don't imagine he's short of a few bob. And at first glance, killing a farmer doesn't seem to do him any good at all. It robs him of a client, for one thing.'

'Do you imagine there's competition among the hierarchy of the Weryers?'

'Cridland might have been challenging his leadership, you mean? Possibly, but from what Hector said, it's First Custodian Moses Peppard who's next in line for High Protector.'

'And Cridland was the lowest of the higher-ups, so he was no threat to the rest of them. Personal animus?'

'That seems more likely,' she said. 'We'll know more once we start speaking to them.'

'We already know half the others – perhaps we should start with them.'

'Yes,' she said, returning to her list. 'Village greengrocer Lawrence Weakley, Old Joe from the Dog and Duck, and dear Septimus Holman, our trusty baker.'

'And Bob Slocomb the dairyman,' I added.

'Yes, although I've never met him.'

'You're never up when the milk arrives.'

'I'm very much of the opinion that the only time one should be up and about at the same time as the milkman is when one is returning home in the small hours after a particularly debauched night out. And nights out are in short supply these days, debauched or otherwise.'

'Remind me of the remaining three?'

'Leopold Lehane – retired bank manager. Noel Gregory – an accounts clerk at the cattle auction house in Chipping Bevington. And Archie Rogers, arable farmer and top tenor in the Littleton Cotterell Male Voice Choir.'

'We had one of those in Aberdare. And a brass band. The miners sang and the men from the iron works played in the band.'

'Oh, how marvellous. I sang in a choir at Girton but there was far too much politics and backbiting for my taste. We should look out for this local choir – I should very much like to hear them.'

'I'd like that – a taste of home,' I said, contemplating the list. 'So those are our runners and riders?'

'Hardly. What about this Grace Chamberlain woman?' She tapped the sketch she'd pinned at the side of the board. 'Where does she fit in?'

'It won't be her.'

'Why ever not? She's the mysterious stranger.'

'The mysterious stranger is always a red herring. You should read more.'

'You're probably right. And then there's everyone else everywhere, of course.'

'We never consider everyone else everywhere until we've eliminated all the people close to the victim,' I said. 'And in practice that means we never consider anyone else anywhere because almost every murder victim is killed by someone connected to them.'

'Wise you are in the ways of the murderer, tiny one. Then we shall continue to attempt to learn more about the Weryers of the Pomary.'

'I concur, my lady.'

'And Grace Chamberlain.'

I sighed and refilled our glasses with cordial.

Later that day we were sitting in the garden, where Lady Hardcastle was fanning herself and complaining about the heat, when Edna appeared at the back door leading two visitors.

'Inspector Sunderland and Dr Gosling to see you, m'lady,' she said.

'How absolutely marvellous,' said Lady Hardcastle. 'Do sit down, gentlemen.'

Edna bustled off and the two men pulled chairs up to the table.

'You'll have to excuse my bedraggled appearance – this heat is altogether too much for me, I'm afraid.'

'You look as radiant as ever, old thing,' said Dr Gosling.

'You're very kind,' she said. 'A frightful liar, but a kindly one.'

He inclined his head in acknowledgement.

'So, then,' she continued, 'what has prompted your most welcome visit? Do you have news?'

'Not news as such—' began Inspector Sunderland.

'I have a cause of death,' interrupted Dr Gosling.

'Which was . . . ?' I asked.

'Exsanguination due to a puncture wound to the left ventricle, caused by a long, thin, sharp metal object.'

'Did we not know that already?' said Lady Hardcastle.

'We surmised, but I am now able to confirm.'

'Any more clues as to what the weapon might have been?' I said.

'Very sharp, very smooth, and probably very shiny.'

Lady Hardcastle frowned.

'Shiny?' she said. 'How on earth . . . ?'

'His shirt above that peculiar bruise on his chest smelled of metal polish,' said the doctor with a smile.

'He might have spilled some on himself at some other time.'

'He might, it's true. But the shirt was otherwise clean and there were no traces of polish elsewhere. I'd have expected his hands to be similarly polishy if he'd been buffing up his silverware in the middle of the night. The weapon, whatever it was, was cylindrical, and about the width of a man's finger.' He held up his own finger just in case we couldn't imagine it for ourselves.

'Does any of this point to a particular suspect? One of the Weryers, perhaps?'

'I like to keep an open mind, as you know,' said the inspector after a while, 'but I'm disinclined to suspect any of the Weryers for now. They're altogether too . . . I don't want to say "noble" – that's far too grand a word. But they're a bunch of old buffers drinking cider and buying clothes for orphaned children.'

'Flo always insists that sort of talk will come back to bite us, Inspector dear,' said Lady Hardcastle. 'The police inspector always rules out the true culprit early on, while he goes haring off after red herrings, she says.'

'I've said something similar but without the mangled metaphor,' I said. 'Are hares fond of smoked herring?'

'They live for it,' she said, 'as do inspectors of police. We have heard from a reliable source, though, that Moses Peppard was seen riding past the dairy on his bicycle on the morning of the murder, so there's at least one Weryer we should be warier of.'

The inspector made a note.

'That's interesting,' he said, 'but he could have been going anywhere.'

'I agree, but I pass it on nonetheless. The Weryers used to be a good deal less noble than you might suppose, by the way.'

'Did they, indeed?'

'Hector Farley-Stroud was once their brave leader, but he wasn't fond of the corruption and power-peddling, so he walked away. It might be that they're still not quite so virtuous as they would have us believe.'

'Almost no one is as virtuous as they would have people believe,' said the inspector. 'But I shall look into it, nonetheless.' He made another note.

'Other than assorted Weryers, the only other person to stand out is Miss Chamberlain.'

'She's actually the person I'd like most to speak to,' he said. 'That's the reason we've come up to the village. Well, it's the reason I came up. Dr Gosling just tagged along.'

'I enjoy your company, old boy,' said the doctor.

'She has a list of Weryers in her notebook,' I said. 'Or their initials, at least.'

'That's interesting, too,' said the inspector. 'I wonder why.'

'Perhaps she's writing a piece on them,' said Dr Gosling. 'Dinah has notes on all sorts of things in her little book.'

'It's possible,' said the inspector. 'Anything is possible at this stage.'

'We believe she travelled here from Exeter, by the way,' said Lady Hardcastle.

'How did you come to that conclusion?' asked the inspector.

'Interrogation and the power of logical reasoning,' she said with a smile. 'There's a convoluted explanation but I'd wager a decent sum on her having come from Devon. Have you made your calls to your contacts yet?'

'Only one,' said the inspector. 'By chance I telephoned my friend at Exeter yesterday afternoon and he promised to let me know if he found anything.'

'But you still suspect her, even though you know nothing about her. A man after my own heart.'

'I didn't say I suspected her, I said I wanted to speak to her. A man was murdered in the early hours of yesterday morning, and everything in his life, and in the world around him, had been the same up to that moment, save for one thing. The only difference in his comfortable, ordinary life was the arrival in your quiet little village of a stranger with no apparent reason for being here.'

'Perhaps she came for the Harvest Festival,' suggested Dr Gosling. 'Or to view the charming Romanesque church. Oh, oh, I know: perhaps she's a murder tourist.'

'A what, dear?' said Lady Hardcastle.

'You know, those people who visit the scenes of tragedies. You can't deny you've had more than your fair share here.'

'Nowhere near as many as the inspector insisted we'd see when we first met him.'

But Dr Gosling was warming to his theme.

'You realize, old thing,' he said, sitting up, 'that most people live their whole lives without ever seeing a single murder. You had one within days of moving in. Then there was the chap at the cattle market—'

'If we're being pedantic, he died at Chipping Bevington.'

'If you insist. But you were living here and you came all the way into town to see me about that one while I was still working at the BRI. Then there was all that unpleasantness at the moving-picture festival—'

'"Unpleasantness" would cover it, yes.'

'Indeed. So you see what might attract tragedy sightseers? And I haven't even mentioned the murders at Riddlethorpe, Bristol, or Weston-super-Mare that you've got yourselves involved in. Perhaps *you're* the reason she's here. Perhaps *you're* the tourist attraction.'

'Pish and fiddlesticks, "old thing". No one would cross the street to see me, much less travel up from darkest Devonshire,' said Lady Hardcastle. Her tone was airily dismissive but I could see from the twinkle in her eye that she was actually rather flattered. 'I do need to know more about this woman, though,' she continued. 'Despite Flo's misgivings, I still think she's up to something, and I should very much like to find out what.'

'You're welcome to come along if you like,' said the inspector. 'You're an adept interviewer.'

'You're very kind, Inspector, but I fear my skills, such as they are, have no effect upon Miss Chamberlain. If I were to return, I rather think she'd just play dumb again. I shall leave her to you.'

'As you wish, but the offer remains.' He turned to me. 'Where would you put your money, if not on the mysterious stranger?'

'I'm an old-fashioned girl,' I said. 'It'll be someone Cridland knew. One of the Weryers, I should say – from everything we've heard, his personal life was quiet and uneventful.'

'I'll certainly be looking into the Weryers' comings and goings.'

'We can give you a list of members.'

'That's very kind, but I know plenty about them already.'

'Oh,' I said. 'We thought we'd been terribly clever finding out who everyone was. We asked Sir Hector Farley-Stroud this morning. We made notes on the crime board and everything.'

'If only you'd waited,' he said with a smile. 'I could have given you all the information you needed. They're a harmless bunch, as far as I know.'

'As far as you know?' said Lady Hardcastle.

'One never knows everything, and I don't want to prejudice my own investigation by ruling out an entire group of suspects just because I have a soft spot for them. One of them might be, as Miss Armstrong often has it, a wrong 'un.'

'One of them is,' I said. 'You mark my words.'

Once we'd seen the inspector and Dr Gosling on their way, Lady Hardcastle suggested that we continue our investigation into the Weryers with a trip to the coopery on the Gloucester Road.

'Even though he could have been going anywhere,' she said, 'I still think it worth our while to speak first to the cycling cooper. I might change before we go, though – I'm positively wilting.'

We set off a short time later and were soon approaching a large painted sign that read: *Peppard's Coopery – casks and barrels made and repaired.*

Lady Hardcastle pulled into the yard and switched off the engine. The only sounds that remained were the singing of the birds, the ticking of the cooling engine, and the satisfying clank of a hammer on iron coming from the workshop.

We approached the huge workshop doors and peered in.

'Mr Peppard?' called Lady Hardcastle.

The clanking stopped.

'Come on in,' called a man's voice from inside. 'It's quite safe.'

We entered the workshop. Frosted windows in the roof admitted a soft, flat light that illuminated the busy room of a master craftsman. There were barrel staves leaning against one wall, with iron hoops beside them. Clean, well-tended tools hung from the walls: draw knives, adzes, chisels, planes, and dozens of other things I couldn't identify. Unprepared timber was stacked in racks at the far end of the room, with yet more curved iron bands ready to be cut to size and riveted together.

In the middle of the workshop was a well-built, handsome man in his forties. He looked like he was constructed entirely of muscle, but there was a gentleness about his eyes and a warmth in the mischievous smile that tempered the potential brutality of his frame. He had been working at a tall anvil, like a polo mallet standing on its end, hammering a hoop into shape. He put down an impressively large hammer and wiped his hands on a cloth hanging from the tie of his leather apron.

'Afternoon, ladies,' he said. 'What can I do for you? A water butt for the garden, perhaps? Repair the ornamental miniature cask you keep your sherry in?'

'I say, what a splendid idea. Perhaps we should replace the brandy decanter with a little oak cask. With a brass tap in the bung. But no, sadly not, Mr Peppard. I'm Lady Hardcastle and this is Miss Armstrong.'

He squinted at us myopically.

'Why, so you are, so you are. I couldn't see you there. I should wear my spectacles but I haven't had them long and I just can't seem to get on with them. What a pleasure to almost see you both, I must say.'

'Thank you,' said Lady Hardcastle and I together.

'But what *can* I do for Littleton Cotterell's most celebrated residents, if not water butts and miniature brandy casks?'

'I'd not rule out the possibility of your supplying both of those at some point,' said Lady Hardcastle, 'but we'd just like a few words with you if we may.'

'Words, eh? I have a good supply of those. Would you like a cup of tea to go with them?'

From Sir Hector's description of a 'bluff fellow', I had been expecting someone considerably less charming than the huge cooper moving gracefully across his workshop to set a kettle to boil on a hotplate beside his furnace.

'It's a little close in here with the furnace going,' he said as he spooned tea leaves into a large tin teapot. 'I've a table and chairs in the yard if you'd prefer.'

'That would be delightful, thank you,' said Lady Hardcastle. 'As long as we're not keeping you from your work.'

'Not at all. A good barrel will last for years if it's treated right. Another half hour to make this one won't make much difference one way or the other. Make yourselves comfortable – I'll bring the tea in a moment.'

Outside, in the shade of a makeshift awning, were four chairs and a table, all fashioned from old barrels. We sat quietly and waited, me basking contentedly in the heat, Lady Hardcastle looking increasingly frazzled.

The tea arrived and we sipped it gratefully.

'So, what sort of words were you after?' asked Mr Peppard. 'Words about the late Claud Cridland would be my guess.'

'You'd guess correctly,' said Lady Hardcastle.

'Terrible shame. Nice fellow. Would have been a dreadful leader of the Weryers, but he was a kind and likeable bloke.'

'Leader?' said Lady Hardcastle.

'Starks is retiring as High Protector soon, so a new one will have to be appointed. He and I were in the running.'

'Ah, I see,' said Lady Hardcastle.

'Why would he have been so dreadful?' I asked.

'Too easily swayed. He couldn't make a plan and stick to it, see? His opinion on anything was the opinion of the last person he spoke to. He changed his mind three or four times a day, like you toffs change your clothes.'

'On a day like today I rather feel I ought to be changing more often,' said Lady Hardcastle, 'but I take your point. But that was your only objection to him?'

'Did I kill him, do you mean? No, I didn't kill him. Like I said, his only problem was that he wasn't up to the job of High Protector. Folk would have seen that soon enough.'

I was even less certain now what Sir Hector had meant by 'bluff fellow', but I wondered if it meant that Peppard was a plain-speaking man. I thought perhaps he might appreciate a little plain speaking in return.

'You were seen riding your bicycle towards the orchard on the morning he was killed,' I said. 'Where were you going?'

'I thought they might have seen me as I passed the dairy,' he said with a smile. 'I wasn't going to the orchard, I was on my way to see a lady friend.'

'At five o'clock in the morning?' asked Lady Hardcastle.

'There's no set time of day for love, my lady.'

'It's love, then?'

He laughed.

'No,' he said, 'it's lust, pure and simple. Her husband leaves the house at around five this time of year and doesn't get back till lunchtime. If I get there not long after he's gone, we can have our fun and I can still be back at work in time to start a decent day's work.'

'Who's the lucky lady?' she said.

'That's not for me to say. I don't mind what people think of me, but it's up to her who knows what she's up to.'

'That sounds surprisingly honourable,' said Lady Hardcastle with a nod.

'Who else might have wanted to kill him?' I asked.

'I honestly couldn't tell you. I can't think of anyone living who bore him a grudge. He was a thoroughly decent man.'

'So we keep hearing,' said Lady Hardcastle.

There being little else to ask him, conversation moved on to other matters, and Lady Hardcastle asked him how much a water butt and brandy cask might cost. She was pleasantly surprised by the price he quoted and, as we clambered back into the Rolls, repeated her promise to send him an order within the week.

◆ ◆ ◆

As we set off back down the Gloucester Road, Lady Hardcastle was in pensive mood.

'What are you thinking?' I asked.

'I'm thinking that his admission of an affair with a farmer's wife might be an excellent bluff. Confessing to something like that is so shocking that we're expected to believe that it must be true. Who on earth would say such a thing and risk a scandal? But what if it's just a way to divert us from an even bigger scandal? While we're busy clucking over his dalliance with the farmer's wife, we're not looking to see if he stabbed Claud Cridland to death in the orchard. We need to find out a good deal more about our charming local cooper before I fully accept his story of illicit early-morning shenanigans.'

'We can do that,' I said. 'We're skilled finders-out of scandalous detail – look how many foreign government ministers we've managed to blackmail over the years. Surely we can track down a cooper's paramour.'

'I have every confidence in us,' she said.

As we approached the turning for Littleton Cotterell I noticed a tall woman striding along the road towards us.

'Is that Grace Chamberlain?' I said.

'It certainly looks like it.'

Lady Hardcastle honked the horn and waved, but the young woman ignored us.

'I wonder where she's going,' I said.

'Perhaps she wants to talk to the cooper, too.'

'He was on her list.'

'He was. We need to try to have another word with her, but we'll leave it for another day, I think. In the meantime, I am in dire need of at least one more bath.'

Chapter Six

On Thursday morning I left Lady Hardcastle to some urgent work in her studio in the orangery, and took a stroll into the village. There had been a mix-up with the meat order and Miss Jones had said she'd drop in to Spratt's on her way home to sort it out. I was keen to go for a walk, though – it would give me a chance to think things through – so I offered to do it myself.

I was surprised to see the village carpenter, Charley Hill, still hard at work with his two labourers on the site of the makeshift stage. We'd seen his lads dismantling the structure earlier in the week but here they were still tinkering with . . . something or other. I had plenty of time so I decided to go and investigate.

Mr Hill saw me coming.

'Mornin', Miss Armstrong,' he said with a smile. 'Come to give us a hand?'

'Good morning, Mr Hill,' I said. 'I'm always willing to lend a hand, but I'm not much of a woodworker.'

'Not many ladies are,' he said, sagely. 'It's man's work, carpentry.'

'So they say. But what are you up to? Your wonderful stage is all packed up, isn't it?'

'It is, miss, yes, but Lady Farley-Stroud's got us workin' on your next marvellous idea. You don't half come up with 'em.'

'My idea?'

He frowned.

'The Harvest Festival supper,' he prompted. 'You know.'

It was my turn to frown, but I decided to play along.

'Oh, yes. Of course. That idea. I'm glad she liked it,' I said. 'Well, I must let you carry on.'

'Right you are, miss. We know where to find you if we come unstuck.'

'Of course,' I said with a confidence I didn't feel. 'Any time.'

I turned away and headed for the small parade of shops.

Fred Spratt was hard at work chopping cutlets from a rack of lamb, while his wife, Eunice, nattered merrily away beside him. With the door propped open in the heat there was no bell to alert them to my presence, but the sound of my summer boots on the sawdust floor had them both looking in my direction.

'Good morning, Miss Armstrong,' said Mr Spratt.

'Hello, Mr Spratt,' I said. 'Hello, Mrs Spratt.'

'Hello, dear,' said Eunice. She was notionally there to keep the books and take the payments, but I always rather suspected that her main reason for going to work every day was to spend more time with her husband.

'Afore you says anything,' said Mr Spratt, 'I knows why you've come, and I've got them here.' He reached below the counter and produced a small packet wrapped in waxed paper. 'I meant to put a note in with the order sayin' the sausages would come later, but the lad took it afore I could get round to it.'

I took the packet with a grateful smile and opened my mouth to thank him.

'I said he should have left it to me,' said Eunice before I could manage it. 'He's got a head like a sieve these days. "Just you get on with your choppin' and trimmin'," I says, "and leave the paperwork to me." But will he listen? Will he, buggery. Course, I don't reckon he hears me half the time. Our Daisy says he's fine but I think he's goin' deaf.'

It was, in fact, Daisy's firm opinion that her father feigned deafness for more than half the time as a means of avoiding conflict and unwelcome invitations to complete household chores. The wink he gave me confirmed that Daisy was at least partly correct.

'Aha,' I said when Eunice paused to draw breath, 'that explains it. I knew it must be something like that.'

'I was expectin' to see young Blodwen Jones come to query it,' he said, 'but we a'n't seen her for a while.'

'Her ma's not well,' said Eunice. 'I told you t'other day. That poor woman does suffer so. Blodwen goes straight home from work to see to her. She don't have no time to be dealin' with your mistakes.'

Miss Jones's mother was, indeed, a little under the weather, and Lady Hardcastle had offered Miss Jones some time off to take care of her, but she'd declined. It was just a summer cold, apparently, and if she were there all the time, her mother would milk it for all it was worth.

'Would you like a couple of these lamb chops to make up for it?' said Mr Spratt as though he hadn't heard.

'Oh, no, I couldn't possibly,' I said. 'A couple of days late on a pound of sausages hardly warrants any compensation. I'll buy four of them, though – they'll make a lovely lunch.'

Mr Spratt wrapped the lamb chops while Eunice took my money.

'I heard you was takin' an interest in Claud Cridland's death,' she said as she handed me my change. 'Terrible business, that. They never seems to have good luck, they Weryers.'

'Do they not?' I said. 'Why, what's happened?'

'Don't take no notice,' said Mr Spratt. 'All that were twenty years ago. 'Asn't got nothin' to do with Cridland.'

'I never said it had,' said Eunice, who didn't seem to have noticed that he'd had no trouble hearing her this time. 'I was just remarkin' on how ill fortune seems to follow 'em, that's all.'

'You can't just leave it at that,' I said. 'What ill fortune?'

'About twenty years ago, one of the Weryers murdered one of the others,' said Mr Spratt. 'No one ever knew why, but they caught him. Tried and hanged him for it, they did.'

'They did,' said Eunice. 'And—'

'And nothin', my love. It's in the past, and that's where everyone wants it to stay.'

Eunice harrumphed and returned to her ledger.

'Where did it happen?' I asked. 'What was it all about? Was anyone else involved?'

Mr Spratt smiled.

'You're as bad as our Daisy with all your questions,' he said, kindly.

And I had so many more of them: How did it happen? How did they catch the murderer? What happened at the trial? Did either man have a family? What happened to them? So many questions leaped to mind, but the look in Mr Spratt's eye told me they weren't welcome and that no answers would be forthcoming.

It seemed to be time to go.

'Thank you for the sausages and the lamb,' I said. 'Cheerio, both.'

I set off for home.

Back at the house, I put the meat in the larder and told Miss Jones that everything had been sorted out.

'Oh, thank you,' she said. 'I knew it would be something simple – Fred Spratt wouldn't cheat anyone. I just never got the time to get over there.'

'Well, it's all done now, we've got some lovely chops for our lunch tomorrow, and you can get straight home to your mother instead of worrying about sausages.'

'Lovely. Although there's little need to hurry home – she's fine.'

'All recovered?'

'Weren't really nothing to recover from. She just likes to make a fuss when she's a little bit poorly, that's all.'

'I know someone like that,' I said with a wink.

She laughed.

'I've just made her some breakfast. I didn't know how long you'd be so I made plenty in case you wanted some when you got back. Edna's just taken it in to her.'

'Marvellous,' I said. 'I wasn't hungry first thing, but I'm starving now.'

I went through to the morning room with a fresh pot of tea and found Lady Hardcastle, dressed in her grimy engineer's overalls, sprawled in a chair in a most unladylike pose.

'You look elegant,' I said.

'Elegance be blowed,' she said, reaching for a piece of toast. 'It's altogether too hot to be elegant. I've always been keen on these overalls—'

'To my enduring dismay.'

'Fuddy-duddy. But they really come into their own in this weather. One would think a trouser would be restricting, but they do allow for a more comfortable sitting position and they're much roomier than one might imagine. Plenty of room for cooling air to circulate. Oh, and I'm mercifully free of the cruel embrace of the corset, too. I might see about having some overalls made in a more fetching fabric. I shall set a trend among fashionable young ladies as I swish about town in my practical but refined daywear.'

'It's worth a try.'

'Right at the moment, though, it's still too hot to be so covered up, even in loose-fitting work clothes and free of the dreaded corset. Do you think perhaps I might get away with those short trousers the runners were wearing at the Olympics the other year? And some sort of short-sleeved shirt?'

'We *could* claim you're in training for the marathon race at Stockholm next year . . . but I doubt anyone would believe us.'

'Why ever not?'

'You're entirely the wrong shape for a marathon runner,' I said, pouring myself a cup of tea. 'And it's a men's event anyway.' I took a fried egg and two rashers of bacon from the serving dish and put them on my toast. 'Even if it weren't, the ladies don't get comfortable clothes. Do you remember the photographs of the women's archery? They were all in their best dresses and hats, as if they were out for afternoon tea with a maiden aunt.'

'Is that why you weren't on the British archery team?'

'Exactly. I couldn't find a suitable hat. And even the ladies who had to move about a bit more were in heavy bloomers and long-sleeved blouses.'

'Pffft. None of it is fair. So if I can't dress as a marathon runner I shall just have to wear something wafty when we go out later.'

'We're going out later?'

'Yes. I was in the orangery making a bowler hat for a badger – he's a solicitor in my new story, you see. Anyway, it suddenly came to me that I'd met Cornelius Starks – Lord High Pooh Bah of the Worriers, and solicitor of this parish – at some dreary civic function a couple of years ago in town. I'd quite forgotten both him and the event until I started thinking about dear little Brock starring in my new moving picture as a solicitor, and then I had a sudden flash of a dull man with a grey streak in his hair, clutching a glass of sherry and telling me we were neighbours.'

'Starks.'

'Even he.'

'You ought to keep a journal of people you meet at these things. You never remember anyone.'

'For the most part I really don't wish to remember them. Honestly, Flo, you'd die of boredom if you had to endure even a minute in their company. But when I do need to remember anyone, they drift back to me eventually, just as Starks did. So I curtailed my musteline hatting endeavours and popped back in here to telephone his office. He was gracious enough to pretend that he remembered me, and further, to pretend that he'd be delighted to see us both.'

'Why wouldn't he be? We're delightful.'

'So you keep saying, but one never knows how people will react.'

'Did either of you mention a particular time?'

'No, we're to drop in whenever we wish – he'll be in his office at Chipping all day. If you'd be an absolute poppet and draw me a bath when we've finished here, I can get out of my scruffy but oh-so-comfortable overalls and into something less suitable for the weather but more suitable for company.'

'I'll find you something wafty,' I said. 'Or floaty at the very least.'

'That's the ticket. How was your village trip? Any new gossip?'

'As a matter of fact, yes. I called in at the butcher's—'

'Has he sorted out the sausage order?'

'That was the reason for my visit. It's not like you to pay such close attention to domestic matters.'

'I always have an eye on these things, dear. I seldom mention them because you always handle them so adeptly, but I take an especial interest in sausages.'

'I'm flattered. Thank you. But anyway. Fred asked me whether we were looking into Cridland's murder and then Eunice—'

'I do love Eunice – she's such a character.'

'She is. Anyway. In the course of a slightly awkward exchange between the two of them it came out that Cridland isn't the first of the Weryers to be murdered.'

'Awkward how?'

'Fred didn't want to talk about it and Eunice . . . well, obviously Eunice very much did. There's not much Eunice won't talk about once you get her going. It all happened twenty years ago, apparently, and I couldn't get anything more from them than that.'

'How interesting. I wonder why we didn't know this already.'

'From Fred's reaction when Eunice brought it up, I'd say it was Something We Don't Talk About.'

'Hmm. Well, it might be nothing, but we should find out more if we can,' she said. 'Pass the bacon, would you?'

◆ ◆ ◆

The address Cornelius Starks had given Lady Hardcastle for his office was on the High Street in Chipping Bevington, a few doors up from Pomphrey's Bric-a-Brac Emporium, and we drove there not long after breakfast.

It was Lady Hardcastle's turn to drive and she arrived in town at some speed, startling an elderly gentleman by honking the horn and then sliding to a halt through a small pile of manure outside the Bengal Tiger pub.

'How many pubs are there in this little market town?' I asked as I stepped on to the kerb.

She totted up on her fingers.

'I make it eight,' she said. 'It does get very busy on market day, mind you – I don't think they want for customers.'

'I don't imagine they do, no. It seems like a lot, though.'

'It certainly does. One for every day of the week, with an extra one on Sundays for a livener before evensong, where they atone for the sins of drunkenness and debauchery.'

The High Street was busy with shoppers, and a mother bustled past with her two children. Lady Hardcastle offered her a cheery greeting but the woman was too distracted by her children and her shopping list to respond. She stopped a few steps up the road and turned back to us.

'I'm so sorry,' she said with a harassed smile. 'It's one of them days. Good morning to you, too.'

And then she was gone.

'Modern life is rather frenetic, don't you think?' said Lady Hardcastle.

'It does seem to move at quite a pace,' I said. 'Imagine what it must be like in the city these days.'

'I do sometimes think we should all just slow down and take time to appreciate the things around us.'

I saw irony in such a sentiment being expressed by someone who invariably drove her motor car as though she were fleeing from a fire, but I decided to say nothing. It was a lovely day and no one's pleasure would be enhanced by starting an argument.

'It's up this way, isn't it?' I said instead.

We walked past Pomphrey's and I was pleased to note that the hookah-smoking moose was still wearing his topi in the window, while at the same time slightly disappointed that no one loved him enough to buy him.

Lady Hardcastle noticed my glance.

'No,' she said, and carried on walking.

We arrived at a dark blue door, beside which was a brass plate proclaiming it to be the offices of *Messrs Starks, Lemmings and Wetmore – Solicitors and Commissioners for Oaths*. For some reason I always mentally added 'and small bets placed', but I had no idea why.

Lady Hardcastle opened the door and entered.

As I followed her in, I was sure I saw Grace Chamberlain on the other side of the street, but when I looked back she was gone.

◆ ◆ ◆

The cramped front office was home to a doughy young clerk with ink-stained cuffs. His desk faced the door and he scrambled to his feet when he saw Lady Hardcastle.

'Good morning, madam,' he said with a tiny bow. 'How may I help you?'

She handed him her calling card.

'Lady Hardcastle,' she said with a smile. 'And this is my associate, Miss Armstrong. I telephoned Mr Starks this morning and he was kind enough to invite me to call.'

'Thank you, my lady,' said the clerk. 'If you'd care to wait here, I shall tell him you've arrived.'

He indicated two visitors' chairs by the window and we sat, looking out at the bustling activity on the busy High Street as he disappeared through a door on the other side of the small room.

Moments later, an angular man, wearing a high-collared shirt in the modern style, a dark jacket and grey trousers, followed the clerk back through the door. From the grey streak in his otherwise almost-black hair, I guessed that this was the man brought to mind by Lady Hardcastle's bowler-hatted badger.

'Lady Hardcastle,' he said, holding out his hand. 'Cornelius Starks at your service.'

I was right.

'How do you do?' said Lady Hardcastle. 'You've not met my associate, Miss Armstrong.'

'Never had the pleasure,' he said, offering me his bony hand. 'How do you do?'

His grip was surprisingly firm.

'How do you do?' I said.

'I gather you two ladies are . . . what's the phrase . . . ? "Helping the police with their enquiries." Maybe not that – makes you sound like a couple of wrong 'uns. I say, you're not wrong 'uns, are you?' He chuckled at what he clearly imagined to be the cleverness of his wit.

We smiled politely.

'I rather imagined you might want to talk to me about the case,' he continued obliviously. 'What with Cridland being a Cider Warden and all. Am I right?'

'You are, indeed,' said Lady Hardcastle.

'Anything to help Inspector Sunderland. Bumped into him a few times over the years.'

'You have a criminal practice?'

'It's certainly criminal the way I practise,' he said with another chuckle. 'No, but seriously, I mostly do wills and a bit of conveyancing. A few business contracts here and there. Keeps the wolf from the door, what? But I've met Sunderland at charity bashes. Very active in the Bristol charity world, our Ollie.'

'I had no idea. He certainly keeps that quiet.'

'Modest man,' said Starks. 'Modest man.'

'So it would appear.'

'Well, now, ladies. I'm happy to answer all your questions, but I've been cooped up in here since eight o'clock this morning and I'm ready for lunch. Would you care to join me? Time was when married chaps couldn't go to lunch with a lady without causing a scandal, but times change, don't they? We've got ladies helping the police with their enquiries now, what?' Again the self-satisfied chuckle.

'We should be delighted to join you for lunch,' said Lady Hardcastle. 'Where do you usually go?'

'There's a tearoom just up the way. They do a marvellous mulligatawny soup. Don't they, White?'

The clerk looked up from his work.

'I beg your pardon, sir?' he said.

'Bixby's Tearoom. Mulligatawny soup.'

'The best in the West, sir.'

'There you are, ladies. What do you think?'

'It sounds splendid. Armstrong?'

'Of course,' I said. In truth I could imagine few things I wanted to eat less than a West Country tearoom's interpretation of a delicious Indian soup, but Mr Starks was a potential source of valuable information and it served no useful purpose to offend him by turning my nose up at his favourite repast.

'Then let us away. I've no appointments in the diary, White, so things should be quiet until my return.'

'Certainly, sir. When will that be?'

'When I'm done, lad. When I'm done.'

We walked back out into the sunshine.

The tearoom was doing a roaring trade but they managed to find a table for their regular customer and his guests. I looked at the menu on the table and toyed with the idea of trying the ham pie, but I still wanted to keep Mr Starks on our side so I didn't demur when he ordered three mulligatawny soups.

'I expect you want to know all about the Cider Wardens,' he said, once the waitress had gone.

'What makes you say that?' asked Lady Hardcastle.

'Everyone wants to know about the Cider Wardens. Actually, that's not quite true. Everyone wants to know about the *Weryers*. We're at once famous and yet shrouded in mystery,' he said in a storyteller's tone. 'Well known, yet hidden from view. There are rumours that we practise arcane pagan rites in the dead of night . . . and yet we hold whimsical events at fêtes and fairs to raise money for charity. We are an enigma. A paradox.'

'You're teasing us now, Mr Starks.'

'A little,' he conceded with a smile. 'But you've already said that it's Cridland's Cider Warden connection that brought you to my humble office, so it's not much of a leap to presume that it's the order you're interested in.'

'I confess you're not wrong,' said Lady Hardcastle. 'We already know a little about the . . . Weryers. Are you acquainted with Hector and Gertie Farley-Stroud?'

'Very well. Very well indeed. Sir Hector was one of my predecessors in the Weryers, for one thing. And he's one of Lemmings's clients now, so I see him often. He always says hello when he visits the office.'

'Oh, how wonderful. They're charming, aren't they?'

'Splendid couple, yes. Lucky to have them in the area.'

'We are. Well, we spoke to Hector the other day, you see, and he told us the tiniest bit about the Weryers – don't worry, he was terribly discreet – but it was just a bit of background information and a list of current members. What we really want is to know a little more about the personalities, the current politics, that sort of thing.'

'The gossip, you mean,' said Mr Starks with a waggle of his unkempt eyebrows.

'As juicy and salacious as you like, yes.'

He chuckled again.

'Not much to tell there, I'm afraid. Just twelve – eleven now – ordinary men who like to drink, and yarn, and smoke a pipe together while making the world a kinder place. I shall miss them.'

'Ah, yes. We met Mr Peppard yesterday – he said you were retiring.'

'I am indeed, I shall be sixty in December and I'm selling my share of the solicitors' practice and moving to Dorset with my wife. We have a cottage near Bournemouth, d'you see? And, of course, that'll also mean resigning from the Weryers of the Pomary.'

'And the post of High Protector of the Pomary will be open.'

I had been ready to jump in and gently correct her, but she could remember the names when she needed to.

'It will, indeed,' he said with a grave nod. 'Ordinarily one of the Custodians of the Arbour would replace me as High Protector, one of the Stewards of the Orchard would be promoted to Custodian in *his* place, then we'd swear in a new Steward and normality would be restored. But obviously there'll need to be more shuffling about with poor Cridland gone. We've two new Stewards to recruit and two to promote to Custodian, as well as the appointment of a new High Protector. We have much to do before the end of the year.'

'Do you have candidates in mind?'

'For the promotions or the new members?'

'Either,' she said. 'Both.'

'Well, there's a hierarchy within each rank, so the traditional way to deal with the promotions was for the senior Custodian and senior Steward both to move up one rank, with everyone shuffling up behind them like a sort of conveyor belt. But over the years we've had to become a little more flexible. Not everyone wants the new responsibilities, so we rely on chaps putting themselves forward.'

'And has anyone done that?'

'Two, yes. Cridland and Peppard – did you say you'd met Moses Peppard?'

'We spoke to him yesterday.'

'Ah, yes, that's right. Well, after poor Cridland's passing, it's just Peppard in the running for High Protector, so as long as he gets the approval of the other members, the post's his.'

'And the Stewards?'

'Fewer problems there – I suspect we'll just let seniority sort it out. That would mean Lehane and Gregory stepping up.'

'I see,' said Lady Hardcastle, who was now taking notes. 'And new members?'

'We have one solid candidate – Sidney Palmer. We've had him lined up for some time in anticipation of my departure. Runs a farming equipment firm. Big showroom-cum-warehouse sort of affair on the other side of Woodworthy. Do you know him?'

'Not well, but our paths have crossed socially.'

'He's a splendid chap and we'll be jolly lucky to have him.'

'That's one,' I said. 'But you need two now.'

'We do. There are always chaps interested – sometimes there's competition for open seats. Sadly, not all are suitable.'

'What happens to the unsuccessful candidates?' asked Lady Hardcastle. 'Can they try again?'

'They can indeed, but there have been very few occasions when reapplication has been successful. None in my time, certainly. But there's nothing in the laws to prohibit it.'

'I only ask because we met one the other evening while you were having your meeting at the Dog and Duck: Pat Swanton.'

Mr Starks made a face.

'Ah,' he said. 'Yes. That all became rather acrimonious. Didn't take rejection at all well. The truth was that he was only marginally less well favoured than Lawrence Weakley, but three of our Custodians voted against him and so Weakley was admitted in his stead. He'd be a fine candidate again, but I fear his antagonistic behaviour towards us has rather ruined his chances there.'

'Who were the three?' I asked. 'Or are you not allowed to say?'

'I shouldn't, really, but . . . well . . . Look, you have a reputation in the district for straight dealing and discretion, so I know I can rely on you to keep it to yourselves. Cridland, Peppard and Mattick were the chaps.'

'What were their reasons?' asked Lady Hardcastle.

'They weren't obliged to give reasons,' he said. 'It's a simple aye or no.'

'I see,' she said. 'This is all very helpful. Thank you.'

I wanted to know a little more about the succession.

'Is High Protector a coveted post?' I said.

'There's some local prestige attached, certainly. One gets a few more invitations to dinners and receptions. There's a small stipend from funds held in trust on behalf of the Weryers. So, yes, I suppose it's a post some would covet.'

'And was there rivalry between Cridland and Peppard?'

'I should say there was a little needling between them, but no rivalry as such.'

'Needling?' said Lady Hardcastle. 'Was this a long-term enmity or something new?'

'I should say "enmity" is a little strong, but they certainly weren't best pals. Never had been. Peppard is what they call a "plain-spoken" sort of a fellow. Doesn't mince his words. Calls a spade a spade, as they say, even when others might prefer to call it a long-handled gardening tool. Most just accept it, but Cridland thought him oafish and rude and wasn't shy of saying so.'

'Which annoyed Peppard?'

'Often. Actually, now you come to mention it, there was a falling-out recently. Peppard expressed an opinion rather too bluntly and Cridland launched quite an attack on his character. Said his behaviour meant he wasn't fit to be High Protector. It all got rather heated. I say, you don't think . . .'

'I shouldn't like to jump to conclusions,' said Lady Hardcastle, 'but I'll be passing this new information to Inspector Sunderland, certainly.'

'I do hope I haven't dropped him in it, but it is a little rum, don't you think?'

'We'll let the inspector speak to him.'

The soup, when it arrived, was as unremarkable as I had feared it would be. It wasn't unpleasant, by any means, but I'd not have recommended it to a visiting friend.

We ate companionably, with Lady Hardcastle subtly probing for further information about the relationships between the Weryers, but Starks had little more to tell, and was far too interested in extolling the virtues of the 'excellent' soup to be of much more use.

Lady Hardcastle allowed him to pay for lunch and we parted on the friendliest terms on the pavement outside the tearoom. He returned to the office; we returned to the Silver Ghost and the journey to our own home.

Lady Hardcastle tore out of town and headed for the Gloucester Road, the quickest way back to the village. A group of young hikers was forced to scatter into the hedgerow as she sped past, but we made it to the main road without further incident.

As we travelled south, I asked Lady Hardcastle what she thought of Cornelius Starks.

'He didn't seem a bad sort,' she said. 'Hector said he was dull, but I've met duller.'

'To be fair,' I said, 'almost everyone appears slightly dull compared with Sir Hector.'

'This is undeniably true. But Starks is merely ordinary, I feel. "Dull" is too harsh a judgement.'

'He makes the case against Peppard even stronger, don't you think? Add the animosity between him and Cridland to the mysterious cycle ride and you've got a tasty suspect for a murder.'

'It's certainly beginning to look that way. Unless . . .'

'Unless what?'

'Well, that whole, "I say, you don't think . . ." thing, and "I do hope I've not dropped him in it." It's all too easy to read that as, "I say, I hope you *do* think he killed him because I most definitely am trying to drop him in it," wouldn't you say?'

'So is he wary of openly accusing his friend, or trying to misdirect us?'

'Well, quite. Or do we take his words at face value? Is he really so dim-witted that it didn't occur to him until that moment that it might be Peppard?'

'He gave us two new suspects, too,' I said. 'I was hoping by this point that we might be eliminating names from our list, not adding new ones.'

'Unlikely ones, though, wouldn't you say? Even if one allows rejection by a rural order of cider men as a motive for murder, I can't honestly see Pat Swanton as a killer. And I can't even see a motive for Sid Palmer.'

'There are only ever twelve Weryers. If you want to be a member you have to wait for someone else to leave. Or die.'

'Granted,' she said. 'But everyone seems to know that Starks is retiring. I don't see it.'

'The law says a person is innocent until proven guilty, but the amateur sleuth has to regard everyone as a suspect until proven innocent.'

'Very well,' she sighed. 'We shall add them both to the list.'

Chapter Seven

We dined early that evening with the intention of giving ourselves time to make a trip to see Abel Mattick.

I had grown accustomed to the light summer evenings and was anticipating a pleasant drive in the balmy dusk. But it was late August so the days were shortening, and by the time we left the house at half past seven the sun had already set. Some of the local farms had begun their harvest, but things weren't yet sufficiently urgent that labourers were being made to work after dark, and so the countryside was quiet as we pootled through the lanes in the gathering darkness.

'Remind me of the etiquette for calling on people in the middle of the night,' I said as Lady Hardcastle swerved to avoid a fox.

'Absolutely not at all the done thing,' she said, 'as you very well know. But it was your idea.'

'I think you'll find that my idea was to see him tomorrow at the cidery.'

'Well, yes, but that was a terrible idea. And it's hardly the middle of the night – it only *feels* like the middle of the night because it's getting dark. I doubt the Matticks will have had their dinner yet.'

'So we'll be interrupting their evening meal.'

'Nonsense. We'll be a welcome preprandial distraction. We might even be offered a glass of his award-winning cider.'

'Oh, well, that's a bonus,' I said, cheerfully. 'Has it won awards?'

'Who knows? I'm not even certain that there even is such a thing as an award for cider. But we shall assure him that were such an award to exist, his malusial fermentation would surely be worthy of the highest accolades, bringing him prizes beyond the wealth of princes. Blue ribbons, gold medals, and ornate trophies set with precious jewels would be heaped upon him.'

'I'm looking forward to it already.'

We were approaching a wide gate, above which was a sign proclaiming the property to be the home of Mattick's Cider.

'There's the cidery,' she said. 'Where do you think the house might be? I've assumed it would be attached to the mill, but there's no sign of it.' She made no effort to slow down as she searched for a driveway or other entrance, so that when she spotted the narrow lane that ran alongside the walled yard of the cider mill we were still travelling at some speed.

'Up here on the right, I think,' she said as she yanked the wheel and sent us swerving, clattering and bouncing along the rutted track, still at a disconcerting pace.

Once past the sheds, the lane opened up and we could see the lights of a cottage about fifty yards away on the other side of a small paddock.

As we drew near, I realized that it was more of a luxurious farmhouse than a mere 'cottage'. Cider making, it seemed, was a profitable business.

Lady Hardcastle parked the Rolls almost neatly on the broad, cobbled courtyard in front of the house, and we trod our way carefully across the stones to the front door. She knocked sharply with her gloved hand.

A few moments later, the door was opened by a round, smilingly attractive woman who looked as though she, like the cider, might be made entirely from the local apples.

'Good evenin', m'dears,' she said. 'What can I do for you? Church collection, is it?'

Lady Hardcastle handed the woman one of her calling cards.

'Slightly less exciting than the church, I'm afraid. I'm Lady Hardcastle, and this is my assistant, Florence Armstrong. Is Mr Mattick at home?'

The woman inspected the card and then looked once more at Lady Hardcastle, a smile of recognition on her face.

'Of course it is. I'm sorry, m'dear, I didn't recognize you. We saw you at the Littleton Cotterell village show t'other day. You plays that piano lovely.'

'Thank you, you're very kind.'

'But I'm afraid you've missed Abel – he's out for the evenin' and he won't be back till late. Is it anything I can help you with? I'm Mrs Mattick, see?'

'I'm not sure, Mrs Mattick. We've been asked by the police to help with their enquiries into the death of Mr Cridland.'

'Oh, terrible business, that. Who'd want to do such a thing?'

'Well, that's rather what we're hoping to help find out. Did you know him well?'

'Not really, m'dear. He was friendly enough, but not very sociable, if you know what I mean. Kept hisself to hisself, like. Him and Abel got on like a house on fire, but I never saw much of him since Annie died. You know about that?'

'Yes,' said Lady Hardcastle. 'My housekeeper told me. He never got over it, she said.'

'No, that was when he closed in on himself. He'd been through a lot, that poor man.'

'It sounds as though it affected him greatly.'

'It did, it did.'

'He was a Weryer, wasn't he?' I said. 'With your husband.'

Mrs Mattick, whose face had grown sombre in the faint light of the lamp in her hallway as she thought about Mr Cridland, suddenly brightened.

'Oh, they does make I laugh, they Weryers,' she said with a little chuckle. 'All their silly nonsense.'

'I thought they just had a few glasses of cider and raised money for charity.'

'Oh, you don't know the half of it, m'dear. Course, I'm not supposed to know – it's all secret, see? But they gots their silly rituals and all that carry-on.'

'Ah, yes,' said Lady Hardcastle. 'The rituals. Do you know anything about them?'

Mrs Mattick chuckled again.

'I i'n't supposed to know nothin' about it,' she said, 'nor about the "robes" he keeps in a silk bag behind the big fermentation vats in the cidery, but a wife always knows. I've no idea exactly what they does, mind. But if they wants to do a bit of play-actin' and prancin' about, then good luck to 'em as long as they're not hurtin' no one. Like you says, they does a lot for charity, and you can't knock that, no matter what other nonsense they gets up to.'

Lady Hardcastle and I exchanged puzzled glances but said nothing.

'But look at me keepin' you standin' out here on the doorstep,' said Mrs Mattick. 'Come on in. I've just made meself a pot of tea.'

'You're very kind,' said Lady Hardcastle, 'but we shouldn't impose.'

'It won't be no imposition.'

'Would it be acceptable to call again when your husband is at home?'

'Of course, m'dears, it would be a pleasure to see you. Perhaps you could come for dinner?'

'Perhaps we could. Thank you, Mrs Mattick.'

'Well, if you're sure you won't come in, I'll get back to me knittin'.'

'You do that, Mrs Mattick. Thank you for your time.'

'It weren't no trouble at all, m'lady. Good night to you and have a safe journey back. I look forward to seein' you for supper.'

'Good night to you, too. Enjoy your tea.'

We returned to the Rolls and set off back down the track.

At the end of the track, Lady Hardcastle turned right on to the lane.

'This isn't the way we came,' I said.

'What do you mean, dear?' she said, distractedly. 'Of course it is.'

'No, we passed the orchard and the cidery on our right and then turned right on to the track. To go back the way we came we should have turned left.'

'I did turn left.'

'You really didn't.'

'Oh, well. We'll see a signpost soon and we can revise our plans from there.'

'Or we could turn round.'

'Nonsense. It's another lovely evening – let's just explore for a while. We so seldom come out this way.'

It was true. We had lived in Littleton Cotterell for a little over three years and we almost never ventured in this direction. Under other circumstances I should have been delighted to explore this unknown part of our neighbourhood. All those 'other circumstances', though, involved daylight. And a map. This current adventure, I felt, was doomed to failure. Or disappointment at the very least. I sat quietly and tried to pretend I wasn't irritated.

An hour later we were still puttering about the lanes of Gloucestershire, searching in vain for a main road, preferably one with a road sign that would point us back towards Littleton Cotterell. It was still warm, and the seats of the Rolls were very comfortable, but my efforts at concealing my frustration were beginning to grow less effective.

'You're sulking, dear, I can tell,' said Lady Hardcastle.

'You were always a very perceptive woman.'

'It's what made me such a useful spy, dear. But cheer up. It's a lovely evening for a drive.'

'I consoled myself with that for the first half an hour,' I said. 'But we're lost. In the dark. And I'm bored.'

'Only boring people get bo—'

'Don't. You. Dare. If you'd just turned round when I suggested it we'd be at home now with a cup of cocoa and a good book. Perhaps you'd be playing the piano. We'd update the crime board. We'd wonder if it was too early for brandy—'

'It's never too early for brandy, dear,' she said, with aggravating cheerfulness. 'And look. Up ahead. There's a signpost.'

Sure enough, a white-painted signpost gleamed in the headlights, a promise of salvation in the gloom. We slowed to take a look. The right turn, it told us, was to Littleton Cotterell. It was fourteen miles away.

'There we are,' she said, still exuding her infuriating brightness and good cheer. 'We'll be home in a jiffy.'

We turned right. I said nothing.

The route was well-signed, and before too long we found ourselves on familiar roads.

'This is going to take us back past the cidery and the orchard, I think,' said Lady Hardcastle.

'It looks like it,' I agreed. 'It'll be just as though we'd turned round when I said we should.'

Sure enough, we drove past the cidery, and then the woodland, familiar from Tuesday's encounter with murder, soon loomed over us against the night sky. For only the second time that evening, Lady Hardcastle slowed down.

'Seen something?' I said.

'I thought I saw lights in the trees.'

I looked to my left.

'I don't see them,' I said. 'Sorry.'

She stopped completely and leaned over me for a better look.

'There,' she said, pointing. 'Flickering. Firelight? Burning torches, perhaps?'

I looked again and caught the briefest glimpse of the glimmering orange lights.

'Got it,' I said. 'Shall we get out and take a loo—'

She was already out of the motor car and heading for the gate.

'Come on, slowcoach,' she said in a stage whisper. 'Don't just sit there with your mouth open.'

I joined her, and together we made our way stealthily along the path through the not-apple trees. As the not-apple trees gave way to orchard, the lights became more obvious.

'They're in the clearing in the middle,' I whispered.

'What clearing? I didn't see a clearing.'

'You were sketching. It's where I found Inspector Sunderland and Dr Gosling. This way.'

As silently as we were able – and we were extremely able when it came to moving silently – we edged among the apple trees until we could see the circular clearing. A table – 'altar' might be a more appropriate word – had been fashioned from tree stumps brought in from outside the orchard. There were four iron braziers set on tall poles providing the light.

All of which appeared perfectly normal and ordinary compared with the group of eleven robed men surrounding the sylvan altar.

The robes had a sheen in the torchlight, as though made of velvet, and were of some dark colour, probably red – it was difficult to tell in the flickering orange light. Each robe had a voluminous hood, and each man's head was covered, his face in shadow. The robes – or perhaps that should be 'cowls' – were embroidered with intricate designs of trees and leaves in pale thread, and tied at the waist with a thick cord in one of, as far as I could make out, three different colours.

The man behind the altar with his arms raised had a golden cord – I could see it glinting in the light as though it was woven through with gold thread. There were two men to his right, and one to his left, each with dark cords, possibly blue. The seven men with their backs to us had red cords, similar to the colour of their cowls.

They were chanting.

I couldn't make out the words, which seemed to be in some other language. It sounded Germanic, or possibly Scandinavian, though there were occasional words that sounded familiar but which I couldn't quite place.

As the chant ended, the man with the golden cord lowered his arms and picked up a billhook from the altar. He held it aloft and loudly spoke a few words in the unfamiliar language. The men responded.

As he put the billhook down, the man nearest us leaned towards his neighbour.

'That i'n't the Sax of the Pomary,' he said. 'What's 'e up to?'

It sounded like the voice of the toothless landlord of the Dog and Duck, Joe Arnold.

'It's gone missing,' said the other man. Lawrence Weakley, the village greengrocer, unless my ears deceived me.

'It never 'as!' said Old Joe. 'What's 'appened to that, then?'

'I don't know, I—'

There was a hiss of impatient shushing from the other red-corded men, and Mr Weakley fell silent. Joe straightened up and turned his attention back to the altar.

The golden-corded leader held up a hammer. The peen was flat, almost like a small, blunt axe.

'That i'n't the Martel of the Rundlet, neither,' said Joe. 'What's goin' on?'

'Will you be quiet,' hissed the nearest red-corded man.

Joe fell silent once more as the ritual continued.

More portentous words. Another response from the congregation.

One of the blue-corded men picked up a folded robe with a blue cord coiled on top of it and showed it to the congregation before handing it to the leader. I couldn't see his face clearly, but he had the same build as Abel Mattick.

More words. Solemn this time. Sorrowful.

A response.

Carved wooden goblets were handed round and raised in salute to the empty robe. The men drank.

And then, suddenly, the spell was broken and the cowled men gathered around the altar and began speaking in conversational tones. They were too quiet to hear, but the few words that floated across the clearing in the heavy late-summer air were definitely English.

Lady Hardcastle tapped my arm and indicated that we should return to the motor car.

We were home by eleven.

◆ ◆ ◆

Once we had settled, I toasted some crumpets and made some cocoa. We sat together in the drawing room, contemplating the day's events by the light of our faithful oil lamps.

'Do you think electricity will ever come to the village?' I asked.

'I like to imagine not,' said Lady Hardcastle. 'I picture the whole country electrified within ten years, with Littleton Cotterell trapped alone in medieval darkness.'

'We got the telephone.'

'The Grange has a telephone line, the police station has a telephone line, and we have a telephone line. And we only have one because I made a most unseemly fuss and then paid a frankly extortionate sum of money to make it happen. But realistically, I see it taking decades before everyone everywhere has access to electricity. It'll be oil lamps and log fires for us for many a long year.'

'And braziers in the orchards.'

'Well, now, wasn't that a thing?' she said. 'One might have imagined we'd stumbled upon an amateur theatrical production if we didn't already know about the Weryers of the Pomary. I can understand Mrs Mattick's amusement – the whole thing was rather comical.'

'Comical,' I agreed, 'and a tiny bit sinister. I didn't recognize the language. Was it made up?'

'That was my first thought, but I also imagined I heard a few Old English words in there, so perhaps it was genuine. I've been trying to remember if I encountered any Dons at Cambridge with an interest in Old English. Harry might know.'

Lady Hardcastle had studied at Girton College while her brother, Harry, was at the university proper. It was at Cambridge that she had been recruited to work for the Foreign Office as a spy – though they never referred to her work as anything quite so vulgar as 'espionage' – while her husband, Roderick, travelled the world as a diplomat. Harry now worked for the recently formed Secret Service Bureau, but he might have language scholars among his contacts.

Lady Hardcastle stood and examined the bookshelf.

'I'm sure there's something useful here somewhere . . . Ah, here we are.'

She took down a thick book with a cover of cracked and faded green leather.

'I do love dictionaries, don't you?' she said as she opened it up.

'I do. I'd forgotten we had that one.'

'I confess I was surprised you chose the other dictionary the other night,' she said. 'This is much more the sort of thing we need. If you're searching for archaic words, this is undoubtedly the place to come. One can't imagine that many people would ever have need of a definition – nor conformation of the spelling – of most of the words in here, yet here they are, catalogued for posterity.' She leafed through the pages. 'Not enough swear words for my taste, but one can't have everything. Now, then . . . what was it Old Joe said? "That's not the something of the Pomary", wasn't it?'

'Sax,' I said. 'The Sax of the Pomary.'

'That was it. Well done, you. Sax . . . sax . . . Oh, it's a knife. But he had a knife, didn't he?'

'A billhook,' I said. 'Or a big pruning knife. We're still assuming "Pomary" is orchard?'

She riffled through the dictionary again.

'It is,' she confirmed. 'But that's not much of a surprise. What was the other thing?'

'The Martel of the Rundlet.'

'They're making these up,' she said as she thumbed through the musty book. 'Hammer . . .' she said eventually, '. . . of the barrel.'

'A cooper's hammer, then. Just like the one the gold-corded man held up.'

'But not the *right* one, we assume.'

'Old Joe's sharper than people give him credit for,' I said. 'If he said it wasn't the right one, it wasn't the right one.'

'I have no reason to doubt him. So the roles of the knife and the hammer were being played by their stand-ins. Intriguing.' She flicked through a few more pages. 'And "weryer" is a guardian. From the Old English *werian*, just as I said. Oh, I say, well done, me. Mrs Wilberforce would be so proud.'

'One of your many governesses?'

'One of the more long-serving ones, yes. I think she lasted for six months before I infuriated her sufficiently that she resigned. But she did make me read *Beowulf*, and her labours, it turns out, were not entirely in vain.'

'So the "Guardians of the Orchard" conduct their rites in Old English and use the "Knife of the Orchard" in those rites, along with the "Hammer of the Barrel", more commonly known as a cooper's hammer.'

'I've never encountered such a thing,' she said, 'but I'll take your word for it.'

'Coopers have the strangest tools. I remember we had to get some barrels repaired for the circus and we called in a cooper and his apprentice. I loved watching them work. And the farriers, too.'

'A cooper's hammer and a knife like a billhook, then.'

'If the billhook was a suitable stand-in,' I said. 'Yes. It's all very appley and ciderish, so it seems appropriate for the Weryers.'

'The "sax" going missing the day Cridland was murdered would be suspicious if it weren't a billhook.'

'My thoughts exactly,' I agreed. 'A billhook wouldn't leave that sort of wound, would it? It's not pointy enough. It's probably just carelessness, isn't it? The sax going missing, I mean. It must be hard being a member of an ancient, secret order. They can't be expected to keep their robes in tip-top condition without the services of a highly skilled maid *and* remember where they put the Sax of the Pomary.'

She laughed. 'Somebody's wife will have popped it in the umbrella stand to tidy it away. "If I trip over the Sax of the Pomary one more time I shall put it out for the rag-and-bone man, don't think I shan't."'

'I fancy another crumpet. Do you want one?'

'Yes please, dear. And some more cocoa.'

I stood to pick up the tray.

'There wasn't nearly enough brandy in mine last time,' she said as I left for the kitchen.

'There wasn't *any* brandy in it.'

'Exactly. That's far too little.'

I returned a short while later with more crumpets and two cups of *Chocolat Chaud Royale*, as I had decided to christen the cognac-laced drink. Lady Hardcastle was looking at the notes she had made.

'You were right earlier,' she said. 'We've not done much to narrow down our list of suspects, have we?'

'Sadly not,' I said. 'And, as fascinating as it was, seeing the Weryers' orchard ritual didn't help much.'

'It would have been nice to have seen the Spike of the Stabbery, wouldn't it?'

'Actually, yes. I'd love it if the killer weren't Miss Chamberlain. She's just too obvious and it would be horribly unsatisfying if it turned out to be her, so I should much prefer to have discovered a connection between the Weryers and the murder weapon.'

'Things are definitely stacked against her, but all that business showed the Weryers in a new light, wouldn't you say?'

'It doesn't quite fit their charitable-charmers image,' I said. 'And it's certainly something they play down. Do you remember Starks trying to suggest it was merely a rumour that they practise arcane rituals in the dead of night?'

'It's definitely not a rumour,' she agreed.

'It was innocent enough, but somehow disquietingly sinister. I can't quite put my finger on it. Oh, and did you notice the coloured cords at their waists?'

'I did. A signifier of rank, I presumed. Gold for the High Protector – he had Starks's build and the voice could certainly have been his. Then there'd be blue for the Custodians and red for the Stewards.'

'That's how I saw it. It doesn't help to make sense of anything, but it's satisfying to work at least one thing out.'

'Nothing at all makes sense to me yet,' she said. 'But it shall – we just need to let it percolate a while longer. And in the meantime, cards or backgammon?'

'We never play backgammon.'

'Then perhaps we should start. Shall we try Go again?'

'Not after Tuesday night,' I said. 'I couldn't bear more sulking.'

'Chess?'

'All right, but only if you promise to be better behaved when you lose.'

'I'll get the board.'

Chapter Eight

Having spent far too many childhood summer days looking out from the back of my parents' circus caravan at the grey-clouded British countryside as our horse – a jet-black Shire that I had named Snowdrop – stoically plodded through the rain to the site of our next show, I was never disappointed by warmth and sunshine. Early adolescence in the Welsh Valleys had dampened my clothes and hair with seemingly endless drizzle, but it had never dampened my enthusiasm for fine weather.

The long, hot, dry spell that had blessed the kingdom (or blighted it, depending upon your personal inclination) since the middle of July was starting to distress many other people, but not me. The customary local greeting of ''Ow bist?' (meaning 'How are you?') had been replaced by 'I'n't it ever 'ot?' (meaning 'I thought eighty-one degrees would be fun but it's really starting to get to me'). I would reply, 'Yes. Yes, it is,' and offer appropriately sympathetic noises while suppressing my urge to say, 'And isn't it glorious?'

Lady Hardcastle was as accustomed to extremes of temperature as I – we had spent several years together in China and India, experiencing the bitter chill of a Chinese mountain winter and the lung-searing heat of early summer in Bengal – but even she had tired of the heatwave.

She arrived for breakfast on Friday morning already heat-bedraggled.

'Good morning,' I said as she flopped into her customary chair in the morning room.

'Good morning to you, too, dear. You're looking annoyingly chipper. Still enjoying the summer?'

'You know me well enough to be able to guess the answer to that one with reasonable accuracy. We should go out and luxuriate in it. It'll be September soon – season of mists and mournful fretfulness. A chilly Flo is a grumpy Flo.'

'Then we should most definitely sally forth in our horseless carriage and take advantage of the Flo-happying weather while it remains.'

'Hurrah.'

'Hurrah, indeed. We were saying only the other evening that we'd like to explore Woodworthy, after all. We could drop in at the Mock of Pommey and take a look at whatshisface while we're there.'

'Griffith Uzzle,' I offered.

'Of course,' she said with a chuckle. 'I do love local names. After a lifetime of Smiths and Joneses, it's delightful to be surrounded by Uzzles, Matticks, Starkses and Peppards.'

'We've been surrounded by Zhangs, Shens, Chandras, Mukherjees, Müllers, Schneiders, Nagys, Vargas, Duboises, Merciers, and a zillion others over the years.'

'True, though everyone's name is exotic and interesting if one is a foreigner visiting their country. But here we've only had to venture a hundred miles or so from London as the crow flies and we're in a world of Mustoes and Flooks, Bingles and Brazingtons. And Uzzles. We must meet Griffith Uzzle, sample his fare and become acquainted with his clientele.'

'We'll not have the same advantages we have here, mind you,' I said. 'We'll be strangers. Incomers. They do look most suspiciously on outsiders round 'ere.'

'Nonsense, dear. We're local celebrities. Most of the denizens of Woodworthy were at the village show last weekend. They'll have seen my bespangled turn at the very least, even if they didn't stay to see Gertie leading them in a round of applause for you at the end. We'll be welcomed with open arms.'

'We'll see,' I said. 'Do you want a fan? You look a bit flushed.'

'I'm finding it a little warm, that's all. Another reason to take a drive, I feel – the cooling breeze afforded by our swift passage through the country lanes will do me the world of good.'

'Well, Edna and Miss Jones have everything properly in hand, so I'm ready when you are.'

'Give me an hour or so to write a couple of letters and we shall away.'

'My turn to drive, don't forget.'

'Is it? Then we shall allow an extra hour for the journey.'

The roads were dusty and we sent up quite a plume as we tootled along. And tootle we did. With me at the controls, all four wheels remained firmly on the ground at all times, and the few horses and bicyclists we passed remained in a state of serenity and calm as the Silver Ghost purred by.

'I'm beginning to think my estimate of an extra hour for the journey might have been a little conservative,' said Lady Hardcastle as she held her arm out lazily and allowed her hand to brush the tall, tufted grass that grew from the bank.

'You'll get hurt if there's anything out there other than grass,' I said.

'Not at this speed, dear. If I see anything dangerous coming our way I'll have time to write to the farmer to get it cut down long before we reach it.'

'At least we're guaranteed to arrive in one piece.'

'I'm disinclined to believe that there are any solid guarantees of safety when one is in a motor car, but I'll allow you "*more likely* to arrive in one piece". The thing is, though, that when we do finally arrive in one piece, everything will be closed and the good folk of Woodworthy shall be abed, dreaming their peaceful, bucolic dreams, and our trip shall have been in vain.'

'Dreams of a peaceful, bucolic life free from the terror induced by the presence of mad old biddies at the wheels of speeding motor cars. You're like a taller version of Mr Toad.'

'Poop-poop,' she said with a chuckle. 'Ow!' She drew her hand sharply back inside the cockpit.

'Told you,' I said.

'Something stung me.'

'Do you blame it? Some industrious bee or wasp was going about its insecty business and you molested it. At speed. I'd sting you.'

'It bally well hurts.'

'I'm no entomologist,' I said, 'but I believe that's the intention. Is there anything left in it?'

'In what?'

'In the site of the sting. Is there any sign of a barb or other pointy insect weaponry?'

She inspected her hand.

'No,' she said. 'It's just red.'

'Then there's nothing to be done other than put up with it like a brave girl. We can see if they'll let us have some ice at the Mock of Pommey if it starts to swell.'

'If we ever get there.'

We tootled along for a few minutes longer. The road to Woodworthy took us past the orchard and the cider mill, but we turned off before we hit the lanes we'd stumbled along after turning the wrong way out of the lane the night before. In the daylight it was difficult to see how we had become so badly lost.

Ahead was a signpost advising us that Woodworthy was a quarter of a mile down a lane to our right. I turned carefully into the lane and, sure enough, we were beside a village green a few moments later.

The green was free of the impedimenta of the cricket pitch, the village team having folded shortly before we arrived at Littleton Cotterell in 1908, and in place of local lads practising their leg spins and cover drives were half a dozen sheep with huge horns and brown patches on their coats, earnestly cropping the grass.

'They're Jacobs,' said Lady Hardcastle, noticing my curious frown.

'Does he know they're here?'

'Ha, ha. It's the breed. They're Jacob sheep.'

'They seem to be the only ones here.'

From our vantage point beside the green we could see a modest church, the pub we were hoping to visit, and a small village shop. The doors of all three were open, but there was no one abroad. There were faint signs of life in the pub, but that was it.

'I'm not sure what I was expecting,' said Lady Hardcastle as I drew to a halt beside the green, 'but it wasn't this.'

'I'd imagined a village more like our own,' I agreed. 'A few shops, a bit of hustle, and a pleasing amount of bustle. No wonder they all come over to Littleton for their fun.'

'Indeed. And they're nearer to Chipping Bevington than we are, so they almost certainly get their supplies there. It's pretty, though.'

It was, indeed, pretty. There was a terraced row of cottages beside the pub, probably dating from the eighteenth century if not before. We could see a lane beside them, with another row of even-older thatched cottages just visible as the lane bent away out of sight.

'No wonder there's only a single pub, shop and church,' said Lady Hardcastle, stepping gracefully from the Rolls. 'One wouldn't need much more to serve these few little houses and the farms around and about.'

'There's another lane leading up behind the church,' I said. 'There'll be a few more houses up there, I'd wager. There has to be a vicarage at the very least.'

'True, true. Country parsons aren't known for their abstemious lifestyles. The local padre will want a handsome house with a formidable housekeeper to take care of him. And possibly a parcel of glebe land upon which to graze his sheep. He'll be a hawk-faced, greedy bachelor, with a line in fire-and-brimstone sermons to make the locals quake.'

'He's a delightful, chubby little fellow with a willowy wife. All smiles and pudgy handshakes. You met him at the Littleton Spring Fayre.'

'He was the vicar of Woodworthy? I had no idea. I thought he was from North Nibley. Lovely chap. We talked about harmoniums.'

'You did. And his wife told a joke about a milkmaid that was much filthier than she thought it was.'

'Oh, that's right. I remember being quite taken aback that a vicar's wife would say anything like that out loud, but it was plain from the innocent look on her face that she didn't really understand it. Well, I take back my disparaging remarks. But you're right – there'll still be a vicarage nearby.'

We strolled across the green towards the Mock of Pommey. The lead sheep looked us up and down as we passed and then returned to her lunch without comment. Her companions, noting her indifference, didn't even pause in their own grass-munching. As we drew near we could hear the murmur of lunchtime chatter from inside the pub. The smell of stale cider and pipe smoke wafted out towards us.

◆ ◆ ◆

As was our habit, Lady Hardcastle entered first, with me a step behind. After years of experience of entering unfamiliar and potentially dangerous places, it was hard not to check over my shoulder that we weren't being followed, but no one was interested in us, not even the sheep. I smiled to myself as I noticed that Lady Hardcastle had been driven by similar habit to place her hand close to her handbag, where she often kept her pistol.

There was no more danger inside the pub than outside, but a disconcerting hush fell upon the patrons as they spotted strangers crossing the threshold of their sanctuary. Behind the bar was a man in his fifties. He had the stocky frame and muscular arms of a labourer, though his broken nose put me more in mind of a prize fighter. I'd seen that face a few nights before at the Dog and Duck, and was reasonably sure we were being given the once-over by the pub's landlord, Griffith Uzzle.

He had been leaning on the bar chatting to one of his regulars, but now he pushed himself upright. As we moved further inside we were no longer mere silhouettes in the doorway, and a smile of welcome lit his face as he saw us properly for the first time.

'Lady Hardcastle,' he said. 'And Miss Armstrong. Welcome to the Mock of Pommey.'

His words broke the spell and the farmhands and villagers returned to their conversations.

'What a charming welcome,' said Lady Hardcastle. 'Mr Uzzle, I presume.'

'In the flesh, my lady. I hope you don't mind the presumption, but I recognized you both from the Littleton Cotterell village show. And from t'other night over at the Dog and Duck. Old Joe pointed you out to us when you came in the bar.'

'Not at all. It's rather flattering, actually.'

'That's handsome, then. What brings you over our way? Old Joe barred you, has he?' He chuckled to himself at the thought.

'It's another lovely day and we thought we'd take a drive,' she said. 'We commented just the other evening that we've lived at Littleton Cotterell for three years and we've never taken the time to explore your charming village. And so here we are.'

'Well, you're most welcome, I must say. I'm afraid we don't have no snug for the ladies like you're used to, nor any of Joe's fancy tables outside on the green, but if you're happy to sit over there by the window I can let you have a glass of the finest cider anywhere in England.'

'Mattick's?'

'The very same.'

'Oh, how delightful. Joe serves it at the Dog and Duck.'

'He does, it's true, but mine's better. He don't store it right, see? Has to be treated just right, does cider, and Old Joe don't have the knack.'

'Well, it would be churlish to turn you down. Thank you, Mr Uzzle.'

'Call me Griff, my lady, call me Griff.'

'Thank you, Griff.'

'Do you have any cordial?' I said. 'I'm driving.'

He looked at me as though this was the strangest reason he'd ever heard, but cast about behind the bar for a moment. He bent down and emerged with a dusty old bottle of brown liquid.

'I've got some sarsaparilla,' he said. 'We had a temperance fella drinking in here a few years ago and I got it for him. I can't guarantee it's still good, mind.'

'I'll try it,' I said. 'Thank you.'

Lady Hardcastle smiled and fished out her coin purse to pay for the drinks.

'Take your seats, ladies, and I'll get the girl to bring them over to you.'

I looked around for any sign of 'the girl' as we crossed to the table by the window, but there was no one to be seen. I checked on the sheep instead, but they were still busy.

Unless we were on a job, I always felt a little self-conscious at the idea of holding a private conversation in a small room filled with strangers, but Lady Hardcastle was seldom self-conscious about anything. She chattered merrily away about the origins of Jacob sheep, speculated upon the history of the church, and asked my opinion on the performance of the Rolls, which she thought had been a little lacklustre this past week.

From the rustle of skirts and the lightness of the footsteps, I knew that a young woman was bringing us our drinks. There was a girl, after all. But she was behind me so I couldn't see her.

'All right, Flo?' she said. 'And Lady H. What are you doin' over 'ere?'

It was Cissy Slocomb. It seemed all my friends were part-time barmaids.

'Cissy,' I said. 'Hello. I might ask you the same question.'

'I works here,' she said, as though she suspected I might be a bit simple.

'Well, yes, I can see that. But I thought you worked at the dairy with your family.'

'Oh, I does. But I earns a few bob over here an' all. Gets me away from the old 'uns for a bit, and I can keep an eye on they handsome farm lads. There's some right bobby-dazzlers comes in 'ere, I can tell you.'

'I can only imagine,' I said, looking over at the lunchtime crowd, among whom there was not a bobby-dazzler to be seen.

She pulled up a chair and sat down.

'Don't mind if I sits with you for a few minutes while Betty's not about, do you? I've been on my feet since five o'clock 'smornin'. Fit to drop, I am.'

'Help yourself, dear,' said Lady Hardcastle. 'It's always lovely to have company. Would you care for a drink?'

'I'd not say no. But . . .' She looked wearily over towards the bar, as though walking those three yards would just about do her in.

'I'll get it,' I said. 'What will you have?'

'A glass of Mattick's would go down lovely, I reckon.'

'Coming up.'

I returned to the bar.

For all that the pub's single room was small and held no more than twenty people, I realized that I needn't have been quite so worried about our being overheard. Now that conversation and laughter had returned to normal it was surprisingly noisy, and it was difficult even to hear Cissy and Lady Hardcastle, who were gossiping like old pals just three yards away.

I returned to the table a few moments later with Cissy's cider.

'Thank you,' she said with a grin. 'Cheers.'

'Cheers,' I said, raising my own glass. Sarsaparilla isn't to everyone's taste, but I rather enjoyed it, and for all Uzzle's misgivings it tasted fine. 'What did I miss?' I asked.

'Nothing much,' said Lady Hardcastle. 'I was quizzing Cissy on the Weryer regalia. She's quite the font.'

'I keeps me ears open is all,' said Cissy. 'I'n't no magic to it.'

'Don't do yourself down, dear,' said Lady Hardcastle. 'The cords on the cowls are colour-coded as we surmised, and the tools are much as we imagined them, too.'

'Have you ever seen the tools?' I asked.

'No, our dad's not senior enough to be trusted with 'em. But he talks about 'em. Gleaming, he says, like silver.'

'Has he talked about them going missing? Do they know what happened to them?'

'They's all of a flap, the lot of 'em. They don't know where they's gone.'

'Where are they usually kept?' said Lady Hardcastle.

'You've reached the limit of my knowledge there, I'm afraid,' said Cissy. 'Our dad only talks about the things he thinks is glamorous and excitin' – he likes to show off. He don't think we're interested in storage. And he's right. Until this minute it never occurred to me to wonder where they kept everythin'.'

'Not to worry,' said Lady Hardcastle. 'You've been most helpful. Thank you.'

While we had been talking, a strikingly beautiful woman of about Griffith Uzzle's age had appeared behind the bar and scanned the room. Her eyes lit upon Cissy taking her ease with us and she smiled.

She approached our table.

'Good afternoon, ladies,' she said. 'How lovely to see new faces here.'

Cissy got up.

'I was just takin' a quick break, Mrs Uzzle,' she said.

'That's all right, dear,' said Mrs Uzzle, 'you're allowed a break.'

'Thank you,' said Cissy, though she made no attempt to sit back down. 'This is Lady Hardcastle and Florence Armstrong from Littleton.'

'I know.' Mrs Uzzle nodded a greeting to us. 'It's nice to have you here with us.'

Lady Hardcastle and I inclined our heads in acknowledgement and raised our glasses.

'You're very kind,' said Lady Hardcastle.

Cissy was still reluctant to resume her seat.

'I'd better be gettin' back to my work, though,' she said, grinning sheepishly at us. She finished off her cider with a heroic final swig and readied herself to return to her duties. 'I'll see you ladies soon.'

She bustled off, and Mrs Uzzle returned to the bar where she turned her attention to her husband. We couldn't hear her above the hubbub but she didn't look anywhere near as friendly now.

Uzzle, looking meekly down at his boots, said nothing.

'That's quite a change,' said Lady Hardcastle with a nod towards the bar.

'The two faces of Mrs Uzzle,' I said. 'So charming to the customers, but I don't think there's much doubt who wears the breeches in their household.'

'As long as they're happy,' she said as she finished her drink. 'Well, tiny servant, the pleasantness of the village pub notwithstanding, I confess myself otherwise let down by my first trip to Woodworthy – I was expecting more of the place. I thought we might pass a pleasant hour or two chatting with its shopkeepers and exploring its side streets, but I fear our walk across the village green has shown us everything there is to see. What say we sup up and return to civilization, perhaps via Chipping Bevington? I need one or two things, so a little afternoon shopping will be just the ticket. Or perhaps lunch at the Grey Goose and then do our shopping in Bristol? Either way, I feel we've exhausted the entertainment possibilities of the village for the time being.'

'If I have a completely free vote, I favour a Grey Goose lunch and a trip into Bristol.'

'Splendid. We can drop in at the Bridewell while we're there and see what the inspector's been up to.'

We finished our drinks, said goodbye to Uzzle and Cissy, and returned to the Rolls which had been kept safe by the watchful sheep.

◆ ◆ ◆

Back at the house that evening, dinner was gurnard, which we had bought from a shop by the fish market on Baldwin Street in Bristol. I roasted it whole and served it with a salad and some new potatoes. Miss Jones's delicious ham pie would keep for the weekend.

Lady Hardcastle had perused the wine in the rack in the larder for some time, most of which she spent complaining that we had no cellar where she could store it properly. When she finally finished grumbling, she settled upon her favourite white burgundy, which worked splendidly. We ate by lantern light in the garden under the apple tree, beset by inquisitive moths.

By nine o'clock we had finished the fish and the burgundy, and were sitting in the drawing room with a bottle of port that her vintner had sent with her last order, to try to tempt her to buy more. To accompany it I had assembled an improbably large selection of cheeses, cream crackers, and fruit, all of which we enjoyed as we contemplated the crime board.

'I shall be buying more of this port,' said Lady Hardcastle as she took another sip. 'I've never really been terribly keen on the stuff, but this is a revelation. Well done, Stodgell and Sons, your cunning plan worked.'

'I can't help but feel that selling wine to you isn't much of a challenge, but they have an eye for a decent drop.'

'Yes, indeed they have. An eye, a nose, and a palate. If you slice some more of that Double Gloucester, I'll pour you another glass.'

I nibbled a cracker and looked at the growing web of information on the blackboard.

'After speaking to Inspector Sunderland,' I said, 'I'm beginning to wonder if all this might be wasted effort.'

'He does seem rather set on it being Grace Chamberlain now, doesn't he?'

'Despite finding out even less when he spoke to her than we did. She's a cagey one, I'll give her that. But does protecting your privacy make you a killer?'

'Killers do tend to keep their killing a secret,' said Lady Hardcastle. 'But I agree that it's not necessarily a mark against her. Although she has been seen in a good few places haunted by Weryers.'

'Granted,' I said. 'But—'

'And then there are the initials and location of the victim in her notebook.'

'Yes, and that's another thing,' I said. 'If I were going to kill someone for a lark, I might well travel a hundred miles from my home, but I'd make sure no one saw me. If I were travelling to kill a specific person for a specific reason, I'd make doubly sure no one saw me. I wouldn't take a room at the local pub, carelessly display my victim's name written in my notebook, and then kill him a day later. And even if I did, I'd not hang about once the deed was done. I'd not want anyone to make any connection between me and the killing. Nor would I want to give them time to think of connections between me and the victim once he was dead. She's still here, and she doesn't appear to be a stupid person, so it can't be her.'

'Unless she plans to kill again.'

'Well, that's a possibility, I suppose. But I'm more interested in the local cooper after what Cissy said, even though the inspector seemed unimpressed.'

'Me, too. Of course, he could simply have been paying someone a visit, just like he said he was.'

'His five o'clock assignation,' I said.

'He said himself that there's no set time for love. And there may be some other, non-murderous reason for his journey.'

'Yes, but still . . .'

'Oh, I'm not trying to pooh-pooh your suspicion, but it wouldn't be right not to consider the more innocent possibilities, even if we're not convinced by the idea of early-morning shenanigans.'

'I'm still struggling to imagine innocent possibilities,' I said. 'It's not as though he might be about his coopering business at dawn, is it? The up-and-about-ness of farmers and dairymen notwithstanding, what would require him to cycle to . . . well, we don't even know where he was cycling to, do we? I imagine the cidery is an important customer, but they'd conduct their business at a more civilized hour. He might have been going to Woodworthy avoiding the hill, but why? What's there for him? Even if we accept his adultery explanation, we don't know exactly where he was off to. It's not enough to condemn him, but a trip to the orchard to see Claud Cridland seems like the least complicated explanation.'

'I wholeheartedly concur,' said Lady Hardcastle with a nod. 'We must make more of an effort to trace Peppard's alleged paramour, but if we can't find her, we need to present a more forceful argument to the inspector. He needs less Chamberlain and more Peppard in his diet.'

'Tomorrow is Saturday,' I said. 'Perhaps we can make some enquiries in the village to see if anyone knows anything about Peppard and his dalliance.'

Conversation turned once more to food and drink, then to international affairs and the increasing tensions on the Continent – something that had occupied many of our conversations of late. By the time we'd got from there to contemplating how the new Official Secrets Act – which had received royal assent the week before – might affect our work with Harry at the Secret Service Bureau, it was well past bedtime.

The next day, though, had other plans for us, and on Saturday morning, discovering the identity of the object of Moses Peppard's adulterous affections abruptly became less of a priority.

At half past seven, while Lady Hardcastle was still asleep, there was a ring at the doorbell.

I opened the door to see Inspector Sunderland standing there. His motor car was in the lane outside with the engine running and Dr Gosling in the passenger seat.

'Good morning, Inspector,' I said. 'You're early. Is there something wrong?'

'I'm afraid so,' he said. 'Is Lady Hardcastle up?'

'Not yet, but I can wake her if you want to speak to her.'

'Thank you, but we need to be on our way. If you can get her up and meet us at the cooper's on the Gloucester Road, I'd be most grateful.'

'Why?' I said. 'What's happened?'

'Moses Peppard has been found murdered.'

Chapter Nine

I woke Lady Hardcastle at once and helped her get dressed as quickly as we both could manage. Within a quarter of an hour she was upright and ready to face the day, which might not have been a world record but was very impressive for someone as slow to rouse as she.

'There's no time for coffee, I suppose?' she said as I hustled her to the door. 'Or even tea? I'd love a nice cup of coffee, though. The inspector won't mind if we're a little late.'

'He wouldn't mind if we didn't make it at all,' I said. 'It's not as though we work for him. But *I* want to be there as soon as possible. I want to see the scene of the crime while everything's fresh and we have experienced and knowledgeable men to talk to about what we see.'

'Right you are, dear, sorry. Let us away.'

She checked that she had sketchbook and pencils in her haversack, then slung it over her shoulder. I handed her our new Thermos flask.

'I made you this while you were in the WC,' I said.

She unscrewed the cap cup and pulled the cork stopper to see what was inside. The hallway filled suddenly with the rich aroma of hot coffee.

'Oh, you absolute poppet,' she said with a broad grin. 'Thank you.'

She reclosed the flask and we stepped out of the front door into the sunshine.

I started the Silver Ghost and was about to roll out into the lane when our driveway was blocked by a familiar red motor car. Our good friend Dinah Caudle, *Bristol News* journalist and the affianced of police surgeon Dr Simeon Gosling, waved from the driver's seat. We both hopped out of the Rolls to greet her.

'Morning, you two,' she said, brightly. 'Lovely day.'

She was, as always, impeccably dressed in the latest fashion. She ought to have been altogether too sophisticated for the little Rover 6 she was driving, but she looked so confident and at ease behind the wheel that it suited her just as well as her exquisitely made clothes. She had bought the friendly little motor car from Lady Hardcastle the year before, and had been seen tootling about the city ever since, reporting on everything from school plays to jewellery-shop robberies.

'Good morning to you, too, dear,' said Lady Hardcastle. 'We'd invite you in for breakfast but we're on our way to a murder.'

'Me too,' said Miss Caudle. 'Simeon called in at my place on his way to meet Sunderland. We were supposed to be going out for lunch together but he thought I might enjoy covering the murder story for the newspaper instead.'

'How very . . . considerate of him,' said Lady Hardcastle.

'Well, quite. I briefly considered giving him hell for waking me so early on a Saturday just to cancel our lunch with only the offer of work to replace it, but he knows me too well. A murder story is *much* more interesting than an indifferent meal in a stuffy restaurant in town. So I got dressed as fast as I could and here I am.' She patted the Rover affectionately.

'Here, as you say, you are. But the body is elsewhere, dear.'

'Yes, I know. Simeon was in a tearing hurry and didn't actually stay long enough to tell me how to get there. I've no idea where this smithy might be, so I thought I'd ask you.'

'It's a coopery and we're on our way there now. If you move out of the way we'll drive down to the village and wait for you at the green until you can turn round and catch us up. Then you can follow us. It's not far.'

Mere moments later we were all three of us on our way out to the Gloucester Road and Peppard's Coopery.

With me at the wheel, the drive was steady enough for Lady Hardcastle to be able to have a few sips of her coffee on the way, and by the time we arrived at the cooper's yard she was quite her old self again.

I parked next to Inspector Sunderland's car and Miss Caudle pulled in behind us. We all disembarked and made our way to the open workshop doors.

◆ ◆ ◆

The scene in the workshop was eerily similar to the last time we had visited, though instead of standing at his tiny anvil – which I subsequently learned was called a cooper's bick iron – Moses Peppard was sitting upright against a workbench with a hideous head wound, his huge fists clenched by his sides. To judge from the blood on the floor, he had been killed in the middle of the room and then dragged to the bench.

Dr Gosling was examining the corpse. Inspector Sunderland was prowling the workshop.

He caught sight of us as we entered.

'Morning, ladies. Bit of a gruesome one today, I'm afraid.'

We nodded sombrely. He must have noticed something in Miss Caudle.

'I know the Littleton contingent have probably seen worse,' he said, 'but no one would think any less of you if you wanted to sit this one out, Miss Caudle.'

'He always calls me Miss Caudle when I'm in trouble,' she said.

'You're not in trouble, dear,' said Lady Hardcastle, 'but you don't look at all well.'

'Come with me,' I said. 'We'll let them get on with their poking and prodding while we try to come up with some explanations in the fresh air.'

I put my arm around her waist to help her to the door, but she shrugged herself free and ran out.

'Is that a clean cup over there by the sink, Dr Gosling?' I said.

'Looks like it. What do you want it for?'

'Listen.'

The sound of retching drifted in through the open doors.

'Pour your beloved a cup of water from the tap,' I said, 'and I'll take it out to her.'

'Ah. Right you are.'

Lady Hardcastle handed me her handkerchief. 'She might want this, too.'

I left her to sketch the scene and the men to do whatever it was they were doing, and went to join Miss Caudle in the yard.

She was leaning over, propping herself against the wall with one hand and holding her skirts out of the way with the other.

'Here you are,' I said, and gave her the water.

'Thank you,' she said, weakly.

She took a sip and then heaved again. I put my arm across her shoulders.

'I feel so bloody stupid,' she said. 'I never knew I'd react like this.'

'Everyone reacts like that the first time,' I said. 'Like the inspector said, no one thinks less of you.'

'Did you?'

'Think less of you? At first, obviously. I thought, "Who's that vacuous ninny in the swanky frock, throwing up in the rhododendrons?"'

To my relief, she laughed.

'It's a hydrangea. But you know what I meant, you oaf. Did you react like this the first time you saw a dead body? One that had met a violent end, I mean.'

'I did. Of course I did. And then cried my eyes out. For hours.'

She stood up and I led her towards the table and chairs under the awning.

'To be fair, though,' I said as we walked, 'I was also having to deal with the fact that I was the one who killed him. Dreadful little Hungarian man in Shanghai. Kept trying to see my ankles.'

'You do have a remarkably trim ankle,' she said, chuckling again.

'Those lucky enough to get a glimpse have remarked upon them,' I said. 'I might have let him get away with his lechery but he was also pointing a gun at Lady Hardcastle. He had to go. A flick of the wrist and my knife caught him in the throat.'

We sat down.

'A lot of your stories end with someone pointing a gun at Emily,' she said as she sat gratefully down.

'You've met her,' I said. 'You can't honestly tell me you've never wanted to point a gun at her.'

Miss Caudle laughed again and sipped her water.

'She's lucky to have you.'

'I keep telling her that. How are you feeling now?'

'Still extremely foolish,' she said, 'but less queasy. Do you know, I'd been grumbling to myself all the way up here about not having had time for breakfast? But it seems to have worked out for the best, after all.'

'You can come back to the house when we're done here and we'll fill you up with whatever you fancy. It'll make you feel better.'

'I might take you up on that. It looks as though Simeon's going to be busy all day. You won't mind if I stop at yours for a while, will you? If it's not too much of an imposition I'd like to sit at your dining table and start drafting my story.'

'Not at all. It's always a pleasure to see you.'

She took out the leather-covered notebook and expensive pen I'd seen so many times before and started writing on a fresh page.

'Who was this Moses Peppard, then?' she said.

'Is this for the newspaper?' I asked.

'It is.'

'Then he was the local cooper and a respected member of the charity organization the Cider Wardens, otherwise known as the Weryers of the Pomary.'

She wrote this down.

'And if it weren't for the newspaper?'

'Put the pen down and I'll tell you.'

She did so.

'Until this morning,' I continued, 'he was our main suspect in the murder of Claud Cridland. He was vying with Cridland for the senior post in the Weryers and they'd fallen out over it. Then he was seen on his bicycle on the morning of Cridland's murder, heading towards the orchard where the body was found.'

'Was he? Was he, indeed?'

'But when we spoke to him about it he said he had nothing to do with it and was actually having it away with a farmer's wife.'

She grinned and reached for her pen but I put my own hand on it.

'Keep it straight and factual for now,' I said, 'and when we know exactly what happened, we'll make sure you get the full story first.'

'Our readers want more than just the dull, dry facts, Flo dear. They want scandal and gossip. They want wild, sensational speculation.'

'Then they're a bunch of prurient fools. Please don't scupper the investigation by pandering to them.'

She looked at me appraisingly.

'Very well,' she said, 'but I'll want everything.'

'You'll have it. You can help, if you like.'

'I can? How?'

'Well, I'm struggling to find a single story to fit all the events of the past few days. We thought things were becoming clearer before we spoke to Peppard – we thought he'd killed Cridland – but his story about the farmer's wife, and now his own murder, have muddied the waters again.'

'Do you think they were both killed by the same person?'

'That would be simplest, wouldn't it?' I said. 'They were both Weryers and it would make the most sense if it had something to do with that. Something they'd both done that made someone want to kill them. But Peppard was seen on his way towards the orchard – he even admitted it was him – so we can't rule him out until we find out more about this alleged farmer's wife he claimed as his alibi. She might be real, but she might just as easily be a yarn he made up to put us off the scent.'

'And even if it was Peppard, we still need to work out who killed *him*,' she said. 'Let's try to think this through. Cridland was murdered by Peppard or "Someone Else". Peppard might or might not have been having an affair with an as-yet-unknown farmer's wife. The farmer might or might not have been aware of what was going on. Peppard was definitely murdered, though. If the farmer knew what was happening in the marital bed while he was out herding his herd, it might have been him. If not, it might be our original "Someone Else", or if not him, "Some Other Someone Else". We need one of Lady Hardcastle's diagrams to get this all straight.'

'Or just Occam's razor,' I said. 'The simplest solution with the fewest assumptions is both murders being committed by the same "Someone Else", surely. Everything else is just silt being kicked up by our own stomping about. I was wrong. It's not the new events that are confusing things; we're muddying our own waters.'

'There we are then, let's go with that. How can I help?'

'"Someone Else" or not, we still need to find out if the farmer's wife is real and, if so, who she is. That'll remove some of the silt from the water.'

'Ah,' said Miss Caudle. 'Yes. I can root out scandal. I'm the scandal equivalent of a truffle pig. I'm a scandal pig.'

'Who's a pig?' said Dr Gosling, sitting down beside us.

'You are, darling,' she said. 'You broke our luncheon date and offered me a corpse with his head staved in as compensation.'

'Ah, yes, sorry. Are you all right?'

'I'll be fine. Flo has taken good care of me.'

'Thank you, Flo,' he said. 'In my defence, Sunderland didn't tell me what sort of state the body was in when he summoned me.'

'I shall let you know when you're forgiven. Are we needed here?'

'No. I've seen everything I need to see until I can get the poor chap on the slab, so I'm just waiting for the mortuary men. Sunderland has some more poking about to do, apparently, and Emily is still sketching. Do you want to go?'

'Flo has invited me back to Littleton Cotterell for some breakfast. I thought I'd take her up on it.'

'Perhaps we could all convene there when you're finished,' I suggested. 'Unless you're in a hurry to get to the mortuary.'

'No, no, a little breakfast will be good before I start slicing. He can wait,' said Dr Gosling with a grin. 'It's not like he has anywhere else to be.'

Miss Caudle glared at him.

'Well, er, yes,' he said, limply, the grin fading. 'We . . . we shouldn't be too long.'

'If you could let Emily know I've kidnapped her maid,' said Miss Caudle, 'I'll drive her home and we'll see you later.'

Dr Gosling stood.

'Right you are,' he said, and set off back to the workshop.

'Sim?' said Miss Caudle.

He stopped.

'Take my cup back in for me, would you?'

She passed him the cup and we got up ourselves.

'Come on, then,' I said. 'I'll help you start the Rover.'

Back at the house, Miss Caudle was still chattering away, bombarding me with questions, as I led her through to the kitchen to ask Miss Jones to start work on a late breakfast for our unexpected guests.

'And what about the other Weryers?' she was saying. 'Have you considered them? Or this mystery woman at the Dog and Duck. I've got some contacts at the local newspaper in Exeter. I'll ask them if they know her. There aren't many people in Devon – I get the impression they all know one another.'

Edna came through from filling a mop bucket at the sink in the boot room.

'Good mornin', Miss Caudle,' she said. 'We a'n't seen you for ages. 'Ow bist?'

'I've been better, Edna, I can't lie. But it'll pass.'

Edna nodded sagely.

'But how about you?' continued Miss Caudle. 'How's your Dan?'

'Oh, mustn't grumble, you know. And he's all right, an' all. Great lummox.'

'Pleased to hear it.'

'Your fella not with you?'

'He's working on a case with Inspector Sunderland.'

'Ooh,' said Edna, putting down her bucket and folding her arms across her ample chest. 'Another murder?'

'I'm afraid so, yes.'

'Juicy one?'

'Very nasty.'

'Some poor unfortunate down in the city?'

'No,' said Miss Jones. 'A local man. Your cooper, Moses Peppard.'

'No,' said Edna in dismay. 'Not Mo. Well I never. That's a terrible shame, that is. He was a lovely bloke. Lovely. Handsome, too.'

I nodded.

'He really was,' I said.

'I tell you, if I'd been thirty years younger I'd have tried my luck there,' said Edna. 'I'd have had to join the queue, mind.' She chuckled fondly.

'Got about, did he?' said Miss Caudle.

'I should say he did, my lover. Not many women between here and Stroud haven't had a tumble with Peppard the Cooper, and them as hasn't have thought about it at the very least. Put a smile on many a face, that man.'

'Had he been seeing anyone recently? Anyone in particular, I mean.'

'Now, see, I think that's one of the reasons he was always so popular. Discreet he was. He wasn't one to kiss and tell.'

'How did you find out about his exploits, then?' I asked.

'Oh, *he* didn't kiss and tell, but some of his ladies was so pleased with themselves that they told everyone.'

Miss Caudle and I both laughed.

'There was always rumours, mind,' said Edna. 'His latest was a married lady down towards Pighill, last I heard.'

'A farmer's wife?' I said.

'That's the only sort of wife they gots down there,' she said with another throaty chuckle. She paused a while in wistful thought. 'They're sure it was murder?' she asked suddenly.

'Definitely,' said Miss Caudle. 'We saw the body. Head smashed in.'

'Oh, you poor loves. No wonder you looks peaky. You go and sit down in the mornin' room and I'll bring you a hot, sweet tea.'

'Just hot for me, Edna,' said Miss Caudle. 'Watching the old figure.'

'Nonsense, you's skinny as a rake. And it don't work for shock if it i'n't sweet. You do as you's told, my lover. Go on.'

'You're very kind, Edna,' she said. 'Thank you.'

'Yes,' I said. 'Thank you. Where's Miss Jones?'

'Here I am,' said Miss Jones from behind us. 'I had to nip to the you-know-where. Hello, Miss Caudle.'

'Morning,' said Miss Caudle with a smile.

'Do we have enough in the house to do a late breakfast for five?' I asked.

'I should be able to knock somethin' together,' said Miss Jones with a smile. 'How long have I got?'

'No idea, I'm afraid. Shall we say an hour?'

She looked at the large kitchen clock.

'Plenty of time,' she said. 'I'll do the eggs when they gets here, and everything else will keep.'

'Thank you.'

'Now you take that young lady through and get her sat down,' said Edna. 'Leave the rest to us.'

We did as we were told.

◆ ◆ ◆

Almost exactly an hour had passed by the time the other three came back. I alerted Miss Jones to their arrival and told them that breakfast was imminent. Miss Caudle's colour had returned and I was pleased to notice Dr Gosling being properly attentive.

Lady Hardcastle had a sketch of the handsome Moses Peppard, pre-head wound, which she pinned on the crime board that Miss Caudle and I had lugged through to the morning room. It had occurred to me as we struggled across the hall with it that we might have been better just having breakfast in the dining room, but the idea of that seemed altogether wrong. Breakfast was in the morning room and anything else would be peculiar.

'There's no doubt about the cause of death,' said Miss Caudle.

'The crushing of the frontal bone of the skull and subsequent damage to the brain would certainly be our best bet,' said Dr Gosling. 'I agree. But I'd not be prepared to swear to it in court until I've taken a look at the rest of him. It wouldn't be the first time someone's smashed up their victim in a fit of rage after killing them much less brutally.'

'I forget the horrors you have to see, Sim. I'm sorry.'

'Nonsense, old girl. Someone has to see them or the evildoers go unpunished.'

'From the size and shape of the wound,' said Lady Hardcastle, who had clearly had time to think about it while sketching the scene, 'I presume he was attacked with a hammer of some sort.'

'That was my first thought,' said Inspector Sunderland. 'A cooper's hammer's a heavy thing – it would make a brutal weapon in the hands of someone strong enough to wield it. The trouble is, in a workshop full of hammers and other suitable weapons, not one had any visible blood on it. The killer might have cleaned it, of course, but that's a rather chilling thought, don't you think? To be able to do something that brutal and then have the presence of mind to calmly wash the murder weapon and put it back with the others? Not to mention scrubbing down the sink – there was no sign of blood anywhere but in the middle of the room, where I believe he was killed, and around his body where it was posed. There was spatter and spray everywhere, and a few drips from the weapon, but—'

He stopped talking when he noticed that Edna had entered with a tray of food. Miss Jones was close behind. They set out the breakfast without saying a word. I thanked them and they hurried out.

'Do you have any idea when it might have happened, Dr Gosling?' I asked.

'Nothing accurate. I took his temperature but I'll have to get to my textbooks to see how this heat would affect things. The larger pool of blood was still quite wet, but some of the individual spots had dried completely, so we know he'd been there for more than an hour. But we knew that anyway – it took us more than an hour to get up here from town after the call from . . .'

'It was Hancock,' said the inspector. 'He'd been cycling home from . . . well, let's just say "elsewhere" to save my blushes.'

'Another rakish scoundrel bringing joy to the ladies of the district, eh?' said Miss Caudle.

'Hancock?' said Lady Hardcastle with a laugh. 'He's more of a charmingly eager puppy than a rakish scoundrel.'

'Some girls go for an eager puppy,' said Miss Caudle, touching Dr Gosling's hand.

'Actually, I'm more interested in the idea of his being "another" rakish whatnot,' said Dr Gosling. 'How many do you have out here in the back of beyond?'

'You'd be surprised, darling,' said Miss Caudle. 'The late Moses Peppard was quite the wild rover, so Edna says.'

'Was he, now?' said the inspector. 'That's interesting. But young Sam Hancock, whatever his boyish attractions, was passing the coopery a little after six when he noticed the doors open. It was unusual for Peppard to be at work so early so he investigated – he has good police instincts, that lad. He found the body, then cycled hell for leather back to the village to telephone the Bridewell.'

'So he was dead before six,' said Dr Gosling.

'Long enough before six for there to have been no sign of the murderer when Hancock arrived,' added Lady Hardcastle.

'Indeed,' agreed Dr Gosling. 'But more than that I'm not yet able to say.'

'No offence, darling,' said Miss Caudle, 'but that's not quite the medically trained insight we'd been hoping for.'

'I leave speculation and wild surmise to minds far superior to my own,' he said. 'I can only draw conclusions from the facts before me. And those are all the facts I have at the moment.'

'We shall mull it further over eggs and toast,' said Lady Hardcastle. 'I'm famished. I say, are those the missing sausages?'

We all sat down to eat.

Chapter Ten

The two men left shortly before noon, but Miss Caudle asked once more if she could stay. Lady Hardcastle cheerfully agreed.

'It's always lovely to see you, dear,' she said. 'We don't come into town nearly often enough and we do so enjoy your company.'

'You're very kind,' said Miss Caudle. 'If you'll excuse me for half an hour while I draft a story for the *News*, I should love to spend the afternoon with someone who doesn't smell of disinfectant.'

Lady Hardcastle laughed.

'And we can always splash some on a cloth if you're missing him,' she said.

'I shall let you know. Oh, and might I use your telephone later, too?'

'Of course, dear. Anything you need.'

'I ought to file the story in person, but it will be quicker to dictate it over the telephone. They'll grumble and moan, especially because it's me. A woman's place is on the society pages, as they never tire of telling me. But I've brought them more than my fair share of scoops since we cracked the suffragette story, so they grudgingly indulge me. And they enjoy the glamour and romance of being first with the news, so they'll take the story even if one of them has to copy it down over the telephone.'

'Our telephone is your telephone, Dinah dear. I'm going to have yet another tepid bath, then we'll be in the garden when you're done.'

With breakfast having been so late I asked Miss Jones not to prepare any lunch, saying that I'd take care of it myself.

'Oh, I don't mind. I can scrub you some taters if you like,' she said. 'Nearly new, I call them. New potatoes are done, but these still i'n't the big knobbly ones we'll get later in the year. They'll boil up lovely. There's peas if you don't mind shelling them.'

'I can do that while we sit in the garden. There are only four cutlets. That'll be enough for three, won't it?'

'I thought you was being a bit generous with two each when I saw the size of them, tell you the truth. Three'll be ample. If you're still hungry there's a summer pudding in the larder. We had some bread to use up.'

'Perfect,' I said. 'Thank you. If you or your mother want the other cutlet, help yourself.'

'I shall. Thank you. Our ma can't abide lamb so I never usually has it. She can have her boiled ham and I'll have a lovely cutlet.'

'It's all worked out well, then. If you want some mint from the new herb garden, do please take some of that, too.'

Miss Jones had become very insistent as soon as they'd appeared in Weakley's greengrocery that we should scrub new potatoes rather than peel them. She'd got a bee in her bonnet about it from something she'd read somewhere and they actually tasted rather nice, so I took a bowl of peas and left her to scrub the spuds.

Lady Hardcastle had returned from her bath and was once more sprawled in her chair, reading a book.

'We've company,' I said. 'Must you really sit with your legs like that?'

'Oh, Dinah won't mind,' she said. 'And it's so very comfortable.'

'It's uncouth.'

'Prig.'

'Slattern.'

'Shut up and shell your peas.'

I left her to her book and set to work on my bowl of peas. There's something immensely satisfying about shelling peas. The way the pod splits open when you squeeze it, the way the tiny . . . what are peas? Are they seeds? The way they feel when you scoop them out with your thumb, anyway, breaking them off from their tiny anchor points. And, of course, sampling them. There's a delicious freshness about a newly de-podded pea that's hard to beat.

I was quite lost in my leguminous pleasures by the time Miss Caudle emerged from the house. The first I knew of her arrival was Lady Hardcastle's greeting.

'Come and join us, dear,' she said, and I was amused to note that she was suddenly sitting up elegantly in her chair.

'Don't mind if I do,' said Miss Caudle. 'This is the life, eh? Summer sunshine, a country garden, a jug of . . . whatever on earth that is.'

'It's elderflower cordial,' I said.

'Just the ticket. May I . . .'

I poured her a glass and she sat with us in the shade of the apple tree.

'How on earth do you do it?' she asked after a while.

'Do what, dear?' said Lady Hardcastle.

'Deal with dead bodies and ne'er-do-wells, day and night. Doesn't it rather crush the spirit, always seeing the worst of people?'

'We see some of the noblest, most heroic of people too, don't forget. People who make great sacrifices for their families, their countries, their principles.'

'But even that must be heartbreaking. You deal with death on a . . . well, I was going to say "daily" basis which isn't right at all.

But you certainly see a zillion times more violent death than the average woman.'

'Someone has to stand up to them,' I said. 'Someone has to stand up to the tyrants and the bullies, the murderers and the assassins. If not us, then who?'

'Yes, but . . .' She trailed off. 'Well, I admire you enormously, that's all. I remember when we first met at the Littleton Cotterell Moving Picture Festival or whatever it was called. I thought you both absolutely insufferable. But after that business with Lizzie Worrel and the suffragettes and now this morning's horrors . . . well . . . you're remarkable, that's all. The pair of you.'

'Thank you,' said Lady Hardcastle. 'You're very kind. But as Flo says, someone has to do it.'

'Some of it, perhaps. You might be able to argue that there are few as well qualified as you for your government work. But this? No one expects you to look at smashed skulls at eight o'clock on a Saturday morning and try to catch the perpetrators. Ollie Sunderland is a capable man. He'll find your killers in the end.'

'He almost certainly will, that's true. I suppose we have to own up to the fact that we enjoy it, then, wouldn't you say, Flo?'

'I certainly do,' I said. 'And we're a team.'

'A remarkable team,' said Miss Caudle. 'If you ever retire from your government work I should like to write your biographies. Share your exploits. Your courage. Your steadfast devotion to your duty. Women in the service of their country and all that.'

'I say, dear,' said Lady Hardcastle. 'Steady on.'

'I mean it. We could explain your methods, too. Try to understand how you work so well together.'

'Oh, that's simple,' I said. 'She annoys people and I stop them from hurting her. It's not a complex arrangement.'

'Oh, nonsense.'

'It's true,' said Lady Hardcastle. 'I'd be dead in a ditch somewhere in central Europe if not for Flo.'

'I've heard you say that before and it's utter rot. Look, I'll not embarrass you further, I just thought someone ought to tell you how marvellous you both are.'

'The same someone who threw up in the begonias,' I said.

'Hydrangeas,' she corrected me.

'You've no chance there,' said Lady Hardcastle. 'Flo, what's that?' She pointed at a spiky flower.

'Zinnia,' I said, confidently.

'No, it's still a dahlia. Hopeless, you see? She can shave an ant's eyebrows with a throwing knife from twenty paces, or bring down a sixteen-stone Bulgarian bodyguard with a flick of her dainty wrist, but she can't tell a buddleia from a bullfrog.'

'They're all just flowers to me,' I said. 'Apart from the bullfrog.' I held up my bowl. 'I do, at least, know how to shell peas. And cook them. When do you want to eat and what shall we do afterwards?'

'Six-ish for dinner,' said Lady Hardcastle.

'And I want to see the orchard,' said Miss Caudle. 'Simeon told me about it.'

'We could go now if you like,' said Lady Hardcastle.

'No,' she said. 'I want to see where they carry out their rituals. I want to see it in the dark.'

With the Rolls and the Rover each being two-seaters, we had to take both of them on our evening jaunt. Miss Caudle had no idea where we were going so I rode with her as navigator after helping her start her engine.

Lady Hardcastle had promised to take it steady, but even by the time we were taking the lane northwards out of the village she had sped ahead.

'Oh, blast,' said Miss Caudle as the single red light at the rear of the Silver Ghost disappeared into the darkness. 'I've lost her. Sorry. Perhaps we might have been better with you driving.'

'It's not far,' I said. 'We'll be fine. And we'd not have kept up with her even if I had been driving – the Rolls is just too fast.'

'It is with her at the wheel,' she said, leaning forwards to peer into the gloom.

'It can be fast with me at the wheel, too,' I said, somewhat too defensively. 'I just choose to be more careful.'

'Oh, my dear, no, that's not what I meant at all. It's admirable that you choose to be careful. Sim, on the other hand, doesn't choose it. He seems physically incapable of driving at more than a walking pace. It's utterly infuriating. Left or right?'

'What?' I was confused.

'Left turn or right?'

'Oh. Yes. Sorry. Left. Right would take you past the dairy and on to the Gloucester Road near the coopery. The orchard will be coming up on our right in about a mile.'

'Righto.'

I could see her leg tense as she pressed her foot hard on the accelerator pedal, but we pootled along at the same sedate pace regardless.

A few minutes later we saw the glow of the Silver Ghost's lights ahead of us. Lady Hardcastle had drawn to a stop a little way beyond the orchard gate for some reason, and we pulled in behind her. She switched off her lights and came to meet us.

'I thought it might be best not to park directly next to the gate,' she said, anticipating the question that was already forming on my lips. 'It's not as though there are many other places the occupants of two motor cars might have gone in the middle of the night, but I thought it might help to cast just a tiny bit of doubt upon what we were up to if we were a few yards up the road.'

'Are people likely to wonder what we're up to?' asked Miss Caudle. 'There's no one about.'

'We know the Weryers come out here in the night. And there's a killer on the loose. Who knows who might be lurking unseen in the darkness?'

'I say,' said Miss Caudle, excitedly. 'A proper adventure. I've not done anything as exciting as this since that day with you lot at the docks. We dressed up as workmen, do you remember?'

'If this is your idea of a fun evening out,' said Lady Hardcastle, 'we ought to take you on more of our "adventures". We can make it official if you like – I'd certainly vouch for you with Harry. You're exactly the sort of person he's looking for.'

'Steady on, Emily dear. Prowling a deserted orchard is enough for now. Let's not get ahead of ourselves.'

'If you change your mind, just say the word. The country's going to need women like you if the situation on the Continent gets any worse.'

'I'll bear it in mind,' said Miss Caudle, with more than a little amusement in her voice.

We had reached the gate by now and Lady Hardcastle looked ahead into the darkness of the woods. The new moon was no help at all.

'We should have brought a flash-lamp,' she said.

'Like this one?' I said as I flicked the switch and illuminated the path.

'If you do decide to get into our line of work, dear,' said Lady Hardcastle to Miss Caudle, 'do insist they partner you with someone like Flo – it will make your life so much easier.'

I led the way through the trees to the first clearing. Our eyes had become accustomed to the gloom so that even the weak yellow light of the flash-lamp brought the orchard magically to life.

'I say,' said Miss Caudle in a low, reverent voice, 'that's quite something, isn't it? You can see why the Ancients might have worshipped here.'

She wasn't wrong. The orchard was impressive enough in the daylight, but in the dark it was even more mystical.

'Wait till you see the second clearing,' I said. 'Come on.'

I led them both across the grassy boundary, wondering briefly how they kept the grass so short. Was it mown? Did they bring some compliant sheep in once in a while to crop it all down? I wondered if I should ask someone. Mattick would know.

The widely spaced apple trees were easier to navigate and we were soon at the inner clearing.

'Oh, my,' said Miss Caudle, looking around. 'Is that an altar over there?'

'It is,' said Lady Hardcastle. 'It looks wonderful in the firelight from those braziers.'

'Which braziers . . . ? Oh, I see them. What a magnificent place. Can't you just imagine them, thousands of years ago, standing on this spot, worshipping their gods? It's just so—'

She stopped suddenly and whipped around.

'What was that?' she whispered.

'What was what?' I said, flicking the feeble beam of the flash-lamp around the clearing.

'There,' she said, pointing. 'Something moved.'

I aimed the light in the indicated direction but saw nothing.

'A badger, perhaps?' suggested Lady Hardcastle. 'A fox?'

'No,' said Miss Caudle, 'it was bigger than that. Look, there it is again.'

This time I saw it, too, but the flash-lamp wasn't bright enough to let us see exactly what it was.

'It was a man,' said Miss Caudle. 'I know it was.'

'A woman, I'd say,' said Lady Hardcastle. 'Long skirt, shawl, above average height. Quite young, to judge from her nimbleness.'

'How could you possibly . . . ?' asked Miss Caudle.

'It's one of her numerous gifts,' I said. 'She can see remarkably well in the dimmest of light. It's got us out of many a pickle.'

'Shouldn't we give chase?' said Miss Caudle.

'To what end, dear?' said Lady Hardcastle. 'What would we do if we caught her?'

'We could find out who she is and what she's doing here.'

'We've a fairly good idea who she is, I'd say.'

'Who?'

'From the description, it's probably Grace Chamberlain,' I said.

'Just so,' said Lady Hardcastle. 'And as for finding out what she was doing here, we can just go to the Dog and Duck and ask her. She's staying in the village.'

'Then what are we waiting for?' asked Miss Caudle impatiently.

'There's no rush. We have two motor cars and she's on foot. Or on a bicycle at best – though I'm not sure where she'd find one. If you've seen everything you want to see here, we can stroll back to our vehicles at a leisurely pace and still be at the village pub before her.'

'Come on, then,' said Miss Caudle. 'Let's not hang about.'

She set off back the way we had come at a much less than leisurely pace. Lady Hardcastle and I followed. Even in the moonlight I could see Lady Hardcastle's grin.

◆ ◆ ◆

Miss Caudle drove back to the village with a good deal more confidence, though her pace was still limited by the tiny engine in the Rover. By the time we arrived at the Dog and Duck, Lady Hardcastle was already inside.

'. . . and whatever these two are having,' she said as we approached the public bar.

'I . . . oh . . . I suppose I'd better have some cordial,' said Miss Caudle. 'I'm not sure about driving after tippling. Do you think it's safe?'

'I've seen no studies,' said Lady Hardcastle, 'but reason dictates that someone in charge of a ton of metal moving at thirty miles an hour ought really to be in full possession of their wits. I'm having cordial, too. Old Joe got some specially for me.'

'Cordial for Miss Caudle, then?' said Daisy.

'I think it best,' said Miss Caudle.

'What about you, Flo?'

'I'll have a brandy,' I said. 'Large one.'

'Two lime cordials and a large brandy coming up.'

'Oh, and get something for yourself,' said Lady Hardcastle.

'Don't mind if I do, m'lady,' said Daisy with a smile. 'A cider would go down lovely.'

Daisy busied herself with the drinks.

'Which door does Grace Chamberlain use?' I asked.

'What do you mean?' said Daisy.

'When she comes and goes. Where does she come and go to and from?'

'Oh, I see. Snug, mostly. She don't like comin' through the public, I don't think.'

'Thanks, Dais,' I said. 'Come on, then, ladies. We should adjourn to the snug if we wish to meet young Grace.'

'Ooh,' said Daisy. 'What do you want her for?'

'We just need to satisfy our collective curiosity,' said Lady Hardcastle as she headed for the door to the snug.

I winked at Daisy.

'I'll tell you later,' I said, and followed.

Miss Caudle took a seat in the corner.

'This takes me back,' she said. 'Sitting here talking to old Whatshischops in the green velvet jacket and that huge cravat.'

'Aaron Orum,' I said.

'That's the chap. How do you remember names like that?'

'That's one of *her* numerous talents,' said Lady Hardcastle. 'Just as correcting people when they get names wrong is one of her very special pleasures. I sometimes get them wrong on purpose just to see the look of glee on her little face when she sets me right.'

I stuck my tongue out just as the door opened and Grace Chamberlain entered, taking off her shawl.

'Good evening, dear,' said Lady Hardcastle.

'Oh,' said Miss Chamberlain. 'Hello again.'

She bustled through the tiny room.

'Stay and have a drink with us, won't you?' said Lady Hardcastle.

'Thank you, no. I'm very tired. I'd like to get to bed.'

'A little nightcap and some convivial company will help you sleep. You can tell us all about your walk. How was the orchard?'

Miss Chamberlain turned sharply.

'I beg your pardon?' she said.

'The orchard, dear. It's so beautiful at this time of night, don't you think?'

'I'm sure I don't know what you're on about,' said Miss Chamberlain, and stalked out through the door by the bar. We heard her footsteps banging on the stairs as she went to her room.

'So much for that, then,' said Miss Caudle. 'We should have given chase after all.'

'Her reaction confirms it was her,' said Lady Hardcastle. 'And she'd have told us to buzz off just as emphatically if we'd confronted her on the road in the dark. We'd have got nothing more from her.'

'Well, you know best, I suppose. What now?'

'There's not much more we can do on the case. We could sup up here and return to the house for cards, if you like. Or music. I've never asked you – do you play?'

'A little.' Miss Caudle looked at the clock. 'But some other time, I think – I ought to be getting home. My landlady does love to make a fuss if I'm out late.'

'Of course, dear. Do please telephone us if you have any brainwaves. We value your insights.'

'I shall. Simeon should keep me abreast of the main developments, but if you could share any information you two come upon, that might help with the brainwaves.'

'It's a deal.'

We finished our drinks, said goodnight to Daisy, and drove our separate ways home.

Chapter Eleven

Shortly after lunch on Monday, Inspector Sunderland arrived at our door with news of the post-mortem. Lady Hardcastle was in the dining room with the crime board, which, to my astonishment, she had lugged over from the morning room after breakfast by herself.

'Don't look so surprised,' she had said in response to my cocked eyebrow. 'I can carry things.'

'Being able to and being willing to are quite different matters,' I said. 'As you often remind me.'

'Needs must when the devil is making the coffee, dear.'

I showed the inspector to the dining room.

'Ah, Inspector,' said Lady Hardcastle. 'Do come in. We've already eaten, I'm afraid, but I'm sure Miss Jones could rustle something up for you if you're peckish.'

'I ate my sandwiches in the motor car on the way here, thank you, my lady.'

'Oh, my dear chap, that will never do. Eating is one of life's great pleasures. You shouldn't absently cram your luncheon into your face while you're doing something else. You should take your time. Savour the joy of it.'

'I can't argue with you, but time is not a luxury afforded us in the police force.'

'I am most disappointed. I shall write to the Chief Constable and demand that his officers be given proper lunch breaks.'

'By all means, my lady, but I doubt he'll have time to read your letter – he'll be too busy.'

'We can surely tempt you to some tea, though? Coffee?'

'A cup of tea would be most welcome, thank you.'

I went through to the kitchen to catch Edna before she left for the afternoon, once again cursing the architect for not including a system of bells, and Lady Hardcastle for not having had them installed once we'd moved in.

By the time I returned, they were examining the crime board.

'. . . definitely up to something,' said Lady Hardcastle.

'I drew the same conclusion,' said the inspector. 'I got nothing out of her at all when I spoke to her last week. I know it's an elementary error of criminal detection to make such assumptions, but I interpreted her reluctance to speak as an eagerness to conceal.'

'Grace Chamberlain?' I asked.

'The very same,' he said. 'You seeing her last night at the scene of the first murder is at least a little suspicious, though, I'm sure you agree.'

'I do,' I said. 'Although it would also fit Dr Gosling's suggestion.'

'Remind me.'

'She might be a murder tourist.'

He laughed.

'I'll buy Gosling and Miss Caudle a slap-up dinner at the restaurant of their choice if he's right,' he said. 'Murder tourist, indeed.'

'Tea will be a few minutes,' I said, sitting down. 'Edna is doing something technical with a mop. I didn't like to enquire too closely.'

'That's fine,' he said. 'I'm in no rush. I'm here to pick your imaginative brains, in fact.'

'Oh, I say,' said Lady Hardcastle. 'How very flattering.'

'As I said at the door, I bring news of the post-mortem. Gosling confirms that death was caused by a single blow to the frontal bone with a heavy, wedge-shaped object.'

'A cooper's hammer,' I said.

'That would definitely be our most likely weapon were it not for the fact that both Peppard's hammers were clean as a whistle. Clean of blood, anyway. Gosling's tests revealed tiny amounts consistent with their being hit by spray, so either he had a third hammer which the killer took with him—'

'Or her,' I interrupted.

'—or her, yes. Or the killer brought his . . . or her own hammer.'

'A rival cooper,' said Lady Hardcastle, 'doing away with the competition.'

'At the moment, my lady,' he said, 'that makes as much sense as any of our other ideas.'

'So far, so ordinary, then,' she said. 'Where do our much-vaunted powers of imagination come into play?'

'I need you to solve a most abstruse puzzle. I need you to come up with a reason why he might have been clutching these in his fists.'

Edna entered at that moment with the tea tray and he waited until she'd gone before fishing in his pocket and producing a pair of silver-plated salt and pepper pots. They were of an old-fashioned design and slightly battered. The plating was wearing off in places. They were identical in size and shape aside from the engraving on the sides. One bore a capital letter S for salt, the other a P for pepper.

Lady Hardcastle reached out and took them from him.

'How very odd,' she said. 'They're not particularly expensive, but neither do they seem sufficiently cheap or unimportant for him to have had them in his workshop. All his other bits and bobs were inexpensive things. Disposable, one might say – the chipped cups and the old tin teapot. Someone loved these.'

She handed them to me.

'My auntie had a pair like this,' I said. 'Part of a cruet set with a little vinegar bottle and a mustard pot with a tiny silver-plated spoon. It was a wedding present – her pride and joy.'

'I remember something similar at my own aunt's house,' said the inspector. 'Now I'm working on the principle that they're significant in some way. Either Peppard grasped them in his dying moment – although I'll grant you that's less likely given the manner of his death and our shared belief that they didn't belong in his workshop – or the killer placed them there. I'm blowed if I can think why, so I've come to you two.'

'Some dining connection?' I suggested. 'Cridland had an apple in his mouth, and they were both sitting upright. Perhaps they were gluttons at a symbolic dinner table.'

'That's certainly a plausible interpretation,' he said. 'If you can come up with a reason why someone might want to say that about them then we could well have a motive for the murders.'

'It's quite the conundrum, isn't it?' said Lady Hardcastle. 'Both men were killed in different ways but, once dead, both were dragged to a new spot and posed sitting upright with some culinary item about their bodies.'

'I shall leave that one with you, then.'

'Of course, Inspector dear.'

An idea suddenly occurred to me.

'Sid Palmer?' I suggested. 'Pat Swanton?'

'I beg your pardon, miss?' said the inspector.

'The initials, S and P. What if they weren't just Salt and Pepper? What if Peppard's last act on Earth was to grab a clue to his killer's identity?'

'Who are these gentlemen? Palmer I've heard of, certainly, but Swanton? And what connection do they have to Peppard?'

'Pat Swanton was rejected for membership of the Weryers and bears them a grudge,' I said. 'Cridland and Peppard were two of the three members who voted against him.'

'I see. And who was the third?'

'Abel Mattick – the cider maker.'

'It does all tie up,' said Lady Hardcastle, 'but I keep coming back to our original thought: the salt and pepper pots didn't belong at the coopery. And not only that. If one were in fear of one's life, would one really have the presence of mind to pick up two objects to point to the identity of one's killer?'

'But we're only assuming the salt and pepper pots weren't Peppard's,' I said. 'And he was a bright chap, after all. What if he'd already thought of the S and P connection at some point and that grabbing them was some kind of subconscious reflex when he saw who was coming at him?'

'He was a big lad,' said the inspector. 'He'd be more likely to try to defend himself than make sure his attacker was identified.'

'Holding those weighty objects in his fists might well have been a defensive act,' I said. 'If he wasn't a trained fighter, having something solid in his fist would have added weight to his punch. He might have known that. It could be both – it could be defensive and accusatory all in one.'

The inspector looked thoughtful for a moment. 'It's a stretch,' he said at length, 'but it's not *completely* out of the question. Other than having similar initials, where does Sid Palmer come into this?'

'He's been keen to join the Weryers for some time,' I said. 'He's just waiting for a vacancy to open up.'

'So you're suggesting he might have killed them to increase his chances of becoming a member? Why those two specifically? And why both of them, for the matter of that?'

'There you have me, I'm afraid. It was just a suggestion.'

'And I asked for imaginative ideas. Thank you.'

'Since it's a tad outré,' said Lady Hardcastle, 'what say Flo and I look into SP and PS while you follow more conventional leads?'

'If you wish,' said the inspector. 'I'm always happy to have help.'

'Then we shall do that very thing. What's your next move?'

'I'm going to speak to one or two of your local shopkeepers' – he opened his notebook – 'Lawrence Weakley, Septimus Holman, and Joe Arnold.'

'The greengrocer, the baker, and the publican,' I said.

'Ah, is that it? Thank you. I knew Arnold was the publican but I had it in my head that Weakley was the butcher. But anyway, the more important thing is that they're all Weryers and I very much agree with you that that particular organization holds the key to all this.'

'They're all good eggs,' said Lady Hardcastle. 'We can vouch for them.'

'You're the one who always says that everyone is a potential suspect until they're not, my lady.'

'Oh, I'm not saying they didn't do it – though I'd be enormously surprised if they had – just that they're decent chaps.'

'I'm sure they are. I shall treat them with respect, my lady, don't worry. But someone knows something about all this and I'll only find out who by speaking to everyone.'

'What will you do about Grace Chamberlain?' I asked.

'To tell you the truth, there's not a great deal I can do. Despite my strong feelings on the subject, Parliament has yet to pass a statute making "infuriating insolence" a criminal offence, and until they do I've nothing else to charge her with.'

'There's "behaving in a decidedly fishy way",' I said.

'Still not on the statute books, I'm afraid. But I've got my eye on her, don't you worry. What's the mood in the village?'

'Regarding the murders, you mean?' said Lady Hardcastle. 'The pub was free of panic last night, but it generally is. They're a sanguine lot, the patrons of the Dog and Duck. But we've not been into the village today. Have Edna or Miss Jones mentioned anything, Flo?'

'Not a word. Obviously they were both upset – you heard what Edna had to say about Peppard – but they've not said anything about the other villagers.'

'Right you are,' said the inspector. 'I was just wondering how to play it, that's all.'

'You'll be fine,' I said. 'You're a popular figure. Sergeant Dobson speaks very highly of you and they all listen to him. You shouldn't have any problems.'

He smiled.

'We shall see,' he said. 'Well, ladies, thank you for the tea. I'd best be on my way.'

'It's always a pleasure to see you, Inspector dear,' said Lady Hardcastle. 'Do let us know how you get on.'

I showed him out and returned to the dining room.

We pondered the crime board for a short while longer, but we made no progress. Eventually, Lady Hardcastle stood.

'Well, Flo dear, we can sit here all afternoon achieving nothing, I can take another cooling bath, or we can go and talk to one of the village Weryers ourselves. What do you favour?'

'There's a fourth option,' I said. 'We could interview Pat Swanton.'

'Or that, yes. Although I'm not entirely sure where he might be on a Monday afternoon.'

'Very well,' I said. 'Of the remaining options, the third seems the most entertaining.'

'I do very much want a bath, though.'

'No, we must take action and talk to a Weryer. But who? The inspector is already speaking to the local ones.'

'He's not talking to Bob Slocomb – the dairyman was absent from his list. We could pootle up to the dairy, have a quick word with Slocomb, and still be back to the village in time to join in with one of the inspector's other interviews.'

'He might not take too kindly to that.'

'Pish and fiddlesticks. We are, as you so often observe, delightful. He'll be pleased to see us.'

'Very well,' I said. 'What about Slocomb?'

'What about him?'

'Will he be pleased to see us?'

'I refer the honourable lady to my previous comment. Everyone is pleased to see us.'

I could quickly name more than a dozen people who would be decidedly displeased to see us, but I let it go. We would be outdoors and doing something useful, after all.

'I thought you knew him,' she continued. 'You're better placed to judge whether he'd be pleased to see us than I.'

'Well, I've met him a few times, certainly, but I'd hardly say I know him. From the little I've seen I'd say that Cissy inherited her sense of humour and general good nature from him, so he might not be unhappy about our turning up out of the blue—'

'There you are, then.'

'—but I wasn't asking him questions about his murdered friends when I spoke to him.'

'We'll be fine. Get your hat on.'

◆ ◆ ◆

The dairy was less than twenty minutes away on foot, and had I not known full well that Lady Hardcastle would have complained about walking in the heat for the whole of those twenty minutes, I would have proposed making the journey by Shanks's pony. As it was, I thought the motor car the more cheerful option, and we were pulling into the dairy's courtyard less than ten minutes after she had first announced her intention to visit the Slocombs.

We found Bob Slocomb inside the dairy, swabbing the decks or whatever the landlubber equivalent might be. He was armed with a hosepipe and a stiff brush and was energetically scrubbing the floor, at any rate.

'Hello there, Flo,' he said with a smile. ''Ere, mind your nice shoes. Let me turn the water off a minute.' He shut the tap and returned to us. 'And Lady Hardcastle, too. It's a pleasure to see you both, I must say. What can I do for you?'

'We were wondering if you might be able to spare us a few minutes to talk about the Weryers,' said Lady Hardcastle.

'Oh, ar,' he said, nodding. 'Our Cissy said as how you was helpin' Inspector Doo-Dah.'

'Sunderland,' I said.

'Like the sausages?'

'That's Cumberland, Mr Slocomb.'

'So 'tis, so 'tis. And call me Bob, m'dear. I keeps tellin' you that. So what is it you wants to know about the Weryers, m'lady? I'n't much I can tell you about ceremonies and that. And the charity work's all public knowledge.'

'We're more interested in the people, Bob,' said Lady Hardcastle. 'What sort of men are they, your fellow Weryers? How well do you all get on?'

'We's a mixed bunch,' he said. 'You knows who we all are?'

'We do. Like the details of your charity work, your membership list seems to be public knowledge, too.'

'It is now, yes. Time was when it was all secret. I remember when I was a lad, no one knew who they was. There was always rumours, o'course, but no one could say for sure. They was quite powerful, too. Had a lot of influence on village life, the Weryers.'

'How did they exert their influence if no one knew who they were?'

'Oh, they'd make their wishes known, m'lady. They had their ways. A whisper here, a comment there. Never revealin' theirselves, but always controllin' things. "Shadowy", our Cissy calls 'em. She reads a lot of books, our Cissy. Comes from bein' the youngest, see?'

'I suppose it does, yes,' said Lady Hardcastle, looking at me. 'And over the years, the Weryers have become less secretive as well as less influential?'

'Two goes together, don't they? Once everybody knows who they all are, people i'n't so frightened of 'em. They start tryin' to tell folk what to do then and they tells 'em to go hang.'

'Was the change gradual?' I asked.

'I suppose it was. Tell the truth I didn't pay 'em much attention back then. Our dad ran the dairy and I worked for him. I had a wife and a young family to take care of. I wasn't much interested in no secret society prancin' about in the cider orchard. All I knows is that twenty year ago we didn't know nothin' about 'em, and now we does.'

'But you knew they held their rituals in the orchard,' said Lady Hardcastle.

He chuckled.

'Oh, everyone knew that. We used to go over there when we was kids and watch. It was scary, see? Kids likes bein' scared, don't they? It was all flickerin' lights and men in cowls murmurin' mumbo-jumbo. It was like one o' they ghost stories our Cissy reads.'

'And what's it like now?' asked Lady Hardcastle.

'Same flickerin' lights, same cowls, same mumbo-jumbo – they tells I it's English, but it i'n't no English I ever heard – so it's just like it always was, only it's less scary now.'

Lady Hardcastle smiled.

'I'm so sorry,' she said, 'I meant what's the order like now?'

'Oh, I see. It's a friendly place now. Nowhere near so "shadowy", you might say.'

'You all get on?' I said. Lady Hardcastle had already asked him the same thing, but I thought he'd sidestepped the question. There must surely be more to tell.

'There's always a bit of argy-bargy, like. Twelve blokes – ten now, of course – from all walks of life. Bound to be some tiffs from time to time.'

'Anything recent?' asked Lady Hardcastle.

'No more than usual. Abel Mattick took the huff with Claud Cridland and Moses Peppard over sommat. But they was gettin' on everyone's nerves, they was. You know the High Protector is retirin'?'

'Yes, we spoke to him the other day.'

'So you knows they two was vyin' for the post? Always arguin'. I ignored it – none of my business – but old Starks was angry with 'em. Said they was bringin' the order into disrepute. Maybe that's what got Mattick's goat, too.'

'Maybe,' said Lady Hardcastle. 'But everyone else was happy?'

'As they ever is,' he said with a smile. 'Get a couple of glasses of Mattick's inside 'em, and everybody's happy, i'n't they?'

'I dare say they are.'

There was a call from outside.

'Dad? Dad, where're you to?'

'In 'ere, Ciss.'

Cissy appeared at the door.

'Oh, hello, Flo. Lady H. I wondered what your fancy motor car was doin' in the yard. I thought our dad had nicked it.'

'I 'ad,' he said. 'I was just about to take it up Gloucester to sell it, when they comes bargin' in to arrest me.'

'They can't arrest you, Dad, they i'n't policemen.'

'Got me there, Ciss. Why were you callin' me?'

'Our ma wants you.'

'What for?'

'Didn't say.'

'Didn't you ask?'

'I i'n't your secretary. You ask her.'

'You'll have to excuse me, I'm afraid, ladies,' said Mr Slocomb. 'Duty calls and all that.'

'Certainly,' said Lady Hardcastle. 'You have much more pressing matters to attend to.'

Slocomb took his leave and we walked back out into the yard with Cissy.

'He i'n't a wassaname, is he? A suspect,' said Cissy in hushed tones.

'No, dear, don't worry,' said Lady Hardcastle. 'We just wanted to hear a little more about the relationships in the Weryers.'

'"Relationships" is right,' said Cissy with a knowing look. 'You should definitely be askin' about them.'

'Oh?'

'Yes. You know I said we saw Moses Peppard cyclin' past here last week – God rest his soul?'

'You did,' I said. 'We saw him the day before he was killed and he told us he was on his way to meet a farmer's wife.'

'On his way to meet someone's wife, that's for sure. But I heard it weren't no farmer's wife. I heard it was Faith Mattick.'

'Abel Mattick's wife?' said Lady Hardcastle. 'Pretty lady? Round of cheek and ample of . . . well, of everything?'

'Yes. That's what they're sayin'.'

'"They"?' I said.

'You know,' she said. 'People.'

'Is there any truth in it?' asked Lady Hardcastle.

'Who knows? She's certainly got a wanderin' eye, though, that Faith. Last year it was Claud Cridland rumplin' 'er sheets while Abel was hard at work in the cidery.'

'Why on earth didn't you mention this before?' I asked, exasperatedly.

'You never asked. I just assumed you knew. Everybody else knew.'

'Is it true, though?' asked Lady Hardcastle. 'Or was that just another thing they were saying?'

'"They", m'lady?' said Cissy with a grin.

'Yes, dear. You know . . . people.'

'Well, no one knows for sure now, 'cept Faith Mattick. And I don't suppose she's in a hurry to tell no one.'

'Does Abel Mattick know?' I asked.

'He'd have to be deaf not to have heard.'

'But he and Cridland were friends, or so he said.'

'People say a lot of things, don't they,' said Cissy.

'They do indeed,' said Lady Hardcastle. 'Flo, dear, I think we need a trip to the cidery instead of joining the inspector in the village.'

'Won't do you no good,' said Cissy. 'They's gone to Gloucester to visit her ma. She's had a fall, she has.'

'What about the cidery?' I asked.

'Nothin' to do there till the apple harvest comes in next week. He's shut the place up and given his workers a few days off to enjoy the last of the sunshine.'

'We shall just have to hope they come back, then,' said Lady Hardcastle.

'They won't be long, I shouldn't think. 'Tweren't serious. She just needs a bit of fetchin' and carryin' for a few days. Abel's only gone up there to fix her lavatory. She a'n't got no one since Faith's dad died last year.'

'How on earth do you know all this, dear?' said Lady Hardcastle, obviously impressed.

'I works in a pub, don't I? People tells me things.'

'They certainly seem to. We should get you a job in a pub, Flo – it would save us all this traipsing about.'

'Why me?' I said. 'It was your idea – you do it.'

'Both of you would go down a storm,' said Cissy. 'Either the Dog and Duck or the Mock of Pommey – wouldn't matter. They loves you.'

'Who do?' I said.

'You know,' said Cissy and Lady Hardcastle together. '"People".'

We left Cissy chuckling to herself and set off back to the village.

I parked outside the Dog and Duck behind Inspector Sunderland's motor car and we set off in search of him.

Daisy confirmed that the inspector had already been in and that he'd spoken to Joe.

'He said he was goin' to see Holman next, but that was ages ago.'

'Thanks, Dais,' I said. 'Oh, did you know Claud Cridland had been tupping Faith Mattick?'

'That's what they said, certainly.'

'Did "they"?' I wasn't going to get involved in that again. 'Why didn't you tell us?'

'I thought you knew. Everyone knew. I mean, I don't know if what we knew was true. But both villages was talkin' about it.'

'When was this?' asked Lady Hardcastle.

'Last summer. It was all over in a flash, mind. One minute they's all talkin' about it, next minute they'd moved on. I tell you when it was – a week or so before the village fête. You wasn't here, I don't think.'

'Ah,' said Lady Hardcastle. 'We were at Weston, dear, do you remember?'

'I'm hardly likely to forget,' I said. 'And you still owe me a proper holiday.'

'Yes, we should do something about that. But it explains why we know nothing about Cridland and Mrs Mattick.'

'It's not gospel, mind,' said Daisy. 'It was just—'

'Something they said,' I interrupted. 'Yes, we understand. We'd better get going, though – we want to catch the inspector before he disappears.'

'Right you are,' she said. 'You comin' over tonight?'

'I don't know. Were we planning a trip to the pub this evening, my lady?'

'I hadn't thought to. Why, is there something happening?'

'Joe's decided that since everyone's out drinkin' on the green, he'd try and provide a bit of entertainment. He's got hold of a skittle alley he can put out there in the evenin', then pack it up and put it in the cellar when we're done – that's what was in the snug t'other night. Loads of wooden boards and hinges and latches. Complicated i'n't the word for it, but it looks good once it's up. There's a competition tonight.'

'In the dark? What's wrong with the skittle alley in here?'

'There'll be lanterns, silly. And it'll be more fun if it's outside. There's teams and everyone can join in, not just the sour-faced miseries in the skittles club. It's signin' up quick, mind, but someone might have a couple of spaces if you's interested.'

'It sounds like fun. If we can make it, we shall.'

We left the pub and strolled along to the baker's, but we could see through the window that Mr Holman was talking to Mrs Grove, the vicar's housekeeper. The inspector had clearly finished there and moved on.

'Who else was he planning to see, dear?' asked Lady Hardcastle as we resumed our walk along the pavement.

'Weakley,' I said.

'Who else was he planning to see?' she repeated in a feeble voice.

I tutted and shook my head as she giggled to herself.

'Very droll,' I said. 'Here we are.'

We entered the greengrocer's shop, where we found Mr Weakley deep in conversation with Inspector Sunderland.

'. . . been very helpful, Mr Weakley, thank you. But I see you have customers, so I'll let you get on. Please tell Sergeant Dobson or Constable Hancock if anything else occurs to you – they'll make sure I get the message.'

'Of course, sir. It's my pleasure to help,' said Mr Weakley. He turned his attention to Lady Hardcastle. 'And how can I help you, my lady?'

'Good afternoon, Mr Weakley,' she said. 'I'm so terribly sorry, but it's actually the inspector we're here to see.'

'That's quite all right,' he said. 'We were just finishing our little chat. Please carry on . . . Unless I can tempt you with a few of these lovely bananas? Fresh off the refrigerator ship at Bristol, all the way from Jamaica.'

'I am rather fond of bananas, it's true. Very well, Mr Weakley, a hand of bananas would be splendid.'

'Certainly. I've got some delicious strawberries, too, mind. Raspberries? How about these greengages? Your Miss Jones makes a lovely greengage pie.'

'You're quite the salesman, Mr Weakley. Yes, to all. We shall gorge ourselves on fresh fruit. I'm afraid you'll have to put it on my bill, though – I haven't come equipped for impulse spending on this scale.'

'That's quite all right, my lady. I know you're good for it. I wish all my customers settled their accounts so promptly.'

Lady Hardcastle left me to deal with the specifics.

By the time Weakley had made up the order there was far too much to carry, but he was sufficiently pleased with the sale that he offered to send his boy to the house with it.

'Edna and Miss Jones have finished for the day,' said Lady Hardcastle, 'so there's no one at home to receive our treasures. Would you ask him to leave it by the front door, please? It's shady there at this time of the afternoon.'

We left Mr Weakley to enter the purchases in his daybook and went back out into the sunshine.

'Oh,' said Lady Hardcastle, suddenly. 'We should have taken three of our bananas with us. We could be eating them now.'

'Please don't worry, my lady,' said the inspector. 'My mother so strongly disapproved of people eating on the street that to this day I can't bring myself to do it.'

'It was one of my own mother's bugbears,' she said. 'But I'm afraid that's precisely the reason I do it as often as I can.'

The inspector chuckled.

'I imagine you were quite a handful when you were young,' he said.

'When she was young?' I said.

He laughed again.

'You told Weakley you wished to see me.'

'I did, indeed,' said Lady Hardcastle. 'We've just spoken to a reliable witness who suggested that our philandering cooper was bedding Faith Mattick. And before that, Faith's lover was Mr Claud Cridland.'

'Both our victims were having affairs with the cider maker's wife?'

'That, at least, is the unproven rumour. Though the Cridland connection was sufficiently widely known that more than one person has told us about it.'

'Your witnesses?'

'Cissy Slocomb and Daisy Spratt.'

'Reliable young ladies for the most part,' he said. 'And both barmaids, too, I understand. They'd certainly hear all the gossip.'

'Quite so. As I say, they neither of them could offer any proof and were both at pains to point out that it was, indeed, just gossip. But it might be worthy of pursuit.'

'It might very well be. Thank you.'

'What have you learned?'

'Weakley has given me another avenue of enquiry to pursue, as it happens. Would you care to join me?'

'We should love to.'

'Thank heavens for that. I need a navigator with local knowledge.'

'Why, where are we going?'

'To see Mr Archie Rogers of Hawthorn Farm.'

'Another of the Weryers,' I said. 'A Steward of the Orchard.'

'Exactly so,' he said. 'Weakley suggested that he might be able to tell us something to our advantage.'

'Did he say what sort of something it might be?'

'No, just that Rogers had a bee in his bonnet about something to do with the Weryers, and that both Cridland and Peppard were troubled by it, too. I'm very keen to speak to him but I have a problem.'

'And that is . . . ?' said Lady Hardcastle.

'I have absolutely no idea where Hawthorn Farm might be.'

Chapter Twelve

We left the Rolls at the pub and made the journey in Inspector Sunderland's motor car. I sat in the front to navigate using the inspector's Ordnance Survey map, while Lady Hardcastle sat in the back and pretended to be important.

'I've always been curious, Inspector dear,' she said as I directed the inspector along the road past the church, 'but I've never had the opportunity to ask: is this your own motor car?'

'No, my lady, it's a police vehicle,' he said.

'Oh, I say, how very modern. I had no idea the Bristol Police Force was so up to date.'

'It's not, I'm afraid. I had to fight tooth and nail to get them to buy this one, and they only grudgingly agreed because I spend so much of my time out of the city.'

'Well, it's jolly nice. Very roomy in the back.'

'Turn left here,' I said.

We drove past the orchard and the cidery, then past the right turn to Woodworthy. Onwards and, gradually, upwards.

'Where are we now?' asked the inspector.

I consulted the map.

'This is Pighill,' I said. 'So named because . . . because it's a hill . . . where pigs lived in medieval times. They had their own porcine community, with swillmakers, wallowwrights, even a court – the Hogs' Bench. They— turn right here for Hawthorn Farm.'

We drove along a track for a few hundred yards until we came to a cobbled farmyard, with sheds on one side and a robust stone farmhouse on the other. Yet another attractive woman of, perhaps, forty-five years old was leaving the house. There must have been a factory in the area turning out these good-looking women by the dozen – I swear I'd never seen so many before. She had a bucket of feed and was on her way to the chicken coops in the small low-walled garden beside the house.

'Mrs Rogers?' said the inspector.

'Yes?'

'Good afternoon, madam. I'm Inspector Sunderland of the Bristol CID and these are—'

'Lady Hardcastle and Florence Armstrong,' said Mrs Rogers. 'We've not met, but I've seen you at Littleton.'

'How do you do?' we said, together.

'Do you mind talking while I feed the chickens?'

'Not at all,' said the inspector. 'We don't mean to interrupt. It's actually your husband we came to see.'

'Oh. That makes more sense. I think he's been wanting to talk to someone in authority. He's in the kitchen having a cup of tea. Let yourselves in.'

We did as we were bidden, and Mrs Rogers walked gracefully on towards her chickens.

'Mr Rogers?' called the inspector.

We found our way to the spacious farmhouse kitchen, where a man of medium build with a ready smile was pouring water from a kettle into an enormous teapot.

'Come on in, Inspector,' he said, warmly.

Inspector Sunderland gave him a puzzled frown.

'Windows are all open,' explained Mr Rogers. 'I heard you introducing yourselves to Franny.'

'Aha,' said the inspector.

'Sit yourselves down. I'm just making a pot of tea.'

We made ourselves comfortable.

'Now then,' he said as he set cups and the teapot on the scrubbed kitchen table, 'what can I do for you?'

'I'm rather hoping you can tell me that, Mr Rogers. I'm investigating the murders of Claud Cridland and Moses Peppard, and I've been making enquiries of your fellow Weryers.'

'Terrible business, that. Terrible. They'll be missed. Great fellas, both of them.'

'I'm sure,' said the inspector. 'And we'll get to the bottom of it. Their killer will be brought to justice.'

'It's the same person, you think?'

'We're keeping an open mind, but that certainly seems the most likely. There are . . . well, I can't go into details, but there are similarities between the two cases.'

'It's a pity you can't hang a man twice,' said Mr Rogers as he poured five cups of tea. 'He deserves that and more.'

'Perhaps. But as I was saying, I've been speaking to other Weryers and they tell me that you seem to know something that was getting various people worked up. Is this true?'

'As a matter of fact, Inspector, yes. It's been much on my mind, and I don't know what to do for the best. I'm not well up on legal matters, and it's all I can do to keep the accounts straight for the farm, so I'm not much use with financial matters, either. So . . . Well, the truth is it might be nothing at all.'

'Perhaps if you just tell us,' said the inspector, 'we can decide for ourselves. It's a financial matter, though?'

'It is, yes. See, like I say, I'm not good with the books, so I might have got it all wrong, but I needed to look at the Weryers' accounts a couple of months ago when we were supposed to be paying for some work at the village school. The builder said we'd not paid him and I needed to check the accounts to see what had happened. I found the payments all right, and he admitted he'd misplaced the cheques, but I noticed some other things. Things that didn't look quite right.'

'What sort of things?'

'Payments, they were, but not for things I knew anything about. I asked some of the lads. I know . . . knew Cridland and Peppard best, so I got them to look at it. They agreed there was something fishy going on.'

'This is very interesting,' said the inspector, who had been taking notes as Rogers spoke. 'Who has access to the Weryers' funds?'

'It's all managed by Lehane. Leopold Lehane, our treasurer. He's a retired bank manager, you see, so he's the best qualified. And Noel Gregory keeps the books – he's an accounts clerk for the auction hall in Chipping. I always thought there was something odd about Lehane. Gregory knew something, too, I think, but he never said what. It must have been the fraud.'

'Did Cridland and Peppard have any suggestions as to what you should do about it?'

'How do you mean?'

'Well, you said you didn't know what to do for the best, but you spoke to those two men and I wondered if they had any ideas.'

'Oh, I see. Well, they were all for taking it straight to the High Protector.'

'Starks?'

'Yes. They didn't see any point in confronting Lehane or Gregory – they'd just deny everything and then try to cover their tracks. Best to go straight to the man at the top, they said.'

'And did they?'

Mrs Rogers had entered and was washing her hands at the sink.

'Fat lot of good that would have done,' she said. 'He's useless, that Starks. It'll be a bright day when he finally retires.' She wiped her hands on a towel. 'Moses would have been twice the High Protector he was.'

'There's a cup of tea for you here, my love,' said Mr Rogers.

She took it with a nod of thanks.

'Is there anything else?' asked Inspector Sunderland. 'Were there any other conflicts within the Weryers, for instance?'

'No, I don't think so,' said Mr Rogers. 'They're a good bunch, aren't they, Franny?'

'Some of them were better than others,' said Mrs Rogers, 'but, yes, they're a good bunch for the most part.'

'Well, we shan't take up any more of your time. You've been most helpful. Both of you.'

'You're welcome, Inspector,' said Mr Rogers.

'You are,' said his wife. 'Drop in any time. Oh, and we're looking forward to what you've got planned for the Harvest Festival, Miss Armstrong.'

'You are?' I said, somewhat nonplussed.

'Oh, yes,' she said. 'It's a marvellous idea. I don't know how you keep coming up with them.'

'Oh, well, you know. Sometimes things just come to me.'

We said our goodbyes and returned to the inspector's motor car.

'What idea is this?' asked Lady Hardcastle as she settled into her seat.

'I honestly have no idea,' I said. 'Apparently I'm a genius, though.'

'I've always said so, dear. And what did we think of all that?'

'I'd like to mull it over for a while,' said the inspector. 'Perhaps I might impose upon your generous hospitality once more? I feel your famous crime board might help me.'

'Certainly, Inspector dear. Come back to the house with us and Flo can tell us more about the pigs of Pighill. I might make a moving picture about them.'

◆ ◆ ◆

Back at the house, the inspector helped me lug the crime board through to the drawing room, and we settled there with yet more tea while he thought things through.

'If Mattick knew about his wife's affairs with Cridland and Peppard,' he said, gesturing with his ever-present, always unlit pipe, 'then that would give him ample motive for murder.'

'If those rumours are true,' I said.

'Even if they were completely false. Even if he only *believed* his fellow Weryers were carrying on with her, that might still incite him to murderous revenge. There's no practical difference in the mind of the slighted between a real slight and a perceived slight.'

'So that makes Mattick a strong suspect,' said Lady Hardcastle.

'What about this embezzlement business?' I asked. 'Everywhere we go these days, someone seems to be stealing something from someone.'

'The vast bulk of my work involves thievery of one kind or another,' said the inspector. 'Even setting aside burglaries and street robberies, I have to deal with everything from clerks pilfering the petty cash all the way to managing directors diverting company funds into their own bank accounts. Greed will never go out of fashion, I'm afraid.'

'I suppose so,' I said. 'And greed and murder often go together, don't they? So that would put Lehane and Gregory in the frame, too, wouldn't it? Cridland and Peppard knew about the fraud and were all in favour of shopping them to Starks – and to the police eventually, I presume – so they'd have ample reason to do away with them to keep them quiet.'

'True,' he said.

'And that might explain the peculiar arrangement of the bodies, too – some sort of coded warning to the others to keep their own traps shut.'

'A retired bank manager and an accounts clerk, though,' said Lady Hardcastle. 'Do we really fancy them for murder?'

'I arrested a charming couple last year,' said Inspector Sunderland. 'A lovely old lady and gentleman from Sneyd Park. They'd murdered their housemaid when they caught her trying to steal some jewellery from the lady's dressing room. Cut up her body with a saw and started feeding it to their dogs. We only caught them because the maid's sister was worried that she hadn't been to church with the family. We found what was left of the remains in the coal cellar.'

'Insane old couples from Bristol notwithstanding,' she persisted, 'I remain unconvinced that our two fraudulent Weryers would brutally murder their friends to cover their tracks.'

'I can't say I strongly disagree,' said the inspector, 'but I shall be talking to them anyway. At the very least we might be able to nick them for the embezzlement.' He leafed through his notebook. 'Do you know Chipping Bevington well?'

'Well enough,' said Lady Hardcastle. 'I tend to rely on Flo for geographical expertise, mind you.'

'I can find my way about,' I said. 'Why?'

'Do you know Swan Lane? Archers Close?'

'As it happens, I do.'

'Splendid. Lehane lives on Swan Lane, and Gregory rents rooms in a house on Archers Close. If you could give me directions, I shall try to catch them at home before I head back to Bristol.'

'If you bring me your map,' I said, 'I'll show you.'

◆ ◆ ◆

We waved the inspector on his way and returned to the drawing room, where we sat together in contemplative silence.

'I wish we'd gone with him,' I said after a while.

'Actually, I do too, now. I'm keen to find out what Lehane and Gregory have to say for themselves. Do you think we should—'

'Barge in uninvited?' I said. 'Probably not. Perhaps we should take a chance on catching Pat Swanton, though. I agree we can't be certain where he might be on a Monday afternoon, but do you at least know where he lives? He might be at home, after all.'

'He might indeed. And if you give me a moment, I might be able to find his address.'

She disappeared, and returned a few minutes later clutching a rather full buff folder.

'Minutes of all the committees I serve on,' she said by way of explanation. 'They're always sent out with a distribution list on the front bearing all the members' names and addresses.' She began riffling through them. 'Now . . . if I can only remember which committee it was . . . Ah, here we are. I wasn't on the Parish Council but I was sent the minutes as a courtesy because I'd been asked to sit in. I was there to advise on the possible effects on village life of the increase in motor traffic, but we spent two hours discussing the best way to repot geraniums.'

'What were the possible effects of increased traffic?'

'I think the general consensus was that it would be bad for the geraniums. But here we are: Pat Swanton, number 12, The Street, Littleton Cotterell. The Street? Which street?'

'You should walk about more,' I said. 'There's a street up behind the shops called The Street. It's quite a common name in this part of the world.'

'How dismayingly unimaginative,' she said. 'But at least you know where it is.'

'I do. It's a fifteen-minute walk and we can pick up the Rolls on the way back.'

'From where?'

'We left it parked outside the pub.'

'So we did, so we did.'

'Shall we go, then?' I said, standing up.

'I just need to have a very quick bath, and then we shall be away,' she said, and swept out of the room.

Mr Swanton's house on The Street was an unassuming whitewashed cottage with . . . with some sort of plant growing over the door. Wisteria? Knowing I would never remember the answer, I was wary of asking.

Lady Hardcastle rat-a-tatted on the cast-iron knocker and, moments later, the door was answered by Mrs Knoff, the Swantons' housekeeper.

'Good afternoon, Lady Hardcastle, Miss Armstrong,' she said with a cheery smile. 'How can I help you?'

'Good afternoon,' said Lady Hardcastle. 'Is Mr Swanton at home?'

'He's not, I'm afraid. He has business at Gloucester. Mrs Swanton is in, though.'

Lady Hardcastle looked at me with a cocked eyebrow and I nodded. I'd met Mercy Swanton a few times and knew her to be rather genial – in truth, she might be prepared to tell us more than her husband would.

'Would you ask her if she'd be kind enough to speak to us?' said Lady Hardcastle.

'Certainly, my lady. Just one moment.'

She returned in less than a minute and ushered us in.

Mrs Swanton was a short woman with a young face but greying hair, which made her age difficult to guess. Her eyes said thirties, her hair fifties, and I had always assumed she was somewhere in the middle. She walked slightly awkwardly and I remembered that Mr Swanton had mentioned she was having trouble with her hips.

'How lovely of you to call,' she said as she waved us to overstuffed armchairs beside the unlit fire in her low-ceilinged sitting room. 'Mrs Knoff said you were hoping to see Patrick?'

'We were,' said Lady Hardcastle. 'We're looking into the recent murders with Inspector Sunderland, and we're speaking to anyone who might help us find out a little more about the Weryers.'

'You think it's got something to do with that lot?'

'Both the victims were senior members of the order, certainly, so it's an angle we're considering.'

'There's comfort in that, I suppose. If someone's killing Weryers it means we're safe. But he wouldn't be able to help you even if he were here. He's not a Weryer. They blackballed him.'

'That's rather the point of asking him, to be honest. We can ask the Weryers themselves, but self-evidently they'll have a rather different perspective on the order than someone on the outside.'

'They do have a very high opinion of themselves, that's for sure,' said Mrs Swanton.

'And Mr Swanton doesn't?' I said.

She laughed mirthlessly. 'He's got as high an opinion of himself as any man, but he'd happily see all the Weryers dead in a ditch, especially those two—' She stopped and looked up at us. 'I didn't mean . . .' she said, hurriedly. 'He didn't. He wouldn't. Not my Patrick. I just meant . . . he was angry when they turned him down in favour of Lawrence Weakley, but not angry enough to . . .'

'What are your own impressions of the order?' asked Lady Hardcastle.

'Until they treated Patrick so poorly it was hard to think too badly of them. They do wonderful work for charity, and most of them are decent fellows.'

'Most?' I said.

'I've never had much time for Noel Gregory – weaselly little man – but the rest are all right.'

'What about the two dead men?' said Lady Hardcastle. 'What did people outside the order think of them?'

'I think that was what made their betrayal hurt so much,' said Mrs Swanton after a moment's contemplation. 'Claud Cridland was a lovely man. He had every right to be bitter after everything that had happened to him – you know about his wife and child?'

We nodded.

'But he bore it all with patience and grace,' she continued. 'And Moses Peppard . . .' She was blushing.

'He was a very popular man,' said Lady Hardcastle.

Mrs Swanton nodded, still slightly flushed.

'He was,' she said, slightly shyly. 'Individually, they're mostly decent men, it's just when they get together that they . . . Well, you know what men are like when they get together.'

'No group of people is in any way similar to the sum of its parts,' agreed Lady Hardcastle. 'Groups take on a personality of their own, and it's not always one the individuals would be proud of. Were there ever any specific incidents?'

'Of bad behaviour, you mean? No, not really. Nothing worse than the farmhands get up to. A little drunken carousing, but nothing you couldn't ignore. Like I said, if they hadn't treated Patrick so poorly I'd never have thought badly of them at all. Do you think it's one of them?'

'The murderer? It could be any of a number of people, but the fact that both victims were Weryers is all we have to go on at the moment.'

'Do you think there'll be more killings? Do you think we might be in danger? Or is someone targeting the Weryers specifically?'

'Again, it's not a possibility we're ruling out. But I shouldn't think there's anything to worry about. Murderers very rarely strike more than once. Twice is rare. Three times is unheard of.'

'Well, I'm just glad we've got you looking out for us.'

'Thank you, Mrs Swanton, you've been most helpful. We ought not to take up any more of your time, though.'

'Oh,' I said. 'Actually there is one more thing before we go. Do you know anything about one of the Weryers murdering another about twenty years ago?'

'No, I'm sorry,' said Mrs Swanton. 'We moved here ten years ago from Bristol. Patrick has business interests in Bristol and Gloucester, you see, so it was handy to be between the two. I vaguely remember something about a murder up this way – it was in the newspapers – but I can't recall the details. I'm sorry.'

'Think nothing of it. We shall let you get on. Thank you so much for your time.'

We stood to leave.

'It was entirely my pleasure, my lady. Oh, but where are my manners? I should have thought to offer you some tea.'

'Please don't worry about that – in this heat we seem to have done nothing but drink tea. Do please give our regards to your husband, won't you. And if you think of anything that might help find the killer, please tell us or Sergeant Dobson – we'll be able to get a message back to Inspector Sunderland.'

Mrs Swanton showed us to the door herself and we set off to pick up the Rolls and head home.

◆ ◆ ◆

Inspector Sunderland dropped in a short while later.

'What news from darkest Chipping Bevington?' asked Lady Hardcastle as I showed him through to the garden.

'None whatsoever,' he said. 'Neither Lehane nor Gregory was at home.'

'I'm so sorry you had a wasted journey.'

'Not entirely wasted,' he said. 'I am at least a little more familiar with the geography of Chipping Bevington.'

'And who knows when that might come in useful?' said Lady Hardcastle. 'We, in the meantime, have been to see Pat Swanton.'

'Have you, indeed? And what did he have to say for himself?'

'Nothing – he wasn't at home, either. But we did speak to his wife, whose name I'm afraid I've never known.'

'Mercy,' I said.

'Oh, how charming,' she said. 'I've known a Faith, a Hope, two Charities, one Patience and a Verity, but never a Mercy. I feel my collection of virtues must surely be nearing completion by now.'

'And did she oblige you with useful information, this Mercy Swanton?'

'Not really, but sort of. Her husband very definitely bears the Weryers a grudge for blackballing him, and they both seem to hold Cridland and Peppard especially responsible.'

'She was quick to deny Mr Swanton had anything to do with it,' I said. 'But then, she would, wouldn't she?'

'But she was adamant they were a nice bunch,' said Lady Hardcastle, 'their rejection of her beloved Patrick notwithstanding.'

'She also vaguely remembered the Weryer murder from the 1890s,' I said. 'She didn't live here but it was in the newspapers.'

'We should have a look at some old newspapers and see what we can find out,' said Lady Hardcastle.

'I shall leave that to you,' said the inspector. 'I should be on my way. Good day to you both, and thank you for your continuing efforts.'

Chapter Thirteen

We could tell from the sound of the sporadic cheers and laughter coming from the village green that the skittles competition was already under way.

'I'm so sorry, dear,' said Lady Hardcastle as we walked along the lane, 'I fear we're late.'

'Not to worry,' I said. 'We can just enjoy the atmosphere. We shall sip our drinks and join in the jollity without the burden of competition.'

The green was lit with a large number of lamps and lanterns, creating an almost carnival-like atmosphere. We approached the crowd and were spotted at once by Jagruti Bland, the vicar's wife.

'Emily,' she said. 'Flo. I'm so pleased to see you.'

'It's lovely to see you, too, Jagruti dear,' said Lady Hardcastle. 'Are you playing?'

'We would be,' said Mrs Bland, 'but it's teams of four . . . and we're two short.'

'Who's your teammate?'

'Clarissa Farley-Stroud. Or Whitman, I should say – I've known her since she was a little girl and I keep forgetting her married name. When Daisy told her you two were coming she insisted we should form a ladies' team, and we've been looking out for you ever since.'

'Oh, I say. What an expectation to live up to. Were there no other ladies at all?'

'Oh, plenty – half the village is here – but Clarissa was insistent. Apparently you'd be our secret weapon.'

'Aha, yes,' said Lady Hardcastle. 'Or Flo would be, at least – she excels at games of skill.'

'So I've heard,' said Mrs Bland. 'Clarissa recounted a lengthy tale about an archery contest at The Grange.'

'I rather enjoyed that,' I said. 'But archery and skittles are hardly the same thing.'

'She's just being modest,' said Lady Hardcastle. 'She has a preternatural aptitude for anything that involves aiming things at other things. We'd be delighted to join your team, dear, though I fear I shall just be ballast.'

'I'd like to say she was just being modest,' I said. 'But I can't lie to a vicar's wife.'

Mrs Bland laughed.

'I'm sure she'll be no worse than I,' she said. 'Come. I'll tell Clarissa the good news.'

Lady Farley-Stroud's daughter, Clarissa, was pleading with Daisy when we found her.

'If you could just move us down the order,' she said, 'we'll have a full team and we can take our turn then. You said yourself that they were coming.'

'I don't mind it myself, Mrs Whitman,' said Daisy, 'and if it was up to me I'd make 'em all wait till you was ready. But I'm gettin' it in the neck from the regulars as it is. Some of these blokes takes it all far too seriously if you asks me, but there's only so many times I can tell 'em to shut their noise before it all starts to get nasty.'

'I understand, but—'

'Have no fear,' said Lady Hardcastle, 'we've arrived. I'm so sorry we're late – it's entirely my fault. When are we on?'

'Right now,' said Daisy, looking at her list. 'Team name?'

'How about The Littleton Lionesses?'

'I'd prefer Tigresses,' said Mrs Bland. 'More appropriate for a Bengali lady, wouldn't you agree?'

'Oh, I say,' said Lady Hardcastle, 'how very splendid. The Tigresses it is, Daisy dear.'

Daisy made the appropriate entry in her list and wrote the team name on the blackboard.

I had learned from watching proper matches in the alley at the back of the pub that skittles could be an interminably long affair. Teams of up to a dozen would play nine hands of three balls each and the whole thing could last all evening. In an attempt to hold the interest of casual players and keep things moving along, they had limited teams to four members who would each play a single hand of three balls.

To my immense surprise, we were the eighth of twelve teams to register. It was a more popular event than I had imagined.

We took our turn and managed a creditable twenty points between us, putting us in fifth place on the scoreboard. Clarissa, it turned out, was the ballast, knocking down only two pins. Mrs Bland managed four overall, while Lady Hardcastle managed to take down five. I threw a lucky second ball that felled the two that had remained standing from my even luckier first go, which earned a cheer from many of the village ladies and some disgruntled murmurs from a few of the regular skittlers. I heard at least one 'She must be cheatin'' and a 'Women shouldn't never have been allowed to play', but when my third ball missed entirely, they were relieved to be able to dismiss the 'spare' as a fluke and the balance of the universe was restored.

Edna and her husband, Dan, had formed a team with Mr and Mrs Spratt, and were up next. As we cheered them on, Mr Weakley approached us.

'Did Inspector Sunderland speak to Rogers?' he asked. 'Did he find out what's going on?'

'He did,' said Lady Hardcastle. 'We went with him. I confess I was hoping it would bring us more directly to the murders, but it might be a step in the right direction. He made certain allegations about Lehane and Gregory.'

'I thought he might,' said Mr Weakley with a nod. 'I'm not part of the inner circle, but I knew there was something up with those two.'

'Why did you not say anything?'

'I don't want to slander anyone. I've no evidence they're up to no good – just a feeling, you know? I couldn't go to Starks with a feeling, still less the police. But I had no problem suggesting the inspector take a look at them without actually saying what I thought was going on.'

'Well, I'm jolly glad you did, Mr Weakley. Thank you. And thank you for the delicious fruit, too. You did us proud.'

'Always happy to oblige, my lady,' he said. 'I ought to get back to my wife before she wonders where I've got to.'

'You ought. Do give her our regards, won't you.'

Daisy had arrived unseen behind us.

'So, come on,' she said. 'Who are your suspects now?'

'Hello, Dais,' I said. 'Shouldn't you be organizing things?'

'There's a break while they argues about whether to have a knockout to decide the overall winner and my head's startin' to spin a bit, so I thought I'd leave 'em to it. So far the Mock of Pommey's team is winnin' by one point over the Dog and Duck, and our captain don't like it. He wants another chance.'

'I see,' I said. 'But as for the suspects . . . assuming we rule out our friends in the village – I don't see Old Joe bumping off Weryers willy-nilly, nor Weakley, Holman or Slocomb – we're down to a disappointing . . . what would you say, my lady? Nine?'

'Unless we look beyond the immediate group, yes,' said Lady Hardcastle.

'Nine?' said Daisy. 'Blimey. And who's they?'

'Starks the solicitor,' I said, 'Uzzle the pub landlord, Rogers the farmer, Mattick the cider maker, Lehane the retired bank manager, Gregory the bookkeeper, Pat Swanton the . . . whatever it is Pat Swanton does, Sid Palmer the farming equipment magnate, and, last but not least, Grace Chamberlain the mysterious stranger.'

'You hasn't narrowed it down much,' said Daisy.

'Dispiritingly, no, we haven't,' said Lady Hardcastle. 'Every time we follow a new line of enquiry we add new suspects rather than ruling them out.'

'And if you had to bet on one right this minute, where'd your money be goin'?'

'At the moment I'd bet on Mattick, with a shilling each way on Pat Swanton,' I said. 'Though I'd not feel I was entirely wasting my money if I put a tanner on Rogers, too.'

'Archie Rogers?' said Daisy with some surprise. 'He's one of the nicest blokes in the county. Why on earth . . . ?'

'Unless I'm being particularly dim – and we should never rule that out – Franny Rogers was the lucky recipient of a visit from Moses Peppard on that morning Cissy saw him cycling past the dairy.'

'She never was,' said Daisy with even more surprise. 'But everyone thought it was Faith Mattick.'

'We can't rule out the possibility that he was treating them both to his considerable charms,' said Lady Hardcastle. 'So he might have been seeing Faith at other times, but I must say I agree with Flo. We have your rumour that he was off to see Faith Mattick, but there was another that said it was a farmer's wife from Pighill. Hawthorn Farm is only a hearty spit from Pighill, and Mrs Rogers is really rather gorgeous. That's not to say that Faith Mattick is without considerable charms of her own, mind you, but a philanderer like Peppard would have been sorely tempted by the fragrant Fran.'

'She is a fine-lookin' woman,' said Daisy, 'I'll grant you that. But I still says Archie Rogers is too soft to hurt no one. I'd put my life's savin's on Mattick. There's sommat about him.'

'How much are your life's savings, Dais?' I said.

'Two shillin's, a silver button from our Sammy's best Merchant Navy uniform, and a rag doll I won at a fair when I was nine. She'll be worth a fortune one day, will Sophie Scruff.'

'A substantial wager indeed,' said Lady Hardcastle. 'Though I'd hold on to your brother's button if I were you – it's a good bet but not a dead cert as yet.'

'When are the Matticks due back?' I asked.

'How the 'eck should I know?' said Daisy.

'You know everything else. I just thought . . .'

'All I know is they went up to Gloucester on Friday.'

'Fair enough,' I said. 'If you hear anything . . .'

'I'll let you know,' she said. 'Looks like they's reached a decision on the knockout, though – I ought to be gettin' back.'

'See you later, Dais,' I said.

Daisy left us and Reverend Bland took her place almost at once.

'I say, well done, ladies,' he said. 'Fifth place. Well done, indeed.'

'Thank you, dear,' said Mrs Bland. 'Dare we ask how you did?'

'Dead last, I'm afraid.'

'Who are your teammates?' asked Lady Hardcastle.

'I have our housekeeper, Mrs Grove, and a couple of my elderly parishioners, Mr and Mrs Sallis. A charming couple, both in their seventies. They've had the most marvellous evening and haven't stopped laughing . . . but they're not numbered among the Lord's natural skittlers. We scored one between us, and that was only because I tripped and mis-threw my final ball. Somehow I fluked a hit.'

'Ah, but you're having fun, though. That's the point of the evening, surely.'

'It is, it is,' he said. 'But just think how much more fun I'd be having if I were fifth on the scoreboard. I wanted Jagruti on the team – at least then we wouldn't be last – but she had other plans. Plans to bring in a ringer, as it turns out.'

'I am entirely innocent,' said Mrs Bland. 'It was Clarissa's idea to team up with Emily and Flo.'

'And a jolly good idea it was, I think you'll agree,' said Clarissa, who had been talking to Mrs Spratt. 'I've seen Flo and Emily in action before.'

'Well, I'm delighted that at least one member of my household is doing so well,' said Mr Bland.

He seemed about to say more, but everyone's attention was rapidly turning to the scoreboard, where Joe Arnold was about to make an announcement.

'Ladies and gentlemen,' he began. 'Unaccustomed as I am to public speakin'—'

'Get on with it,' shouted a woman's voice, probably Daisy's.

Joe chuckled.

'I s'pose I should, really, shouldn't I? I just wanted to thank you all for comin' and to say that there will be a knockout competition between the top four teams to decide the overall winner. The first semi-final will be the Mock of Pommey A Team against the Dog and Duck B Team. The winner will play either the Mock's B Team or the Dog's A Team for a place in the final. And the winner of the final will get a barrel of cider kindly donated by Mattick's Cider, and a ham from Spratt's the Butcher's right here in Littleton Cotterell.'

'How about some money?' shouted Daisy.

Joe ignored her – something he'd had to do quite a lot over the years.

'The first semi-final starts in five minutes and there's sandwiches on sale at the bar.'

There was a minor stampede towards the pub door but we left them to it.

'Shall we stay?' asked Lady Hardcastle.

'We've come all this way,' I said. 'We might as well watch the local boys win.'

I joined the throng at the bar to secure drinks for our team, and we found ourselves a spot to watch the unfolding contest.

Back at home after a resounding victory by the Dog and Duck A Team, I made some cocoa and took it through to the sitting room where Lady Hardcastle was sprawled in an armchair, fanning herself with a copy of the *Bristol News*.

'I'n't it ever 'ot?' she said, in a frankly dreadful impersonation of the local accent.

'It's quite close, yes,' I said. 'Do you not want this delicious hot cocoa?'

'Want? No, dear, I *must* have it – it'll help me sleep.'

I handed her the cup and made myself comfortable in the other chair.

'What are we going to do tomorrow?' I asked.

'I'm not entirely certain. After today's excitement I'd rather like a rest, but I feel we ought to press on. If we don't hear from Dinah by lunchtime I shall telephone her at the newspaper office. Didn't you say she was going to look into the mystery of Peppard's assignation for us?'

‘Like a “scandal pig”, she said – a truffle pig but with scandals.’

‘I got it, dear, thank you. Some people use dogs, you know.’

‘For snuffling out scandals?’

‘Undoubtedly, yes, but more commonly for truffles. Dogs will seek them out for the price of a piece of sausage and being told they’re such a very good girl. Pigs, on the other hand, like to eat what they find, and then one finds oneself wrestling six hundredweight of hungry hog for possession of the precious fungus.’

‘I don’t think we’ll have to wrestle six hundredweight of hungry journalist for news of Peppard’s Pighill Paramour, though.’

‘Good lord, no. I’d be surprised if she weighed as much as eight stone wet through.’

‘You need to tell her our suspicions about Franny Rogers,’ I said.

‘Perhaps, but not yet. I thought I might withhold that for a short while, lest it colour her investigations.’

‘Fair dos. And she told me she was going to ask a friend at the newspaper in Exeter about Grace Chamberlain. She might have some news for us there, too.’

‘Not a chance, dear. How on earth would anyone she knows manage that?’

‘If Daisy Spratt turned up unexpectedly in . . . oh, I don’t know, a village near Reading, let’s say.’

‘Arborfield,’ said Lady Hardcastle, confidently.

‘Really?’

‘Yes, I once met a girl from Arborfield. She was engaged to a friend of a friend at Cambridge.’

‘I see. So Daisy pops up in Arborfield, and someone says, “She’s got a Gloucestershire accent. I’ve got a friend who works at the *Bristol News* – I’ll telephone them and see if anyone’s heard of her.” And Dinah Caudle will pipe up and say, “I know a Daisy Spratt from Littleton Cotterell. Dark hair. Good-looking. Charming as you like but never stops talking."'

'You've carefully picked a very specific example there, dear,' she said. 'I'm not sure that proves anything.'

'It casts doubt on your "not a chance", though, doesn't it? There *is* a chance.'

'Well, yes, but a jolly slim one.'

'You're the one who chastises me for my imprecise use of language.'

'You're right, dear, of course,' she said. 'So I shall ask her if anyone at the *Exeter Post* or whatever it's called has heard of Grace Chamberlain.'

'Thank you. What else shall we do?'

'I rather thought we might go over to the cidery.'

'The Matticks are away,' I said. 'And everyone's been sent home.'

'An ideal time to visit, then. Bring your picklocks.'

The road past the orchard and cidery was quiet as we drove towards the Matticks' house on Tuesday morning.

We'd had a lengthy discussion about practicalities and logistics before we left the house. So many of our professional activities were carried out in cities where we could travel discreetly by cab, or even on foot, and we were unused to having to concern ourselves with concealing a motor car. Out in the villages of Gloucestershire, though, cabs were rare and distances too great for comfortable walking, and so the Rolls was both a necessity and a liability in more or less equal measure.

We had eventually decided that since the Matticks were away, it would draw less attention to park the motor car in the courtyard of their house than to leave it in the lane. If we were seen coming and going, we could convincingly claim that we were calling on them and had no idea they weren't at home. If we left the Rolls in the lane, we reasoned, people might wonder what we were up to – and they'd be right to wonder.

Lady Hardcastle parked on the cobbled courtyard with uncharacteristic neatness, and we alighted to investigate our surroundings.

'No smoke from any of the chimneys,' I said. 'And all the windows are closed.'

'They're not back from Gloucester, then,' said Lady Hardcastle. 'Let's snoop.'

We walked all the way round the house, looking in through the windows.

'I'm happy to break in if you want,' I said once we'd returned to the front door, 'but what do we expect to find? A confession? A notebook full of deranged ramblings and drawings of his enemies?'

'That would be most helpful,' said Lady Hardcastle. 'Though I'd settle for a long, thin pointy thing and a massive great hammer.'

'In that case, I suggest we try the sheds and then stroll down to the cidery. I'm not squeamish about burgling people's houses if the circumstances demand it, but it's a bit rude to go poking about just because we can.'

'I agree, actually. With so many other places to store incriminating evidence, he'd be a fool to leave it where his wife might bump into it.'

There were two stone-built outbuildings, both protected by padlocks that managed to keep us out for an additional ten seconds. We found an assortment of gardening tools inside one, but nothing that fitted the description given by Dr Gosling of either of the murder weapons. The other contained two bicycles, a rusted bedstead, and a few items of unwanted household furniture, including a hat stand, two broken bentwood chairs, and a steamer trunk. The trunk was empty.

'So much for the sheds,' said Lady Hardcastle. 'If I sat in the wheelbarrow would you wheel me to the cider mill? It's too hot to walk.'

'Not on your life.'

'I don't know what's become of modern servants,' she grumbled. 'I'm sure my parents' servants would have carried them on their backs and been grateful for the work.'

'Times have changed,' I said. 'Herr Marx pointed out that I'm an oppressed mass, I am. I shall be rising up any day now, and casting off the yoke of the capitalist bourgeoisie.'

'And about time, too. But would you still carry me? It's too hot.'

'No,' I repeated. 'Best foot forward, come on. The walk will cool you.'

'Now, I know that's nonsense.'

'It'll get you in the shade, at least. If you're a good girl I'll buy you an ice cream from that tearoom at Chipping Bevington.'

Still grumbling, she led the way down the rutted track towards the cidery.

The cider mill yard was deserted and all the doors locked. The locks were much more substantial than on the house and its sheds, but you'd expect that, given that one of the two main buildings was full of very desirable, very valuable cider, and the other contained everything necessary to make more. We stood contemplating what we presumed was the main brewing building.

'We ought to see if there's a back door,' I said. 'If anyone should happen to come into the yard looking for Mattick or his workers,

I don't want to be stuck inside with these enormous front doors wide open.'

'You make a compelling point,' said Lady Hardcastle. 'There's bound to be another way in and out, even if just for safety's sake.'

We skirted to the right of the tall, stone-built . . . was it a shed? A barn? Or was it the cidery? Or the cider mill. It was, we presumed, the main building with the presses and fermentation vats, whatever it was called.

A stone shed built on to the rear of the building appeared to house a steam engine, but there was little else to see apart from a single, normal-sized door of green-painted wood, with a conventional and insubstantial lock. I took my best picklocks from the pocket of my linen jacket and set to work. Within moments, the door was unlocked, but still stubbornly unopenable.

'Bolted from the inside?' asked Lady Hardcastle.

'Seems that way. We should have guessed, I suppose. How about a new plan: I leave this one unlocked and we go in through the front doors. We close them behind us and if there's any trouble we unbolt this back door and hop it before anyone even knows we were there?'

'That should work. But I can't imagine anyone coming out here – the whole county seems to know the Matticks are away at her mother's.'

'Perhaps that's why we should be careful,' I said as we returned to the yard.

I made short work of the lock and, once inside, I closed and locked the door behind us. There were windows in the roof and all along the walls above head height, so the space was brightly lit by the late-August sunshine.

There were barrels everywhere, and four large oak fermentation vats like the ones we'd seen in wineries in France. An impressive and slightly terrifying press stood at one end. Built in an iron frame, two great screws would push an iron plate downwards to crush whatever sat between the heavy wooden block mounted on it and the sturdy wooden base. From my reading so far I guessed this would be mocks of pommey. There were holes in the screws, presumably for rods or poles so they could be turned by hand, but there was also a complicated system of gears and drive shafts connecting them to the steam engine we'd seen outside.

Incriminating evidence, though, was in short supply. The room was tidy and clean, and all the tools and equipment neatly stored. We searched it thoroughly and ended up by the still-bolted back door with nothing to show for our endeavours but a pleasant appley smell up our delicate hooters.

'I'm not at all certain what I hoped to find,' said Lady Hardcastle, disappointedly, 'but whatever it was, it definitely isn't here.'

'It's an interesting place, though, isn't it?' I said. 'That cider press is magnificent.'

'It is indeed. You know, when I was at Girton we—'

She stopped suddenly and looked at the single window beside the large front doors.

There was a woman outside, her hands cupped around her eyes to help her see in through the window. We froze. At the back of the shed we were partly in shadow, but she would immediately notice any movement.

'Grace?' I whispered.

Lady Hardcastle nodded.

Grace Chamberlain moved away from the window and tried the door. I was glad I'd locked it behind us, but the rest of my plan – sneaking out through the back door should anyone come – seemed hopelessly inadequate in the presence of a real visitor.

We took advantage of her absence from the window to conceal ourselves from view behind one of the large vats. We waited in silence.

A minute or so later she tried the back door and I was once again thankful that we'd not unbolted it. It rattled in its frame but the bolts held and she moved on.

We gave her a few minutes more to give up and go away before I slid stealthily to the window and looked out. Miss Chamberlain was walking out of the yard and back towards the lane, so I signalled to Lady Hardcastle that it was safe to open the back door.

As I walked across the room I noticed something half-hidden beneath a trestle holding up a huge cask – or 'tun', as I later learned it was called. I didn't know how we'd missed it before, most especially since it was exactly the sort of thing we'd been hoping to see.

It was a cooper's hammer.

I signalled Lady Hardcastle to come and join me.

'Look,' I said, quietly. 'The murder weapon?'

'Possibly,' she mused.

'Dr Gosling would be able to tell if it has blood on it with his mystical potions.'

'Phenolphthalein,' she said, absently.

'Exactly what I said.'

I reached for the hammer.

'No, wait,' she said. 'If we take it and it does indeed prove to be the murder weapon, Mattick will be able to say it's not his, that he's never seen it before, and that we must have found it somewhere else. He'll claim we're trying to "fit him", as the Australians have it, by providing false evidence. The police need to find it here. We need to leave it where it is and tell Inspector Sunderland that it might be worth his while having a good look around the cidery.'

I nodded my agreement and we left quietly by the back door.

It took slightly longer to relock than to unlock, but the job was soon done and we were fairly confident that no one would notice that it was unbolted. Even if they did, we reasoned, they'd just assume that someone forgot to throw the bolts. The door would be locked, so no alarm would be raised.

We set off up the track, back to the Rolls.

As we rounded the last bend, I once again saw movement ahead. I stopped dead and motioned to Lady Hardcastle that we should melt as best we could into the hedgerow.

'Grace again?' she said quietly once we were reasonably well concealed.

'It looked like it,' I said. 'It was a woman in a blue dress.'

'Almost certainly her, then. What's she doing out here, I wonder?'

'What are *we* doing out here?'

'Looking for clues to the murders.'

'Might she be doing the same?'

'She might. But why?'

'We could always ask her.'

'We've tried to have two conversations with her already, and Inspector Sunderland has had a go, as well – I'm not at all sure we'd get anywhere no matter what we asked her.'

'True, but—'

I stopped talking as I caught a glimpse of a figure leaving the courtyard of the Matticks' house and coming back down the track towards us.

We waited, still and silent, as Grace Chamberlain passed us and walked briskly back to the lane. From our hiding place it wasn't possible to see all the way to the end of the track, but we gave her what we thought was an appropriate length of time and then emerged, brushing leaves, cobwebs, and one particularly energetic beetle from our clothes.

'I'm so sorry,' I said. 'There really wasn't any point in us hiding then, was there?'

'Why not?'

'She knows we must be here somewhere – she's seen the Rolls outside the house.'

'Ah, yes,' said Lady Hardcastle with a smile. 'Oh well. At least it saved us from an awkward encounter. "I say, how marvellous to see you. Snooping on the Matticks? Yes, us too. It's a lovely day for it, don't you think? Well, we can't hang about chatting all day. Things to do, you know. Cheerio."'

'I think we could have done better than that,' I said. 'Still, what's done is done. Home for tea? I'm gasping.'

'I thought you were going to buy me an ice cream at Chipping.'

'I suppose you have been good,' I said. 'But I still need a cup of tea. And then we need to get home so we can telephone the inspector and get him to find an excuse to search the cidery.'

'Good point, but there's no real rush for that. Home via Chipping Bevington for tea and ice cream.'

We set off, with Lady Hardcastle once more at the wheel. A few hundred yards down the lane we saw Grace Chamberlain, striding purposefully back to her lodgings at the Dog and Duck. Lady Hardcastle slowed as we approached her.

'I say, dear, would you like a lift? We're going your way. You'd have to perch on the luggage rack but it would save you a walk in this heat.'

'No, thank you,' said Miss Chamberlain, her eyes still fixed on the road.

'As you wish. Good day.'

She drove on.

'We're not going her way,' I said.

'No, but if an act of kindness might warm her to us I'd forego my ice cream in favour of a conversation and a little information.'

As we approached the junction with the Gloucester Road, we were passed in the opposite direction by the dog cart whose owner plied his trade at Chipping Bevington railway station. In the back were the Matticks. Mrs Mattick saw us and gave a cheery wave.

'Cooee,' she called. 'I haven't forgotten about dinner.'

We returned her wave and carried on towards Chipping.

Chapter Fourteen

Tuesday afternoon proceeded very much as planned, with treats eaten at the tearoom and Inspector Sunderland alerted to the need to search the cidery. He had assured us that a search warrant would be forthcoming and that he would be visiting the Matticks in the morning.

Wednesday morning arrived without fanfare and I took up Lady Hardcastle's coffee and toast at around eight o'clock. To my surprise, she was sitting up in bed, reading.

'Good morning, Flo dear,' she said as she set the book down on her bedside table.

'What ho,' I replied.

'What ho? We've been spending altogether too much time with my brother. "What ho", indeed.'

'You used to say it all the time.'

'That was until I realized how absurd it sounded.'

'Well, I thought I'd try it out,' I said.

'Did you? And how does it feel?'

'Utterly ridiculous. I don't know how Harry does it without feeling foolish.'

'Well, that's Harry for you. Have we heard from the inspector yet?'

'Not yet, no. But give him a chance – it's only eight.'

'I know, but I'm impatient to know whether that hammer has anything to do with things. I'd imagined a dawn raid with dogs, and burly constables armed with revolvers.'

'I had, too,' I said. 'But I suspect it'll just be the inspector and an assistant—'

'Probably Simeon – those two seem to be working together a lot lately.'

'Probably, yes. And they'll present their search warrant, happen upon the cooper's hammer by the barrel and say, "What's all this, then?" Mattick will say, "It's a hammer. We use it for minor repairs on the barrels." Inspector Sunderland will say, "We'll test it for blood, if you don't mind," and Dr Gosling will rummage in his bag for his mysterious potion—'

'Phenolphthalein.'

'You know I'm never going to remember that, don't you? So, Dr Gosling tests the hammer for bloodstains and—'

I could hear the telephone ringing.

'I'd better get that,' I said. 'Edna's terrified of it – she's convinced it will electrocute her. And Miss Jones doesn't think it's her place to be answerin' no telephones. "Suppose it was someone important, what would I say?"'

Lady Hardcastle laughed.

'It's probably for me, though,' she said. 'I ought to come with you.'

We hurried to the hall and I picked up the telephone earpiece.

'Chipping Bevington two-three,' I said. 'Lady Hardcastle's residence.'

'Miss Armstrong,' said a familiar voice. 'Is that you?'

'Yes, Inspector,' I said.

'Is that how you answer the telephone now?'

'I'm just trying it out. Do you like it?'

'Not a great deal. Is she up?'

'She is,' I said. 'Would you like to talk to her?'

'I always enjoy talking to her, but it's not necessary. Can you both come to the cidery? There's something you ought to see.'

'What sort of something?'

'It's Abel Mattick,' he said. 'He's dead.'

I drove to the cidery, glad to be out in the fresh air, while Lady Hardcastle sat in the passenger seat, fussing with her sketch bag and musing on our failures as detectives.

'It all seemed so reasonable,' she said. 'The cuckolded husband murdering his two rivals, one of whom was also his competitor for the post of Grand High Poobah of the Mystic Order of Apple Worriers. He was the perfect suspect.'

'It's always like that,' I said. 'We suspect a string of wrong people, some of whom end up being murdered themselves, until it finally dawns on us who the real killer is. That's exactly how it works every time.'

'Yes, I suppose so. The frustrating part is that we never know how many false suspects we'll have to get through before we find the truth. It's not a fixed length of time between being informed of the murder and fathoming the identity of the killer.'

'I think you'll find it is. If you go back through our recent cases, I think you'll find they all wrap up in about the same length of time.'

'Be that as it may,' she said, finally closing the haversack, 'I am displeased with my conclusion-jumping failure. Quite aside from anything else, two men have died while we've been floundering about suspecting them. If I'd had my wits about me, we might have saved them.'

'We didn't kill them. It's not our fault, it's the killer's fault.'

'I suppose you're right,' she sighed. 'But, still . . .'

I parked in the courtyard and we alighted to find Inspector Sunderland, Dr Gosling, Sergeant Dobson, and Constable Hancock surrounding a wet corpse lying beside an overturned barrel in a large puddle of liquid. The air smelled of cider.

'Ah, good morning, my lady,' said the inspector as we approached. 'And Miss Armstrong, of course.'

'Good morning, Inspector,' we said together.

'Gentlemen,' said Lady Hardcastle with a nod.

The others acknowledged us, and I suppressed a smile at the absurdity of this prolonged social ritual taking place while we all stood around a puddle of death.

'I'm sorry to drag you out here in these awful circumstances,' said the inspector.

'That's quite all right,' said Lady Hardcastle, who had already started sketching the scene. 'Was he in the cider barrel?'

'I'm afraid so,' said Dr Gosling. 'From the look of him he was clouted over the back of the head with something flat – a plank, perhaps – and then lifted into the barrel with that.' He pointed to a hoist mounted on the side of the building. 'They use it for getting the heavier barrels on to wagons.'

'I see,' she said. 'Did he drown?'

'I can't say at the moment. With a knock like that it's possible that he was already dead, but I'll know more when I've got him back to the mortuary.'

'Did you find him or . . . ?' I asked.

'We found him,' said the inspector. 'Mrs Mattick was spared that, at least, but she's in a terrible state, as you can imagine.'

'Is she alone?'

'No, miss. Hancock fetched one of her friends from the farm over yonder.' He pointed across the road. 'She's being looked after.'

'Good,' I said.

'Do we know when it happened?' asked Lady Hardcastle.

'Mrs Mattick says he got up at dawn to go and make a start on checking the cidery. The harvest was delayed by Cridland's death but they've organized some help and they're hoping to start at the end of the week. And that means everything in the cidery had to be clean and ready, which is why he wanted to get an early start. We arrived shortly before eight with the search warrant. There was spilled cider all round the barrel and the lid was slightly askew, so Sergeant Dobson took a look inside.'

'How awful. Was there a man's worth of cider on the ground?'

'How do you mean, my lady?'

'Well, Mattick would have displaced almost his own volume in cider when the killer lowered him into the barrel. I was wondering how much was left. If there was just a little it would mean it had dried out and we might assume he was killed shortly after getting here. If there was a lot it might be more recent.'

'Good thinking, Emily,' said Dr Gosling. 'I say. Well done. There was quite a bit, I'd say, but I'd not be confident of guessing the evaporation rate of cider, so I'm not sure how much it would tell us. Body temperature would be my usual method but water conducts heat much more quickly than air, so I'm not sure of the calculation until I can see my textbooks again. I'll take the temperature of one of the other barrels, though, so I might be able to make a decent stab at it.'

'Poor old Mattick,' said Lady Hardcastle. 'What's that?' She pointed to what looked like a medicine bottle lying on the ground next to Mattick's body.

'That, my lady,' said the inspector, 'is the reason I asked you to come. It was in the barrel with him.'

We approached and squatted to examine the bottle. The label had begun to peel off where it had been soaking in the cider, but it was still legible: *Hardiman's Elixir.*

'An apple in the mouth,' she said, 'salt and pepper pots, and now a bottle of some sort of medicine. Probably of questionable efficacy.'

'Our ma swears by it,' said Constable Hancock.

'My apologies. But there's meaning in this. These can't be random additions. The killer is telling us something.'

'Someone is telling someone something, at least,' I said. 'It could be a message for someone other than us. And do we no longer think the salt and pepper pots were a message from Peppard himself?'

'It's less likely now, don't you think?' said Lady Hardcastle. 'Now we have three food-related objects left with the victims – it seems much more like the killer's work.'

'Well, if you can fathom it out,' said the inspector, 'we might be a little closer to finding out who's responsible for all this.'

'Preferably before he kills again.'

'Or she,' I said.

'Well, quite,' she said. 'We saw Grace Chamberlain out here yesterday afternoon.'

'What were you doing out here?' asked the inspector.

'Snooping. Don't worry, we didn't break any laws. And the house and cidery were securely locked up so neither did Miss Chamberlain.'

Inspector Sunderland smiled. He was clearly unconvinced by her bland assertion that no laws had been broken, but he made no comment.

Instead, he said, 'Did you speak to her?'

'No, we thought ourselves terribly clever by hiding in the hedgerow so that she wouldn't know we were here.'

'Until we remembered we'd left the Rolls parked outside the Matticks' house,' I said. 'Then, obviously, the jig was up.'

'We passed her on the road and offered her a lift home but she turned us down,' said Lady Hardcastle.

'I shall have a word when we get back to the village,' said the inspector.

'Good luck,' I said.

'Indeed,' said Lady Hardcastle. 'Is there anything useful we can do?'

'No, thank you, my lady,' said the inspector. 'I just wanted you to see the elixir bottle *in situ* in case it sparked anything, but we have everything else well in hand.'

'In that case, we should leave you to your work. We have a conundrum to solve.'

'I appreciate your help, my lady.'

'It's flattering to be involved, Inspector. Good day, gentlemen.'

We clambered back aboard the Rolls and set off for home.

As we drove around the village green, Mr Weakley was arranging trays of beetroot, cauliflower and broad beans outside his shop. He waved to us, beckoning me to stop.

He hurried towards the motor car, still holding a handful of broad beans.

'Is it true?' he asked anxiously.

'Good morning, Mr Weakley,' said Lady Hardcastle. 'Is what true?'

'Edna Gibson told me they found Abel Mattick drowned in a barrel of cider.'

'Did she, indeed? News does travel fast. Yes, I'm sorry to have to tell you your friend has been murdered.'

'We're none of us safe.'

'I usually try to steer clear of alarmism, Mr Weakley,' she said, 'but in this case I rather fear you might be right. I urge you to take precautions. And if you can think of anything – *anything* – that might help the police catch the perpetrator of these awful crimes, you must speak up.'

'And what if he comes for me?'

'Does that mean you know something but are afraid to say?'

'I've been wondering if—'

He stopped as he caught sight of Septimus Holman, who had come out on to the pavement to paste an offer of cut-price custard tarts on his shop window.

'Perhaps you'd like some more strawberries, my lady,' said Mr Weakley, a little too loudly. 'I could bring them round myself.'

Lady Hardcastle nodded.

'If it wouldn't be too much trouble, that would be most agreeable. Thank you.'

'Let me see . . . It's half past ten now . . . I can take a break at eleven if that's not inconvenient for you.'

'No, that would be splendid. We can have them for lunch. Thank you, Mr Weakley. Cheerio.'

I drove on.

◆ ◆ ◆

We had time to rid ourselves of hats and ask Miss Jones for coffee and cake in the drawing room, where we updated the crime board.

'Three murders,' said Lady Hardcastle as she pinned up a sketch of the cidery. 'All Weryers. All with food-related items on or near the body. And now our local greengrocer is in fear of his life.'

'Not unreasonably,' I said. 'Given the circumstances.'

'Well, quite. I'm sure the others are on edge, too.'

'All except one.'

'I'm still not ruling out some other party. I know I've been insistent that it must be one of the Weryers, but I'm no longer so certain. One murder is a quarrel between fellow members. Two is a much more significant argument. But three murders? Three murders of men who all belong to the same association . . . That has more of an air of vendetta about it, wouldn't you say? Someone who bears the Weryers a grudge for some past wrong.'

'It could be anyone in the village, then,' I said. 'Or beyond. The Weryers have dealings all over the county, and down into Bristol, too.'

'It could, indeed. But it has to be someone who can get to the orchard, the coopery and the cidery in the early hours of the morning, so it's more likely to be someone local.'

'Or someone from Devon who just so happens to be living locally.'

'Yes . . . but . . . I struggle to see what motive she might have. She's from Exeter or beyond. What possible connection could she have to the village?'

'We've been far too easy on her,' I said. 'We've just shrugged our shoulders and accepted her silence as though that's the end of the matter. We need to go hard on her.'

'I cling to the hope that we can circumvent her reluctance to talk by finding out the truth in other ways. I haven't given up on Dinah's research. Actually, I said I was going to telephone her today, didn't I? Perhaps I can do that before Mr Weakley arrives.'

At that moment, the doorbell rang and she didn't get a chance. I glanced at the clock and saw that it was still some way short of eleven o'clock, so it couldn't possibly be the greengrocer. Not yet.

I went to answer it.

'Mr Weakley,' I said as I opened the door and took the proffered punnet of strawberries. 'Thank you very much indeed.' In a quieter voice, I said, 'We're just having coffee in the drawing room. Would you care to join us?'

'That's very kind of you, miss,' he replied, just as quietly.

As stealthily as we could both manage, I led him into the drawing room. I loved Edna like a favourite aunt but we'd already had renewed evidence that morning of her propensity to gossip, and it was obvious from Mr Weakley's earlier demeanour that he didn't want anyone to know he was talking to us. Better for all concerned if she didn't know he was there.

I ushered him in to the drawing room and shut the door behind us.

'Good morning again, Mr Weakley,' said Lady Hardcastle from beside the crime board. 'Do take a seat.'

'There's coffee,' I said. 'Would you like some?'

'That's very kind of you, miss,' he said, sitting awkwardly in one of the armchairs, 'but I'm afraid it's not to my taste. I never could get on with coffee.' He smiled nervously.

'I can fetch you some tea,' I offered.

'No, miss, thank you. To be honest I feel like I might turn into a teapot some days. It's this heat. It's making me so very thirsty all the time. And . . .'

'And you'd rather I didn't give Edna cause to wonder who had arrived to drink our tea.'

'That, too,' he said. 'I'm very fond of Edna, and her Dan, but she does tend to—'

'Gossip?' said Lady Hardcastle.

'If you want a bit of news spreading round the county you can tell Edna or you can take out an advertisement in the newspaper. Only difference is you'll have to wait a day or two for the newspaper to print it, but old Edna can make sure everyone knows before nightfall.'

'It's a useful skill. We rely on her for news from the village. But you're right. Discretion is important here – as, I suspect, is haste. You don't want to be missing from your shop for too long, do you? So what is it that troubles you?'

'"Troubles" isn't quite the right word, my lady. I'm troubled by the murders, of course. Terrified, in fact. But actually the thing that's been on my mind has been a minor source of comfort. Or reassurance, perhaps.'

'I see. And what is it?'

'We're just four days away from the twentieth anniversary of one of the blackest days in Weryer history. Well, it was the blackest day until recently, at any rate. I'm not sure how you'd choose now. But on the third of September, 1891, a young member of the Weryers was murdered. No one talks about it and I wasn't living here then, but I do know that it was one of the other Weryers and he hanged for it.'

'Do you know who they were?' I asked. 'Or what happened? Why he did it?'

'No, like I say, they don't talk about it. It's like the village's secret shame. Both villages, in fact – they're just as tight-lipped up at Woodworthy. I only managed to get this much out of Fred Spratt the other day. I heard him and Eunice talking about "the anniversary" and I thought there was a celebration coming up so I asked when the happy day was.'

'And why is this news reassuring?' asked Lady Hardcastle.

'Because I wasn't here then. I'm from Chew Magna – other side of the city. I moved here ten years ago with my wife. She's from over this way, you see? It was her father's shop. But that means I wasn't involved in any way.'

'And Cridland, Peppard, and Mattick were?'

'Yes, they were Stewards then, of course – junior members like me – but they were all Weryers when the murder took place.'

'Are there any other members still around from that time?' I asked.

'Just Uzzle and Starks. The rest of us are comparative new boys. I don't think—'

There was a noise from the hall and we all fell silent.

We waited until we heard Edna's footsteps on the stairs.

'I don't think any of the others paid much attention to the Weryers back then,' he finished.

'This is all very interesting,' said Lady Hardcastle. 'Thank you so very much for telling us about it.'

'I felt I ought, my lady.'

'Thank you all the same. Now, I don't mean to throw you out, but would you like to take advantage of Edna being busy to slip out unnoticed?'

'I would appreciate that, yes. I hope you and the police manage to stop the killer.'

'We shall try. Good day, Mr Weakley. And thank you for the strawberries.'

'I'll show you out,' I said.

I opened the door to check that the coast was clear and then hurried him across the hall and out the door.

I returned to the drawing room and flopped into an armchair as Lady Hardcastle continued to make her notes on the crime board.

'Of the twelve Weryers of 1891,' she said, 'two died at the time – one killed by the second, and the second hanged for the crime. Until very recently, five remained associated with the order, of whom three are now dead. If their deaths are in any way connected with the events of twenty years ago, the two survivors – Grand

High Muckamuck Cornelius Starks, and Woodworthy pub landlord Griffith Uzzle – ought both to be in fear of their lives.'

'Unless one of them is the murderer.'

'That's a possibility we'd be foolish to rule out, of course. But what would be their motive? The only thing I can think of is Starks trying to protect the good name of the order by eliminating the people who knew the details of its dark, secret past.'

'By creating a dark, secret present,' I said. 'It's not very convincing. And why now? He's had twenty years to cover all that up.'

'He's mindful of his legacy, perhaps? Wanting to leave the order with its secrets still concealed?'

'Hmm. Perhaps. But what about Swanton?'

'What indeed? We can't get away from the fact that the dead men blackballed him.'

'You met him. Did he seem like the sort of person who would go on a killing rampage because some nasty boys wouldn't let him join their gang?'

'I confess I find it unlikely. But I wonder how many other killers seemed like perfectly reasonable chaps right up to the moment they ran amok. I'll keep him on the list until we can prove it wasn't him.'

'And the others?'

'I've got nothing at all for Uzzle. And he wouldn't do anything without permission from his wife, anyway.'

'She was nice enough to us, but she seemed very much the one in charge, didn't she? Betty.'

'Was that her name?'

'I think that's what Cissy called her,' I said. 'It might be Griff's name above the door, but she was the one running the place.'

'Perhaps she . . .'

'Again,' I said, 'why?'

'That's just it, isn't it? Why indeed?'

'And if it does have anything to do with the events of twenty years ago,' I said, 'then Grace Chamberlain can't have anything to do with it. She's, what, five-and-twenty? Not much more. She would have been a small child ninety miles away, in Devon.'

'In which case I come back to some other local or . . . Well, I'm afraid I'm rather talking myself into the idea that it might be Cornelius Starks. Do you fancy a trip to the solicitors' office at Chipping Bevington? If nothing else, Mr Starks might be persuaded to shed some light on the twenty-year-old Weryer murder.'

'I'll get our hats.'

Chipping Bevington High Street was a pleasant place on a Wednesday. Market day wasn't until Thursday – at which point the town went completely mad – but, with no market, Wednesday's commerce was a very genteel affair.

Obviously, Lady Hardcastle arrived with all the grace and calm of a swarm of angry wasps, and the Rolls slid to a halt outside the offices of Messrs Starks, Lemmings and Wetmore – Solicitors and Commissioners for Oaths through yet another pile of manure. It was fast becoming her speciality.

We entered through the nondescript door and were once again greeted by the pudgy-faced clerk. He looked at the clock.

'Good . . . afternoon, ladies,' he said, double-checking that the minute hand had, indeed, just passed twelve. 'Lady Hardcastle and Miss Armstrong, is it not?'

'It is, yes,' said Lady Hardcastle. 'Good afternoon, Mr White. Is Mr Starks available?'

'He's busy with a rather complicated land transaction this morning and has asked not to be disturbed, I'm afraid. I can take a message and ask him to telephone you later. You have a telephone?'

'We do. But would you be kind enough to interrupt him anyway. Tell him I wish to speak about the twentieth anniversary.'

'I'm afraid I—'

'I really must insist, Mr White. I shouldn't have driven all the way here were it not extremely urgent.'

He sighed.

'Very well, my lady,' he said. 'The twentieth anniversary of what?'

'He'll know.'

The clerk left through the rear door and we heard his footsteps on the stairs.

A few minutes later, the footsteps returned and the door opened once more.

'I'm afraid Mr Starks cannot be interrupted,' said the clerk.

'Did you give him my message?' asked Lady Hardcastle.

'I did, my lady. He says he has no idea what you might mean and respectfully suggests that you make an appointment if you wish to speak to him.'

'I see. Very well, we shall be in touch. Good day, Mr White.'

And with that, we swept out.

I expected that we'd simply drive off, but Lady Hardcastle stood on the pavement with her hand on the windscreen frame.

'No idea what I might mean, indeed,' she said.

'Mr Weakley did say it was something they don't talk about,' I replied.

'He did. But one would have thought that he would have wanted to help us even more, now there's a possibility the murders are linked to the anniversary and he might be next.'

'Unless . . .'

'My thoughts exactly. Unless he's involved in some way. What we need, dearest Florence, is a trip to the offices of the *Bristol*

News. We told the inspector we'd look in the newspapers, and their archives should have reports of the original murder and the trial.'

'If they let us look,' I said. 'Newspapers have never been terribly helpful to us in the past. *The Times* wouldn't even let us in the door that time we were trying to research the Duke of Taunton's involvement in the Hungarian affair.'

'Ah, but we have a contact at the *Bristol News*, don't forget. Dinah will look after us.'

'Home to telephone her, then?'

'No,' she said. 'Ice cream first, then home.'

We walked up the High Street to the tearoom.

Miss Caudle had been very keen to help but couldn't arrange for us to visit the archive until the following week at the earliest. We were holding the telephone earpiece between us so that I could listen.

'The problem, Dinah dear,' said Lady Hardcastle, 'is that we're beginning to wonder if the murders are connected to the anniversary on Sunday. If that's the case, then next week is too late, I'm afraid. Starks and Uzzle might be in danger.'

'Oh, I see,' said Miss Caudle's distorted voice. 'I suppose you've already tried your local library?'

'We don't have a library . . . oh, the one at Chipping Bevington, you mean?'

'I didn't mean that one specifically, but if there is one there, then yes. They might have kept copies of old newspapers, especially if the story was of local interest.'

'I feel such a fool,' said Lady Hardcastle. 'We've used the Bristol library in the past for research, but I forget that we have a library of our own nearby. We've just returned from Chipping – we could have made our enquiries while we were there if I'd had my wits about me. We shall have to return.'

'Are you able to go over there tomorrow?'

'The sooner the better, I think. The killer doesn't seem to have a timetable as such, but if it has any connection at all with the 1891 murder, I can't imagine he'll let Sunday's anniversary go by. I rather fear some sort of final flourish, but as long as we have some ideas before then we might be able to keep Starks and Uzzle safe. That's why we were hoping to visit your archive tomorrow, you see. But if that's not possible, we're very much free to visit Chipping.'

'Splendid. It's just that I'm going to be out your way tomorrow to talk to someone about a story I'm working on. It just so happens she knows Franny Rogers, so I was hoping to kill two birds with one stone and get the tittle, and possibly even the tattle, on Mrs Rogers's extra-matrimonial shenanigans while I was at it. If I can provide an additional pair of eyes for your newspaper research that will be three birds and I shall consider it a very efficient stone indeed.'

'That would be splendid,' said Lady Hardcastle. 'We welcome any help we can get at this stage, thank you.'

'I don't have the first idea where the library is, but I'm sure I'll find it.'

'It's at the bottom of the High Street,' I said. 'On the left if you're coming into town from the Gloucester Road. But Thursday is market day, don't forget, so you might have to park a little way out of town and walk in. And keep your wits about you – there'll be cows.'

'There'll be what?'

'Oh, take no notice,' said Lady Hardcastle. 'Just be aware that it'll be busy.'

'Righto. I should be there sometime in the middle of the afternoon if that suits.'

'We'll see you there, dear,' said Lady Hardcastle.

Chapter Fifteen

Thursday morning got off to a slow start. I had been raring to go and was up and doing shortly after six. Lady Hardcastle, though, proved typically resistant to the notion of getting up. She wasn't a lazy woman by any manner of means, but for all her energy and industry, once abed she was reluctant to rouse herself to action.

One of a servant's principal tasks – one of any employee's principal tasks – is to manage their employer to ensure that their behaviour remains acceptable. Over the years I had devised many strategies for dealing with the gravitational pull of the bedstead, and the one that had always proven the most successful was the provision of what her friend Horatia called 'the starter breakfast'.

In the big houses, ladies were usually served breakfast in their rooms, but Lady Hardcastle had always preferred to eat at the table. Despite this preference, the question remained of how to actually get her to the table in the first place. I managed to solve this, for the most part, by taking a minimal breakfast tray to her room and gently nagging her until she was sufficiently upright to partake. Once fortified with coffee and a round of buttered toast, she was usually able to shamble blearily to the breakfast table and the day could begin in earnest. In the early days it had been tea with toast and honey, but she had developed a preference for coffee and plain buttered toast over the past few years. I was happy with whatever she wanted, just so long as she got up.

On Thursday, though, she wasn't having any of it.

'Good morning,' I said brightly as I entered the room.

It had long been her habit to sleep with her head under the covers, and although the warm nights had meant a rejection of the usual blankets, she was still completely covered by a sheet. She looked like an unseasonal snowdrift.

I placed the tray on the bedside table, being careful to clatter the cup and saucer a little, but there was still no response from beneath the sheet.

I opened the curtains, letting in the glorious morning sunshine. The view across the lane and to the fields and woods beyond never failed to lift my spirits, but the increase in the brightness of the room only brought forth a groan from the bed.

'What time is it?' she mumbled.

'Nine o'clock,' I said.

'Nine? But we have things to do.'

'I know. I came in at seven and you wouldn't stir at all. At eight you were amusingly foul-mouthed and left me in no doubt about where I should put the coffee and toast. And so here I am at nine with fresh coffee and even fresher toast, being moaned at for not waking you earlier.'

The sheet came down with a snap to reveal a face scrunched up against the light, surrounded by a cloud of dark hair. I had long since given up trying to persuade her to plait her hair before bed. I said it would make it easier to style in the morning; she said it would be lumpy and uncomfortable to sleep on. We compromised by letting her have her way.

'I was rude?'

'Colourfully so. Language to make a navvy blush. And as for the instructions on where to "shove" the toast . . . well.'

'I'm so sorry, dear, I was only barely conscious. I wasn't really aware of what was going on. Do please forgive me.'

I laughed.

'You're forgiven,' I said. 'Now eat your toast and then get up, you idle mare. Miss Jones will have breakfast on the morning room table in a quarter of an hour. If you don't come down, I'll feed yours to the dog.'

'We don't have a dog.'

'I'll go out and get one specially.'

'That's fair. Thank you for the coffee and toast, dear.'

I left her to it.

We were finally ready to leave for the library at about eleven o'clock, but just as we were heading for the door the telephone rang.

'Chipping Bevington two-three,' I said in my best telephone voice.

I listened to the caller for a few moments and then said, 'One moment, Inspector, I'll check.' I attracted Lady Hardcastle's attention with a click of my fingers, which prompted a cocked eyebrow but no comment. 'Are we able to accompany the inspector when he visits Leopold Lehane this morning?'

'Rather,' she said enthusiastically. 'Tell him about the library visit, though.'

I passed this on and listened to the inspector for a few moments more.

'He's setting off soon and will meet us at Lehane's house on Swan Lane in about an hour and a half,' I said. 'But he wonders if we might have a word with Sid Palmer on the way, "just to rule him out".'

'I'm sure we can manage.'

The inspector thanked me and hung up.

'Well, then,' said Lady Hardcastle as she bustled towards the door. 'Enough of your shilly-shallying. We'd better get cracking.'

I shook my head and followed her out to the Rolls.

Palmer's Farming Equipment was housed in two converted barns on one of the larger lanes between Littleton Cotterell and Chipping Bevington. There was a sizeable yard outside, already busy with farmers looking for the latest equipment, and we parked next to the smaller building that obviously served as the sales office.

A farmer I recognized from the Dog and Duck was being shown a three-wheeled Saunderson tractor by an enthusiastic young salesman. He gave me a big grin and a thumbs-up as Lady Hardcastle led the way into the office building.

Inside, she was greeted by another young salesman.

'Good morning, madam,' he said, somewhat dubiously. 'How may I . . . help you?'

'Good morning,' said Lady Hardcastle, utterly unfazed. 'My name is Lady Hardcastle. I wonder if I might have a word with Mr Palmer.'

'Mr Sidney Palmer, madam, or Mr Richard Palmer?'

'Sidney.'

'Is it a . . . social call?'

'Business,' she said.

He didn't seem convinced, but made a show of looking in the large desk diary on the table beside him.

'I'm afraid Mr Palmer is busy at the moment. Would you like to make an appointment?'

Before Lady Hardcastle could answer, a man appeared from a door behind the young salesman.

'Has Philips been in, Densley?' he asked. 'He said he'd drop in on his way to— Oh, Lady Hardcastle. Good morning. What brings you to our humble establishment? Are you in the market for a new tractor? A plough? We have an interesting range of harrows just in.'

'Good morning, Mr Palmer,' said Lady Hardcastle. 'I'm afraid one of your tractors would fill our back garden on its own. No, I have another matter to discuss. Is there somewhere more private where we might talk?'

He frowned slightly, but his manner remained affable as he said, 'Certainly, my lady. Follow me. And Densley? See if you can track down Philips for me, would you? There's a good chap.'

He turned back through the door and led us along a short passageway to another, more spacious office. He indicated two chairs and we sat while he perched on the edge of his unostentatious desk in front of us.

'I'm so sorry,' said Lady Hardcastle, 'where are my manners? Do you know Florence Armstrong?'

'By reputation only,' said Mr Palmer. 'Most recently as the saviour of the Littleton Cotterell show. How do you do, Miss Armstrong?'

'How do you do?' I said with a smile and a nod.

'Now then,' he continued, 'what can I do for you?'

'We're trying to find out all we can about the Weryers,' said Lady Hardcastle. 'I gather from Cornelius Starks that you've applied to join.'

'I have, but I'm not a member yet. So I'm not sure . . .'

'Ah, it's the very fact that you're not a member that makes you the ideal person to ask. They've been forthcoming enough – at least they've seemed to be – but one always wonders if they might be holding something back.'

'What sort of something?'

'The recent murders have all been of senior members of the Weryers, as you know, and we – that is to say Armstrong, Inspector Sunderland, and I – are very much of the opinion that that's not mere coincidence. Something is going on in the Weryers, and we're looking for any information we can find that might tell us what.'

'Ah, yes, of course,' he said. 'I should like to help in any way I can, but I fear I know little about them that isn't already common knowledge. I didn't even learn of the murders until yesterday afternoon, when my wife and I returned from our holiday.'

'What a terrible thing to come back to,' said Lady Hardcastle. 'Were you somewhere nice?'

'Very nice indeed. Or very Nice, you might say. We spent a few weeks in the south of France.'

'Oh, how wonderful,' said Lady Hardcastle.

'Very wonderful indeed,' he said with a smile. 'I can wholeheartedly recommend it.'

'I've visited the area before, but it was many years ago now. I remember it being most invigorating.'

'It is. I feel like a new man. We even spent a couple of nights in Monte Carlo. Won a packet. So it was profitable as well.'

'How delightful,' said Lady Hardcastle. 'I seldom win at the gaming tables.'

This was a flattering lie. For all that I was often able to best her in our card games at home, it was usually because she wasn't properly concentrating. In truth she was an extremely skilled baccarat player and had an uncanny knack for working out which cards remained in the shoe at vingt-et-un. She seldom lost money at the casino.

'Oh, my wife usually has to drag me away before I lose the house, the company, and all our savings,' said Mr Swanton, 'but this time Lady Luck smiled on me. I think it almost paid for the entire trip.'

'Oh, that's even more wonderful. But I hadn't realized you'd only just returned – you must have a lot of work to catch up on, and here we are asking you about the Weryers.'

'Not at all, my lady, not at all.'

'Nevertheless, we should let you get on.'

'Thank you, but please don't worry. Young Dickie has been handling things in my absence. He's a quiet lad, but a conscientious one. He's kept things ticking over nicely.'

'Then I feel less guilty for intruding on your time. But if you hear of anything Weryer-related that you think might have a bearing on things, do please let me or Inspector Sunderland know.'

She stood and handed him her calling card.

'I shall, my lady. Now, are you sure I can't interest you in a nice new tractor? A cider press, perhaps? We have some small ones that would be ideal if you have a couple of apple trees in your garden.'

Lady Hardcastle smiled. 'I shall bear it in mind, Mr Palmer. Thank you.'

We said our goodbyes and he saw us out to the Rolls.

We set off for Chipping Bevington.

Leopold Lehane's home was a handsome stone-built house set a little back from the road on Swan Lane. We arrived just as Inspector Sunderland was parking his own motor car, and we approached the door together. We left the inspector to knock on the impressive brass knocker. He was the one with the credentials, after all.

A woman of late middle age in a black dress answered the door.

'Good afternoon,' said the inspector, holding up his warrant card. 'I'm Inspector Sunderland of the Bristol Police and this is Lady Hardcastle and Miss Armstrong. Is Mr Lehane at home?'

The woman looked us all up and down, her expression somewhere between impatient and hostile.

'Wait here,' she said, and slammed the door.

'Thank heavens for that,' said Lady Hardcastle.

'For what?' asked the inspector.

'Servants have been doing that to us a lot lately. I thought it might be something we'd done. But if they do it to an actual rozzer, it's clearly the fashion.'

'If I had a penny for every time I've had a door slammed in my face after showing my warrant card, I'd have retired to the coast long ago.'

The door opened.

'What's it regarding?' asked the black-clad housekeeper.

The inspector was generally known for his equanimity, but I could tell from his weary sigh that his patience was wearing thin.

'Fraud, madam,' he said. 'And possibly murder. May we come in?'

'I . . . Well . . . Wait here.'

She slammed the door again.

'Oh, for the love of—'

The door opened again almost immediately to reveal a bespectacled man in his late sixties, in an immaculate but slightly dated suit. His lined face wore a nervous expression.

'Inspector Sunderland, is it?' he said, quietly.

'Yes, sir. And you are . . . ?'

'Lehane,' said the man. 'Leopold Lehane. You'd better come in.'

He turned and walked across the small hallway without saying another word, clearly expecting us to follow. I closed the front door before hurrying after them into what turned out to be the drawing room.

Mr Lehane invited us to sit but seemed unwilling – or unable – to make himself comfortable. He began to pace the room, anxiously wringing his hands.

'I thought it would only be a matter of time before you called,' he said. 'You, or someone like you. Someone from the police, I mean. I've done terrible things and it weighs heavily on my mind.'

'What things, Mr Lehane?' said the inspector.

'I'm so sorry, where are my manners? Would you care for some tea?'

The inspector looked at Lady Hardcastle and me, and we shook our heads.

'No, thank you, Mr Lehane. What have you done?'

Lehane stared at the floor. He was struggling with his conscience, that was certain, but he didn't look like a killer. Then again, as we said so often, killers seldom do.

'Mr Lehane?' said the inspector. 'What have you done?'

'Well . . . I . . . you see . . .'

'The courts tend to look more leniently upon people who confess and show remorse for their crimes.'

'They do?'

'They do.'

'Then I suppose . . . It started last year, do you see? It was Gregory. He made me do it. He found out about . . . Well, he found out about something. Something no one must know. A private thing. Caught me, do you see? Caught me with . . . I didn't want to do it, but he made me. Blackmail, do you see? There would have been a scandal. Gaol. I'd be ruined.'

'What did he make you do, Mr Lehane?'

'It was just a few shillings at first. He needed my signature. It was from the Weryers' account, do you see? I'm the treasurer. Trusted. I was a bank manager, you know.'

Lady Hardcastle looked as disappointed as I was. If the inspector felt the same, though, he kept it well hidden.

'So Gregory was taking money from the Weryers,' he said, 'and he made you sign the authorization?'

'Yes. I had to, do you see? Had no choice. Couldn't risk . . . I'd be ruined.'

'What else did he make you do, Mr Lehane?' asked Lady Hardcastle.

'Else, my lady? Else? Isn't that terrible enough? That a former bank manager, a trusted official of the Weryers, should be party to fraud and embezzlement . . . I shall never forgive myself.'

'So you had nothing to do with the murders of Mr Claud Cridland, Mr Moses Peppard, or Mr Abel Mattick?' said the inspector.

Mr Lehane stopped pacing, his mouth hanging open.

'Murder? Why . . . I . . . Good lord, no. Why would you say such a thing? On top of all my agony, you accuse me of . . .'

'What about Gregory?' asked Lady Hardcastle. 'Did he kill them?'

'No, no, you don't understand,' said Mr Lehane. 'We had nothing to do with the deaths of those men. Our crimes were much worse.'

'Worse than murder, sir?'

'Common ruffians commit murder, Inspector, we expect nothing more of them. But I counted myself a gentleman. A man of honour. And I have betrayed a trust placed in me by an ancient and noble order. Betrayed my friends. No crime could be greater than that. I have been tormented by it these past months. Every day I expected the knock on the door, the clank of the darbies as I was chained up and led away for my crimes. It was almost a relief to find you there at last. It is over.'

'How much did Gregory steal?' asked the inspector.

'One pound, three shillings and fourpence-halfpenny,' said Mr Lehane, solemnly.

It was all Lady Hardcastle and I could do not to laugh. It was to Lehane's credit that he was so troubled by his part in the theft, but a theft of half a week's wages hardly warranted the kind of reaction we had just witnessed. Fortunately, Inspector Sunderland was a great deal more professional.

'I see, sir,' he said. 'Well, I shall obviously have to consider what action to take, and I should warn you that you may well be charged with a minor offence—'

'A minor offence?' protested Mr Lehane. 'But it was a terrible breach of trust.'

'Be that as it may, sir, the sums involved are relatively small and you were being coerced. If you would be prepared to attest to the . . . the blackmail, then it's more likely that Gregory will face full responsibility for the theft.'

'But I can't. It would all come out. I'd be undone. And if I implicate him, Gregory will carry out his threat. Better to face a charge of theft than . . .'

'Oh,' said the inspector. 'Oh, I see. In that case I shall see what I can do.'

'Inspector,' I said, 'would you be kind enough to step out of the room for a short while?'

He looked at me curiously for a moment, but then nodded.

'Mr Lehane,' he said, 'might I make use of your WC?'

Mr Lehane was similarly confused.

'Certainly, Inspector,' he said. 'At the top of the stairs and turn right.'

I waited until the inspector had gone.

'You seemed to know us, Mr Lehane,' I said.

'Your reputation precedes you, Miss Armstrong. You are our local celebrities.'

'And so you're aware that I possess, shall we say, certain skills?'

'I had heard something to that effect,' he said, nervously.

'I shall speak to Mr Gregory to ascertain the accuracy of your version of events. If I am satisfied that you have told us the truth,

I shall describe to him in graphic detail the terrible things that will happen to him if he breathes a word about your secret. He will be persuaded that he will live a longer and much less uncomfortable life if he confesses all to the magistrate but substitutes a threat of violence for the threat of ruination.'

'But—'

'Blackmail is a terrible thing, Mr Lehane, especially when ensuring a conviction requires that the secret be revealed anyway. In what you've said so far to the inspector, you haven't openly admitted to breaking any laws other than theft, and in this case I don't believe you should have to. Gregory might not have stolen very much money, but the way in which he did it makes his crime ten times worse in my eyes. He deserves to be punished for it, but I shall make it my business to ensure that he keeps his trap shut about his real method of extortion.'

'Well, I . . .'

'We shall say no more about it,' I said. 'In fact, this conversation never happened.'

We sat in silence for a few minutes until Inspector Sunderland returned.

'Mr Lehane was just saying that he's happy to confess to his part in the embezzlement,' I said, 'but that he will make it plain in his statement that he was acting under duress, having been threatened with physical violence by Noel Gregory.'

'That's most gratifying,' said the inspector. 'Thank you. I shall be in touch to make an appointment for you to attend a police station to make your statement. It should be possible to do it at Littleton Cotterell, which would suit me since I'm working with the officers there, and would save you from having to involve your local police at Chipping Bevington. That should help to minimize the gossip. I should warn you that based on the advice I receive it might be necessary at that point to arrest and charge you, but

I would be happy to release you on bail pending the magistrates' hearing. I shall be charging Gregory with theft and extortion.'

Mr Lehane nodded. 'Thank you, Inspector. And thank you, Miss Armstrong.'

'I've done nothing, sir,' I said.

He showed us out and we returned to the motor cars.

'Thank you for your help, ladies,' said Inspector Sunderland. 'Did you manage to speak to Palmer?'

'We did,' said Lady Hardcastle. 'It's almost certainly not him – he has an extremely good alibi. He was out of the country for all three murders, or so he claims.'

'Do you believe him?'

'It's far too easy to check,' I said. 'His employees would know if he'd been at home all this time. And even if the railway or the ferry companies have no record of his crossing, you could make a quick call to the Nice Police and they would check all the hotel registrations for you.'

'You have a charmingly optimistic view of the level of international cooperation between police forces, but you make a good point. So that's a third name off the list.'

'A good day's work, then,' said Lady Hardcastle. 'How shall we do this next part?'

'I'll go with the inspector,' I said.

Once I'd helped crank the engine to life, I hopped into the inspector's vehicle and he set off.

'I never want to know what was said in that room,' he said.

'And nor shall you. All I ask is that when we get to Gregory's house, I be allowed to go in first. Alone. I'll leave you to arrest him and take him down to the Bridewell after that. I'll go home with Herself.'

◆ ◆ ◆

Back at the house, we took a few moments to eat a sandwich and update the crime board.

'We're down to . . . six suspects now,' said Lady Hardcastle, counting up the remaining names. 'Starks, Uzzle, Rogers, Swanton, and Grace Chamberlain. That's still quite the field, wouldn't you say?'

'It is,' I agreed, 'but I've a feeling this library trip will help.'

'I do hope so.' She checked her watch. 'We'd better get going. I'll drive.'

Chapter Sixteen

With Lady Hardcastle at the wheel as we drove through the village, I was able to take a good look at the activity on the green.

'Oh,' I said, as realization dawned. 'They're building a temporary dining hall, aren't they?'

'That's what I've assumed all week,' said Lady Hardcastle. 'What did you think it was?'

'I don't know. Some sort of building, certainly – that much is obvious – but I couldn't think what it was for.'

'You told Gertie she should hold the harvest supper on the green.'

'In the open air, I said. I hadn't thought they'd go to all this trouble.'

The timber from the stage for the village show had been reused to build a vast frame, to which Charley Hill and his lads were nailing canvas sheets to form walls and a roof. Even if the weather turned, we should all be snug and dry within.

Lady Farley-Stroud was inside the new structure, directing her volunteers as they positioned tables and chairs. She caught sight of us as we zoomed round the green and waved urgently. Lady Hardcastle braked with alarming suddenness and I had to brace myself against the dashboard to prevent myself from being thrown through the windscreen and over the bonnet.

'What do you think of our realization of your wonderful idea?' said Lady Farley-Stroud as she approached the Rolls. 'Mr Hill has done a splendid job, don't you think?'

'I do,' I said. 'It looks magnificent. But I can't really claim any—'

'The supper is on Sunday evening, straight after the Harvest Festival service. The parade will be at twelve. You'll both be here?'

'We wouldn't miss it for the world,' said Lady Hardcastle.

'Good,' said Lady Farley-Stroud with a smile. 'It'll be good for village morale. They're terrified, poor things. Three men murdered and no sign of an arrest. They're all wondering who will be next. They're putting a brave face on it, of course. One does, doesn't one?'

'One does, dear. What else can one do? Did the men have many friends in the village?'

'They were all well liked, certainly. Especially dear Moses Peppard. If I were thirty years younger . . .'

'Would that we were all a little younger,' said Lady Hardcastle. 'Think of the fun we could have had then with the knowledge we have now.'

'Oh, I had plenty of fun,' said Lady Farley-Stroud with a wink. 'What are you two up to this afternoon? Can I press you into service? We've a lot to do.'

'I'm afraid we're still helping Inspector Sunderland. We're off to the library at Chipping.'

'Valuable work, m'dear, valuable work. I shan't detain you any longer. Catch the killer and set us all free.'

'We'll do our utmost. Cheerio for now.'

With a wave, Lady Hardcastle threw the Rolls into gear and accelerated briskly away.

◆ ◆ ◆

I took my own advice and guided Lady Hardcastle to a suitable parking spot on the outskirts of the small town. I had a notebook and pencil in the pocket of my linen jacket. She had elected to bring her sketch bag.

We made our way towards the library through the throng of traders and shoppers. Peering through the crowds we could just about see livestock being marshalled towards the auction hall in the distance. Meanwhile, stalls had been set up on the broad pavements of the High Street. It was a lively and exciting place on market day, with only the ever-present threat of cattle to cast a shadow over the fun.

We stopped a few times to look at the stalls, and I was tempted by some hand-woven shawls made by a farmer's wife from Nupdown.

'Keep you lovely and warm in the wintertime, that will,' she said as I fingered the surprisingly smooth fabric.

'I should think it would,' I said. 'And such lovely colours. Will you be here all day?'

'All day, my lover, yes.'

'I'll stop by on our way home – I won't want to carry it about all day and risk ruining it.'

'I'll put it aside for you if you likes.'

'Oh, in that case, I'll have it. Thank you.'

I rummaged in my pocket for some change and she scrawled a receipt on a scrap of paper.

'Just pick it up when you leaves,' she said. 'I'll be here till me 'usband is done. And 'e'll be in the Hayrick till 'e's too drunk to stand, so I doubts you'll miss I.'

Lady Hardcastle handed her one of her calling cards.

'In case we do,' she said, 'you can reach us there.'

'Oh,' said the woman as she examined the card. 'Thank you, m'lady.'

We left her and walked on through the cheerful crowd. I could still hear cattle lowing in the stock pens by the auction hall, but there was no room for them on the High Street so I was able to put my fears aside and just enjoy the exuberant atmosphere.

We eventually reached the library and, to our horror, found that the door was closed.

Lady Hardcastle pushed hard. It was locked.

I looked around and found a bell pull. I pulled it.

A few moments later we heard the clonk of bolts being drawn, then the door opened a crack to reveal a small, elderly lady with reading glasses perched on the end of her nose. If I'd been casting the role of Librarian for a music hall skit, I'd have hired her on the spot.

'Yes?' she said, nervously.

'Good afternoon,' said Lady Hardcastle. 'Is the library open today?'

'Oh, yes, dear, do come in.'

She opened the door just wide enough for us to slip inside, and then immediately closed and bolted it behind us.

'We have to keep the doors locked on market day,' she said as she led us to the main desk. 'Things can get a little . . . rowdy, do you see? We had an incident last year when . . . Well, let's just say that poor Mr Jones will never look at the collected works of Thomas Hardy without some painful memories completely unconnected with the fictional events in Wessex.'

Mr Jones, I surmised, was the bird-like man behind the desk, lost in concentration as he repaired the binding on a battered copy of *Middlemarch*.

'Is there something in particular I can help you with?' asked the woman. 'Or are you just seeking sanctuary from the market-day madness?'

'We were hoping you might have an archive of local newspapers,' said Lady Hardcastle.

'Oh, my word, yes. Yes, we do. I'm delighted you should ask. I insisted we keep them, you know. The town council has tried more than once to force us to dispose of them, but I ignore them. What are you looking for?'

'September 1891 to . . . oh, I don't know, early the following year? When would the next assizes be?'

'The Bristol Spring Assize would have been in early 1892, yes.'

'We'll start with September to November 1891 then, please, with whatever local news you have. And then jump to anything at all that might have covered the Assizes in '92.'

'You're looking for news of a crime, I take it?'

'A murder, yes.'

'Not the Weryer Murder?'

'The very same,' said Lady Hardcastle. 'You know of it?'

'I was only thinking about it the other day when I heard about poor Abel Mattick. You don't think there's a connection, do you?'

'We've no idea yet – we know nothing about the 1891 crime. That's very much why we're here.'

The librarian seemed puzzled by our interest in the case.

'You have some connection with the police?' she said.

'Not a formal one,' said Lady Hardcastle, 'but we help out from time to time.'

The librarian looked at us both for a few moments and then suddenly smiled.

'You're Lady Hardcastle and Florence Armstrong,' she said. 'Oh, my dears, I'm so sorry for not recognizing you. What an honour to be involved in one of your investigations. Do please find yourselves a table and I shall bring the newspapers to you at once. Oh my word, how wonderful. My sister Flora will be tickled pink – we've been following your exploits for some time.'

She bustled off in search of newspapers and we found ourselves a reading table away from the three other library patrons, who were poring intently over their own researches. Two of them were, at least. The third had fallen asleep with his copy of Caesar's *Gallic Wars* on his face.

We got out our notebooks while we waited for the librarian to return.

She took quite a while, but eventually I caught sight of her pushing a trolley stacked with newspapers. She had made it about halfway towards us, smiling excitedly, when we heard the tinkling of a bell. One of the other readers tutted and shook her head at the interruption.

The librarian looked to her passerine colleague to answer the door, but his concentration was total. That or he was intoxicated by the fumes of the glue he was using. Either way, it fell to our new friend to see who was there.

A minute later we were joined at the table by Dinah Caudle. She looked as glamorous as ever and greeted us warmly.

'Hello, darlings,' she said. 'What have I missed?'

'Shh,' said the tutting woman.

'Oh, shush yourself,' said Miss Caudle. 'You're not even reading that book. You're only in here to get away from your husband for an hour.'

'Well!' said the woman, indignantly. But she made no further complaint.

The librarian arrived with her trolley.

'I have the *Bristol News* for all the dates you mentioned,' she said in more hushed tones. 'And the *Stroud Herald* and *Gloucester Chronicle* for the period just around the murder itself.'

Lady Hardcastle smiled. 'You're very kind, Mrs . . .'

'Miss. Miss Francis. Fauna Francis.'

'Thank you, Miss Francis.'

'I'm delighted that someone has vindicated my decision to keep these.' She patted the newspapers affectionately. 'If you need anything else, please do come and ask.'

She left us to it and we dished out the newspapers between ourselves.

'I have news of Moses Peppard and the Lady of Pighill,' said Miss Caudle as she opened up her leather-bound notebook. 'It was, indeed, Francesca "Franny" Rogers of Hawthorn Farm.'

'I thought it was,' I said.

'I confess I had my suspicions, too,' said Lady Hardcastle. 'That's interesting, though. And what of Faith Mattick?'

'She had been a regular recipient of Peppard's favours, but that ended in the spring.'

'And how does your source know this?' I asked.

'Because she took over when Faith Mattick called it a day.'

'Good heavens,' I said. 'He had a waiting list?'

'So it would seem. But it means he really was on his way to Hawthorn Farm the morning Cridland was killed. It doesn't really help us much now that he's dead, but at least it adds weight to the single-killer hypothesis.'

'It does, dear, it does,' said Lady Hardcastle. 'Thank you for your efforts. I think we need to concentrate on the possibility of a link to the 1891 murder now, though.' She indicated the newspapers piled on the table. 'Shall we?'

It took a long time. The news was densely printed, often without a headline, and I found myself distracted by a story from the Eastbourne police court telling me that Harry Brimble, a hotel proprietor from Winchester, and William Moore, a licensed porter, had been charged with wilfully smashing Salvation Army instruments, causing damage in the amount of £10. They were also charged with assaulting James Blackman, who had been carrying the instruments in a sack. I learned also that Dr C. Hubert H. Parry's new musical setting of *De Profundis* had been performed at the Three Choirs Festival at Hereford. It was all utterly fascinating, but had nothing to do with our own case.

Eventually, though, I found a reference to the Weryer murder, and over several editions the details began to emerge. My notes became a tangled mess of crossings-out, arrows, annotations and questions, but slowly I was able to piece together a version of the story.

As I worked my way through my allocated newspapers, what struck me most was that, when the story appeared in later editions of different newspapers, they were usually reprints of the original version, sometimes with added sensational commentary. It seemed that a lot of news reporting actually involved simply reading other newspapers and copying their stories.

I was disturbed to note, though, that one newspaper actually added some details of its own which appeared nowhere else and were not mentioned in the evidence given at the trial. I shouldn't like to 'cast nasturtiums' on them, as Lady Hardcastle might say, but I did wonder if they'd just made it up in order to add some spice to the story.

An hour and a half later, I had read as much as I could bear to read about the Weryer Murder of 1891, and I got up to explore the library and stretch my legs.

It housed an impressive collection for a small library in a provincial market town, and I wandered for a while among the shelves. I found myself in the history section, where a careless reader had left a book on medieval warfare on the floor. I picked it up and took it back to the table for something to look at while the other two finished their newspaper research.

Another half an hour passed by before they, too, had finished, and I gratefully set my book down.

'I believe I'm done,' I said, quietly. 'And my back is killing me. Do you think we might call it a day and get some fresh air?'

'I quite agree,' said Lady Hardcastle, a good deal less quietly, 'though it's not my back that's troubling me. This seat could definitely do with a cushion.'

'Shh,' said the tutting woman.

Miss Caudle shook her head.

'I think we ought to return to the land of the living where we can discuss our findings without being shushed,' she said.

'Thank heavens for that,' said the woman.

'Oh, for heaven's sake,' said Miss Caudle. 'We've not said a word for two hours and you're *still* staring at the same page of that blessed book. I'm not at all convinced that we're the problem.'

The woman's expression was furious but she made no reply.

We packed up our things and restacked the newspapers on the trolley before making our way back to the desk.

'Thank you so much for all your help, Miss Francis,' said Lady Hardcastle. 'Your newspaper archive is an absolute boon. If you ever have any more trouble from the town council, do let me know.' She handed over her calling card. 'I shall write to them at once.'

'I'm delighted, my lady. Thank you,' said Miss Francis. 'Are you sure there's nothing else I can do for you?'

'No, I think we have everything we need. You've been more help than we could possibly have hoped for.'

'I'm so pleased. Do call again if you need anything further. And good luck. I hope you find out who's doing all . . . all this.'

She let us out through the barely open door and we stood on the pavement, blinking in the sun, as she locked it behind us once more.

'Where shall we go?' asked Miss Caudle.

'The tearoom?' suggested Lady Hardcastle.

'We can try,' I said, 'but I'd bet it'll be busy today. I doubt we'll get a table.'

'The pubs will all be crammed, too,' said Miss Caudle.

'We could sit in the park,' I suggested.

'Or we could just go back to the house and have sandwiches in the garden,' said Lady Hardcastle.

'It would be more comfortable,' I said.

'And quieter,' said Miss Caudle.

'Come on, then, ladies,' said Lady Hardcastle. 'Let's go.'

I made a few rounds of sandwiches and a jug of elderflower cordial while the other two made themselves comfortable in the garden. Miss Caudle had offered to help, but I politely and diplomatically declined. She'd only get in my way, and I'd have spent more time telling her where things were than it would have taken me to do it all myself.

I carried the tray out.

Lady Hardcastle was holding forth.

'. . . without even pausing to put her stockings on,' she said. 'Ah, there you are, Flo dear. I was just telling Dinah about that time in Paris when we had to flee the hotel before the Austrians caught up with us.'

'The finest silk, they were,' I said as I set the tray on the table.

'The Austrians?'

'Yes,' I said. 'Yes, the Austrians were made of silk. Do you see what I have to put up with, Miss Caudle? If you really do fancy working for the SSB you can have my job.'

'You'd miss me horribly,' said Lady Hardcastle.

'Horribly,' I said. 'Tuck in. These are cheese, those are ham, and these are egg and tomato. I'd have made some mayonnaise but I wanted to get out and hear what you both had to say about the Weryer Murder of '91.'

'I'm sure they'll be lovely, dear,' said Lady Hardcastle. 'And I want to hear it, too. Who shall start?'

'I don't mind going first,' said Miss Caudle, taking out her notebook. 'Now then . . . The first report I found was from the Monday edition of the *Bristol News*.'

'Yes,' I said. 'The others didn't pick it up until a few days later. A whole week later in the case of the *Gloucester Chronicle*.'

'We're always first with the story at the *News*. Samuel Puddy, of Woodworthy—'

Lady Hardcastle let out a sudden 'Hah!' but I shushed her.

'Let's hear everything first,' I said.

Dinah frowned and cocked her head questioningly, but carried on.

'Samuel Puddy, of Woodworthy, was found strangled to death in the garden of his house by . . .' She flicked through her notes.

'By the local handyman-cum-gardener who had called round to tidy up the flower beds,' said Lady Hardcastle.

'Ah, yes, thank you,' said Miss Caudle, making another quick note on the page to link the sections together. 'I see it now. He wasn't a poor man, then, if he could afford to get someone else to tend his garden, but I don't seem to have made a note of his line. Some sort of merchant, wasn't it?'

'He was a timber merchant,' I said.

'And, obviously, a Weryer,' added Lady Hardcastle.

'Actually, well done, me,' said Miss Caudle. 'I had both of those. My notes are a shambles. Sorry.'

'Mine, too,' I said.

'Don't worry,' said Lady Hardcastle, 'I'm summarizing as we go, so we have a coherent version.'

'So the gardener found the body and alerted the pub landlord, Griffith Uzzle,' continued Miss Caudle.

'Do we know why he chose the pub landlord and not some other local worthy?' asked Lady Hardcastle.

'He was asked that at the trial,' I said. 'Apparently Uzzle was known to be a friend of the victim and was also, crucially, the owner of a dog cart. That meant he could come to Littleton Cotterell to fetch the policeman—'

'Sergeant Goodfield,' said Lady Hardcastle.

'Tsk,' said Miss Caudle. 'The *News* reporter missed that. Anyway, Uzzle harnessed his horse and set off to come down here to the police station. Why would he not go to Chipping Bevington, by the way? Surely a serious crime like that would make a fellow think of the police in the town.'

'When we first moved here,' I said, 'Constable Hancock was very disdainful of the police at Chipping. Perhaps it's a longstanding mistrust. Perhaps the villagers always preferred the village bobbies rather than "they idiots over at Chipping".'

'Perhaps they did,' she said. 'But whatever the reason, Sergeant Goodfield was summoned and the legal processes were begun.'

Lady Hardcastle made a few more notes and then took her turn at recounting the events.

'The coroner returned a verdict of unlawful killing,' she said, 'and the police inquiry continued. On the twenty-second of September, William Hardiman – a farmer and fellow Weryer – was arrested. He was indicted by the magistrate at Chipping Bevington to stand trial for murder at the Spring Assize at Bristol.'

She made some more notes.

'At the trial,' I said, reading from my own notes, 'it was alleged that Hardiman and Puddy had quarrelled over a debt. Hardiman's farm had suffered terrible losses following an outbreak of . . . splenic fever?'

'Anthrax,' said Lady Hardcastle without looking up.

'Aha,' I said. 'Where was I? Oh, yes . . . following an outbreak of splenic fever among his cattle the previous year – he lost more than half his herd. Puddy had given him a loan but, unsurprisingly, Hardiman had difficulty paying it back. The prosecution called Griffith Uzzle, Moses Peppard, Claud Cridland, and Abel Mattick, who all testified that they had witnessed multiple arguments about the debt between their two fellow Weryers, at least one of which had come to blows. The accused's wife, Mrs Ann Hardiman, testified that no such quarrel existed and that the two men were on good terms. She also insisted that her husband had been at home on the night of the murder, but under cross examination she admitted that while he was "at home", he did spend an hour or more in the cattle sheds checking his remaining herd. This, said the prosecution, would have given him ample time to murder Puddy and return home, with her none the wiser. The jury returned a verdict of wilful murder. Hardiman was convicted and sentenced to death by hanging. The sentence was carried out two weeks later.'

There was a moment's silence while Lady Hardcastle finished making her notes. When she was done she put down her pencil and looked up.

'Well, ladies,' she said, 'that answers quite a few questions, wouldn't you say?'

Chapter Seventeen

Some questions might have been answered by the account of the Weryer Murder, but further questions needed to be asked, and the sandwiches and cordial were all gone.

'Coffee?' I said. 'I think Miss Jones has made a Madeira cake, too, if you fancy it.'

I tidied away the wreckage of our late lunch and returned a few minutes later with coffee and cake. Lady Hardcastle had taken advantage of my absence to tell another highly embellished tale of derring-do. I set the tray down and wondered whether to correct her on a few salient facts.

'That was the seamstress,' I said as I sat down. 'The prostitute was the one in Dubrovnik who distracted the head of the secret police for us while we did a bunk out of the brothel window.'

'What on earth were you doing in a brothel in Dubrovnik?' said Miss Caudle with a laugh.

'Well, now,' said Lady Hardcastle. 'It all began when—'

'Some other time, perhaps?' I said. 'I'm keen to know what you both think about the current case.'

'My first and most urgent thought is that we need to alert Inspector Sunderland to the potential danger to Griffith Uzzle,' said Lady Hardcastle. 'The other three witnesses for the prosecution have met gruesome ends and there's a very real possibility that he might be next.'

'Agreed,' said Miss Caudle. 'Assuming we definitely think the cases are connected.'

'There's no doubt about that,' I said. 'Has Dr Gosling told you about the items found with the bodies?'

'An apple, a bottle and a cruet set?'

'More or less,' I said. 'We'd been working under the assumption that the S and P on the salt and pepper pots referred to Sid Palmer or Pat Swanton. But Palmer, at least, has an alibi. And since Mattick was found with a bottle of Hardiman's Elixir, I think we can assume all the items were connected with the Weryer Murder, so that means the S and P are for Samuel Puddy and not Pat Swanton.'

'Oh, he didn't tell me all that. Well, that's certainly suggestive. What about the apple?'

'I'm not at all sure about the apple,' I said. 'There's no apple in the murder.'

'There's not,' said Lady Hardcastle. 'He was dragged from the spot where he was killed and placed against a tree where . . . Oh, my word, how stupid we've been.'

She rummaged in her haversack for her sketchpad and opened it to the pages where she'd sketched Mr Cridland's body in the orchard.

'There,' she said at length. 'I thought so.'

She pointed to a drawing that showed the body in relation to the other trees. Miss Caudle and I shrugged in unison.

'The orchard is more or less a grid,' she said. 'He's leaning against the third tree. I'd be awfully surprised if it wasn't in the ninth row.'

'It was,' I said. 'I counted the rows when I went to look for the spot where he was stabbed.'

'I don't see the significance,' said Miss Caudle.

'The third of the ninth,' said Lady Hardcastle. 'The date of the murder.'

'It's a stretch,' said Miss Caudle, 'but if you put it together with the other items, it does make sense.'

'So we have references to the 1891 murder and each of them was killed in a Weryerish way,' I said.

'Each of them?' said Miss Caudle. 'I can see being beaten with a cooper's hammer or drowned in cider, but what's Weryerish about the way Cridland was killed?'

'I've been meaning to tell you,' I said. 'While you two were still dawdling over your newspapers, I picked up a book about medieval warfare.'

'You did,' said Lady Hardcastle. 'I thought it an odd choice of reading material at the time.'

'It had fallen off the shelf,' I said. 'It chose itself. But as it happens, it was most fortuitous. I found a reference to a billhook.'

'A pruning knife?' said Miss Caudle. 'Long thing like a hooked machete?'

'Yes, but when they mounted them on poles to use as weapons, they added a spike for stabbing. They could slash with the hooked blade, or thrust forward with the spike.'

'And Cridland's wound,' said Lady Hardcastle, 'was cylindrical, as though caused by a long, thin spike.'

'With bruising on his chest where it would have been stopped by the dull outside edge of the blade,' I said. 'I'd bet ten bob the missing Sax of the Pomary is a ceremonial billhook.'

'The Martel of the Rundlet is missing, too,' she said.

'The which of the what?' said Miss Caudle.

'The Weryers seem to have one or two ceremonial implements,' said Lady Hardcastle. 'In my imagination they're polished steel, or possibly even silver-plated. They're certainly shiny, because Simeon found traces of polish on Cridland's shirt. One is this putative bill-hook – the Sax of the Pomary. The other, I'm assuming, is a cooper's hammer – the Martel of the Rundlet. I'd bet ten bob of my own that they're missing because the killer has them.'

'And who,' said Miss Caudle, 'is the killer?'

'Well, that's the crucial question, isn't it? We have our eye on Cornelius Starks. He was a Weryer in '91 but I'm struggling to come up with a motive. He isn't mentioned in any of the accounts as a witness on either side, so he doesn't seem to have been involved in the original crime at all.'

'So why would he want to start killing the witnesses now, twenty years later?'

'There you have me. Why, indeed?'

'Clearing out the last memories of the Weryers' disgrace before he retires to Dorset?' I suggested. 'That might make sense to a deranged mind.'

'Is he deranged?' asked Miss Caudle.

'Ordinary,' said Lady Hardcastle. 'Hector Farley-Stroud thinks him dull, but we merely found him unremarkable. There are those wild souls who might think commonplacedness and conformity a form of derangement, but I'd be fibbing if I said I thought he was in any way mad.'

'Who else?' said Miss Caudle.

'The only other person on our list is Miss Chamberlain,' I said. 'But she would have been no more than about five or six years old in 1891, anyway.'

'Shall I tell the inspector that, then?' asked Lady Hardcastle. 'He needs to protect Uzzle and arrest Starks?'

'If he arrests Starks, won't that protect Uzzle anyway?' said Miss Caudle.

'Only if we're right. If we're wrong, we leave Uzzle exposed to attack. He'll be sacrificed on the altar in the orchard.'

'Or run over by a dog cart,' I said.

'Or that. I shall make my call.'

◆ ◆ ◆

Miss Caudle and I were discussing the best place in Bristol to buy kippers when Lady Hardcastle came hurrying back into the garden.

'There's a telephone call for you, Dinah dear,' she said. 'It's one of your colleagues at the *Bristol News*. I'd just finished my call to Inspector Sunderland when the telephone rang again immediately. I suppose the ladies at the exchange can see when the line becomes free. I wonder if she was listening in.'

'Thank you,' said Miss Caudle. She hurried inside.

'The inspector says he'll be "pulling Starks in for questioning" as soon as he can get out here,' said Lady Hardcastle.

'Did you tell him what we'd learned?'

'I did. He was most intrigued. He remembered the Weryer Murder once I mentioned it, but he would never have thought of a connection. He's rather pleased with us.'

'As he should be. We're his unpaid lackeys.'

'Well, His Majesty's Government is paying our wages, so in a way we're his paid lackeys. Or, at least, we're his lackeys and we're being paid. Either way, we're both very good girls.'

'He didn't say that, surely?'

'Good lord, no. He would never say anything so thoroughly awful. But we *are* very good girls.'

'We really are,' I said.

Miss Caudle had returned.

'What are you?' she said.

'Very good girls,' I said.

'The absolute best. I have news that might make you think that I'm a very good girl, too.'

She sat down.

'Well?' said Lady Hardcastle. 'Don't leave us on tentacles. Tell us the news.'

'That was, as you said, one of my colleagues on the telephone. He had taken a message from my contact at the *Exeter Advertiser*. He apologized for taking so long to reply to me but it took some digging.'

'And what did his digging unearth?'

'He made calls of his own to various friends and colleagues throughout Devon, but he could find no one who had heard of Grace Chamberlain. She had been accused of no crimes, she had appeared at no public meetings, she had sung in no choirs, nor won a prize for the most adorable bunny rabbit at a village fête. Like most people, she had never featured in the news at all.'

'And yet . . . ?'

'Well, now. No one had heard of Grace Chamberlain, and he was all set to telephone me and tell me the bad news. He was chatting to a friend at the *Dawlish Gazette* and said something to the effect that one would think a tall, auburn-haired beauty with a port-wine stain on her temple would have made some impression on the world. And the friend said, "That sounds like Grace Hardiman. She works at the library." From what they've both said, I'm inclined to think Grumpy Grace is William Hardiman's daughter. And since the Weryers' testimony got her father hanged, she has a very good motive for travelling all this way to bump them off in time for the twentieth anniversary.'

'That's remarkably good work,' said Lady Hardcastle. 'Thank you.'

'It wasn't anything to do with me – it was the lads at the *Dawlish Gazette*.'

'We're still grateful to you for urging them on, dear. Though you're right and we should send them a case of champagne.'

'Don't go overboard.'

'Too much, do you think?'

'Just a bottle or two, perhaps.'

'Very well. But it's precious information. She really does have a perfect motive.'

'And that means we've sent the inspector after the wrong person,' said Miss Caudle.

'We'll set him straight,' said Lady Hardcastle.

'Well, yes, obviously. But should we go after Grace ourselves? It seems foolish to let a killer run free when we could just stroll up to the pub and detain her.'

'We've no authority,' I said. 'We can't hold her and she'd be well within her rights to tell us to shove off. If we were more . . . forceful, she'd be justified in bringing charges against us for false imprisonment. We're on very shaky ground.'

'Not only that,' added Lady Hardcastle, 'we don't actually have any hard evidence that she's done anything wrong. She has a jolly good motive, but we've no proof of anything.'

'Then we should get some,' said Miss Caudle indignantly.

'We shall. But we have to leave the rest to Inspector Sunderland. He said he wanted to call in here on his way to Chipping Bevington.'

It took the inspector the best part of an hour to get to us from the middle of Bristol, and he wouldn't have caught Starks at his office at all – he'd already have gone home. As it was, we were able to stop him going to either his office or his home.

Rather than letting the poor man relax in the garden with a cup of tea, we corralled him into the drawing room with the crime board and told him of our latest discoveries. We began with the story of the Weryer Murder of '91 while he made notes.

'This is most compelling,' he said when we'd finished.

'You haven't heard the best part yet,' said Lady Hardcastle. 'Tell him your news, Dinah, dear.'

Miss Caudle recounted her conversation with her colleague and our own supposition that Grace Hardiman and Grace Chamberlain were one and the same.

'Well, now, that's much more like it,' he said. 'Thank you very much. I've had half the police stations in Devon looking for any mention of Grace Chamberlain but none of them knows anything, though to be fair I hadn't tried Dawlish. I should have thought of telephoning the newspapers myself – they always know all the comings and goings.'

'We have our uses,' said Miss Caudle.

'You do, indeed.' He reviewed his notes. 'Well, I don't have enough to arrest her, but I certainly have enough to insist most forcefully that she explain herself.'

'You think it's her?' asked Miss Caudle.

'I have an open mind as always,' he said. 'But with Patrick Swanton out of the running—'

'Oh?' said Lady Hardcastle.

'I interviewed him this morning at his office in Bristol – he has cast-iron alibis for all three murders.'

'The field narrows,' she said.

'It does,' he agreed. 'And the more I thought about it on the way here, the less I was convinced that Starks has anything to do with it, either.'

'Well, quite. Even less so now,' said Lady Hardcastle.

'Indeed. I'm glad I dropped in. Instead of wasting my time with a trip to Chipping, I shall go to the Dog and Duck and speak to Miss Grace Chamberlain. Would you care to join me? If she's innocent she might feel more inclined to talk if there's a woman or two present. And if she's guilty, it won't make any difference because she probably won't talk anyway.'

'It's a sound idea,' said Lady Hardcastle, 'but I fear our presence would only irritate her. She's rather taken against us, I'm afraid.'

'All three of you?'

'Yes,' said Miss Caudle. 'Even me. I didn't actually speak to her, but I could see the hostility in her beautiful green eyes when she looked at me. Or it might have been a reflection of the lamps in the Dog and Duck. Either way, she didn't have any time for us.'

'Then I shall have to go alone,' said the inspector with his familiar chuckle.

'Right you are,' said Lady Hardcastle. 'Are you going to warn Uzzle?'

'I wasn't planning to, no. I don't see a great deal of benefit in worrying the poor fellow at this stage.'

'But he's the last remaining prosecution witness from the trial,' I said. 'Actually, for a time I thought he might be the killer.'

'Did you?'

'Yes, but I couldn't work out what motive he might have had. Now, though, he seems more like the next potential victim. Surely it's worth at least mentioning it to him.'

'I take your point,' he said, 'but I'm sure he's already worked that out for himself. Why don't I just make sure Sergeant Dobson cycles out that way to check on things? I'm sure Dobson will enjoy a trip to the pub, and he's not the sort of chap to cause alarm. A visit from the genial local bobby will give us all peace of mind without startling anyone.'

'An admirable compromise,' said Lady Hardcastle. 'Thank you.'

'My pleasure.'

He made to leave.

'Oh, before you go,' said Miss Caudle, 'have you seen Simeon today?'

'No,' he said. 'He's been busy at the mortuary.'

'Ah, yes, of course, he did say something about a death in the east of the city somewhere. A wife finally got fed up with being belittled by her husband and smashed a soup tureen over his head, I think he said.'

'He said something similar to me, yes. Which means I've been denied the pleasure of his company, I'm afraid.'

'Poor you. In that case he won't have passed on my invitation to you and Dolly to come with us to dinner next Wednesday evening. There's a new restaurant in town that I'm simply dying to try.'

'That's very kind of you. I shall double-check that she hasn't got anything else on the calendar, but I'm sure we'd enjoy that very much.'

'Splendid. How about you two? We could make a party of it.'

'I'd be delighted,' said Lady Hardcastle.

'Me, too,' I said. 'Is it the one owned by that French chap? It's been advertised in the *News*.'

'It is, and he has quite the reputation. The place is booked solid for the next month but I managed to bag a table for Sim and me. I'm sure he can cater for six as easily as two.'

I wasn't sure of anything of the sort, but I wasn't going to turn down the opportunity to dine at an exciting new restaurant. And while Miss Caudle might not have been confident of her ability to charm Grace Chamberlain into telling us who she was and what she was up to, I didn't doubt she could charm an ambitious French chef into setting a few extra places at the table.

'I shall confirm the arrangements with Gosling tomorrow,' said the inspector. 'But for now, ladies, good evening to you all, and thank you very much for the new information.'

With a wave of his notebook he was gone.

'Should we warn Uzzle ourselves?' said Miss Caudle as we returned to the garden and settled back into the shade under the apple tree.

'It's a tricky one,' said Lady Hardcastle. 'I thought someone ought, but I'm coming round to the inspector's point of view. He'll have twigged much sooner than we that the others were the witnesses, so he'll be on his guard by now anyway. And if Grace is involved she'll be less of a threat once the inspector has marked her card.'

'True,' I said. 'But we could pop up there anyway. You know, just by way of being neighbourly. At the very least we could have a word with Cissy and ask her to keep her eyes open.'

'All right, why not? A spot of dinner then a trip to Woodworthy.' She turned to Miss Caudle. 'Would you care to join us, dear?'

'No can do, I'm afraid,' said Miss Caudle. 'My affianced is picking me up at seven. We're going to a concert, then on for dinner.'

Lady Hardcastle checked her watch.

'Oh, my dear, you should have said. It's gone half past five already. You'd better get a move on.'

'Nonsense. I can be home in an hour and getting changed will be the work of a moment. I really don't mind if we're a little late, if I'm honest – the programme opens with a Beethoven string quartet and I could live a long and happy life without ever hearing another of those.'

'Still, you'd better get going. Poor Simeon is insecure enough as it is without thinking you've forgotten your tryst.'

Miss Caudle laughed. 'I think "tryst" is taking it a little too far. There'll be little trysting going on in a formal dress in a stuffy concert hall. But I'd better be on my way. If I can get to a telephone I shall call you tomorrow to see how you got on with Uzzle.'

'Right you are, dear. Give my love to Simeon.'

'Of course.'

'Would you like a hand starting the Rover?' I said.

'That's kind, thank you, but I've very much got the hang of it now. Talk to you tomorrow.'

A moment later, she, too, was gone.

'I can do a nice salad for dinner if you fancy it,' I said.

'That would be splendid. Is there pie?'

'I believe so. And there are some hard-boiled eggs, too. I made a few for the sandwiches but we didn't eat them all. And if you can bear to wait an extra couple of minutes, I'll make that mayonnaise I was threatening.'

'Splendid. Thank you. I'll update the crime board and join you presently.'

By the time we drew up outside the Mock of Pommey, the sheep of the Woodworthy village green had gone wherever sheep go in the evening. The thought that they might have their own ovine pub to go to made me smile.

'What's amusing you?' asked Lady Hardcastle as we made our way to the pub door.

'The Flock of Pommey,' I said.

She frowned, but said nothing.

The pub was noisily busy and there were no tables to be had. There were also no women present apart from the landlady, Betty Uzzle, and Cissy Slocomb, both of whom were looking frazzled. We drew unwelcoming looks from the regulars, and one of them attracted Betty Uzzle's attention and nodded our way.

'Good evening, my lady,' she said. 'What can we do for you?'

'Good evening, Mrs Uzzle,' said Lady Hardcastle. 'We were hoping to have a quick word with your husband. Is he here?'

'No, I'm afraid he's out.'

'Where has he gone?'

'I told you: out.'

Lady Hardcastle looked at me and cocked an eyebrow. This was a sudden change of mood. We knew she didn't take any nonsense from her husband, but she'd previously gone out of her way to be polite to us.

'When will he be back?' asked Lady Hardcastle, calmly.

'Later.'

'I see. Would you be kind enough to give him a message when he gets in, please?'

'I shall try.'

'It's really rather important that you do, Mrs Uzzle. We believe he might be in danger. Tell him . . . tell him the anniversary is approaching, and we believe the recent killings are connected. Tell him to be on his guard.'

'Anniversary?' she said with what seemed to me to be an affected air of ignorant innocence.

'Yes, he'll know. Has he not mentioned it? How long have you been married?'

'I beg your pardon?'

Her manner had fully changed now, from understandably-put-out-at-the-intrusion to openly belligerent. Her hands were on her hips.

'I'm curious,' said Lady Hardcastle, still impeccably calm and well mannered. 'Indulge me.'

'Thirty years this June.'

'So you were married to Mr Uzzle at the time of the Weryer Murder of 1891.'

'So what if I were?'

'I was merely trying to establish whether you would be familiar with the crime, Mrs Uzzle, that's all. The anniversary of the murder approaches, you see, and the three murdered men were witnesses for the prosecution at the subsequent trial of William Hardiman. As was your husband. There are too many coincidences for us to overlook. We wanted to be certain that Mr Uzzle was aware of the connection and was taking the necessary precautions to ensure that he didn't become the fourth victim.'

'And who do you think is doing this? Who would murder witnesses from a twenty-year-old murder trial?'

'If we knew that, Mrs Uzzle, there'd be no need for this visit.'

'I'll tell him. Are you stopping for a drink? We've no room set aside for ladies, mind.'

'We can see you're busy,' said Lady Hardcastle, 'so we shall leave you to your work. Do please pass on the message, though, won't you. We wouldn't have come all this way if we didn't think it was terribly important.'

'I'll tell him.'

Mrs Uzzle turned away to see to a customer and we left.

We got as far as the Rolls and leaned against it as we contemplated our next move.

'She was a good deal less affable than I remembered,' I said.

'One can't really blame her for being a little offish,' said Lady Hardcastle. 'There she was, fearfully busy, and a couple of strange ladies bustle in and start asking her impertinent questions about her husband. I'm not sure I'd have been any more welcoming in her shoes.'

'Granted,' I said. 'But once she knew we were only concerned for his welfare . . .'

'Well, we *said* we were only concerned for his welfare, but she's not obliged to believe us. We could just as easily be working for His Majesty's Customs and Excise, come to snoop on them for non-payment of . . . whatever duties it is publicans have to pay. Booze is always subject to that sort of thing and I'd lay good odds most of the publicans round here are working some sort of fiddle.'

'I suppose so. But at least we can go home feeling virtuous. We've done our bit to try to save his life.'

'I only hope it's enough. There's a part of me that wonders if we shouldn't just make ourselves comfortable out here and try to catch him when he returns.'

'Well,' I said slowly. 'We could . . .'

She laughed.

'I know,' she said. 'It would almost certainly be a waste of time. But now we've finally identified the next potential victim, it feels a little anticlimactic to abdicate responsibility for his safety to his sceptical wife.'

We were interrupted by the arrival of Cissy Slocomb.

'What on earth did you say to 'er?' she said.

'We told her Mr Uzzle might be in danger,' I said. 'Why?'

'She's got a face like thunder, she has. Slammin' glasses, snappin' at poor old Tom Johnson. He only asked her for the dominoes.'

'Sorry, dear,' said Lady Hardcastle. She quickly explained about the Weryer Murder and how we believed it to be connected to the recent killings.

'She already knew about that, I reckons,' said Cissy when she had finished. 'I 'eard 'em t'other night talkin' about "witnesses" and "that girl".'

'"That girl"?' I said. 'Grace Chamberlain? Do they know who she is?'

'No idea, Flo, sorry. Why? Who is she?'

'She's William Hardiman's daughter. Or, at least, we think she is.'

'And who's he when he's at home?'

'He's the man who hanged for the murder of Sam Puddy twenty years ago. The original Weryer Murder. The three murdered men were witnesses for the prosecution at Hardiman's trial. And so was Griffith Uzzle.'

'Oh my word,' said Cissy. 'So you reckon . . . ?'

'It's a distinct possibility,' said Lady Hardcastle. 'But it's something of a relief to find that they think there's a connection, too – they'll be on their guard. We were worried . . . *I* was worried – Flo here has a good deal more faith in people. I was worried Mrs Uzzle might not pass on the message and that he'd be found dead one morning.'

'Is it all right for you to be out here with us?' I asked. 'I don't want you to get into trouble if she's already in a foul mood.'

'I told her I had to piddle,' she said. 'Can't deny me a piddle.'

'She's not the cheerfully welcoming woman we met before,' I said. 'So she might try.'

Cissy laughed. 'She's usually all right to me. But Griff, mind . . . she treats him terrible. I don't know how he puts up with it sometimes, the way she talks to him.'

'People endure worse for love,' said Lady Hardcastle. 'Do you know where Uzzle has gone?'

'He's meetin' someone, he said. But that's all I knows. Didn't say who, didn't say where. Probably one of his shady deals, if you asks me. He's always got some fiddle goin'. Last month he sold half a dozen brand-new bicycles and twenty yards of blue serge to customers in 'ere, and I know he didn't come across none of it lawful, like.'

'Even better. If he's up to no good, he'll definitely have his eyes open for trouble. We can sleep easy.'

'Cissy!'

Mrs Uzzle was standing at the pub door with her hands once more on her hips.

'Get in here, you idle girl,' she shouted. 'I don't pay you to stand out here gossiping with nosy parkers from Littleton Cotterell, no matter what la-di-da titles they've got. Get back to work.'

'Yes, Mrs Uzzle,' said Cissy. She gave us a grin. 'And I never did get my piddle.'

'And as for you, *my lady*,' continued Mrs Uzzle, 'if you've said all you've got to say, I shall thank you to sling your hook. We don't like strangers hanging about the village at night.'

'On our way, Mrs Uzzle,' said Lady Hardcastle, cheerfully. 'Do remember to pass on our message, won't you?'

Mrs Uzzle snarled angrily and turned her attention to Cissy, who gave us another grin and a cheeky wave as she was ushered inside.

'Not cheerfully welcoming at all,' I said.

'Indeed not,' said Lady Hardcastle as she started the engine. 'But our work here is done. Home for cards and a nightcap, I think.'

We set off back to the house.

Chapter Eighteen

On Friday morning I was having a cup of tea in the kitchen with Edna and Miss Jones. They had both been curious about the murders but not overly worried. The victims thus far had all been men, and Weryer men at that.

'Our Dan didn't want me walkin' about on me own in the dark,' said Edna. 'But I told 'im, I said, "Seems to be you're in more danger than me," I said. "It's only blokes what's been done in. Maybe you's the one as should be stayin' at 'ome." Course, he didn't like that. But it's right, i'n't it? No women's been killed. Makes a change if you asks me. You hears of plenty of men gettin' killed in fights and arguments, but if it's somethin' creepy and frightenin' it's always a woman with 'er throat cut.'

'Our ma was worried just the same,' said Miss Jones. 'But . . . well, I'm sorry, but I just ignored her. If I locked myself away every time something bad happened in the world I'd never leave the house.'

'I think you've both got the right idea,' I said. 'We think it's all connected with the old Weryer Murder.'

'Oh, my word,' said Edna. 'I'd forgotten all about that. Twenty-odd year ago, weren't it? Quarry owner up at Woodworthy.'

'Timber merchant,' I said.

'That's it. It's all we could talk about for weeks, then twenty years go by and it's gone clean out of my head. They said 'e was carryin' on with someone, but they always says that, don't they?'

'Sam Puddy was?'

'Sam Puddy,' said Edna, nodding. 'That was his name. I haven't heard that for years. It was only a rumour, mind, and I i'n't one to gossip, as you knows—'

Miss Jones rolled her eyes at this, but neither of us said anything.

'—but they did say as how he was diddlin' one of the other Weryers' wives, and that's what got him killed.'

'Ann Hardiman?' I suggested.

'Might have been,' she said. 'Wasn't Hardiman the one they hanged?'

'He was.'

'That must be it, then. I tell you, it's not like me not to remember these things, but I've got almost nothin' left of all that. No one talks about it, see?'

'No, we noticed that. We had to get the story from old newspapers.'

Further discussion was halted by the ringing of the doorbell. Edna looked at the clock.

'Whoever can that be at this hour?' she said. 'No decent person would call before ten. The mistress a'n't even 'ad her mornin' coffee yet.'

'There's only one way to find out,' I said, and hauled myself to my feet.

I opened the front door to find Inspector Sunderland smiling at me.

'Good morning, Miss Armstrong,' he said. 'What a lovely day it is again.'

'Good morning to you, Inspector. Would you care to come in? Herself is still asleep but I can shake her to consciousness if needs be.'

'No, don't trouble her. I just wanted you both to know I had no luck with Miss Chamberlain last evening.'

'Still not talking?'

'She wasn't there,' he said. 'Gone out shortly before I arrived and no one knows where. Not that she ever told them where she was going, mind you.'

'And you're back this morning for another try?'

'Exactly so.'

'We had no luck with Griffith Uzzle last night, either.'

'You went up to Woodworthy?'

'We thought we ought to warn him, but he was out, too. We left a message with his wife and came home.'

'Ah, yes, Betty Uzzle – a formidable woman. I interviewed them both a few days ago. Uzzle might be the licensee as far as the magistrates are concerned, but she runs the place. And runs him, as well, from what I can make out. I swear he called her "ma'am" once.'

'She wasn't pleased to see us, but we put that down to the place being jam-full and only her and Cissy Slocomb serving.'

'A charitable view, but you might be right.'

'Are you sure you won't come in?'

'Perhaps on my way back. I'd like to beard Miss Chamberlain in her lair before she has a chance to go out for the day.'

'I shall have Miss Jones put the kettle on,' I said.

'Thank you. Cheerio for now.'

I shut the door and returned to the kitchen. Lady Hardcastle would want to be up for his return, and a pre-breakfast tray was needed.

◆ ◆ ◆

By the time Inspector Sunderland returned an hour later, Lady Hardcastle was washed, dressed, and thoroughly presentable in a white cotton frock. I'd even managed to get her hair to behave.

We invited the inspector to join us for breakfast and he gratefully accepted.

'You must think my wife doesn't feed me,' he said as he helped himself to a grilled tomato.

'Actually, I was thinking your poor wife never sees you,' said Lady Hardcastle. 'A policeman's lot might not be an 'appy one, but a policeman's wife doesn't have it much better.'

'It's not so bad since I've been in the CID, but when I was on the beat I was out at all hours.'

'Well, as long as she doesn't mind you eating at strange women's houses, you're always welcome here.'

'Thank you, my lady,' he said. 'Though I'm not sure she thinks of either of you as strange. Well, not *very* strange, at least.'

Lady Hardcastle laughed. 'She mustn't worry – I've been thought a little strange all my life. And will you ever be able to bring yourself to call me Emily, do you think?'

'I shouldn't think so, my lady, no.'

Another laugh. 'Very well, Inspector dear, I shan't press you. Now, tell all: what did Grace Chamberlain have to say for herself?'

'Not a word.'

'She really is becoming most tiresome. I think we ought to send Flo round to intimidate her a little.'

'Me?' I said. 'I am sweet and delightful. The very cheek of it.'

'You are utterly terrifying, dear, and you know it,' she said.

'I'm afraid it would do none of us any good,' said the inspector. 'She hadn't returned to her room. Joe sent young Daisy up to check and got no answer. He was reluctant to intrude but I was concerned that she might be unwell, so he eventually unlocked the door and let me look inside. The room was tidy and her few possessions still there, but the bed hadn't been slept in.'

'Curiouser and curiouser. I wonder—'

The doorbell rang.

I found an agitated Cissy Slocomb and her equally concerned friend Daisy Spratt on the doorstep.

'What's the matter, ladies?' I said.

'Thank goodness you's in,' said Daisy. 'Cissy wanted to tell you sommat, but I's nosy so I tagged along.'

'Come in,' I said. 'We're having breakfast.'

'Oh,' said Cissy, dismayed. 'I don't want to interrupt Lady Hardcastle while she's eatin'.'

'Nonsense. Come on. Inspector Sunderland is here, too.'

They reluctantly followed me in. It occurred to me that neither of them had ever been inside the house, and they both goggled at the size and comparative luxury of the place.

'So this is how the other half lives, eh?' said Daisy with uncharacteristic awe. 'I never thinks of Lady Hardcastle livin' in a place like this. She's just the nice lady who comes in the pub and teases Old Joe. I never thought of her as actually bein' a proper toff.'

'This is just the hallway,' I said. 'Wait till you see the morning room.'

'The mornin' room?' said Cissy. 'You has rooms for different times of the day?'

I laughed and ushered them in.

'Cissy and Daisy have come to see us,' I said.

'Good morning, girls,' said Lady Hardcastle. 'Do make yourselves comfortable. Help yourselves to food if you wish. Would you like coffee? Tea?'

'No, thank you, m'lady,' said Daisy, settling awkwardly on the edge of a chair.

Cissy just sat with her hands folded on her lap.

'What brings you both here?' asked Lady Hardcastle, cheerfully. 'What can we do for you?'

'It's about Mr Uzzle,' said Cissy, quietly.

'Oh, dear. Is he all right?'

'That's just it, m'lady, we doesn't know.'

'Did he not return last night?' asked the inspector.

'No, sir,' mumbled Cissy. 'He went out last night and he never come back.'

'I see,' he said. 'And how do you know that?'

'Well, sir, our dad drops me off at the pub on his rounds some days, so I'm there early, like. Griff takes delivery of the milk and has a chat with our dad while I gets in and starts work on the cleanin'. But he weren't there. So we asked Mrs Uzzle where he was and she said he weren't back from his appointment and we should mind our own business. But she was all on edge, so our dad said I should come down here and tell you, like. Mrs Uzzle weren't happy about that, but he insisted. By the time I got down here, though, I felt a bit silly so I got our dad to drop me at the butcher's so I could ask Daisy what she thought. And . . . well . . . here we are.'

'Well, we're jolly glad you came, dear, thank you,' said Lady Hardcastle. 'Now, are you sure you won't take some tea? Flo dear, get some extra cups, would you?'

I went to the kitchen to fetch cups and saucers.

Moments later, I returned to the morning room where Daisy was talking.

'. . . think they's connected?' she said.

'With the two of them going missing on the same night, it's a possibility, isn't it?' said Lady Hardcastle. 'And I'm not terribly fond of coincidences. Not ones like that, anyway.'

'You don't think she's done him in?' said Cissy. 'I always thought there was somethin' fishy about her.'

'Again, it's a possibility. What do you think, Inspector?'

'I think I need to get Sergeant Dobson to send Constable Hancock out looking for them,' he said. 'I'll take a drive round the area, as well.'

'Would you think us interfering if we returned to the Mock of Pommey and asked Mrs Uzzle some questions?'

'I'd be most grateful if you would. If you find anything, get word to the sergeant – I'll have him coordinating things at the station in the village.'

'Can I have a lift?' asked Cissy.

'Back to the pub?' asked Lady Hardcastle.

'Yes, please. She'll have my guts for garters if the pub i'n't clean by openin' time.'

'Of course, dear. As long as you don't mind sitting on the luggage rack. We've only two seats, you see?'

'No, I don't mind.'

'I'd better drive,' I said. 'You'll have her off into the hedge on the first bend.'

'She's right,' said Lady Hardcastle. 'She drives like my grandmama, but that can be a blessing when there's a precious cargo on the back.'

With apologies to Edna for leaving her all the clearing up, we were on our way within five minutes.

◆ ◆ ◆

'Faster!' yelled a voice from behind me as I nursed the Rolls carefully along the twisty lanes. I smiled and shook my head as the giggling entreaties continued, but kept my speed steady.

'You could stand to go a little faster, dear,' said Lady Hardcastle. 'Let the girl have a bit of fun.'

I tutted again, and was about to enumerate the many possible dangers of excessive speed when two young farmhands rounded the bend ahead of us on the wrong side of the road, mounted precariously on a single bicycle. I slammed on the brakes and the lads swerved clear, laughing their heads off as they wobbled on towards Littleton Cotterell.

Cissy, meanwhile, was laughing even more loudly than the departing farmhands. She had been catapulted into the cockpit and was lying upside down between Lady Hardcastle and me, with her legs in the air and her skirts round her waist.

'Are you all right, dear?' asked Lady Hardcastle.

'Never better, m'lady,' said Cissy through her giggles. 'Pardon my bloomers.'

We had to get out of the motor car to help her right herself, and it took some amount of pulling and heaving to extricate her from beneath the dashboard. I wanted to check her for injuries, but as soon as she was upright again she just smoothed her dress and hopped once more on to the luggage rack, still wearing the broadest grin.

'Onwards!' she yelled and, as soon as I had the Rolls in gear, onwards we went.

We arrived at Woodworthy without further incident and I parked on the opposite side of the green from the Mock of Pommey, just as we had on our first visit. The sheep had returned and were grazing contentedly. The flock leader eyed us suspiciously for a moment but seemed to recognize us and, with a nod of her horned head, returned to her breakfast.

Cissy hopped gleefully down on to the road, as though being thrown into the footwell of a moving motor car was all in a day's work.

'I hope you don't mind us stopping all the way over here,' I said. 'But I thought it might give us the advantage of a little tiny bit of surprise if Mrs Uzzle didn't hear us pulling up outside.'

'I's just grateful for the ride,' said Cissy. 'Thank you.'

We started to walk across the green.

'Before we go in,' said Lady Hardcastle, 'do you think we might have a quick scout around outside? What's in those sheds, for instance?' She indicated two stone outbuildings beside the pub. 'And is it possible to open the cellar door from out here, or does one have to be inside?'

'As long as Mrs Uzzle don't think I had anythin' to do with it, you can look wherever you likes,' said Cissy. 'I'll just go in like normal, though, if you don't mind – I could do without 'avin' another row. She can be a right mare sometimes.'

'She does seem to be something of a virago,' agreed Lady Hardcastle.

'No, I don't reckon she can be,' said Cissy with a puzzled frown. 'Not after all this time. They's been married for years.'

Lady Hardcastle laughed.

'And the sheds?' she said.

'They's just sheds. One used to be the stable, but when the 'orse died they couldn't afford another one so it just got used for storin' junk. And the cellar door only opens from the inside, sorry.'

'No matter. Thank you, dear. You get yourself back to work and we'll join you presently as though we've dawdled while you hurried eagerly to return to your labours.'

Cissy skipped off and we made our own way, with reasonable but not-too-obvious stealth, to the outbuildings beside the pub. When trying to be inconspicuous it's always best, I feel, not to be too conspicuous about it.

The sheds were secured with the usual chunky, clunky padlocks, and I had the first of them off in a few seconds.

We found spider webs, rat droppings, rusted tools, and the broken wooden handles of two shovels and a pickaxe. There were battered lanterns with cracked glass, and a stack of old beer crates bearing the name of a brewery I knew to have gone out of business while Queen Victoria was still alive. The only thing of any value was a gleamingly well-maintained Rudge-Whitworth ladies' bicycle.

'Once again, I'm not at all certain what I expected to find,' said Lady Hardcastle, 'but I'm quite sure we haven't yet found it.'

'I half expected Griffith Uzzle's corpse,' I said. 'Bludgeoned to death with a skittle.'

'The same thing was on my mind, I have to confess. Though not a skittle. I can't imagine how one might hold it to use it as a weapon – it's such an awkward shape.'

'I'm sure I could find a way.'

'I'm sure you could, dear. That's a handsome-looking bicycle, though, don't you think?'

'Very nice indeed. I still think we should have bicycles.'

'We most definitely should,' she said.

'But I think that's it. If we're quick we can have a look round the other shed before we go in to speak to Mrs Uzzle.'

'Oh, there's no need to rush,' said Lady Hardcastle. 'We shall say we went to look at the church. People never dare doubt one if one says one has been looking at the church.'

'"One",' I said.

'Yes, sorry. Sometimes one's ones run away with one.'

We left the bicycle and the rats and I relocked the padlock.

The other building had once been the stable and was no more tidy. A few items of cracked and neglected tack hung from hooks on the wall, with a cartwheel, two of its spokes missing, leaning beneath them.

Lady Hardcastle poked at a hessian sack in the corner, and I half expected angry rats to come scurrying out to admonish her for disturbing them. Instead there was a metallic clonk from beneath the sack and an 'Ow!' from Lady Hardcastle.

'There's something under there,' I said.

'My bruised toe would tend to agree with you,' she said, crouching down to lift the sacking. 'Hello. And what do you suppose we have here?'

I couldn't see past her.

'The Crown Jewels?' I said. 'A chest containing a map to the lost city of Atlantis?'

'Oh, so much better than that.'

She shuffled aside to reveal a cooper's hammer with an ebony handle and a gleaming, polished head, and a similarly gleaming, ebony-handled billhook complete with a wickedly pointed four-inch spike. She dropped the sacking and stood up.

There was a noise from the doorway behind us.

'And what the bleedin' 'ell do you think you're doin' in my stable?' snarled a woman's voice.

It was Mrs Uzzle. And she was armed with a shotgun.

'Put the gun down, Mrs Uzzle,' said Lady Hardcastle. 'There's no need for that.'

'There's every need when I finds burglars on my property,' said Mrs Uzzle.

'Come to steal your . . .' Lady Hardcastle looked around. 'Perished harness? Your broken wheel?'

'Don't come the clever breeches with me, *my lady*. I has a right to defend my property.'

'You keep emphasizing my title in that impertinent way, dear. I do wish you'd stop. It really is most awfully rude of you.'

'Oh, I'm so sorry, *my lady*. Wouldn't want to be rude to a burglar, now, would we?'

'Do you not see how childish it is? I mean, really. What do you expect to gain by it?'

As I had explained to Miss Caudle as we sat in the garden on Saturday, our working methods were quite simple. Most of our adversaries were aggressive, adrenaline-fuelled thugs of one sort or another who were keyed up for a fight and expected their opponents to take the whole thing as seriously as they did. What they never anticipated was light-hearted inanity and childish taunting, so when we found ourselves in a tight spot, Lady Hardcastle would use her unique talent for infuriating people while I egged her on. This would distract them while I carefully manoeuvred myself into a position where I might exercise some of my own talents and prevent them from hurting her. There was always a danger, of course, that she would irritate them to such an extent that they'd kill her just to shut her up, but human nature is a curious thing. Most people were so confounded by the upending of the expected order of things – the person with the gun should be the one holding the cards, after all – that they found themselves arguing with her rather than simply shooting her.

It was an uncomplicated arrangement but it usually worked.

Usually.

'That's close enough, *Miss Armstrong*,' said Mrs Uzzle, swinging the shotgun round to point it at me.

'It doesn't really have the same effect when you do it to me,' I said. 'I actually *am* Miss Armstrong. It's not like it's an affectation or anything – it's my name.'

Mrs Uzzle frowned and shook her head as though trying to clear it of our nonsense.

'Don't try and get clever with me,' she said, somewhat uncertainly.

'Oh, she doesn't have to try, dear,' said Lady Hardcastle. 'It comes quite naturally. She really is most devastatingly clever, you see? Sharp as a tack. Smart as a whip, as our American cousins have it. Do you know, she once—'

The shotgun swung once more in her direction.

'If I have to tell you to shut up once more, I shall shut you up permanently.'

'If we're being pedantic, dear – and I really think accuracy is very important in these situations for the avoidance of doubt – you haven't actually told me to shut up at all. You gave us some non-sense about defending your property from burglarious ne'er-do-wells in summer dresses, but my silence has never been called for.'

'Well, I'm tellin' you now. Shut—'

My right hand grabbed the barrel of the gun and hoisted it upwards as I drove the open palm of my left into the side of her face. She managed to squeeze the trigger as she fell, but the deafen-ingly loud blast of the gun merely blew off a handful of roof slates and brought a shower of dust down on us.

I wrested the shotgun from her limp fingers and broke it open. I pulled out both the spent and unspent cartridges and put them in the pocket of my jacket.

'Are you all right, my lady?' I said.

'Quite all right, dear, thank you. The roof might be a little less weatherproof than it once was, but I am unharmed.'

Mrs Uzzle groaned woozily.

'Don't point guns at people, *Mrs Uzzle,*' I said. 'Someone *always* gets hurt.'

'She's right, dear,' said Lady Hardcastle. 'It never ends well.'

Mrs Uzzle gingerly felt her face.

'You've broken my cheek, you cow,' she mumbled.

'Oh, don't be such a baby,' I said. 'I barely tapped you. You'll have a black eye by tomorrow but there's no lasting damage. Do at least credit me with knowing how to do my job.'

'I'll bloody kill you,' she said, struggling to get upright.

I pushed her down with my foot.

'Not yet,' I said. 'You just lie there and recover.'

'Well, not *just* that,' said Lady Hardcastle. 'Recovery is important, of course, but while you're taking your ease you might care to spend a few moments trying to explain to us just exactly what on earth's going on.'

'And why would I want to do that?'

'Well, let me see. Your husband is missing. Grace is missing. And until a few moments ago everyone had been assuming that Grace was responsible for the murders of three Weryers. We all thought your husband was next. But that was until we found what I very much suspect are two of the murder weapons hidden under a sack in your shed. At that point I began to change my mind. Just as we were about to leave to summon the police, you stomped in waving your silly gun around – why do you even own such a thing, by the way? I know it's the countryside and everyone seems to think they need one, but you're publicans, not farmers.'

'We have a problem with rats,' said Mrs Uzzle. 'And snooping busybodies.'

'At least that's a little more honest than your claim that you thought us burglars. How do you explain the presence of the murder weapons?'

'I don't see no murder weapons. There's some items of Weryer regalia in here for safekeeping, but no murder weapons.'

'The police surgeon will be able to test for the presence of blood—'

'With phenolphthalein,' I said.

'Oh, I say, dear. Well remembered. The police surgeon will carry out his tests and we'll know soon enough whether the tools have even tiny traces of blood on them. And then what shall we be forced to conclude?'

'You're the detective, *my lady*, you tell me.'

'When I first saw the weapons I immediately began to think we'd been wrong about Grace and that your husband was the killer.

But when you arrived with your blunderbuss I wondered whether it might be you.'

'Now look here—'

'Well, we know it's not Grace Chamberlain.'

'Is that what the little witch is calling herself?'

'It is.'

'And you believe her?'

'We have learned that she was formerly known as Grace Hardiman, of course. We've not been entirely idle. We also know that her father was hanged for the murder of Samuel Puddy in 1891. But as for what she calls herself now . . . that's rather her own affair, I think.'

'She's obviously tryin' to hide her true identity.'

'Well, yes, that's what we thought once we learned of her connection with the original murder. We'd come to believe she was seeking revenge on the witnesses whose testimony had seen her father convicted.'

'So why are you standing there arguing with me instead of out saving my husband?'

'As I say, Mrs Uzzle – the murder weapons and your own attempted assault with a deadly weapon rather altered my opinion.'

'We were just looking after the hammer and billhook. Griff found them at the orchard. They've been missing. The Weryers have been looking everywhere.'

'And rather than keep them in the house until he could tell his fellow Weryers that they were safe and sound, he chose to hide them under an old sack in the shed?'

'He was afraid of burglars.'

'You're both rather afraid of burglars, it would seem. Do you get burgled a lot?'

Mrs Uzzle began to struggle once more to regain her feet.

'We can sort this out,' she said, sitting up but still looking groggy. 'It's all just been a misunderstanding. I'm sorry I pointed the shotgun at you – I was frightened.'

The sudden change of mood was jarring.

'Where has he taken her?' I said, suddenly.

'Where has who taken who?' she asked, her voice calm and reasonable now.

'You're trying to keep us here. Your husband has Grace Chamberlain somewhere and he means to kill her, so you're deliberately delaying us so he can get on with it. Where?'

'I'm sure I haven't the first idea what you're talking about.'

I stepped forwards and grabbed her arm, twisting it into a painful lock. She tried to swat at me with her free hand but I held fast.

'If I twist like this,' I said, gently demonstrating, 'I can dislocate your elbow.'

She yelped and I relaxed my grip.

'But if I twist like this' – again I demonstrated – 'I can dislocate your shoulder. Either on its own would be very painful. Both together would be excruciating. And it's been such a long time since I had to do it to someone that I'm not at all sure I remember how to put them back. You'd be in agony until we could get you a doctor.'

I twisted a little harder.

'Bugger off,' she said.

I twisted in the other direction.

'The cider mill,' she gasped. 'He's at the cider mill.'

'Thank you,' said Lady Hardcastle, picking up the shotgun. 'Come along, Armstrong, we need to hurry.'

We left Mrs Uzzle nursing her arm and hurried outside, where we collided at once with Cissy Slocomb.

'Oops,' said Lady Hardcastle. 'Sorry, dear. We're in a bit of a rush. Mrs Uzzle is in a small amount of pain—'

'I heard,' said Cissy.

'She shouldn't be too much trouble, but keep your wits about you. Does anyone out here have a telephone?'

'They just got one installed in the pub a few months ago. It's in their flat upstairs but I doesn't know how to use it.'

'It's really quite straightforward, dear. You just lift the earpiece, jiggle the doo-dah a few times, and when the operator answers you just . . .' Lady Hardcastle saw Cissy's pained expression and decided to try a different tack. 'Not to worry, we'll think of something else. You're a proficient cyclist, aren't you, dear?'

'You knows I am – you seen me. But I a'n't got mine with me.'

'A minor concern. Take Mrs Uzzle's and get to Littleton Cotterell as fast as you can. Tell Sergeant Dobson that we believe Uzzle is at the cider mill with Grace Chamberlain. We're on our way there now.'

'The bicycle's locked in the shed, though. They's afraid of burglars.'

'They really are, aren't they? Flo will take care of it, dear, don't worry. But for heaven's sake, do hurry. I fear Miss Chamberlain is in danger.'

It was the work of a moment to get the shed door open again, and we helped Cissy on her way with a hearty shove.

At a run, placidly observed by the grazing sheep, we returned to the Rolls and set off for the cidery with Lady Hardcastle at the wheel.

The lanes were narrow and our speed excessive, but I made no complaint as we hurtled along. I appreciated the need for haste and, despite my usual nagging, was actually rather confident of Lady Hardcastle's ability to get us there quickly and safely. It was making me more than a tiny bit nervous, though, so I distracted myself by taking off my jacket and folding it neatly on the floor beside the shotgun. There was the possibility of a scuffle in our near future and I wanted to be as unencumbered as possible.

We arrived in one piece in what might very well have been record time, had records of the journey between Woodworthy and Mattick's Cidery ever been kept.

The courtyard was empty as we squealed to a halt. Lady Hardcastle stopped the Rolls to one side of the huge main doors so that we could approach them indirectly. The doors were partially open, which meant there was almost certainly someone inside. They had probably arrived on the battered old bicycle leaning against the wall.

The Silver Ghost's engine purred to a stop and the reassuringly luxurious sound of Rolls-Royce engineering was replaced by the unceasing noise of the countryside. City-dwellers imagine the country to be a place of peace and quiet, but it's nothing of the sort. The trees rustle in the wind, insects hum, and the birds – there are so many birds – never, ever shut up. My ornithological knowledge was still limited but I knew that sparrows were by far the worst, chirping angrily at each other in the hedgerows. The chattering of a blackbird as it takes flight or the endless cooing of amorous wood-pigeons can give them a run for their money, as can the screech of a swift or the yapping of jackdaws and magpies. It sometimes made me nostalgic for the endless clatter of cartwheels on cobbled streets, and the cries of street vendors.

We alighted and moved cautiously to either side of the open doors. I looked in but could see nothing unusual. Lady Hardcastle, though, had spotted something. She silently signalled that she would enter and that I should follow.

She stepped with her customary nimbleness through the door and I saw her put her finger to her lips as she cleared the threshold. My job in these situations was to guard the rear, keeping an eye open for danger coming from behind. Lady Hardcastle would enter the dangerous place, often armed, and all I had to do was watch her back. It usually worked splendidly.

Usually.

I was turning to check that there were no threats to our rear, but other than a blinding explosion of pain at the back of my head, I remember nothing else.

Chapter Nineteen

I came to, reasonably proficiently tied, lying on a wooden slab. I tested my bonds by wiggling my fingers and made contact with another hand. We might be in trouble, but at least Lady Hardcastle and I were still together. I opened my eyes.

I could see a massive iron screw. My head screamed in protest as I turned to look up, but I saw what I expected to see: another wooden slab, stained with decades of apple juice. We were in the steam-powered cider press.

I tapped a message on Lady Hardcastle's hand in our personal code.

'It's all right, dear, he's outside,' she said. 'He's round the back trying to start the steam engine. He has a plan, apparently.'

'What the hell happened?' I croaked.

'He was hiding round the back of the building when we arrived. There's a telephone here – do you remember? Mattick used it to call the police station. So dear, sweet Betty telephoned to say we were on our way. He heard the Rolls and waited till we'd started inside, then he sneaked up on us from behind, armed with the shotgun we'd taken from his wife – I shouldn't have left it in the Rolls. You took the butt of it to the back of your tiny head, then he pointed the loud end at me, and here we are.'

'It's not loaded, though,' I said.

'He took the cartridge from your jacket pocket. It's just the one, but a single shot from one of those ghastly things is enough.'

'Oh, for heaven's sake. I'm so sorry. I was expecting trouble inside – I hadn't thought he'd be outside.'

'Not to worry. We've been in trickier scrapes. And poor Grace has it worse. She's balancing on top of a barrel with a noose around her neck.'

'Why hasn't he killed her?'

'He was all set to do just that when his wife telephoned. It seems there's a new plan. We are to be crushed in the cider press and then Grace, racked with guilt at all the terrible things she's done, will hang herself.'

'How do you know all this?'

'He's quite a voluble fellow, and rather pleased with himself. I just asked a few simple questions and it all came tumbling out.'

'And why did he do it?'

'We didn't get that far, I'm afraid. The telephone rang again and after a few "yes, ma'ams", he scuttled out to try to get the steam engine lit.'

'That's a shame.'

'It is, but I'm sure we'll get to the bottom of it. And speaking of bottoms, would you keep yours still for a moment, please – I think I might be able to make some progress with this knot.'

'It was me,' came a woman's voice from behind me.

'We thought perhaps it might have had something to do with you, dear,' said Lady Hardcastle as she fiddled with the ropes at my wrists. 'Which is why we were so keen to speak to you.'

'Our dad didn't kill Sam Puddy,' said Grace Chamberlain, defiantly. 'Our ma knew it. And they all knew it, too, those Weryers. They knew he was innocent, but they all lied in court. Our ma spent her whole life trying to clear his name. She died last month, still saying he didn't do it, so I decided to come up here and find out the truth.'

'And what did you find?'

'Nothing. Every time I went to talk to one of the "witnesses" they were dead. And then you were snooping around me, too, getting in my way.'

'We might have been able to help you if only you'd let us.'

'Well, I didn't know that, did I?'

'No, dear, no you didn't. But now isn't the time for recriminations. We have to get us all out of this tiresome predicament we find ourselves in. Oh, I say.'

'What now?' I said.

'We should have known right from the start that dear Grace was familiar with Littleton Cotterell. Do you remember that first day we met her and she said, "Does the pub still have rooms?" *Still* have rooms, do you see? She must have known that it had rooms in the past. Oh, I feel such a fool.'

'You look like a fool, too,' said Uzzle, gleefully. He had returned and I could hear the wheeze of the steam engine outside in the shed as it built up its deadly pressure. 'But don't worry, no one will see your shame. They won't even be able to recognize you once Miss Chamberlain has crushed you to death.'

'Well, that's a comfort, at least,' said Lady Hardcastle. 'One does so hate to look foolish.'

'Well, aren't you the cool one?' he said. 'Betty can't stand you, but I always had a soft spot for you, I must say.'

I could hear him moving around and he came into my eyeline, one hand on the control lever of the cider press. He grinned at me and winked.

'Since we're not long for this world,' said Lady Hardcastle, 'would you indulge the condemned with an explanation of just what the blithering blue blazes is going on here?'

'I don't see why not,' he said, still grinning. 'It all started in the spring of 1891, when my beautiful young wife took a fancy to Sam Puddy, the local timber merchant. He was a handsome man, and rather well off, and she quite fell for his charms. She told me what she was up to, of course—'

'And you didn't object?'

'Why should I object? I enjoyed the thought of it. She rules the roost, as they say, and what she wants, she gets. She loves me, and I love her, and I know she'll always be by my side. If she wants to dally with other men, then who am I to say no?'

'Well, I mean—'

'Do you want me to tell you or not? If you're just going to keep interrupting, I'd just as soon get on with more pressing matters.'

'No, do please carry on. I'm all ears.'

'She enjoyed her affairs – she's had many over the years—'

'She's a beautiful woman.'

'She is, indeed. But she always wanted them on her own terms. When she tired of her conquests she told them to sling their hooks and off they went. Except, poor Sam Puddy was smitten. Utterly besotted. And he wouldn't go quietly. He began pestering her, begging her to leave me and run away with him. Well, she couldn't have that, now, could she?'

'I suppose not. And so she killed him?'

'Good lord, no. Why would she dirty her hands with something like that when she could just tell me to do it? No, I arranged to meet him, to sort things out man to man. He agreed at once. He thought he might persuade me to let her go. We said we'd meet out of sight in the field behind his house at midnight. I arrived early, of course, and jumped him as soon as he came out of his back door. He died quietly enough, and I was home and in bed with Betty before his body was cold.'

'And then you persuaded the others to lie in court and swear that it was a quarrel over money and that William Hardiman was to blame.'

'Betty persuaded them. She can be very persuasive.'

'I'm sure. And then Grace arrived in the village and . . .'

'We recognized her at once, of course. She was always such a pretty little girl, I'm sure we'd have known her for the woman she's become, even without that birthmark on her temple. And we knew. And with the anniversary approaching, the others began to go soft on me. A "crisis of conscience", Claud Cridland called it. They were threatening to go to the police, to admit they'd lied.'

'And you couldn't have that.'

'Betty couldn't have that at all. Like I said, she loves me. She didn't want to see me hanged, so she told me I had to get rid of Cridland and warn the others off. I knew he'd be at the orchard just after dawn, checking his precious apples, so I took the Sax of the Pomary and the Martel of the Rundlet from the display case at the Weryer Lodge and . . . and I killed him. There was a scuffle, but he succumbed in the end. And I dragged the body—'

'To the third tree in the ninth row to signify the third day of the ninth month – the date of the original murder.'

'It was Betty's idea. We needed to give them a message, you see. To make them aware of the consequences of speaking out. Sadly, they weren't nearly so clever as you and they didn't work it out at all. We tried to be a bit more obvious with Peppard and the salt and pepper pots, but Mattick still didn't twig. Or he didn't seem to, anyway. We gave him plenty of chances to reassure us that he wasn't going to go to the police, but he just played dumb so he had to go, too. I miss those salt and pepper pots – they were a wedding present.'

'But with all your co-conspirators dead, why leave the Hardiman clue with Mattick's body?'

'Betty realized we could lay the blame on Grace. If we made it even more obvious that it was all connected to Puddy's murder, we could suggest that she'd come up here seeking revenge for her father's hanging. She's written a tearful note explaining everything. Or Betty has, at any rate. No one will check the handwriting.'

'That's all very ingenious,' said Lady Hardcastle. 'But why would she have killed us and let you go free? Surely she'd want to get all the prosecution witnesses.'

'Because you stumbled upon her plan. She had to kill you to . . . to . . .'

'No, dear,' said Lady Hardcastle, 'it just doesn't make sense. The police aren't nearly so stupid as you suppose. They'll not be convinced that she had any reason to kill us if she was already planning to take her own life. Especially not since she would leave you unharmed.'

'Ah, but you're assuming that by the time she's discovered I'll still be unharmed. Betty will take care of that. She'll make it look convincing.'

'I'm sure she will.'

'Is your curiosity satisfied now?'

'Quite satisfied, thank you, dear,' she said. 'You may proceed.'

He laughed. 'Arrogant to the last. I can see why Betty dislikes you, but I have to say I admire you in a way.'

He pulled the control lever and the two giant screws began to turn, bringing the press plate slowly towards us.

◆ ◆ ◆

The plate descended slowly, but I took little comfort from that. Lady Hardcastle had taught me enough about mechanics for me to know that there was usually a choice in machines between strong and fast. The plate might not be moving quickly, but that meant that the steam engine's power was being used to produce the maximum crushing force. When it finally reached us, the plate would squash us slowly but very thoroughly to an unrecognizable pulp. And there would be no way for us to fight against it – it was too strong to be stopped by mere humans.

Luckily, it wasn't just the machine we had to fight against. We had been placed in it by a human, and humans can always be defeated.

I was greatly relieved that Uzzle had turned out to be such a windbag. While he'd been needlessly telling us everything, Lady Hardcastle's nimble fingers had loosened my bonds sufficiently that my hands were free.

I had to choose my moment. Even the most slow-witted person can shove a struggling woman back into a cider press if he has time to act, so I had to be patient. Patience wasn't easy with the press plate already only inches above us, but I had to wait.

Just a little longer.

The plate was close enough now that Lady Hardcastle was having to try to twist her body to get clear of it, and I knew I had to take my chance.

Finally, Uzzle turned his back on us to finish the murder of Grace Chamberlain. I reached out to grab the edge of the slab and, with a mighty heave, pulled myself free. With my ankles still tied, I landed awkwardly but I managed to twist myself round to see the crushing plate now in contact with Lady Hardcastle's upper arm.

I grabbed the shoulders of her dress and tried to haul her free of the press. I felt the ripping as a couple of seams gave way and somehow my mind decided it had time to contemplate the repair job that awaited me when she and the dress were home.

As she thudded noisily to the floor, Uzzle finally realized what was happening.

He turned away from Grace and rushed towards us.

I left Lady Hardcastle trying to wriggle to safety on the stone-flagged floor, and flipped on to my back. In a few short moments I considered many options for our defence, but Uzzle's own inexperience made my decision easy. He wasn't a fighter and, like all non-fighters, considered his size his principal advantage. He imagined that he could simply overwhelm us with speed and bulk and return to his work.

I, on the other hand, had other ideas.

As he closed in, I drew my knees towards my chest and waited another split second until his leading leg was straight. I thrust my bound ankles towards his knee. I felt the sickening, grinding crack of breaking bone and tearing ligaments, but the sound of it was drowned out by his scream.

His momentum carried him forwards but I managed to roll clear, and he pitched headlong into a barrel, knocking himself unconscious. Sitting up, I freed my legs and left Lady Hardcastle to wriggle a little more while I hopped up on to the barrel to free Grace from her noose. I untied her wrists and helped her down before freeing Lady Hardcastle.

As we all three checked ourselves and each other for damage, we heard a motor car arriving outside. Inspector Sunderland had arrived just in time.

Once he had ascertained that Grace, Lady Hardcastle and I were all right, Inspector Sunderland used the cidery's telephone to call for Dr Fitzsimmons. Uzzle's right leg was badly damaged and he would have to spend the first few weeks of his incarceration in hospital. I tried very hard to feel remorse but I just couldn't summon the requisite emotion. He had killed four people over the past twenty years and had been in the process of trying to kill three more. If it took a smashed knee to stop him, then so be it.

Constable Hancock was standing guard over Uzzle while we waited for the doctor, not that he was going anywhere. The inspector took a statement from Grace while Lady Hardcastle and I kept discreetly out of the way in the corner and, when he had finished, Lady Hardcastle beckoned him over to us.

'How is she?' she asked.

'Rather shaken up, as you can imagine,' he said.

'Only too well. I know you have to see to Uzzle, but you don't really need us here, do you? I thought one of us could take her back to our house, or even the pub if she prefers. She could do with a nice cup of tea and a sit-down. She needs someone to look after her while she has a good cry.'

'That's a very kind thought, my lady. Perhaps you could do it?'

'Oh, of course. I was going to suggest Flo – she's nearer her own age – but if you think . . .'

'I do. She's taken something of a liking to you. She couldn't stop singing your praises.'

'But it was dear Flo who did all the hard work.'

'It always is,' he said with a smile. 'Nevertheless, she seems to admire you. I think she needs a mother figure—'

'Grandmother figure, more like,' I said.

'I keep telling you, I'm the disreputable-aunt figure,' said Lady Hardcastle. 'I'm only forty-three.' She turned to Inspector Sunderland. 'I'm forty-three, Inspector, that's all.'

He chuckled. 'You don't look a day over forty-two, my lady. But regardless of age, I think she needs someone to look after her.'

'I agree. I shall invite her back to the house.'

'Good idea,' I said. 'I'll make my own way home later. You won't mind dropping me off, will you, Inspector?'

'Not at all. In fact, I'd welcome your assistance with something, if you wouldn't mind.'

'Always happy to help the local gendarmes,' I said. 'Never hurts to have friends in the rozzers.'

'You'll always have friends in the rozzers, Miss Armstrong, don't worry about that.'

◆ ◆ ◆

Lady Hardcastle took Grace out to the Rolls. I had thought Grace to be aloof and self-assured when we first met her less than two weeks before, but now she seemed fragile and small. The confident woman was still there, but so was the little girl who had lost her father to a cowardly man and had lived twenty years in the shadow of the shame he had brought on her family.

The cowardly man in question was ministered to by a professional but entirely unsentimental Dr Fitzsimmons before being loaded on to his carriage and transported back to the police station in the care of Constable Hancock.

I assisted Inspector Sunderland in gathering the ropes that had been used to bind us and the one that had been fashioned into a noose for Grace, and placed them in the boot of his motor car.

'Is this what you wanted me for?' I asked with a grin. 'I know I'm a dab hand at tidying up, but . . .'

He laughed.

'I need to arrest Mrs Betty Uzzle,' he said. 'From what you told me, she's an accessory at the very least.'

'And a nasty piece of work.'

'I'll have to take your word for that. I met her when I interviewed her husband a few days ago and I found her to be utterly charming.'

'You need to be careful there,' I said. 'You're exactly the sort of chap she goes for.'

He chuckled again.

'I rather doubt that,' he said. 'I'm not the sort of chap anyone goes for, much less a beautiful woman like that.'

I gave him a puzzled frown but said nothing.

'Anyway,' he said. 'After hearing your account of Uzzle's story, I get the impression that she wouldn't take a blind bit of notice of any orders given her by a mere man, even if he does have a warrant card issued by the Bristol Constabulary.'

'She won't take any notice of me, either,' I said. 'She's not the sort to take orders from anyone.'

'Perhaps not. But I'm both ethically and professionally prohibited from giving the arrogant so-and-so a smack in the chops if she decides to cause trouble . . .'

'I understand you completely, Inspector,' I said. 'Have no fear. I have no such qualms. In fact, after everything she's put me through today, she'll be lucky if I don't belt her one just for the pleasure of it.'

'I shall be looking the other way if you do, thank you.'

'Would you like a hand starting your motor car again?'

'If you wouldn't mind, that would be most welcome. No one else ever helps me with that.'

'Not even Dr Gosling?'

He clambered into the driver's seat and then held up his hands.

'Surgeon's hands, dear boy,' he said in a passable impersonation of his friend. 'Can't risk the tools of the trade.'

I laughed and cranked the engine to life before hopping in beside him.

◆ ◆ ◆

We arrived at Woodworthy to find the Mock of Pommey closed and no one in sight. There never seemed to be anyone abroad in Woodworthy, with the only sign of life out of doors being the Jacob sheep on the green, but the pub was usually open and the sounds of conversation and laughter from within would give the reassurance that this wasn't some eerily deserted ghost village.

Inspector Sunderland hammered on the pub door with the side of his fist.

After a few moments we heard the clatter of a key in the lock and the sound of several bolts being drawn.

The door opened a crack, but from where I was standing I wasn't able to see who was there. The voice told me, though.

'Oh, Inspector,' said Betty Uzzle. 'Thank goodness you're here. I didn't know what to do. That Chamberlain girl has Griff. I think she means to kill him. Look what she did to me when she came here looking for him.'

She opened the door a little wider and stepped out into the sunlight, indicating the blossoming bruise on her face. She looked almost as tiny as Grace had – the perfect damsel in distress. Until she caught sight of me, that is. The timid expression was replaced by one of shock, and then she seemed to grow back to her normal stature.

'You,' she snarled.

'Yes,' I said, sweetly. 'Me. Still alive. Still kicking. That must be quite a surprise after what you told Griff to do to me.' I turned to the inspector. 'Grace didn't cause the bruise, by the way. That was me.'

'You hear that?' she said. 'She admits assaulting me. I want her arrested.'

'I'm so sorry, Mrs Uzzle,' said the inspector, 'there was a bee buzzing in my ear. I didn't hear a thing. But you'll be relieved to know that your husband is alive and well, as are the three women you told him to kill. He sustained some injuries but he's in police custody and on his way to the Bristol Royal Infirmary.'

'It was all him. I had nothing to do with it.'

'We shall let the courts decide that. Elizabeth Uzzle, I am arresting you as an accessory in the murders of Samuel Puddy, Claud Cridland, Moses Peppard, and Abel Mattick, and as an accessory in the attempted murders of Grace Chamberlain, Emily, Lady Hardcastle, and Florence Armstrong. You have the right to remain silent. You do not have to say anything, but anything you do say will be taken down and may be given in evidence.'

There was a flurry of movement as she stepped back inside the pub and slammed the door. We heard the bolts being shot and the key turning in the lock.

'This will just count against you, Mrs Uzzle,' called Inspector Sunderland. 'Open the door.'

There was no response.

The inspector sighed.

'Would you do me a service and wait here, please, Miss Armstrong,' he said. 'I'll go round the back. If she sees me and decides to scarper out this way . . . Well, I leave it to your discretion, but don't damage her too badly, will you. If I look the other way too much I'll be in danger of dislocating my poor neck.'

'Leave it to me, Inspector,' I said. 'I can be subtle.'

He set off towards the outbuildings and the rear of the pub, while I positioned myself against the wall so that I couldn't be seen from inside. After a moment's thought, I moved to the other side of the door so that, as before, I'd be partially concealed if she opened it and peeked out.

I relaxed and watched the sheep. They're peculiar creatures, sheep. They're soft and woolly, and as timid as a junior chambermaid, but they have evil little faces. And with the terrifying curly horns of the Jacobs, the Woodworthy sheep would surely haunt my nightmares were they not already full of cows.

I paused in my contemplation of malevolent livestock to ready myself for the imminent arrival of the malevolent wife of a murderous innkeeper, as the clonks of the door's heavy bolts cut through the sound of summer birdsong.

Betty Uzzle wasn't used to fleeing – I judged she was more the stand-her-ground-and-stare-her-enemies-down sort of a woman. She gave her surroundings only the most cursory of glances and didn't notice me at all until I was upon her.

By the time the inspector returned she was lying prone on the ground with her wrists neatly bound with a ribbon I'd taken from her hair. As an extra flourish, I'd tied a bow in it.

'Present for you, Inspector,' I said as he approached.

'Thank you, Miss Armstrong,' he said. 'That's just what I wanted. How did you know?'

He replaced the ribbon with a pair of police-issue darbies, and together we hauled her into the back of his motor car.

The journey back to Littleton Cotterell was a swift, and mercifully quiet, one. The fight had finally gone out of Betty Uzzle and she sat silently in the back seat of the motor car, staring sullenly out of the window.

As we approached the village green, I asked the inspector if he wouldn't mind dropping me off at the pub.

'I can't see the Rolls,' I said, 'but Grace might have insisted on being left here. I'd like to check on her if she did. And if she didn't, it's but the shortest walk back to the house.'

'As you wish, miss,' he said, pulling over. 'Thank you for your help today. And over the past two weeks, actually. I'll call on you tomorrow to take your statements.'

'It's an honour to be allowed to help, Inspector. I only wish we'd fathomed it all out much sooner – we might have saved those other men.'

There was a derisive 'Hah!' from the back seat.

'Are you sure I can't hit her?' I said as I got out.

'Few things would give me more satisfaction,' he said, 'but we'll let the courts deal with her now. She'll get what's coming to her.'

She was sneering out of the car window at me as I made my way to the Dog and Duck.

Daisy was sweeping the old sawdust from the floor of the public bar as I entered.

'All right, Flo,' she said. ''Ow's it goin'? Caught any villains lately?'

'One or two,' I said. 'I take it you've seen Herself?'

'Not this afternoon. Sergeant Dobson dropped in. Full of it, he was. You'd've thought he'd caught Uzzle hisself from the way he was goin' on. I'm glad you's all right, mind.'

'Takes more than a couple of murderous bedlamites to put me down, Dais, you know that.'

'Takes three, at least.'

'At least. Can you let me into Grace Chamberlain's room?'

'Course. Why?'

'If they didn't stop here, it looks like Lady Hardcastle has persuaded her to stay with us for a while. I'll settle her bill and then I'd like to get her things so she can be comfortable.'

Daisy stopped brushing and looked at me.

'I forgets how kind you are sometimes,' she said, fondly.

'I'm what?'

'Never mind. Come on, you – let's get Miss Chamberlain's carpet bag packed up.'

Chapter Twenty

We spent a quiet afternoon and evening with Grace. She ate very little at dinnertime, but she did at least eat. She said almost nothing and we didn't pressure her to.

She did, though, sing. After dinner we sat in the drawing room, reading by lamplight. After a while, Lady Hardcastle put down her book and settled herself at the piano where she began to play. As usual, she had no particular pieces in mind, she just sauntered lazily from tune to tune as the mood took her. When she started to play Schubert's 'Nacht und Träume', Grace joined in. She had a beautiful contralto voice, and I put down my own book and shut my eyes as I listened. It was one of those glorious, spontaneous moments that could never be anticipated or repeated, and I found myself deeply moved. I don't believe in magic, but there's definitely something magical in the air when musicians perform together.

When the song ended and the last notes died away, we all sat for a few moments in silence, with only the ticking of the hall clock to tell us that time hadn't stopped completely.

Lady Hardcastle played a good many more pieces, but Grace had returned to her book and said nothing more until we all said goodnight and she retired to her guest room.

◆ ◆ ◆

By the time I rose on Saturday morning, Grace was already sitting in the drawing room, reading a book.

'Good morning, Grace,' I said. 'Did you sleep at all?'

'Not well,' she said. 'But I'm very grateful for the room. Thank you. That bed is wonderful. Old Joe is nice enough but the Dog and Duck was never what you might call homely. It's neat and tidy, but you couldn't say it was properly comfortable.'

'No. I stayed there for a night myself once.'

'But you only live round the corner.'

'It was for a case. I was attacked by a ghost while I was there.'

'You were not,' she said, admonishingly.

'Well . . . I ought to write some of these stories down, actually. We've had some interesting adventures since we've lived here.'

'"Interesting" isn't a word I'll use if I ever tell anyone what happened to us yesterday. I'll never be able to thank you both enough for saving me.'

'It was the very least we could do,' I said. 'We should never have let it get that far in the first place.'

'I didn't help. I . . . I just didn't think I could trust anyone here. Our ma always said both villages were in on it. They knew what the Weryers were up to, she said, and they were all part of getting our dad convicted. So when you two started nosing around, and those girls at the pub . . .'

'Cissy and Daisy are all right,' I said with a smile.

'I know that now, but that Cissy's father is a Weryer. I thought if I let anyone know who I was or what I was looking for, they'd clam up at the very least. At worst . . . well . . . you saw what happened at worst.'

'Which is exactly why I said we should have worked it all out sooner.'

'What's done is done,' she said. 'And I'll get my day in court. I'm going to petition . . . whoever it is you petition, to get our dad posthumously pardoned.'

'I hope you manage it,' I said.

'They can't un-hang him,' she said, 'but they need to acknowledge that he wasn't guilty. They don't even have to say they were wrong – they can say they got it right based on what they knew, but they were lied to. I don't care, as long as it says in the public record that he didn't kill Sam Puddy.'

'You'll have a fight on your hands,' I said. 'No one likes admitting they were wrong, and the Establishment likes it even less, but if there's anything we can do to help, you need only say. Lady Hardcastle knows people. Some quite powerful people, as it happens. And if they're no good, she knows people who have the ear of other powerful people. It's not like you're asking for a special favour; you're asking to amend the record to correct a terrible miscarriage of justice.'

'Thank you. I don't know why on earth you'd want to help me, but I'm grateful for it.'

'Think nothing of it. It's what we do. Are you comfortable talking about what happened?'

'On Thursday?'

'Yes. Inspector Sunderland called on you at the Dog and Duck – he was all set to accuse you of the murders – but you weren't there. We went to the Mock of Pommey to warn Uzzle, but he wasn't there, either. We saw Betty Uzzle and tried to get her to pass on a message but she gave us short shrift and we came home.'

'"Accuse" me?'

'Of course. We'd discovered your real name – Miss Caudle has a friend at the *Dawlish Gazette* and he recognized your description.'

She touched the birthmark at her temple.

'This is a bit of a giveaway,' she said. 'As if the red hair wasn't enough.'

'So we knew the story of the Weryer Murder, and who you were – we put them together and presumed you were up here for revenge on the men who got your father hanged.'

'I was just looking for answers. And that was why I got a village lad to take a message to the Mock of Pommey on Thursday. Uzzle was the last one of them and I needed to know what he had to say. I got a note back at lunchtime telling me to meet him at the cidery at five o'clock. I got there on time but there was no one about. I hung around for a quarter of an hour but it didn't look like he was going to show up so I made to leave. The next thing I knew there was an old sack over my head and I was tied up and dragged inside. He left me there overnight.'

'You're lucky he didn't do away with you there and then,' I said.

'I was terrified he would, I can tell you. But now I know a little more about the Uzzles, I don't reckon he had permission to act on his own. I think he went back to ask for instructions. And then in the morning . . . well, you saw what he did in the morning.'

'We did. You're going to have to go through all this again with the police, and again at the trial, so it's good that you remember. But don't dwell on it. None of it is your fault and there was nothing you could have done differently to stop it.'

'That's easy to say . . .'

'I know. But cling to it. It will save you from destructive doubt and self-recrimination.'

'I shall try.'

'Good,' I said with a reassuring smile. 'Now, then. About this time in the morning I usually make Herself a round of toast and a cup of coffee and take it up to her. Would you like something now or would you rather wait for breakfast?'

'That's not breakfast?'

'No, that's become known as her "starter breakfast". The real thing comes later, once she's had a chance to come to.'

'I'm not sure I could eat two breakfasts. Would you be offended if I waited?'

'Not at all. Will you take coffee, at least?'

'I prefer tea first thing. That coffee we had last night was delicious, mind you.'

'We get it from Crane's in Bristol. Crane himself is a horrible little man – we had a run-in with him last year – but his coffee is first-rate. You should take a pound or two with you when you go.'

'Thank you. I think I read about Crane in the newspaper – I keep an archive of them at the library. No one ever looks at it but I always feel it might be useful one day.'

'We'll have to introduce you to the librarian at Chipping Bevington before you leave with your coffee. You and she are of one mind when it comes to the saving of old newspapers.'

'It's always useful to meet people in my line of work. Do you need a hand?'

'No, I can manage some tea and coffee – that's very much in *my* line of work. You just relax. Miss Jones will be here soon to take care of the real breakfast.'

I left her to return to her book and got to work in the kitchen.

Inspector Sunderland called round to take our statements shortly before lunch, then we spent a lazy Saturday afternoon in the garden, with both Lady Hardcastle and dear, sweet Grace mocking my botanical ignorance.

After dinner we retired once more to the drawing room, where this time the mood was much jollier. I was persuaded to play the banjo and we giggled our way through a selection of popular songs.

Grace's voice was just as well suited to music hall as to Austrian Romanticism, and she even knew additional – hilariously filthy – verses to a couple of our favourites.

Sunday was the day of the Harvest Festival.

Having never managed to attend the event before, we were unsure of the programme or the protocol, but Lady Farley-Stroud had said that the procession was at noon, so we strolled out to the village green together shortly after half past eleven, dressed for celebration.

The canvas-covered, timber-framed construction had been bedecked with ribbon and bunting, with corn wreaths hanging above the huge opening. Villagers in costumes were assembling behind a large farm wagon, ready for the procession. The two enormous Shire horses pulling the wagon were wearing woven corn decorations of their own, and the bed of the wagon was heaped with all manner of fruit and vegetables.

The villagers' costumes ranged from old-fashioned smocks and red neckerchiefs, to animals – the stag I liked, the cows not so much – and one particularly eerie representation of the Green Man. Children were in their Sunday clothes for the most part – several of the girls had garlands of flowers in their hair – though one was an apple and one was some sort of generic root vegetable.

'What's that lad dressed as?' I asked as we crossed the green to where Cissy and Daisy were standing.

'Mangel-wurzel,' said Grace.

'You're pulling my leg,' I said. 'That's not a word.'

'It's a type of beet used as cattle and pig feed,' said Lady Hardcastle. 'It's from the German *Mangoldwurzel*.'

'Is it, by crikey?'

'It is. It's astonishing the things one picks up.'

'Consider me astonished and not a little impressed.'

We approached my old friends.

'How do, Dais,' I said. 'Cissy.'

'Afternoon, all,' said Daisy. 'Finally made it for the Harvest Festival, then?'

'Finally,' said Lady Hardcastle. 'If it's always as marvellous as this, I shall be sure to try to come every year.'

'Oh, if you think this is marvellous, you wait till later. There's dances and all sorts.'

Cissy put a hand on Grace's arm.

'Are you all right, Grace?' she asked. 'I sort of feels a bit responsible with it all goin' on under my nose at the pub, like.'

'Don't be silly,' said Grace. 'You couldn't have known.'

'But still.' Cissy withdrew her hand and gave a shrugging smile. ''Ere, can we get you a drink? I knows the barmaid – we might get a discount.'

'That would be lovely, thank you.'

The three younger women walked off towards the pub, leaving us to watch the procession alone.

'I think she'll have some difficult times ahead,' said Lady Hardcastle as we watched them go, 'but she seems like a resilient girl. I think she'll be all right.'

'I think so, too,' I said.

As the church clock struck twelve, a tambourine trilled outside the fire-damaged village hall, and the assembled villagers formed into a more orderly line behind the wagon. With another tambourine roll, the procession set off around the green, accompanied by Fred Spratt on the fiddle and Sergeant Dobson – out of uniform and wearing, instead, the ubiquitous smock and neckerchief – on tin whistle.

They proceeded twice round the green, clapped and cheered on their way by the rest of the villagers – many of whom threw flowers on to the wagon – before disappearing up the road beside the church.

'That was short and sweet,' said Lady Hardcastle as the last little girl ran to catch up with the rest of the procession, proudly clutching a flower she'd retrieved from the road.

'There's more to come,' I said. 'Daisy mentioned dancing, don't forget.'

'How could I? I love a country dance. I remember a rather dour Scottish governess trying to teach me Strip the Willow and the Dashing White Sergeant. I'm sure English country dancing will be just as much fun.'

'You may yet be disappointed,' I said. 'Look.'

The seven remaining Weryers – Noel Gregory had been gaoled for six months by the magistrate – were walking towards the middle of the green, led by Cornelius Starks. They were dressed in black knee breeches with white silk stockings and buckled shoes. Their shirts were white, and their waistcoats the same red as the ceremonial robes we had seen at the orchard. They each wore sashes over their shoulders and across their bodies, coloured to signify their rank – Starks's in gold; the six Custodians, red. On their heads they each wore a crown, woven, I presumed, from the finer branches of the apple trees. They carried wooden staves in their right hands.

They lined up in two rows, facing each other, and a man I thought I recognized from the Mock of Pommey approached carrying a concertina.

The dance involved a lot of complex weaving about and the banging of sticks. I felt certain it would have been a great deal more impressive with twelve of them, but with three dead and two in gaol, they had to make do.

There was something about the dance that spoke of centuries of tradition, and I found myself hoping they'd weather the current storm and manage to rebuild their membership. Inspector Sunderland had spoken with admiration of their good works, and it would be a shame if the past fortnight's events – and the memory of the twenty-year-old murder – put an end to it all. Some traditions were worth preserving.

◆ ◆ ◆

By the time we were all summoned into the – it wasn't a marquee, exactly, but I shall call it that for convenience – by the time we were all assembled in the marquee for supper, it was eight o'clock and I was absolutely starving. It was lit with dozens of lanterns and I briefly worried that the whole thing might go up in flames, but it did look very pretty.

I had imagined that the evening would be a very egalitarian affair, with long communal tables and the whole village celebrating together, but I had reckoned without Lady Farley-Stroud. The long tables were there, but so was a 'top table' where she and Sir Hector sat with the vicar and Mrs Bland, Cornelius Starks and a lady I presumed to be his wife. There were two empty chairs. I had been hoping we might sit with Daisy, Cissy and Grace, who were in the middle of one of the long tables and laughing fit to burst at something one of them had said. I was moving to join them, but my hopes, as I feared they might be, were dashed when Lady Farley-Stroud caught sight of us and beckoned us over.

We were seated with great ceremony between the Farley-Strouds and the Blands.

'You've done us proud again, young Florence,' said Lady Farley-Stroud.

'I can't honestly say I did anything, my lady,' I said.

'Nonsense,' she said. 'This was all your idea.'

'But I just said—'

'There's no use arguing, dear,' said Lady Hardcastle, quietly. 'Just take the praise and bask in the glory of your achievement.'

'But—'

'Shush, dear. You're a marvel. Just accept it.'

And so I accepted it.

We were treated to a hearty meal of a pork stew cooked in cider, served with dumplings. It might not have been entirely suited to the warm weather, but it was much easier for the real heroines of the evening – the village ladies and farmers' wives whom Lady Farley-Stroud had persuaded (or, more likely, ordered) to take care of the catering – to cook and serve. To drink, of course, there was more cider. Barrels and barrels of cider.

We chatted to Mr and Mrs Bland, congratulating the reverend on the wonderful service and Jagruti on the beautiful church decorations. They were charming company, and I soon forgot the small disappointment of having been dragged away from the girls.

When the apple pie and custard had been served and we were all tucking in, Sir Hector leaned round his wife's ample frame and waved his spoon at us.

'Damn shame about the Weryers,' he said. 'Wouldn't have happened in my day.'

'What will become of the order?' asked Lady Hardcastle.

'Not sure, m'dear, not sure. You see—'

Lady Farley-Stroud reached out and grabbed Sir Hector's wrist.

'Hector, dear,' she said, 'are you going to talk round me for the rest of the evening, waving your spoon in my face?'

'Just talkin' to Emily and Florence, my little plum duff.'

'I can see and hear very well what you're doing, Hector, and I fear for the safety of my dress if you lose control of that custard-covered spoon. Why don't we swap seats?'

'Right you are, my precious love. I say, I've an idea. Why don't you sit here? Then Emily can sit there. I'll sit where Emily was sitting . . .'

A brief game of musical chairs played out, accompanied by the shuffling of bowls, spoons and cider glasses. When the music stopped, Sir Hector sat between Lady Hardcastle and me, leaving Lady Farley-Stroud to talk to the Starks about their plans for Mr Starks's retirement.

'Where was I?' said Sir Hector as he took another spoonful of pie. 'This is splendid pie, wouldn't you say? Don't breathe a word to Mrs Brown, but I think this pastry might be better than hers.'

'You were talking about the Weryers, dear,' said Lady Hardcastle.

'So I was, m'dear, so I was. The thing is, you see . . . It's not just that they've been around for centuries, but there's been an unbroken line of membership and succession since the order took its present form.'

'In 1721,' I said.

'I say, well remembered. Yes, one hundred and ninety years of Stewards being promoted to Custodian, of a trusted Custodian being promoted to High Protector. Retirements and more than one death in office meant new recruits, but always one at a time. Always slow and steady, d'you see? And now here we are with three Custodians murdered and the fourth certain to hang for it. They've a Steward in chokey for fiddlin' the books and the High Protector is all set to retire to the seaside with his good lady wife. Six Weryers down and no Custodians left to promote. I'm sure they could get four decent Custodians from the current crop of Stewards – Lehane, Holman and Weakley would be fine candidates. Bob Slocomb, too – he's a solid, dependable fellow. But who would lead them? And where will they find six new men?'

'Mr Starks said he had a few names in mind,' I said.

'Not six, though, I'll be bound. And what about a leader? Who among the current crop could take control?'

'Why don't you do it, dear?' said Lady Hardcastle. 'Steady the ship, as it were.'

'I don't know,' he said, slowly. 'It's a lot of work.'

'But it's work you know. And you only need do it for a year or two, until everything has settled down.'

'Perhaps, perhaps. But they'd still have a recruitment problem. Not many men of good standing left.'

'There are plenty of women of good standing,' I said. 'Why not Weryer women?'

Hector thought for a while.

'Women in the Weryers?' he said. 'I'm not sure, m'dear, I'm not sure.'

'It's something to think about, though,' I said.

He chuckled.

'It most certainly is,' he said. 'You know, I'm not entirely certain it's actually forbidden by the charter . . .'

'There you are, then. There are plenty of competent women of fine character in the area, many of whom are excellent drinkers. Your recruitment problems would be solved overnight.'

'I can't imagine anyone apart from you thinking it a good idea, but I might mention it if I decide to stick my oar in at any point. I say, would you consider . . . ?'

'Not in a zillion years,' I said. 'Quite aside from anything else, I look dreadful in red.'

He laughed again.

When supper ended, the tables were pushed aside and the floor was cleared for dancing. With Fred Spratt once more on fiddle, Sergeant Dobson with his tin whistle, and the unknown Woodworthy man – whose name I later learned to be Bill Miller – on concertina, we danced the night away. I knew none of the old country dances, but I managed to pick up enough to enjoy myself.

It was well past midnight by the time we rounded up Grace Chamberlain and staggered home.

◆ ◆ ◆

We all rose late on Monday, slightly the worse for wear, though I, as so often, was the first one up.

Anticipating their own fragility, I had given Edna and Miss Jones the day off, and I confess I rather enjoyed cooking breakfast. Grace arrived at the kitchen door next and gratefully poured herself a cup of tea from the pot I had made as soon as I heard her moving about upstairs. By the time Lady Hardcastle appeared, yawning and bleary-eyed, we were already carrying things through to the morning room.

'What are your plans for the day, dear?' she asked Grace as we all sat down.

'I was going to go home,' said Grace. 'I've done what I came for, and I really ought to be getting back to my job.'

'I quite understand, but you know you're welcome to stay as long as you wish, don't you?'

'I do, thank you. I miss home, though, and my library. The police have my address, so they can contact me when they need me.'

'Do you have a train in mind?'

'There's a direct train to Dawlish from Chipping Bevington at twelve minutes past one. Is there anyone in the village with a cart for hire?'

'The dog cart chap from Chipping Bevington can sometimes be found supping in the Dog and Duck, but you needn't worry about that – I'll run you to the station in the Rolls.'

'Oh, that's very kind, but there's really no need.'

'Nonsense. It's no trouble at all. If we leave in plenty of time I can introduce you to the librarian, then once I've dropped you off I can pick up a few things in town without Flo nagging me.'

'I do not nag,' I said. 'I occasionally point out the needless extravagance of some of your purchases, but I do not nag.'

'She nags me about my driving, too.'

'And if you value your life, I advise you to do the same, Grace.'

Grace laughed.

'It can't be that bad,' she said.

'Remember you said that as you round a blind bend on two wheels and your life flashes before you.'

'You see what I'm forced to endure?' said Lady Hardcastle. 'Other people don't have to put up with this from their servants.'

'I'm unconvinced by both of you,' said Grace. 'I've never met two better friends. You're lucky to have each other.'

Lady Hardcastle and I both said 'Pfft' together, which did nothing to persuade Grace that she might be wrong. Helping herself to another sausage, she decided to change the subject.

'Do you think . . .' she began. 'Do you think it was all my fault?'

'All what, dear?' said Lady Hardcastle.

'The murders. If I hadn't come here, Uzzle would never have killed those men.'

'You can't think like that, dear. I was told off for expressing similar feelings of guilt when we were unable to work out what was going on. You didn't kill those men, Griffith Uzzle did.'

'Yes, but if I hadn't come here—'

'And if Uzzle hadn't killed Sam Puddy, Betty Uzzle would never have panicked when she heard you were back. And if he wasn't so weak, he would never have followed her orders and murdered his friends. You can blame Griffith Uzzle. You can blame Betty Uzzle. But you absolutely cannot blame yourself. I doubt we could find a doctor to certify that they're mad, but they're dangerously unstable and quite without morals or conscience. Anything could have panicked them into a similarly tragic and destructive course of action.'

'Yes, but—'

'Why will no one simply take my advice?' said Lady Hardcastle. 'It really is most irritating. You know I'm right.'

'I do, but—'

'Butts are for archery and rainwater. I shall hear no more about it.'

With a sigh, but smiling, Grace returned to her breakfast.

Lady Hardcastle returned from Chipping Bevington with an armful of books – several of which were for me – a new hat, a pair of tennis shoes, three sketchbooks, an assortment of ironmongery and other hardware items for her latest moving-picture project, a silk scarf, something unidentifiable and very technical from the photographer's shop that had just opened next to the Grey Goose, and a bag of Gloucester Lardy Cakes for tea.

'I see you took full advantage of being nag-free,' I said as she returned from her second trip to bring her purchases in from the Rolls.

'It was only a temporary respite, though, I notice,' she said, dropping the books on the table next to me.

'I'm not nagging,' I said. 'Just commenting.'

'In a disapproving way. I bought you some books in a pre-emptive attempt to mollify you.'

'And I'm very grateful, thank you very much.'

'Cakes, too.'

'So I see.'

'Have you made any plans for dinner?'

'Not yet – I was waiting to see what you fancied.'

'Splendid. I've booked us a table at the Grey Goose for seven o'clock.'

The doorbell rang.

'That's very lovely of you,' I said. 'I'll just see who's at the door.'

It was Dr Gosling and Dinah Caudle.

'Hello, Flo,' said Miss Caudle. 'Sorry to call unannounced but we—'

'We wanted to make sure you were all right after your ordeal,' interrupted Dr Gosling.

She glared at him momentarily.

'We've weathered worse,' I said with a smile. 'Come in, won't you? We're in the drawing room.'

They knew the way so I stayed to shut the front door.

As they crossed the hall I could hear Miss Caudle muttering. 'I can speak for myself, you know, Simeon. You're always doing that.'

'Sorry, old sport. Just trying to be helpful.'

'It's patronizing and you're to stop it at once.'

'Right you are, dear.'

He led her into the drawing room.

'Hello, old thing,' he said. 'Just paying a house call, you know what we doctors are like.'

'As long as you don't charge me for the privilege, you're welcome any time, dear,' said Lady Hardcastle. 'Are you able to stop? Perhaps we might have some cider in the garden?'

'That would be splendid,' said Miss Caudle.

I bypassed the drawing room and went straight to the kitchen to fill a jug of cider.

By the time I joined them in the garden they were all sitting comfortably around the table beneath the apple tree.

'And here's the heroine of the hour,' said Dr Gosling. 'I hear you saved the day again, Flo.'

'All in a day's work,' I said.

'You're altogether too modest. Sunderland is full of praise, too.'

'He's very kind,' I said. 'You both are. Is there any news?'

'The Uzzles were both indicted by the magistrates today to the Spring Assizes. They were remanded to Horfield Prison pending trial. Or, at least, she was. He'll be sent there once he's been released from the BRI. There was quite a bit of damage to his right leg by all accounts.'

'Needs must,' I said.

'Well, quite. He'll not get any sympathy from me.'

'Nor from me,' said Miss Caudle. 'I'm in awe of you both. Once again you solved an actual murder.'

'We just happened to be at the wrong place at the right time,' said Lady Hardcastle. 'The inspector would have been on to Uzzle pretty soon.'

'Not until after he'd killed Grace Chamberlain,' said Miss Caudle. 'You're marvels, the pair of you.'

'You helped, though, don't forget. It was your diligent work that discovered who Grace really was. Your contacts would come in useful if you ever did decide to join us.'

'Well, I . . .'

'What's all this?' said Dr Gosling. 'Join them?'

'I'll tell you later, dear.'

'Right you are. Now, then, I have some important business to attend to and I mustn't forget or I'll be in trouble.' He cleared his throat. 'In my official capacity as police surgeon, I have been asked to pass on the grateful thanks of the Bristol Police Force for your assistance in capturing the murderer Griffith Uzzle and his accomplice.'

'His controller, more like,' I said.

'That, too. There's talk of a commendation from the Chief Constable.'

'Oh, I don't think we could accept that,' said Lady Hardcastle. 'We don't work for medals, dear. Well, I don't – I don't like to speak for Flo.'

'No, I'm just in it for the lardy cakes,' I said.

'Lardy cakes?' said Miss Caudle. 'I haven't had one of those for years.'

'I bought some this very afternoon if you'd like one,' said Lady Hardcastle. 'Perhaps with some tea?'

'I'll put the kettle on,' I said.

'Thank you,' said Miss Caudle. 'And when you get back, you owe me something.'

'I do?' I said, with a frown.

'You do. While I was being sick in the hydrangeas at Peppard's coopery, you promised me the full, exclusive story. I've a pen full of ink and a head full of questions. Tell all, my tiny friend.'

'Oh, that. Of course. I'll be but a moment.'

As I left, I heard Lady Hardcastle say, 'If the lardy cake doesn't fill you too much, perhaps you'd care to join us for dinner, too. Unless you have other plans, of course. We have a table booked at the Grey Goose in Chipping Bevington. I'm sure they'd make room for two more.'

'That would be lovely,' said Miss Caudle. 'Now, about this murder investigation . . .'

Life was back to normal. For now.

Author's Note

1911 had a scorching hot summer, both in the world of Lady Hardcastle and in real life. The heatwave made life unbearable in many parts of England, though its effects were less unpleasant in Littleton Cotterell (everything is less unpleasant in Littleton Cotterell, apart from the murder rate, which is horrific), but it did affect the harvest.

Harvest time is a moveable feast – farmers bring in the crops when they're ready. In Britain the harvest usually begins around the end of September but it can vary, and it was unusually early in 1911. At the end of July, for instance, a farmer in Monmouth in South Wales reported gathering his earliest harvest since 1865. I've pushed the Littleton Cotterell harvest to the end of August.

'Weryer' is a real word, though the Oxford English Dictionary cites just one use in a Middle English text. It means 'guardian' and comes, as Lady Hardcastle surmises, from the verb 'to were' (to guard or protect) – now obsolete in English but still in use in Scots – which in turn comes from the Old English *werian*.

Whereas I'm able to browse the Oxford English Dictionary for obscure words, that luxury wouldn't have been afforded to Lady Hardcastle. In 1857, the Philological Society of London decided that existing English dictionaries were insufficient, and proposed a new project to completely re-examine the English language from

Anglo-Saxon times onwards. They reached an agreement with the Oxford University Press in 1879 to begin work on this new dictionary, an undertaking that they thought would take ten years. Five years later they had reached the word 'ant' and the realization dawned that it was going to take much longer than they had originally envisaged.

The *OED* was published in volumes (or 'fascicles') between 1888 and 1928 as *The New English Dictionary*. Volume 7 (O and P) was published in 1909, while Volume 8 (Q to S) didn't appear until 1914. In 1911, Lady Hardcastle would have been able to look up 'pomary' but not 'weryer' or 'sax', so I invented an esoteric dictionary for her.

In Britain (and, indeed, most places outside the USA), the word 'cider' refers exclusively to the alcoholic drink made from fermented apple juice, known to Americans as 'hard cider'. We do use the term 'sweet cider', but even that isn't the same as in the USA and is simply alcoholic cider that happens to be sweet, rather than the unfiltered apple juice you might be expecting.

Aberdare does have a male voice choir, the Cwmbach Male Choir, but it was founded in 1921. There is a brass band based in the village of Llwydcoed, a mile or so north of Aberdare, but that was founded in 1912. In our world, though, both existed in the town in the 1880s when Flo returned to her mother's home. Flo has mentioned in the past that her mother is actually from Cwmdare, a mile or so up the mountain to the west of Aberdare, and I picked that village because it's where my own grandmother came from. Like Flo, she worked in domestic service – but she was a cook, not a lady's maid, and her father was a miner, not a circus performer.

Whenever I need names appropriate to a particular part of the country, I use lists of the most popular names by county, as compiled by britishsurnames.co.uk from the 1881 census. From the list for Gloucestershire, for instance, the most common surname was

Smith, much as you might expect, but you were forty-four times more likely to find a Brazington in Gloucestershire than anywhere else. And that's handy to know.

Nempnett Thrubwell is a real place south of Bristol, and sits just to the north of Blagdon Lake (known at the time of the story as the Yeo Reservoir) on the edge of the Mendip Hills. North Nibley, Nupdown, and Chew Magna are also real, but most other places and their names are made up.

Flo doesn't remember why she might think of the phrase 'Solicitors, Commissioners for Oaths, and Small Bets Placed', and there's no earthly reason why she should. It's a line from an episode of *The Goon Show* ('The Treasure in the Lake', later issued on a BBC LP and retitled 'The Treasure of Loch Lomond') and wouldn't be broadcast on BBC radio until 1956. I've no idea why it sticks in my own mind, but if an opportunity to shoehorn in a *Goons* reference appears somewhere, I'm never going to turn it down. Incidentally, there was no Author's Note in the third book in the series, *Death Around the Bend*, but Flo's comment there about being named after 'the Lady with the Lump' is also taken from a *Goon Show* ('The Phantom Headshaver (of Brighton)' – 1954).

The layout and history of Chipping Bevington is loosely inspired by the real market town of Thornbury in South Gloucestershire, which has had so many pubs along and beside its High Street over the years that it's difficult to keep track. Five of those pubs remain at the time of writing (or six, if you include a pub that was originally a butcher's), with three restaurants or coffee houses in buildings that have been pubs within the past ten years. It's a number that has continually changed over the centuries, but eight isn't in any way an unreasonable number for fictional Chipping Bevington.

'Where's it to?' is a West Country formation, common in the Bristol area, and simply means 'Where is it?' I've written before about my hopes that the regional quirks of our language can survive, and this one (as well as the South Walian response, 'It's over by there') is a particular favourite.

Skittles is still a popular pub game in Britain. The West Country variation, as played at the Dog and Duck, involves nine pins set up on a wooden alley no less than thirty feet long. Bristol-style pins are about ten inches high, flat at both ends, and about three inches in diameter with a five-inch-wide bulge in the middle. They're set up in a diamond shape and arranged in such a way that it's possible for the ball – 'about the size of a cannonball' – to pass between them without hitting anything. There are many variations around the country in rules and equipment, but the villagers of Littleton Cotterell would know only the Gloucester or Bristol game.

It occurs to me that I might never have said that the *Bristol News* is fictional – the main local newspaper in the area in Lady Hardcastle's time was the *Western Daily Press*. I mention it now because I thought I ought also to say that the *Stroud Herald*, *Gloucester Chronicle*, *Exeter Advertiser* and *Dawlish Gazette* are also made up.

The story Flo finds about the damage to the Salvation Army instruments at Eastbourne, though, is real, and is from the *Western Daily Press* dated 8 September 1891. News of the performance of Hubert Parry's (of *Jerusalem* fame) brand-new musical setting of *De Profundis* at Hereford is from the same edition. Adjusted for inflation, the £10 damage to the Salvation Army instruments is about £1,300 in 2021 ($1,840). If old newspapers interest you, a subscription to the British Newspaper Archive might prove entertaining.

The Weryers' dance is related to what we now remember is called Morris dancing. It dates back to at least the fifteenth century but declined in popularity after the Industrial Revolution, so that by the end of the nineteenth century it was all but forgotten. Folklorists started a revival of the traditional English dances around the turn of the twentieth century, but at the time of our story it hadn't quite reached the level of recognition it would later achieve, and I decided that though the Weryers' dance was an old one, no one would refer to it as a Morris dance.

About the Author

Photo © 2018 Clifton Photographic Company

Tim Kinsey grew up in London and read history at Bristol University. *Rotten to the Core* is the eighth story in the Lady Hardcastle Mystery series, and he is also the author of the Dizzy Heights Mystery series. His website is at tekinsey.uk, and you can follow him on Twitter @tekinsey, as well as on Facebook: www.facebook.com/tekinsey.